SENTENCED TO TROLL 5

S.L. ROWLAND

AETHERVALE
PUBLISHING

ALSO BY S.L. ROWLAND

Tales of Aedrea

Cursed Cocktails

Sword & Thistle

The Halfling's Harvest

There Be Dragons Here

Pangea Online

Pangea Online: Death and Axes

Pangea Online 2: Magic and Mayhem

Pangea Online 3: Vials and Tribulations

Sentenced to Troll 1-6

Path to Villainy: An NPC Kobold's Tale

Collected Editions

Pangea Online: The Complete Trilogy

Sentenced to Troll Compendium: Books 1-3

Sentenced to Troll Compendium 2: Books 4-6

Sign up for S.L. Rowland's Newsletter

For signed copies and advanced chapters visit Patreon at patreon.com/slrowland

 Formatted with Vellum

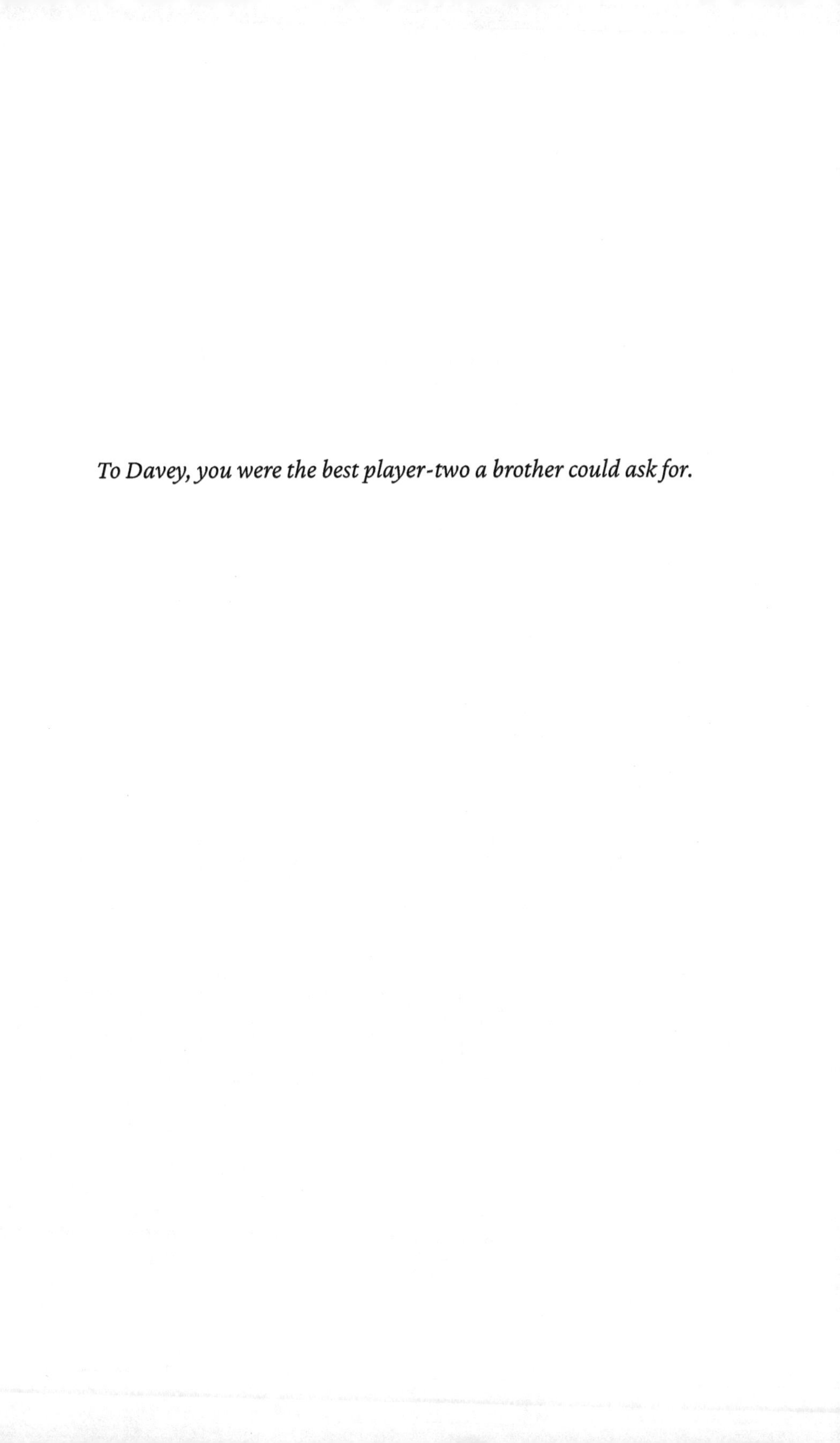

To Davey, you were the best player-two a brother could ask for.

CURRENT STATS

Chod, Level 25 Barbarian/Summoner Forest Troll
    HP: 6235/6235
    Mana: 5000/5000
    Rage: 0/100
    XP: 673,291/735,000

Strength: 42
    Dexterity: 24
    Constitution: 43
    Intelligence: 10
    Wisdom: 15
    Charisma: 6

+1 Strength and Constitution racial bonus per level.

+1 Ability point per odd level.

6 stat points available.

0 ability points available.

Abilities:

Bite. *Using your massive tusks and powerful jaw, you take a bite out of an opponent, dealing immense damage. Cost: 10 rage. Level 2.*

Claw. *You attack with sharp claws, swiping at an opponent and dealing extra damage. Cost: 5 rage. Level 2.*

Intimidation. *You stare down your opponent, confusing them so that they are unable to attack for two seconds. Cost: 10 rage.*

Berserker Rage. *(Ultimate) Attacks and physical damage build your rage meter. 5 rage per attack. Rage meter deteriorates over time when out of combat at a rate of 5 rage per second. Activating Berserker Rage fills rage meter. For 30 seconds, rage meter does not decrease, deal increased damage, health regenerates at 5x the normal rate, cannot be stunned, slowed or otherwise affected. Cooldown: 10 minutes.*

Increased Regeneration. *(Passive) Regenerate health at a faster rate. Level 2.*

Rapid Regeneration. *(Passive) When below 10% health, regeneration is doubled.*

Nightvision. *(Passive) Increased vision in darkness and low light.*

Thick Skin. *(Passive) Take 10% less damage from physical attacks.*

Savage. *(Passive) Ability to eat uncooked meat without consequences.*

Camouflage. *(Passive) When out of combat and not moving for 20 seconds, trolls blend in with their surroundings.*

Sweeping Slash. *Form a sweeping arc in front of you, dealing damage and knocking your opponent off balance. Cost: 5 rage.*

Conceal (Passive). *Hides level from anyone who is not a guard on city grounds.*

Summon Horror (Passive). *Ability to summon a horror. Each horror grants a unique ability. For every horror active, gain 1% increased damage and health points. Horrors decay 10% for every minute outside of combat.*

Horror of Power. *Summon a horror with 20% of your strength. Cost: 100 mana. Cooldown: 30 seconds. Bonus: Your next attack deals double damage.*

Horror of Vitality. *Summon a horror with 20% of your health points. Cost: 100 mana. Cooldown: 30 seconds. Bonus: Opponents near Horror of Vitality are slowed by 20%.*

Horror of Finesse. *Summon a horror with 20% of your attack speed. Cost: 100 mana. Cooldown: 30 seconds. Bonus: Your next attack heals you for damage dealt.*

Sacrifice. *Sacrifice X amount of horrors to receive a temporary buff. Horror of Power: +1 Strength. Horror of Vitality: +1 Constitution. Horror of Finesse: +1 Dexterity*

Kamikaze. *Sacrifice a horror to deal a burst of damage.*

Champion. *Summon a copy of the most recent enemy you have defeated. Decays 10% every minute out of combat. Cost: 50% of mana pool. Cooldown: 6 hours.*

Spirit of the Beast. *The Spirit of the Beast path is composed of five phases.*

Phase 1: Spirit Inquiry. *A spirit animal is a guide from the spirit world, possessing traits similar to those of the individual. Unlocking one's spirit animal leads to a better understanding of the self and one's place within the world.*

    Spirit Animal: *Frost Goat*

Phase 2: Spirit Embodiment. *Bonding with a spirit beast is only the beginning of the Spirit of the Beast path. By finding an amulet that connects you to your beast, the bond between the two will grow stronger, unlocking further advancements.*

    Spirit Embodiment: *Ram Horns*

Phase 3: Spirit Enhancement. *Just as your body has undergone a change reflective of your spirit beast, your spirit may be enhanced in the same manner. Gain a new passive ability based on your spirit beast.*

    Spirit Enhancement: *Ram Rage: Barbarian rage now lasts twice as long. Physical attacks deal splash damage.*

Phase 4: Spirit Guide. *Your body and spirit have undergone great changes, but your bond with the spirit world is only beginning. Summon a spirit guide of your spirit beast.*

    Spirit Guide: *Summon a frost goat spirit guide. The spirit guides may lead you through darkness and guide you to locations you have previously visited, even if you do not know the way. Spirit guides may* be consumed for a 50% increase to Wisdom for 10 minutes. Cooldown: 24 hours.

Available Abilities (*1 ability point to unlock*):

Massive Bite. *Deals double damage. Cost: 20 rage.*

Claws. *Swipe at opponent with both hands, dealing extra damage. Cost: 10 rage.*

Multi Attack. *Bite and Claw at the same time. Cost: 20 rage.*

Iron Will. *Immune to slows and stuns for 30 seconds. Cost: 50 rage. 180 second cooldown.*

I'm Always Angry *(Passive. Available at level 10). Once rage meter is at 50%, it will not deteriorate below 50% when out of combat.*

Perception. *For 10 minutes, gain increased awareness of your surroundings. Spot hidden objects, as well as unusual sounds, odors, and tastes. Cooldown: 6 hours.*

Cleave. *Your next attack causes bleed damage, dealing 1% of opponent's health per second for 5 seconds. Cost: 10 rage.*

Battle Cry. *You let out a ferocious roar, increasing rage by 20. No cost. 60 second cooldown.*

Class Advancements. *Upon reaching level twenty-five, you have unlocked a class advancement. You may only advance one class at a time. A second class may not be advanced until completion of primary advancement.*

Barbarian Advancement.
Spirit of the Beast. Unlock for further details.

Summoner Advancement.
Dreadbeasts. Unlock for further details.
Dual Subclass. Unlock for further details.

Current Items:

Item. Phoenix Feather. 10% resistance to fire-based attacks. *A very rare item, phoenix feathers can only be gathered if they are willingly given by the host. Feathers plucked from unwilling birds turn to ash.*

Item. Tiger's Eye Pendant. Removes one debuff. Cooldown: 10 minutes. *A rare stone believed to ward off evil and bring balance to life.*

Item. Aquatic Boots. *Allows user to walk on water.*

Item. Petrified Staff. An enchanted staff capable of taking on the properties of up to 3 attached stones. +3 Intelligence. +3 Wisdom. Bonus: *While holding Petrified Staff, the user can cast ranged physical attacks once every 10 seconds.*

Item. Forlorn Scepter. +5 Intelligence. *Increases the range of summoned creatures by 50%.*

Item. Glouwseeker Venom. *When injected into the bloodstream, glouwseeker venom immobilizes target. Length of stun dependent on size of target, resistances, and amount injected.*

Item. Sea Scorpion. +3 Strength. *An enchanted trident capable of taking on the property of 1 enchanted stone. Bonus: deals splash damage.*

Legendary Item. Angel of Death Brandy. *When drinker falls below 1HP, a metaphysical event will occur, rewinding time for the user to two seconds prior to death.*

Item. Brimming Tankard. *A magical tankard that, once filled,* *will never go empty. Warning: Once filled, contents cannot be changed. Only works on beverages.*

__Item. Expandable Satchel.__ A bag capable of holding enormous content and only burdening the wearer with ten percent of its weight. Simply focus on the item inside and it will appear in your hand.

__Item. Destroyer. An enchanted warhammer capable of taking on the properties of up to three stones. +2 Strength, +3 Constitution.__ This ancient warhammer was forged in the heart of a volcano. __Bonus Ability: Inferno.__ With each consecutive hit, Destroyer grows hotter, allowing it to warp or pierce through even the hardest metals. Multiplier works when hits are less than five seconds apart. Cost: 10 mana per attack. Cooldown: 10 sec.

__Item. Spaulder of Swiftness. +1 Constitution, +1 Dexterity.__ Lightweight, durable leather mail designed to protect the off-hand shoulder during battle.

__Item. Green Dragon Egg.__ Green dragons rule with impunity over the forests they inhabit. They are the most territorial of all dragon species, and capable of spewing toxic gas in lieu of flames. Wherever a green dragon calls home, a dense fog is said to follow. Green dragon eggs may only be hatched in the heart of an ancient forest.

__Item. Halite Shield.__ A lightweight translucent shield capable of taking damage without reducing visibility.

__Item. Frosted Buckler. +2 Constitution.__ A lightweight and small shield capable of deflecting blows as well as being used offensively. __Bonus Ability:__ Physical attacks blocked with Frosted Buckler cut attacker's Dexterity in half for ten seconds.

PROLOGUE

The elevator opened with a gentle swish, and every head in the laboratory turned in that direction. Valery scowled at the disturbance. Nobody was scheduled to visit today, and she wanted her team focused. The last thing they needed were distractions.

Polished leather shoes clacked with each step as a broad-shouldered man wearing a custom-tailored suit exited the elevator and stepped into the lab. Valery's lips curled down at the edges as she noticed the thin twenty-something blonde falling in step beside him.

"Back to work, everyone," she ordered.

There was stilted movement as eyes darted between Valery and the head of Mythos Games.

"Daughter." The man came to a stop in front of Valery, unnaturally white teeth flaring with his smile. His purple eyes gazed into her own.

"Father."

He winked at Valery. "If you keep frowning like that, you'll end up with wrinkles like your mother."

Bastard. Valery gave him the fakest smile possible, doing little to conceal its disingenuousness. "To what do I owe this unexpected visit?"

His smile widened. "I've been following along with your little project."

Valery felt her chest tighten. This was her project, and the last thing she needed was her father meddling.

"And?" She tried to sound as calm as possible, but she knew her father could read her like a book. That was one of his strengths—the ability to figure people out with ease and use that information to play them like a fiddle.

"Don't worry." He winked again. "Your little secret is safe with me. I love what you've done with the game—creating your own lore and integrating it into the real-time evolution of the game-world. It's beautiful. Especially the trolls, they might play a bigger part in this story than anyone imagined."

Her father might be a dick and a shrewd businessman, but he still had a childlike fascination with lore and world-building. But there was no way in hell he was here with his new side-piece just to tell her this.

She gave him a knowing look. "Should she be here?"

The young woman pursed her lips but said nothing. This entire lab was highly classified among the company. Aside from the general details of the program, none of this was public knowledge, and she doubted her father had made the woman sign an NDA. Bringing an outsider into the lab was asking for trouble, but as the head of Mythos Games, no one could stop her father from doing as he pleased. Not even Valery.

He laughed. "Oh, it's not like that. Let me introduce you to Miss Dorothy Jordan. I expect you'll get to know each other very well in the coming months."

CHAPTER I

WANDERMERE

A HEAVY FOG spreads across the forest floor of Wandermere. The name is fitting because we've been wandering aimlessly for almost two days. There's been evidence of centaurs—well-trodden paths and empty outposts—but it's like they've abandoned the forest.

The entire vibe of this place sits uneasy with me. All around us, birds chirp and bugs rattle, but it's hard to see clearly for more than ten feet in this fog. In every direction, massive trees tower over us in perpetuity. Each tree trunk is wide enough to carve a car-sized tunnel through it.

But aside from wolves and warthogs, every animal we've come upon has bolted, even from Taryn.

"I get that it's ancient, but I thought there would be a little more action," I say to no one in particular. Living in New York City, I know what it's like to feel small among buildings that touch the sky, but this is different, somehow peaceful and terrifying at the same time.

"It's beautiful." Taryn tilts his head back, staring into the canopy overhead.

Taryn hasn't been very talkative as of late, especially toward me. Since losing Stompy, most of our communication consists of things we see or which direction we should take rather than actual conversation. I don't press the issue, though, hoping that giving him space will heal things between us.

There's a sparkle as two small, brightly-colored fairies peek out from behind a tree and point slender fingers in our direction. When they speak, it sounds like wind chimes, their language clearly not translated by my communication stone. Before I have a chance to point them out to the others, they bolt away into the forest.

We come across a small stream, and Berry walks down to the edge for a drink. He grunts before returning to Taryn's side. Ruby has her eyes focused in the direction the fairies disappeared, while Jordy stands stoically on Taryn's other side.

Even though it's midday, the forest feels like twilight. The massive leaves are easily the size of my head, and their branches tangle and intertwine, forming a canopy that nearly blocks out the sky, only allowing light to penetrate in small doses.

There's a loud caw as a massive golden bird takes flight. Limery grows warm against my shoulder before bolting into the foliage overhead.

"Be careful!" I shout behind him, but he's already out of range.

As I gaze at the towering trees of this ancient forest, I imagine this is what it feels like to be an ant walking among giant blades of grass. How do they navigate being stuck in a towering world without a map?

I just hope that if we run into any real monsters that they aren't proportionate to the gargantuan trees. Occasionally, wind hits the canopy and piercing beams of light give the forest a magical quality, like the heavens are reaching down with radiant fingers. When the light hits the fog, it glows gently, giving the appearance of dozens of troll-sized wisps.

While we walk, I pull the green dragon egg from my satchel and examine it for the hundredth time, hoping it might give us some inkling of direction.

Item. Green Dragon Egg. *Green dragons rule with impunity over the forests they inhabit. They are the most territorial of all dragon species and capable of spewing toxic gas in lieu of flames. Wherever a green dragon calls home, a dense fog is said to follow. Green dragon eggs may only be hatched in the heart of an ancient forest.*

The egg is slightly smaller than my fist and bright green even in the dull light. Thick, diamond-shaped scales lap over one another like a pinecone. It could be my imagination, but it seems slightly warmer than before.

Maybe we're getting close to the heart of the forest.

I place the egg back in my satchel. A week ago, I had no idea that it was a dragon egg. Now, it's the entire reason we're in Wandermere.

But we'll need to find the heart of the forest if we want any chance at hatching the dragon.

With the fog obscuring everything that isn't directly in front of us, it's almost impossible to make an educated guess. I assumed this would be a foggy area based on the egg's description, but the reality is beyond anything I could have imagined.

I cast Spirit Guide, and a frost goat formed of orange and white energy appears in front of us. Its presence pushes back the fog for several feet in all directions, revealing ground covered in wet leaves, moss, and rich dirt. Small creatures scurry back into the foggy depths.

My guide makes the immediate vicinity clearer but does little to help our navigation. Watching it walk like a beacon while pushing back the fog is a beautiful sight, though. There's also comfort in knowing that no matter how lost we get, it can always guide us back to the portal.

Taryn's own frost goat approaches my spirit guide, lowering his head in a show of respect.

I turn to Taryn. "Looks like mine is the top dog."

"When it comes to pets, I'll take substance over style," he says flatly.

He rolls his eyes as he pats Berry's back for Ruby to join him. The jackal leaps into his lap with surprising finesse and curls up between Taryn's legs.

After everything that has happened over the past few days, my jokes don't seem to have the same effect that they used to. Taryn brushes them off more times than not. I don't expect him to get over losing Stompy any time soon, but I think staying busy will help. If we can ever find anything worthwhile in this sprawling maze of trees, we still have objectives to complete.

It might be a while before things are truly normal again between us. I know it's selfish of me, but I miss goofing around with my best friend. I've replayed what happened in Boneholde a hundred times in my head, wondering what we could have done differently. I've always been itching for a fight, and even though Stompy made his own decisions, I know it was my choices that put us in a bad situation to begin with. That's something that will never change. Taryn's grief will take time, but I just want to keep it from consuming him in the meantime.

I give his shoulder a firm squeeze as we look out into the murky beyond. "Do your druid senses tell you if we're getting closer?"

"Do I look like a GPS?" He sighs. "Judging by the size of the trees, this is a giant forest, and we've barely populated any of our map. Without a village or manned outpost to give us directions, we can't even fill in the markers on our map. The heart of the forest could be anywhere."

I summon a few more horrors and we continue our journey through the woods. I wish we had done more research before coming here. I bet the troll library in Hornryx probably had information on Wandermere. We followed the most well-traveled path out of the portal, but it's possible we went in the wrong direction. All I know right now is that this is one of the few ancient forests in Mythos. Supposedly, it's the home of the centaurs, and most likely a scary green dragon as well.

Limery returns after a few minutes wearing a mischievous smile.

"Find anything good?" I ask.

He lands on my shoulder. "Limmy likes this place. The birds is bigs." He wipes a string of drool from his chin.

"Just don't get yourself eaten. We don't want Limmy being bird food." I poke the bulge in his stomach, and he cackles.

By early afternoon, we come upon an underground spring that empties into a bubbling pool. Fog gathers at the edge of the water like there's some unseen force keeping it at bay. In the center of the spring, there's a giant stone with a jeweled sword buried nearly halfway up the blade. A stream of sunlight breaks through the canopy, igniting the jeweled pommel in a dazzling display against the surrounding trees.

Limery's bulbous yellow eyes fill with greed.

"Hold up." I raise my hand in front of the imp before he has a chance to fly over. "There's no way we're this lucky. Let's play this smart."

Taryn gives me a look that I can't quite make out, like a mixture of sadness and uncertainty. Maybe my sudden caution is a painful reminder of how things could have gone in Frostmoor.

He turns away. "I'll scan the area and make sure it's not some kind of trap."

Before I have a chance to argue, he transforms into a red bird and flies away. His feathers are no longer white now that we're in a more temperate climate.

I ignore his brash behavior and step closer to the pool. The bubbling spring is relaxing. If we weren't searching for the heart of the forest, I could see myself losing hours soaking my feet in the cool water.

There's no telling how long the sword has been in that boulder, but it looks to be in pristine condition. When I try to analyze it, all I receive are question marks. If this isn't a trap, then we could have stumbled onto a pretty powerful weapon.

I stare into the spring. Tiny ripples distort my reflection, but I can still make out the massive horns that sprout from my head. A gift from my Spirit of the Beast path, I trace my finger from the black base to the icy blue tips. They are practically identical to the horns on Taryn's frost goat.

I tap the tip of my left horn. It's not sharp, but it could still do some damage, though they would be more effective smashing than goring. It looks cumbersome in the reflection, but I hardly notice they are there most of the time. Sleeping on them was a bit of an adjustment, though.

Somehow, I've managed to look even more badass. I can't wait to see Gord's face when we return to the troll forest. No doubt he'll be jealous of my new look.

There's a flutter of red feathers as Taryn returns, transforming back into his dwarven form. "I didn't see anything. There are some paths nearby that look like they were recently traveled by something with hooves, but that's it. I went up high, but the forest goes on forever. If there's a town or village anywhere near, it's hidden beneath the trees. And if someone is waiting to ambush us, their Camouflage is on par with the trolls."

I'm not sure if I should feel comforted by that or not. "Trolls are the only race I know that have Camouflage as an ability, but we don't really know much about the races outside the Isle. I've always been able to see trolls as translucent figures when they have it activated, but I doubt it would work on another race. Ruby's perception should spot anything out of the ordinary, right?"

He nods. "In theory."

I place a hand on his shoulder. "You cool with this?"

He sighs. "Yeah. I think it's going to be a bit before I'm back to myself, but that doesn't mean we should stop adventuring. I owe it to Stompy to make sure his death means something." He turns to face the sparkling sword. "It looks like a good sword. Go ahead and see if you can pull it out. We'll keep watch."

I wade into the spring, where the water is even colder than I imagined. Goosebumps erupt over my entire body.

Surprisingly, the pool is only waist deep when I reach the boulder.

I glance at Taryn before wrapping my hand around the hilt. He nods, and I give the weapon a hearty pull. It doesn't budge, so I grab it with two hands, plant my feet, and yank.

Water sloshes in the pool just as a massive boulder slams into my side. Several of my ribs crack, and pain flares through my midsection as I'm rocketed from the spring. I crash into an unforgiving tree and fall to the ground, stars dancing at the edge of my vision.

I grunt as I fight against the shooting pain to stand, unable to see above the fog. "What the hell was that?"

Limery hovers in front of me saying the words I've heard all too often. "Is yous okay, Chods?"

"Ungh. Yeah, I'm fine." I grimace as I equip Destroyer and use it as a crutch to stand, searching the area for enemies.

"It's not a treasure, it's a monster." Taryn guides Berry back from the spring, and I notice what he means.

A golem-like creature stands in the center of the pool, its arms and legs composed of several boulders stacked on top of one another like those little rock statues I would always see in Central Park. Only I think it will take more than a stiff breeze to knock this guy down. One giant boulder forms the golem's body, which is also where the sword is buried. The blade gleams in the ray of sunlight as the monster thrashes about.

Sword-wielding Stone. *Unique Monster. Level 32. An enchanter of great renown, Kathwyn the Benevolent traveled far and wide across Mythos hiding her enchanted objects in challenging locations where only the brave and worthy could retrieve them. The Sword of Repercussion was tested by many, but none proved capable of removing it from the stone she had placed it within. As the portals closed and the sword was lost to time, its enchanted properties began to fuse with the life aura in the heart of Wandermere. As life aura passed through the stone to the sword, the stone grew sentient and has been seen wandering the forest ever since, searching for rays of sunlight to bask in.*

The faceless golem reaches with fingers formed of stacked pebbles and pulls the sword from its backside. Even though it has no eyes, it points the sword in Taryn's direction. At level thirty-two, this might be more of a challenge than we bargained for. A sword that has feasted on life aura for years and years—there's no telling what abilities a monster like this has. With a name like The Sword of Repercussion, they can't be anything pleasant.

Jordy lowers his head and paws at the earth.

"Easy, buddy," Taryn orders as he guides Berry a few more steps backward. "I'm not sure you want to headbutt this monster."

I touch my tender ribs, still feeling the discomfort. "We're off to a rocky start, but I think we can handle it."

Taryn frowns at my attempt at humor, but then his face softens. "Yeah, but I've heard it's best to let sleeping stones lie."

I laugh at his pun and try to keep it going. It's been too long since we've bantered. "Maybe, but I thought dwarves were boulder than this."

He shrugs, smirking. "Your call, but don't cry to me when you're stuck between a rock and a sharp blade."

I summon a round of horrors and gather them at the edge of the spring while Limery hovers next to me. The sword-wielding stone stands in the center of the bubbling pool, but it hasn't attacked. Not yet.

"Would you like to do the honors?" I gesture toward the monster.

Taryn raises his staff and a bolt of lightning rips through the trees. Thunder rumbles as the bolt hits the spring. Electricity arcs along the golem's body, and I'm certain that it's stunned in place.

I charge in with my horrors to get in a few free hits, but the golem shudders and the tiny arcs of electricity are absorbed into its stone body. Two of Limery's fireballs explode against the monster's chest, leaving scorch marks but barely doing any damage. A yellow aura surrounds the sword, and electricity trails from the hilt down the blade. At the tip, the electricity merges together and three massive bolts arc in our direction.

Limery zips out of the way, avoiding the attack, but one of the bolts catches me straight in the chest. My insides vibrate with energy as I'm stunned. I hold off on activating my Tiger's Eye Pendant. If the monster isn't attacking, then there's no point in wasting it.

Taryn grunts as he jumps from Berry's back and disappears

beneath the fog. The bolt meant for him zigs by and explodes against one of the massive trees.

A moment later, Taryn crawls into the fogless area around my spirit guide. "What was that?"

Once again, the stone warrior stands sentry in the spring. It's not aggressive, but it packs a hell of a punch.

I grimace at the charred flesh on my chest. "It has to have something to do with the sword. If the life aura has made it sentient, then I bet the enchantment from the sword has morphed into some kind of ability for the monster. It must absorb the attacks and send them back."

He frowns. "Then what do we do?"

I grip Destroyer even harder. "We crush this rock into rubble."

Hooves pound against the earth behind us and I take a defensive position, ready for another fight. Three centaurs, two male and one female, come to a halt a dozen feet away, their weapons raised in our direction. They stand proud, mighty warriors that rival me in height. The males both have broad shoulders and thick torsos, with their equine halves reminiscent of powerful draft horses. The female is more slender, with the lower half of a racing horse.

The two fairies I saw earlier peek out from behind the centaurs and chimes once again fill the air.

The centaur on the left has a dark chestnut coat on his lower half, with matching hair that drapes over his shoulders and olive skin. Runic tattoos cover his shoulders and arms, and he wields an ornately-carved wooden bow pointed in our direction. The centaur in the center has a charcoal coat, hazelnut skin, a forked black beard, and braids similar to my own. A massive ornamental shield tattoo covers his chest, swirling around his pecs and onto his shoulders. He holds a long spear tipped with a carved tusk. The female has a palomino lower half that's tan and speckled with white splotches. Her ivory skin is much paler than the other two centaurs, making the blue tattoos that run down her arms much more prominent. Flowing auburn hair drapes across her ample chest. She also wields an ornate bow with an arrow pointed at Taryn.

My grip tightens around Destroyer, and I call the horrors to my side, not sure what to expect.

The middle centaur raises a fist and the other two lower their weapons.

He rests the butt of his spear on the ground. "That's not a fight you'll win. Come with us if you're looking for a worthy challenge."

CHAPTER 2

DARK TIDINGS

"Dude, quit staring," I whisper as I nudge Taryn in the arm.

He shifts his gaze from the female centaur to the trees overhead, not the least bit inconspicuous. "Sorry, it's just that this is not how lady centaurs look in games. She's a little...distracting."

He has a fair point, but he could still be a little less obvious about it.

The female centaur watches us with curiosity while the two small fairies hover around her shoulders. Not much smaller than Limery, the fairies stand out in sharp contrast against the muted tones of the forest. At first glance, they look adorable. One is pink and the other purple, they both have translucent lacy wings, and a trail of glitter follows wherever they move.

There's something unsettling about them, though. They're almost angelic in appearance, but their arms and fingers are spindly, not unlike Limery's. While their eyes are proportionate to their faces, the lack of pupils makes their beautiful faces almost creepy, like a wolf in sheep's clothing. They murmur melodically to one another, laughing and pointing.

I focus on one of them and a description appears.

Celestial Fairy. *Level 21. Though not native to Wandermere, celestial fairies have thrived in the aura of the ancient forest. When an adventurous party of gnomes perished while searching for gold and glory, their fairy companions were left to their own devices. They quickly reproduced, becoming an invasive species and overtaking much of the forest. With sufficient numbers, the celestial fairies waged war on the native woodland fairies, eradicating them from the forest. Wandermere is now home to the largest celestial fairy population across Mythos.*

I blink rapidly as I read the description over once more. I've never pictured fairies as conquistadors, especially ones looking like they just slid down the rainbow bridge. But I should know better than most not to judge solely on appearance. Limery might be mischievous at times, but I get the feeling that these two are always up to something.

I gesture toward the two fairies. "Did these two warn you we were here?"

The female centaur smirks. "There are many eyes throughout the forest."

"That's not ominous at all," Taryn mumbles as he narrows his eyes.

The bearded centaur laughs. "I doubt you have what it takes to scare a forest troll, Sylvie." He turns to Taryn. "The dwarf on the other hand..."

Taryn scowls in their direction. "I'm sorry, but aren't you the ones who just asked for our help? Who are you all, anyway?"

The bearded centaur places his hands together and bows slightly. "Apologies. We meant no offense. Our leader, Swift Thundercrest, told us a tale of encountering a blue forest troll traveling with a dwarf while he was in Seascape. He said that heroes have returned to Mythos once more. While he made no mention of horns, the pairing is such an oddity that we had to assume it was you two. Were we misguided?"

I think back to the council meeting with King Orso. I never spoke with the centaurs, but they were there along with a half-dozen other races. If we can meet with this Swift Thundercrest, maybe he can help point us in the direction of the heart of the forest so that we can hatch the dragon egg.

I shake my head. "No, it was us. I'm Chod. This is Taryn, and this is Limery. We're here on a bit of a time-sensitive mission. Any chance we can meet with Swift?"

He nods. "Very well. I am Thannis Smokehoof. This is Daimun Stonewhisper." He gestures toward the chestnut-colored male wielding the bow. "And this is Sylvie Redmane. The two fairies are Starlight and Sunbeam. Together, we scout the forest for threats and—"

Water splashes behind us, and I look over my shoulder where the stone-wielding golem has retaken its slumbering position in the center of the spring.

"Do not worry about the Wanderer." Thannis follows my gaze. "It is a powerful but simple creature. Unless provoked, it will spend the entirety of its days basking in the sunbeams."

Taryn scoffs. "Sounds like a cushy life."

Thannis's eyes narrow. "It is a peaceful life, more than I can say for the centaurs of late."

The demeanor of the other two darkens, and Starlight and Sunbeam chime in agreement from behind.

"What do you mean?" I focus on Thannis intently, uneasy about what news he may have.

"There have been dark tidings from abroad, and mysterious occurrences within the forest. It is no longer safe to travel at night in Wandermere."

Taryn and I exchange nervous glances before I speak. "We've

been out of contact while on our travels. What's the news from abroad?"

Thannis's hooves paw at the ground, his tail flicking in agitation. "There have been more sightings of dark creatures. A handful have now made their way through various portals even though Mosstar, the shadowlands, and others remain closed on our end."

A chill runs down my spine. If Valmar is able to send monsters through the portals without risking invasion into his own, that puts us at a major disadvantage.

Taryn looks over his shoulders as if searching for threats. "And what about the forest? Why is it no longer safe?"

Daimun huffs, his body language mimicking Thannis's as his fingers tap against the bow nervously. When he speaks, his voice is deep and boisterous. "Mysterious holes have begun appearing across the forest. Holes that are too small for centaurs to explore and too dangerous for fairies. The fairies who have ventured into their depths have not returned. We don't know what resides within, but shadowy figures have been spotted moving through the forest after twilight. Many centaurs and fairies have gone missing at night, to the point where Swift has ordered us all to stay at camp after nightfall."

Taryn strokes his beard and the clasps jingle against one another. "Is that why all of the outposts were abandoned? We've been traveling for almost two days without seeing anyone."

Sylvie is angry when she answers. "The forest is too big to patrol without our outposts. By forcing us to retreat to our camp, we are cutting our legs out from under us. The shadows are expanding, and if we don't act soon, I fear we will face a battle we cannot win."

"What's your plan?" The plight of the centaurs isn't lost on me. It wasn't that long ago that the trolls were in a similar predicament.

Thannis scans our party. "That depends on whether the mighty heroes will offer their assistance."

I step forward and extend my hand. "If you will help us locate the heart of the forest, then we will help you in whatever way we can."

Thannis nods as he grips me firmly around the forearm. "It will be done."

Sylvie whispers something to the fairies, and they dart off deeper into the forest leaving a whimsical trail in their wake. After a few moments, the fairy dust dissipates.

"Follow me," Thannis orders as he turns in the opposite direction of where the fairies disappeared.

Our party falls in line behind Thannis along the well-trodden path, while Sylvie and Daimun bring up the rear. The fog grows thicker as we walk. My spirit guide pushes back the fog around us but offers little additional visibility. The centaurs are tall enough that they can see above the fog with ease, but I have a feeling they know these paths well enough that it wouldn't hinder them if they were buried in fog.

We walk for half an hour in near silence before Thannis comes to a halt. He reaches into a pouch strapped around his lower abdomen and pulls out a bronze talisman in the shape of a starburst. A yellow stone glows gently in its center. Thannis places the talisman around his neck and a moment later, a gust of wind explodes from his body, pushing back the fog for close to thirty yards in all directions. Leaves and dirt tumble away toward the edge of the boundary, revealing an assortment of holes several feet in diameter.

"That's cool!" Taryn grins, eyeing the talisman. "What is it?"

Thannis grabs the amulet by one of its points and holds it

toward us. The stone in its center now glows brightly. "It is an Amulet of Sight. At night, it will cover the area in light. In areas such as this, it keeps the fog at bay. But come here." He motions toward one of the holes in the ground.

Taryn climbs down from Berry and we both join Thannis at the hole's edge. It reminds me of my battle with the mana-infused wyrm, only these holes are filled with pure darkness that not even my night vision can penetrate. I pull one of Jon's enchanted rocks from my satchel and activate it, but the light has no effect against whatever is causing the shadow. It's unsettling how the darkness can persist even in the presence of light.

I kneel and shine the light closer with no success. "You have no idea what's in there?"

Thannis shakes his head. "Some shadow creature, but we know nothing more than that. We've not been able to catch one out in the open, and anyone who has seen one up close has not returned to tell the tale."

A raspy sound comes from within the hole, like someone straining for breath. "Shh." I hold up a hand for the others to quiet and lean a little closer, tilting my head sideways to hear better.

"Chod," Taryn whispers.

I brush him away, closing my eyes to better make out the noise. It sounds almost like words.

Limery grows warm against my shoulder, and Taryn calls my name again as I try to make sense of the words.

"Chod." Taryn pulls at my elbow.

"What?" I snap and turn to see what the problem is. "I can hear something in there."

He points into the hole and my gaze shifts to the darkness where two orange eyes are staring back at me.

CHAPTER 3

THE HIDDEN VILLAGE

A THICK, black, slime-covered tongue lashes at the air, and I dive out of the way. Limery squawks, conjuring fireballs in both hands, and I equip Destroyer as I crawl to my feet.

The tongue disappears as quickly as it came, but when I shine Jon's enchanted light into the hole, the glowing eyes are nowhere to be seen.

"What the fuck was that?" I turn to Thannis for answers, my heartbeat pounding in my ears.

Daimun and Sylvie have their bows pointed at the hole, faces grim, but their leader stands stoic.

"Your guess is as good as mine. Whatever they are, these creatures are not native to the forest." Thannis shakes his head and purses his lips. "But at least we have a clue as to what happened to the missing fairies. Whatever foul monsters lie within these holes are multiplying, but whether it is from their own accord or some parasitic infestation, I don't know."

My grip tightens around Destroyer. "You think they could be turning other monsters into these shadow tongue things?"

Thannis nods. "It is a possibility. They could also be using the life force of those they kill to power their replication. We don't have enough information to know for sure. What matters is that they are stopped before they overtake the forest."

Taryn creeps toward the edge of the hole. "If that was its tongue, I'm not sure I want to see the body."

I take a step back, and Limery returns to my shoulder. "We'll do our best to help you with these monsters, but we require something in return."

Thannis raises a brow. "If it is within my power, it will be done."

I put away my weapon and pull the green dragon egg from my satchel. Its vibrant exterior gleams in the aura of Thannis's amulet.

Daimun and Sylvie both gasp when they see the egg, but Thannis is more reserved.

He watches the egg intensely before speaking in a low voice. "Where did you find that?"

I pull the egg closer to my chest. "That doesn't matter, but we were told that it could only be hatched in the heart of an ancient forest where life aura is most concentrated."

He nods, his eyes never leaving the egg. "You were told correctly. This is a rare and powerful item indeed. I cannot recall the last time a dragon egg has entered Wandermere." He slowly extends both hands. "May I?"

I hesitate for a moment before letting him take the egg. If they were going to rob us, they could have done so far easier when we were fighting the Wanderer. The way he stares at the egg, I'm not sure if it's greed or reverence, or maybe a little of both, but we need his help if we're going to hatch it at all.

Thannis holds the egg like it's the most precious object in

Mythos, and the other two centaurs gather around him like kids on a playground.

Taryn leans in close and whispers, "I have a feeling King Orso might not be happy you took that."

I shrug. "I'm pretty sure he has bigger problems at the moment. Besides, he gave us full access to his treasures. It's not our fault if his advisor wasn't paying attention."

Thannis hands the egg back to me. "I hope you understand the power that lies within this egg."

I think back on Senzala's totem—Nesira, the white dragon from Frostmoor—and the abilities it granted her. How it shrouded everywhere it went in a blizzard. Even the mana-infused wyrm from my first quest displayed immense power. There's no telling how big the three in the troll forest have grown by now. "I think I've got an idea."

Taryn steps past me to shine one of Jon's flashlights into the hole again. "So, what's the plan here? Make a few bombs, toss them in, and call it a day?"

"The shadows can wait." Thannis flicks his tail. "Swift will want to hear of the dragon egg. First, we will take you to our camp."

Even with Taryn casting Strong Wind, I have to sprint to keep up as the centaurs gallop across the forest. Berry traipses along fast but clumsily, his golden armor clinking, while Jordy charges in sync beside him. Limery flies next to me, my shoulders too jostling for his comfort.

Before long, I'm completely lost among the towering trees with no way of telling which direction we came from or where the portal is located. Only my instincts keep me calm, assuring me that this isn't a trap.

My mind wanders as we travel, and when Thannis comes to a halt, I nearly barrel into his hindquarters.

The fog here is denser than anywhere else in the forest, and without Thannis's amulet to keep it at bay, it forms a towering wall in front of us.

The charcoal centaur turns toward us. "Very few outsiders have been granted access to our ancestral home. I hope you respect what an honor this is."

Taryn bows slightly. "We appreciate the honor."

I nod in agreement.

"Very well. Welcome to the Hidden Lake." He gestures toward the wall of fog, and both Daimun and Sylvie step back, taking sentry positions. "Follow me."

He steps between the two centaurs and through the wall of fog. Taryn follows close behind, and I pull up the rear.

For a moment, the fog is so dense that I can't see anything, but then it clears to reveal a vibrant village bustling with fairy and centaur activity. Several fairies chime overhead, watchful guardians among the trees. Compared to the rest of the forest, this is like an entirely different world. The trees are spread much further apart, with sprawling fields full of lush grass in between. There are gaping holes in the canopy where sunlight spills through, and trails of glittering dust follow dozens of fairies as they zoom around.

Several hundred yards away, there's a village of mostly stable-like structures that are fitting for centaurs, almost like an outdoor flea market. There are no doors on the entryways between buildings, and everything is big enough for a full-grown centaur to move through with ease.

Next to the village, a sparkling blue lake shimmers in the sun. In the center, large bubbles erupt from beneath the surface, bursting to emit smoke that travels in wisps toward the wall of fog surrounding the village.

This place isn't all that different from the troll village. There must be some powerful ley lines running beneath the lake if it's the source of all this fog.

In one of the open fields, two centaurs spar with wooden spears. Several more take aim with bows at a nearby target, where two pink fairies retrieve the arrows once the quivers are emptied.

I join Thannis on his right side. "This place is amazing! Do you not need guards to protect the boundary?"

He huffs. "Normally, we have scouts posted throughout the forest, but Swift has ordered them all to remain within the boundary of our village until we have a plan. The fairy patrol keeps a constant presence at the border concealed within the fog, but it is no longer safe for them to venture out alone. Only certain of us are permitted to leave, and only to where we can make it back by nightfall. That is the only reason we were fortunate enough to come upon you." He turns to face the wall of fog. "We are safe while within the boundaries of the Hidden Lake. While we do not worship in the ways of men or dwarves, this is sacred ground among centaurs and all those who roam the forest. Only once we leave do we become susceptible to the creatures that have invaded our forest."

I brush my fingers through the wall of fog. It reminds me of the barrier around the troll forest that casts illusions to keep trespassers from entering the village. The fog flows around my hand as I move but whatever I displace is immediately filled by more fog. "Does the barrier protect the village from outsiders or is it simply for concealment?"

"I have heard of the protection surrounding the troll forest." Thannis smiles. "Though ancient, that is a different type of magic. Centaurs cannot work with raw mana in the same ways as trolls. Our barrier conceals us, but the grounds within are its real power. They were blessed many years ago to protect the heart of the forest from corruption. No creature of shadow or death may set foot within our boundary without suffering a terrible fate."

Taryn gulps. "What about shadow druids?"

Thannis's hooves pound against the earth as he laughs heartily. "It is one thing to practice magic formed by darkness. It is quite another to be forged from it. You will be fine."

Sylvie coughs as she attempts to conceal her own grin.

"What?" Taryn leans forward. "It was a fair question."

A stampede of approaching centaurs draws everyone's attention from Taryn's embarrassment. A half-dozen fairies hover around them, one for each centaur.

I recognize the largest of the centaurs from King Orso's council. He's stout with a silver lower half and a matching gray beard trimmed to a point. A massive broadsword hangs from one side of his body and a bow on the other. His chest is covered in a detailed tattoo depicting a dragon curled around the base of a towering tree.

He raises one eyebrow as he takes us in. "We've not been formally introduced. I am Swift Thundercrest, leader of the Wandermere centaur herd. You've changed since I last saw you." His lips curl as he stares at my horns. "It is a mighty look befitting a hero troll and one that will strike fear into your enemies. Finding you here bears even more credence to the claims of King Orso."

Thannis clears his throat before I have a chance to respond. "There is something you must see." He turns to me. "Show him."

I once again pull the egg from my satchel, and it definitely feels warm against my fingers this time. The centaurs surrounding Swift gasp, but Swift's expression doesn't change. His eyes move from the egg to me and then back to the egg.

"I see." His right hand trails up his side, resting on the dragon tattoo covering his midsection. "You wish to hatch it here?"

My fingers trail over the warm scales of the egg. "Is this the heart of the forest?"

His hand falls back to his side and his expression is once again jovial as if laughter is on the edge of his lips. "Mighty, but still with much to learn. Come with me. Time may be of the essence, but some things are worth an explanation." He nods to the other five centaurs surrounding him. "I will be in my private quarters with the heroes. Thannis, Sylvie, Daimun, I trust you can make the necessary arrangements?"

Thannis nods before galloping off toward the lake with his companions. The other centaurs disperse, and we follow Swift toward the village.

Swift grins at me as we take the well-trampled path through the village. The architecture boasts a primitive design combined with modern items and fairy magic. While most of the buildings are stables with open-air walls on at least one side, there is a forge, a tavern, a tannery, and shops not that different from what I would find in Lynchton or some other small town. There also seems to be a maze of stables for sleeping throughout the center of the village. One of the stables has a massive grill where two fairies cook meat and vegetables. My mouth drools at the smell. All around, fairies zip to and fro, completing tasks that the centaurs are incapable of.

We pass by the tavern, and I have to physically restrain Limery from darting to the bar. "I'm sure there will be time for a drink before we leave."

"But Limmy is thirsties." He gives me his best pout.

Swift laughs. "Centaur brew is not for the faint of heart."

"I can assure you, Limery has more courage than the lot of us combined." Taryn winks at Limery, eliciting a blush from the imp.

Swift catches me as I slow to watch a fairy grinding herbs at the potion shop. "I'm sure the village is a sight to behold for an outsider. When the celestial fairies began reproducing, they changed the trajectory of the herd. We were a simple people in many aspects, content to live our lives among the trees, but by working together, we've become a force all over Mythos."

The fairy notices us and chimes at Swift. I'm still surprised that their language isn't advanced enough for my communication stone to translate.

I wave at the tiny creature, and it sticks its tongue out. Limery mimics the fairy, blowing a raspberry of his own.

I fight not to laugh. "How does that work?"

"We look out for one another. Centaur bodies are built for strength and power, but it comes at a cost. Fairies are smart, cunning, and industrious. Their magic allows them to do many things that their size would not. We harvest materials, they put them to use, and we trade with the other kingdoms across Mythos. They are more than just companions; we coexist. We give them a purpose and protect them from those that would do them harm...until recently. Now both of our races are in danger of isolation from the outside world."

He stops in front of a stable and gestures for us to enter. "My private quarters."

Taryn starts to climb down from Berry, but Swift stops him.

"You may enter with your pets. All are welcome here."

Taryn grins as he guides Berry into the building, scratching the bear behind the ears. Ruby sleeps peacefully between Taryn's legs and Jordy trots behind them, head held high.

We pass through a wide hall that empties into a sprawling open-air room. The walls give privacy while still feeling at one with nature. There's no roof, and the sky is unimpeded save for a few fruit-bearing trees that grow within the room. Tiny hammocks stretch between several limbs, probably for the fairies to sleep in.

Small blue melons with purple dots dangle from the branches. Swift plucks one and tosses it to Taryn. Juice explodes across his beard as he takes a bite, followed by a loud groan of pleasure.

Taryn wipes the juices from his beard. "Wow, that's so good. Like a blueberry and a grape had a baby."

I focus on one of the melons until a description appears.

Item. Twilight Gusher. *+1 Constitution for 1 hour. A hybrid melon found only in Wandermere, the Twilight Gusher was cultivated by celestial fairies and has become one of the most sought-after treats in Pruxford and Antadale.*

Swift offers me one, but I decline. Going into battle, I might eat one just for the stats, but not here.

"Trolls don't have much of a palate for sweets."

Taryn takes another bite and speaks with a full mouth. "Dude, you're missing out."

Berry snatches the gusher from Swift's hand but quickly spits it on the ground, apparently not a fan of the sweetness either. Jordy doesn't waste any time eating it off the floor.

"Don't worry," Swift laughs. "We have an assortment of meats that are sure to be more to your liking. But first, let us get down to business. I would offer you a seat, but we don't get many two-legged visitors."

A pile of hay rests in one corner, but the remainder of the floor is nearly empty aside from a handful of spears and other weapons propped in another corner. Shelves line every wall and are filled to the edge with potions, scrolls, books, and trinkets. Everything is at least four feet off the floor, making it easy for a centaur to reach.

"It's no problem. We're used to standing." I lean in close to Taryn. "Good thing you're on Berry or you might miss all the action."

He rolls his eyes. "You used to be such a good trash talker. What happened?"

I search for a witty retort, but the words don't come, leaving my mouth gaping like a fish. I can tell by the smirk on Taryn's face that he knows he got me.

"Fair enough. My jokes have been rather short-sighted as of late."

Taryn smirks. "I'm sure you'll have plenty of new ones inside that big, empty head of yours."

Swift's tail flicks as he watches us. "I used to bicker with my brother in much the same way. It is a blessing to have such a bond."

I give Taryn's shoulder a soft squeeze. "What happened to your brother?"

Swift stares off into the treetops for a moment, eyes distant as he relives some memory. "Draydon was an adventurous spirit, even for a centaur. Where action and adventure awaited, he answered the call. He explored far and wide, and when Wandermere offered no more secrets, he traveled through the portals. He became a fan of prize tournaments, competing against the best warriors for gold and glory. He won many, but he perished in a tragic accident when a broken lance caught him in the chest. The gnomes honored him with a glass sculpture outside of their tournament grounds."

I grimace at the thought of taking a lance through the chest. "I'm sorry to hear that. He sounds like an amazing competitor."

"That he was." Swift clears his throat. "But that is enough idle chat. The night grows ever closer, and we have urgent matters to discuss. I'm sure Thannis has informed you of our situation?"

"The formless monsters with glowing eyes and super-long tongues," Taryn says dryly. "Yeah, we've seen them."

My skin crawls at the memory. "You want us to find a way to kill them. What have you tried already?"

"Not enough, I am afraid." He sighs. "Since the disappearances, I have ordered everyone to return to the village after night-fall. Limited scouts go out during the day, but that is when the creatures are hidden. We've discovered the holes but have no understanding of how deep they go or what lies within. We can't fit inside, they are impenetrable to light, and the fairies who've investigated never returned. Once we witnessed a tongue snatch a fairy from the air, we haven't risked their safety since. We've tried dropping fire and fairy explosives, but with no luck. I feared our only option was to meet the monsters at nightfall, a fight we are most assuredly not prepared for."

I trace my horn as I think, running its pointed tip beneath my claws. "That's something to work with. We'll do what we can."

Swift nods slowly. "That is all we ask. While you are here, you will have access to any of our items, elixirs, and explosives."

Limery claps his hands together at the last part.

Swift grins at the imp. "In exchange for your help, we will hatch your dragon."

As soon as he finishes, I receive a notification with a quest alert.

Quest Alert: *You have been offered the quest "Tit for Tat." Shadow monsters are overtaking Wandermere, and mysterious disappearances have occurred throughout the forest. Identify the threat and eliminate it, bringing peace to the forest once again.*

Reward: *Increased favor with Swift Thundercrest and the Wandermere Herd.*

Bonus: *In exchange for your efforts, Swift Thundercrest will guide you through the process of hatching a green dragon egg.*

When I accept the quest, Swift releases a sigh of relief.

I remove the egg once more, and it's still warm to the touch. "Chief Laojin of the arctic trolls said that we needed to hatch it in the heart of an ancient forest. How far are we from there?"

Swift laughs again, the same as the first time I mentioned the heart of the forest.

I raise an eyebrow. "What's so funny?"

He lifts his arms, spreading them wide as he gestures at the surroundings. "The Hidden Lake is the heart of the forest. It is our ancestral home and has the highest concentration of life aura throughout Mythos."

Taryn raises a finger, a confused look on his face. "I thought there was supposed to be an adult green dragon living here."

"You are correct. For over one hundred years, Verdaria has slumbered in the depths of the Hidden Lake. The life aura nourishes her while in her stone form, and the fog that coats the forest is thanks to her."

Taryn's mouth hangs open. "So, you're telling me there's a dragon sleeping at the bottom of your lake that has been there for over a hundred years?"

Swift nods. "And if your dragon egg belongs to her, it is all the more miraculous that no one has attempted to hatch it until now."

I keep the fact that it belonged to King Orso to myself. "What do we have to do to hatch it?"

He smiles. "Tell me, are trolls known for their patience?"

Taryn snickers, and I hold back a groan. The trolls might have patience, but it's certainly not my strong suit.

CHAPTER 4

WHAT DREAMS ARE MADE OF

WORD TRAVELS FAST and there are hundreds of centaurs surrounding the Hidden Lake by the time we arrive. An equal number of fairies dart through the air, and some dive low against the lake, letting their spindly fingers trail against the water's surface. One sprinkles fairy dust onto the dragon's bubbles, and glittery fog wisps through the village toward the wall.

This place must be even bigger than I thought because I only saw a few dozen centaurs when we first entered the village. I wonder just how many of them used to be spread across all of the forest. Their tails swish and hooves paw at the ground, and I get the feeling that this is a once-in-a-lifetime opportunity for them.

The forest has darkened since our arrival, and the sun lies hidden somewhere beyond the treetops. Dozens of torches blaze around the edge of the lake, and occasionally, pink embers soar into the air. Night will come soon and with it our promise to find out what exactly has overtaken the forest.

Thannis and Sylvie stand back from an open space where a large raft rests on the lake's edge. The raft is made from freshly-chopped trees roped together with vines, and leaf-covered branches protrude in a few areas, giving it a more natural look than anything built by humans or dwarves. In the center, there's some sort of altar where vines intertwine into a cradle for the egg.

The herd goes quiet when they notice our approach, but the chiming of fairies still carries across the lake. Swift leads the way, followed by Taryn and Ruby riding Berry. Jordy flanks his right, and Limery and I pull up the rear.

Limery adjusts himself on my shoulder. "Limmy is exciteds for the baby dragons."

"I think we all are. A dragon can't be more trouble than you, right?" I gently poke him in the stomach.

"Limmy isn't troubles." He cackles. "Limmy will shows the baby dragons how to makes fire."

Just what we need, a wild and powerful imp teaching an untrained dragon how to breathe fire in the middle of the forest.

"How about we discuss that when the time comes?"

When we arrive at the raft, Swift pulls a horn from his satchel and blows. Deep sonorous notes echo through the forest and even the fairies quiet.

He speaks, and his voice is amplified across the gentle waves of the lake. "A shadow has loomed over the forest of late but today, we have reason to see the light. For when we are at our darkest, the forest has brought two heroes into our village."

"And me's," Limery interrupts.

"And a brave imp." Swift winks at Limery before returning to his speech. "While the heroes will fight to push these monsters of shadow and death back to whence they came, we are granted something even more miraculous—the opportunity to witness the birth of a dragon."

Whispers and gasps start around the lake as the rumors are finally confirmed.

Swift raises a hand and they quiet once again. "None of us here have witnessed Verdaria in her living form. For over a hundred years, she has slumbered, and it has been two generations since a dragon was last hatched in Wandermere. But the winds of Mythos are changing and today, we will play a part in that change."

As if on cue, a gust of wind rips across the village. Branches shake violently and waves spread across the lake.

"Now that's spooky." Taryn looks around for the source of the gust, but there's nothing there.

Swift speaks in a low voice. "Chod, please place the egg on the altar."

When I remove the egg from the satchel, the wind dies down immediately. I can't help but wonder if the forest can sense the power within the egg? Or perhaps Verdaria's presence extends beyond the bottom of the lake. Whatever the reason, the egg is warmer than I have ever felt it, and the green scales are as vibrant as fresh grass. We're definitely in the right place. The altar cradles the egg perfectly as I set it down.

Swift nods to Thannis, Sylvie, and Daimun before continuing. Each of the centaurs steps forward with an item.

"Hatching a dragon takes time, but we have gathered some items that should help boost the concentration of life aura around the egg."

Sylvie holds a plain gray stone in her palm. A dull rune is etched across the top of the stone, and it's small enough that it could fit into one of the sockets on Destroyer or one of my other enchanted weapons.

She kneels and places the stone at the edge of the raft closest to the water. "This is a Regeneration Stone. It increases the healing and health regeneration of whoever holds it. It can also transfer its properties to enchanted weapons when equipped."

Item. Regeneration Stone. *Increases health regeneration by 20%.* **Bonus:** *When paired with Shield of Vigor and Renewal Spear, user will be granted a ten-foot aura that provides 20% increased regeneration for companions within its radius.*

That's a hell of an attachment, especially combined with the full set. By having all three pieces, it's basically like the entire party has a Regeneration Stone. I wonder if the aura would work on my horrors to keep them from dying when out of combat? Even if it kept them at one percent health, the amount of health they have doesn't matter when casting Sacrifice or Kamikaze. I'll need to talk to Swift about these items when this is all said and done.

Next, Daimun holds up a dull gray shield. The shield is massive, with a shimmering green tree engraved into the front, eerily similar to the tattoo on Swift's chest. In the center of the tree, there's a socket that's the perfect size for the Regeneration Stone.

He places the shield in the bottom left corner of the raft. "The Shield of Vigor increases the overall health of whoever wields it. When paired with the Regeneration Stone, healing and health regeneration are increased even further."

I quickly examine the shield.

Item. Shield of Vigor. *Increases HP by 30%.* **Bonus:** *When paired with Regeneration Stone and Renewal Spear, user will be granted a ten-foot aura that provides 20% increased regeneration for companions within its radius.*

Now, this is an item I would love to have. A thirty percent health increase combined with the bonus from my horrors would make me pretty tough to kill. Not to mention the Rapid Regeneration passive I already have when below ten percent health. With these items, I could fight with low health for even longer. I could even bait opponents into continuing a fight by playing weak before exploiting the rapid healing.

Thannis showcases the final item, a spear in the same dull gray color as the other two items. The weapon is tipped with an emerald spearhead.

He holds it in our direction. "The Renewal Spear is the final piece of the set. On its own, the spear gathers aura while not in use, but it also saps life force when it touches a living being. The aura is stored within the weapon and can be transferred to the wielder on command. When all three items are combined, they produce an aura that buffs companions within a ten-foot radius."

Item. Renewal Spear. Capable of holding life aura equivalent to 500 HP. The Renewal Spear gathers aura passively while equipped and can steal health from enemies during battle. Life aura may be absorbed by the wielder at any time. **Bonus:** *When paired with Regeneration Stone and Shield of Vigor, user will be granted a ten-foot aura that provides 20% increased regeneration for companions within its radius.*

This one makes me giddy with excitement. I can already see a hundred different uses for the Renewal Spear. It would synergize with the passive from my Horrors of Finesse perfectly. Part of me wishes that we could use these for our quest to clear the forest, but if Swift is putting them on the altar, there has to be a good reason.

Thannis places the spear in the bottom right corner of the raft, forming a triangle around the altar. As soon as he releases it, a trail of energy zips from one item to the other, forming some kind of magical current that produces a deep green aura. The runes along all three items pulse with energy, and the aura travels up the altar to where green ghost flames surround the egg.

"These items will further increase the already potent aura in the lake." Swift moves to the front of the raft and picks up a rope attached to both corners.

Stepping into the lake, he hauls the raft in. It bobbles for a second before resting on the calm water. With a final tug, the raft floats gently toward the center of the lake. As the daylight continues to fade, the ghost flames reflect on the water's surface and add an eeriness to the bubbling fog, making it look more like a cauldron than a lake.

After a few final words, the rest of the centaurs begin to disperse.

"What now?" I ask.

"For the dragon, we wait. For you, we must gather provisions for your quest."

***

Inside the armory, I place an ornately-carved spear back into its bin. "Do you have any more item sets like the one on the altar?"

The centaurs have well-made items in their armory, but very few of them are enchanted, and not at all suited for either mine or Taryn's playstyle and abilities. The spear is sturdy and beautiful but offers me nothing that I don't already have with my trident, but even Sea Scorpion's enchantment no longer provides much value thanks to the passive from Ram Rage that allows me to deal splash damage on all physical attacks.

Swift runs his finger over the tip of the spear I just passed over. "We make fine bows, arrows, and spears, but we have little need for the weapons of the two-legged. Very few of us prefer plate armor, and we aren't built to be agile sword wielders. This one—" He grips the hilt of the broadsword hanging from his side. "—was a gift to our herd long ago. Our blacksmith primarily forges arrowheads and shoes for our hooves. The item set on the altar was a gift from abroad."

"Makes sense." I stop in front of a rack of intricately-designed arrows displayed on the wall. They are made from a variety of materials—some wood, others metal, and the feather fletchings come in various sizes and colors. I'm sure Archard would have a field day testing out how they all work. "I prefer a more in-your-face approach, and Taryn has leaned into his druid abilities more and more. We're magic and mayhem. Bows and spears just aren't a good fit for us right now."

Swift motions for us to leave. "Do not worry. Our fairy companions should have some items to help you with your quest."

The next stable we enter is coated with enough glitter that it could pass for the backstage of a drag show. A half-dozen fairies scurry about. Up close, they're somehow both beautiful and terrifying at the same time. Each fairy has flawless skin and perfectly proportioned features, but their spindly arms and fingers seem out of place, and there's something unsettling about their eyes. They're opalescent and without pupils, so it's impossible to tell if they are watching me or not. Each one is a slightly different shade of pink or purple with lacy wings that look like they could blow away in a stiff breeze.

Two stand together mixing a potion in the corner. One holds the container while the other stirs it with a long stick. Colors swirl together, and I catch the faint aroma of cotton candy. Another ladles the contents of a completed batch, carefully measuring each scoop as it pours the vibrant liquids into vials.

On the other side of the stable, another fairy looks drunk as it stumbles across a raised platform before lying down on a small pile of straw. Three others already lie there asleep. A second fairy looks about to pass out as it clenches its palm over an empty vial. A moment later, a sparkling pink powder appears in the vial.

It takes me a moment before I realize what the others are up to. "Are you harvesting fairy dust?"

Swift cups the dazed fairy in his palm and strokes it between the wings. The fairy nuzzles against his thumb and chimes so softly it almost sounds like a purr.

He places the tired fairy on the straw pile next to the others just as two new fairies fly in and take their seats. They chime with delight as they clench their fists and streams of fairy dust fall into the container.

"They've been working overtime since the invaders appeared. The males produce Dream Dust, and the females produce Sleep Dust. It's a draining process for them to provide so much dust, but we are well-stocked even though we haven't had the opportunity to use them yet."

"What do we have here?" Taryn lifts a vial filled with a purple, glittery substance. As he tilts it, the substance moves like sand.

Swift grins. "Celestial fairies have some of the most potent dust of all the fairy races. Where other fairy abilities are often tied to the elements, celestial fairies are known for their sparking trails and the magical dust they produce. This—" He taps the vial in Taryn's hand. "—is Dream Dust. A few sprinkles of this can lead to vivid dreams while sleeping. An entire vial can make one experience dreams as if they were real."

"So, like hallucinations?" I pick up a vial and give it a shake.

Item. Dream Dust. *A powerful, potent substance capable of unlocking hidden realms of the mind. Effects are dependent upon amount ingested.*

Swift nods. "Exactly, those affected are unable to distinguish dream from reality until it wears off. We have no idea if it will affect the shadow monsters, but it was our next course of action before you arrived."

"It's worth a shot." Taryn adds a few vials to his satchel, and I do the same. "What else are we working with?"

"While the Dream Dust may disorient an opponent, Sleep Dust is capable of immobilizing them outright." Swift points to a collection of vials containing a light pink substance. It's less vibrant than the Dream Dust and much less glittery.

Item. Sleep Dust. *Often mixed with liquid and drank as a tonic, Sleep Dust offers effects ranging from drowsiness to instantaneous deep slumber.*

"Now, that could be useful." Even if we don't use it here, you never know when you might need to sneak past a guard or bypass a dungeon mob.

Swift showcases some of the other items containing fairy dust before we leave. Small amounts are mixed into potions, elixirs, and tonics. Some offer increased or modified dreams; others help with relaxation. There seem to be countless options for using these two types of dust depending on how they are brewed. Before the shadow monsters invaded Wandermere, these concoctions were the herd's most-traded items with other kingdoms.

We load up on as many vials of Dream and Sleep Dust as we can find, but most of the other items are unlikely to help us in battle. Still, we pack a few more that might prove useful once we find ourselves back in a city again. While we still have some gold from our time on the Isle of Mythos, we've spent more than we've earned lately so we might need to trade soon.

The fairies return to their glittery escapades, and we follow Swift to a row of empty stables at the edge of the village. From our vantage point, the torches blaze around the Hidden Lake. In the center, the raft sways gently and the green aura from the three items reflects off the calm surface.

Swift's tail swishes as he watches the raft. "The days always pass too quickly of late. For your safety, I would wait until daybreak before beginning your quest. The less time you spend under darkness, the better. We have plenty of open stables for you to sleep in, and if you wish, you may watch the ceremony as one of our colts is branded a stallion."

Taryn shifts his gaze to the ground. "That is a generous offer, but I'm going to call it an early night. We have a long road ahead of us tomorrow."

I'm sure he's not in a partying mood, but it would probably do him some good to be around others for a while.

"Oh, come on." I squeeze Taryn's shoulder. "We've never been known to turn down a good party." I laugh.

He doesn't answer, guiding Berry into one of the open stables. I offer Swift a shrug before joining Taryn. Maybe he just needs a little convincing.

Swift nods his understanding. "Very well. Settle in. You will find the herd down by the lake if you choose."

Limery smiles devilishly. "Oh, yes, Limmy loves to parties."

At least he won't take any convincing.

CHAPTER 5
THE SCARS OF LIFE

TARYN FLUFFED the pile of hay before collapsing onto it. Berry nestled beside him, jostling Taryn as the bear positioned himself until his head rested on his owner's lap. Jordy tucked his legs and sat down on the druid's other side while Ruby cuddled in the warmth of Berry's rust-colored fur.

"What?" He raised his head to meet Chod's eyes. "Can't we rest for just one night?"

Chod frowned. "Bro, come on. When are we ever going to have the opportunity to party with centaurs again?" He knelt in front of Taryn, his massive horns making his threatening presence even larger. "I think it would be good for you."

Taryn clenched his jaw, fighting the urge to snap at his friend. Chod was only trying to help, but comments like that always made him sound like a dick. Taryn didn't need anyone telling him what was good for him, especially the person who was a large part of the reason things felt so shitty. He took a deep breath, letting the moment pass.

"I've got everything that's good for me right here." He

scratched Berry on the head, eliciting a groan. "Isn't that right, Berry?"

Chod sighed, but it wasn't from disappointment. It was more like a sigh of failure, and it matched his sunken shoulders as he shook his head. "Alright, suit yourself. Limery and I are going to see what all the fuss is about."

"Yeah, Limmy wants to parties!" The imp threw his hands in the air and pumped them, a move Taryn had taught him not long ago.

Taryn smiled. "You show them how it's done, little dude. I'll be here if you guys need me."

As the two were leaving, Taryn called after Chod. "Thanks for trying."

Chod gave him a half-smile before disappearing into the village.

Taryn stared at the empty space where Chod had stood. Underneath all the rage and wise cracks, he was a good person—it was part of the reason they'd remained friends for so long—but Taryn wasn't ready to put himself out there just yet. He'd exchanged a few wisecracks with Chod earlier, but everything was still raw. Too raw. Like someone had scraped out his heart with a rusty spoon.

He wasn't ready to let his guard down again. Not yet.

He laid back against the straw. It wasn't the same as a bed at the inn, but since the hay was piled on soft earth, it was surprisingly comfortable. Plus, it was always more enjoyable to lay next to his pets, something Berry and Jordy wouldn't be able to do once they were back in the cities.

Taryn imagined the duo clamoring through a busy tavern, Berry knocking chairs aside with his massive size and Jordy's hooves clacking against the wooden floors. They'd be kicked out in a heartbeat.

He pulled the last of the carrots Gherhardt had given him in Frostmoor and fed it to Jordy. The frost goat crunched on it loudly, his jaw moving back and forth as he ground it against his blocky teeth. He'd been on death's doorstep when Chod first brought him down the mountain. Jordy was old, but since they'd bonded, it was like the goat had turned back the clock.

Good, because Taryn couldn't handle losing another pet.

He scratched the bridge of Jordy's nose, and the goat lowered his head in a show of respect. He was an interesting creature—stubborn and proud, but not in the same way that Stompy had been. More like if Berry's affectionate qualities and Stompy's heroic qualities had been combined.

"He would have liked you a lot." Taryn wiped a tear from his cheek. The two pets had only spent a handful of days together before Stompy passed.

He closed his eyes and leaned back to keep from crying. At least he was alone. Chod felt bad enough without seeing Taryn's inner turmoil. As upset as he might be, what was done was done, and he didn't want to hold a grudge against his best friend.

Squeezing his eyes tighter until they started to tingle with pain, he focused on the world around them. Anything to distract himself from what was happening inside his head. Distant chimes told of fairies coming and going. Owls hooted somewhere high in the trees. Branches hissed in the night, and faraway laughter could be heard.

Hooves clopped through the village as a latecomer raced to join in the fun.

Then a wet tongue licked Taryn on the nose. He opened his eyes to find Jordy's nose inches from his own. Jordy snorted, followed by another slimy lick as his outrageously-long tongue darted for Taryn.

He moved out of the way, leaving the frost goat licking at air. "Fine. We'll go down for a few minutes."

Berry and Ruby were on their feet in an instant. Berry's stump of a tail wagged like an excited dog and Ruby paced between Taryn and the stable entrance.

Taryn placed his hands on his hips. "Message received. How to tell me I'm a party pooper without telling me I'm a party pooper."

They came to a stop at the edge of the village, and Taryn inhaled deeply as he took in their surroundings. This truly was a beautiful place. The way the torches and dragon altar reflected off the lake was mesmerizing. Not to mention the fairies that zipped around, blurs of bubblegum and lavender against the night sky with trails that sparkled in their wake.

Down by the lake, a large fire blazed. Several deer roasted on three spits constantly rotated by a group of fairies.

Chod's hulking frame was noticeable immediately, even next to the large centaurs. He held a slab of meat in one hand and a drink in the other. Limery swayed in the air, both hands wrapped around a beverage much too big for him.

"Oh, man." Taryn laughed. "I really hope we aren't turning him into a delinquent." He turned to his pets. "Go on and have some fun. It's safe here. You don't have to stick around me all night."

Berry nuzzled Taryn's leg before frolicking off toward the lake with the others in tow.

For the moment, Taryn wanted to sit and observe. He'd go talk to the others when he was ready. While there were plenty of centaurs feasting and drinking, there were other activities taking place all around the village.

A group of younger-looking centaurs were tossing spears to see who could throw one the farthest. Dozens of spears stuck in the ground over a hundred yards away. Every time a new record was set, cheers echoed across the forest. Another group practiced archery, they shot at a tree playing a game where the goal was to shoot an arrow directly above the previous shot. A trail of arrows zigged and zagged halfway up the towering oak.

"I sense there is great trouble within you."

Taryn jumped at the sudden sound, turning to see a dark-skinned centaur with a forked beard only feet away. He'd been so focused on the centaur games that he hadn't heard Thannis's massive hooves approaching from behind.

"It's been a tough week." Taryn sighed.

"I do not doubt it. Dark times are ahead for all of us, I fear." He placed a hand on Taryn's shoulder. "But for now, we still have nights like these. Come, I will show you how some centaurs have made peace with the pain inside their hearts."

Taryn couldn't explain why, but he followed Thannis. They took a roundabout way, sticking close to the village but bypassing Chod and the most raucous of the herd.

They stopped next to a smaller fire, where a few centaurs sat on their haunches. It was an odd sight, seeing them sitting. Several more stood around the fire chatting and drinking. Sylvie and Daimun were both there, and Taryn tried his best to avert his gaze from her exposed chest. The duo tilted their mugs to him as he passed.

Closest to the water's edge, an older centaur with a bluish-gray coat and long gray braids appeared to be chiseling into the chest of a much younger centaur. Upon closer inspection, he could see the outline of a tattoo. Almost all of the centaurs had tattoos, and this one looked to be the outline of two spears crossed over the young centaur's chest.

He took a moment to examine some of the other's tattoos.

The elder was covered more than any of them, from his neck all the way down to his waistline. Trees and flowers, weapons and shields, even runes and designs that seemed to only be decorative; he'd left no space empty.

Sylvie had blue tattoos along both arms. They swirled into wispy ends like gusts of wind. Daimun also had tattoos along his arms, but his were intricate symbols and runes. Thannis had an ornate shield over each pec with ornamental embellishments that ran onto his shoulders and a quarter of the way down his arms.

Thannis placed a hand on his chest as if feeling his own tattoo. "Armun has etched the bodies of every centaur on their name-day for as far back as I can remember. And now, young Danetro has joined our ranks."

Danetro grimaced as Armun tapped the end of a short metal needle with a hammer, slowly moving it across the young centaur's chest.

Taryn had watched documentaries on traditional tattoo design. There was usually a trail of blood and ink as the design took shape one dot at a time, but Danetro's body was healing as soon as the needle was removed.

Taryn scrunched his brow. "How is he healing so fast?"

Armun raised the needle, and Danetro immediately relaxed. "The life aura from the lake increases regeneration, allowing the body to heal almost as fast as the ink is applied."

Danetro groaned as Armun resumed the tattoo. "It still hurts like a banshee."

Taryn stepped closer. "You do amazing work. So much detail for only using a single needle."

Armun's tail swished. "That is high praise coming from a dwarf. Dwarven craftsmanship and attention to detail are the finest I have had the pleasure to witness. I would love to see their skill with a needle."

Taryn smiled at that. "I can't say I've ever seen a dwarf with a tattoo, but maybe now that the portal to Isle of Mythos is opened that will change. Is there a reason you all have tattoos?"

Armun stopped again, giving the young stallion a moment of reprieve. "The reason is different for each of us. In ages past, the tattoos depicted great victories or tallied enemies defeated in combat. Swift's brother, Draydon, held onto that tradition and would return to the forest after every tournament to mark his victories. There was a time when those tattooed would ingest Dream Dust and watch the scene play out as it was etched into their bodies. Nowadays, some choose to honor their history, others their goals and ambitions, some choose to honor those they have lost. While others do it for no other reason than to honor the history of the herd."

Taryn choked up for a moment. *Some choose to honor those they have lost.* There was something beautiful in that sentiment.

He cleared his throat. "When you are done, I would be grateful if you would tattoo me."

"You're doing what?" Chod stood up so quickly that his drink sloshed over the edge of the mug. A pile of bones sat at his feet, remnants of the roasted boar.

Taryn straightened, his conviction set. "I'm getting a tattoo."

Chod stared at him for a moment, body swaying from the effects of the centaur mead, before extending a fist. "Badass! What are you getting?"

"I don't want to ruin the surprise. Just thought I would let you know what was happening in case you went looking for me." Taryn looked around, where centaurs were drinking and laughing. "Is the party everything you thought it would be?"

Chod placed a hand on Taryn's shoulder more forcefully than

he would have when sober. "It's great! I'm next up in the spear toss, and Limery has made friends with the fairies. They're putting on quite the show."

He pointed over the lake where Limery and a handful of fairies hovered over its surface. Limery held a fireball in each hand. When he tossed it, the fairies threw up a handful of dust. As the fireball passed through the dust, it exploded into a colorful blaze of light that crackled like fireworks.

Taryn laughed. "I'm not sure I want to know how they discovered that trick."

"Chod!" Swift yelled from the field where nearly twenty centaurs had gathered to toss spears. "Time to show us some of that barbarian troll strength."

Taryn slapped Chod on the side. "Good luck with the spear toss. Time for me to go get stabbed repeatedly with a needle. They tell me it's fun."

Danetro stood proudly, shoulders back to push out his chest as he showed off his new tattoo. He trotted like a show-horse, tail swishing as he spun in a circle. It had taken hours, but the tattoo was finished. Finely-detailed spears that had been painstakingly designed one dot at a time.

The two spears crossed over one another in an X, taking up the majority of Danetro's chest. Taryn had learned that they represented the young stallion's role in the tribe—a hunter during times of peace and a warrior in times of unrest. One spear was uneven and knotted in places, with a stone spearhead lashed together with leather and adorned with feathers—a symbol of the past. The other was polished wood, sleek and perfectly balanced, fitted with a metal spearhead—a symbol of the present. Both played their part in centaur society.

"It looks amazing." Taryn gaped in awe. Soon, he would have his own tattoo. "You really killed it, Armun."

The elder centaur dipped his head. "Practice leads to perfection. Now tell me, what tattoo is worthy of a hero dwarf?"

Taryn cleared his throat. "I would like to honor the pet I lost in Frostmoor."

Armun's brow furrowed as he focused on Taryn's words. "Tell me about this pet of yours. Tattoos tell a story in themselves, and the better I understand your connection to the tattoo, the better I will be able to uncover the story within you."

Taryn took a deep breath. He'd known this moment would come. If he was getting Stompy's memory tattooed onto his flesh, he should be able to talk about him. But it wasn't just talking about what had happened at Boneholde that was hard. Since that day, anything that reminded him of Stompy was also a reminder that his pet was no longer around.

A strong hand rested on his shoulder.

"Not all tattoos are created equal." Thannis's gaze lingered on him with a soft expression that contradicted his powerful appearance. "My tattoo honors those I lost as well. These shields that cover my chest are my promise to defend the Hidden Lake so that it never happens again. Dream Dust helped me to make peace with the demons in my head."

Thannis looked to Armun and the elder nodded. Reaching in his satchel of tattoo supplies, Armun pulled out a vial that swirled with a purplish-brown liquid.

Item. Manifestation Potion. *Brewed with Dream Dust and psychedelic mushrooms, this potion has the ability to intertwine the subconscious with reality.* ***Warning:*** *Highly potent. Do not use while working or operating contraptions.*

Armun lifted the vial for Taryn to see. "Take this while I am tattooing you and whatever you choose to focus on will revisit you once again."

Taryn reached for the vial, but Armun pulled it back. "But first, tell me about your pet."

Taryn steeled himself. He could do this.

"His—" Another deep breath. "His name was Stompy. He was a moulhaug, the most stubborn creature I've ever met, but he was mine. He saved my ass on more than one occasion. He died saving my ass."

Armun's face was grave. "He sounds like a very loyal companion, but I am afraid I'm not familiar with, what was it, moulhaugs?"

Taryn's chest tightened. If Armun didn't know what a moulhaug looked like, then how was he supposed to tattoo it?

He would try his best to describe it. "They're native to the Isle of Mythos. I guess with the portals being closed, it makes sense you wouldn't see them here. He was big, easily two to three times as large as a centaur, with gray skin that had patches of green so that he looked like a moss-covered boulder when sleeping. He had a massive horn on the tip of his nose, kind of like a rhi—"

Taryn stopped himself. Of course, they wouldn't know what a rhino was.

Armun sighed. "I'm sorry, but I am not familiar. Perhaps if there is something that reminds you of him, that is all that truly matters. Tattoos are a symbol, after all, nothing more."

Taryn closed his eyes. He could get a horn, but there was no telling if it would look like Stompy's. Maybe he should just give up on the idea. It had been worth a shot, but it didn't sound like this was meant to be.

Something hard pressed against Taryn's side.

He opened his eyes to find Jordy with his horns lowered. Berry and Ruby stood behind him. They were always there when he needed them.

"Your pets have great affection for you." Armun petted Berry behind the ears, and the bear groaned in pleasure. "They can sense when you are in distress."

Taryn lifted Jordy's chin until their eyes met. "Thanks, Jordy," he whispered. He turned back to Armun, grinning. "I think I know just what to get."

CHAPTER 6

BITTERSWEET GOOD-BYE

Taryn rested on a raised platform lying on his back. He clenched the Manifestation Potion in his palm as he lay there shirtless, staring at the night sky. He would take the potion soon, but he wanted to feel these first few pokes.

Armun leaned over him, needle in one hand and the small hammer in the other. "Ready?"

Taryn nodded and then focused his eyes on the starry sky overhead. Many a night he had gazed up at the same sky as he rested on Stompy's tough hide. Somehow, it felt appropriate.

He winced as the needle jabbed into his chest. The pain flared but dulled almost immediately. Half a second later, the next tap came, followed by more pain.

He'd chosen to have the tattoo over his left pec, over his heart. It might have been cheesy, but he didn't care what anyone else thought. This tattoo was for him and him alone.

His family had never had any pets growing up, there was precious little money to go around as it was. Bonding with Stompy, Berry, Ruby, and now Jordy, he'd made up for lost time rather quickly. In the same way Chod had bonded with Limery, he'd found a real connection with these bits of data that rivaled any relationship he'd had outside the game. Their companionship and vastly-different personalities filled a void in his heart that Taryn hadn't even known he'd had.

As each successive stab of the needle built on the last, Taryn embraced the pain. He let it course through his body, mingling with the suffering already inside him. The more he embraced the pain, the less intense the emotional hurt seemed to feel, until he came to appreciate the physical pain. Was this how people felt about tattoos in real life? He'd never once thought that physical pain could help heal emotional wounds.

Armun stopped for a moment, and Taryn felt invincible at the brief reprieve.

"How are you holding up?" the centaur asked.

"I'm good." He lifted the vial. "Time to see what this is all about."

Taryn downed the potion, and it tasted like candy that had been dropped in the mud, simultaneously sweet and disgusting. It only took a few seconds before the world went hazy.

The pain of the needle resumed, but it felt distant. He sat up and was surprised when a ghostly copy of himself rose from his own body, leaving the corporeal version under the needle and hammer of Armun's experienced precision.

The world swirled around him in a watercolor tide of purples and pinks. Aside from the immediate vicinity around his body, all shape and form left the world.

He hovered over Armun's shoulder, watching the tattoo come to life. Laughter coursed through his chest unbidden at how silly the design was.

A deep bellow echoed behind him, the sonorous tones reverberating in his chest.

Taryn froze, and whatever ghostly version of a heart he currently had halted as well. A second bellow erupted, much closer now, followed by a massive snout resting on his shoulder.

He refused to move, refused to turn around in case this was all some clever trick. There was a snort, and a warm gust of air huffed against the side of his face. When Taryn turned, Stompy watched him with large moss-colored eyes.

Taryn wrapped his arms around the moulhaug, burying his face into the creature's side. "I'm so sorry, boy." His body shook with waves of emotion.

Stompy huffed again, his nostrils flaring before taking a step back. When Taryn tried to follow, Stompy lowered his horn, blocking Taryn's approach.

Their eyes locked again.

"What?" Taryn's voice cracked. "I didn't mean for any of this to happen. I tried to get you to come with us, but you wouldn't listen." He clenched his fists. "What do you want from me?"

Stompy lowered his head, sniffing at Taryn's leg. Suddenly, there was something firm in his pocket that hadn't been there before.

"Of course." Taryn laughed when he reached inside. "A carrot. Is this my dream or yours?"

The carrot glowed with energy as he held it out to Stompy. The moulhaug snatched it up, grunting as he crushed it between his sledgehammer teeth. When he was finished, Stompy lowered himself to the ground so that Taryn could climb on his back.

Taryn settled in, and Stompy kicked off from the ground, floating into the air as the world shifted around them once again. The purples and pinks shrunk back, revealing a star-speckled vastness. Far away, Taryn could faintly feel the prick of the needle against his skin.

Stompy soared through the heavens like some god-powered

beast. Scenes began to appear around them, ghostly holograms depicting events from Taryn's time in Mythos.

The fight with Stompy where they'd first bonded. Their travels through the Greystone Mountains. Relaxing by the beach in Sandholde.

Stompy slowed, groaning softly at the image of them soaking up the sun.

Then there was chaos as a scene showed Stompy smashing through the stable in Seascape and running through the streets to find Taryn and Chod battling Glenn outside the portal.

One by one, Taryn revisited the memories he had created with this magnificent beast, all the way up until the gates of Boneholde.

Stompy slowed down.

"Don't stop," Taryn whispered softly. "I can't watch this one. Not again."

Stompy snorted, lingering in front of the image as the hobgoblins spilled over the gate.

"I said no!" Taryn yelled, and his voice echoed through eternity.

Stompy responded with a bellowing trumpet of his own, bucking Taryn from his back. He turned on the druid as he hovered in space, steam pouring from his nostrils and fire blazing in his mossy eyes.

He bellowed again, as if telling Taryn this was not an option.

Taryn forced himself to watch. He watched as Chod tried to slow the horde down with his horrors. Watched as Stompy turned back. He witnessed his own face contorted in desperation, and Chod's bulging muscles as he pulled with all his might to try and turn the moulhaug around.

For the first time, he saw the mirrored desperation in his

friend's face as Chod realized he'd finally met his match in a battle of wills.

Stompy wasn't scared as he ran into the horde of hobgoblins. He was mad as hell and determined to make sure his master made it away safely.

Tears streamed down Taryn's face as he watched it all unfold, but he finally understood why Stompy had brought him here. It didn't matter if Chod had been reckless. In the end, it was Stompy's choice to sacrifice himself—not just for Taryn, but for Berry and Ruby and Jordy. For Chod and Limery. He'd done what family was supposed to do—look out for one another.

The scene faded and the starry night morphed back into the forest of the Hidden Lake. Taryn saw himself lying on his back as Armun finished up the last lines of the tattoo.

There wasn't much time, and Taryn didn't want to waste a second of it. He leaned forward and wrapped his arms around the moulhaug's side, listening to the slow heartbeat for the last time.

CHAPTER 7
HUG IT OUT

THE FAIRIES and centaurs are equally fascinated with my horrors as the grumbly creatures scurry around the open field. Horrors of Power and Finesse grunt and groan as fairies poke and prod at them.

Limery seems to be having fun with a group of rowdy fairies over by the lake, and occasionally, streaks of flame zip across the night or an explosion rains down a trail of colorful sparks.

"I expected more from a hero troll," Swift goads me. "But I guess technique is more important than strength for spear throwing."

The centaurs are pretty good trash talkers, and they've been gloating all night. They must get a special pleasure from beating a hero at something.

I finish my drink and toss the mug aside. "I wouldn't count your dragons before they hatch."

Compared to all the centaurs competing in the spear toss, I've been in the middle of the pack each turn. But little do they know that I have a few tricks up my sleeve.

I pull one of the spears from the ground and ready my throw, calculating the best angle to release. Taking a deep breath, I cast Sacrifice, and all my horrors vanish in a puff of smoke. My muscles bulge as the added Strength and Dexterity floods my being.

I cock the spear behind my shoulder and take three steps, launching the weapon through the air. It arcs high into the night sky before sticking into the earth with a wet thud, some twenty meters further than the next closest.

Several centaurs murmur behind me.

I flex my muscles, giving my bicep a kiss before winking at Swift. "You were saying?"

He laughs. "Well done. Well done indeed."

"Thanks for the competition," I tell the group. "I might have won this bout, but I don't think there's any chance of me winning a footrace against any of you."

Several of them laugh and offer me congratulations before Swift and I step aside.

"I'm going to check on Taryn and call it a night. We'll head out first thing in the morning."

Swift leans in a little too close, and I can tell the mead has him feeling good. "If there is anything you need before you go, ask and it shall be done."

We grip one another's forearms, and then I head back down to the lake while the fairies retrieve the spears from the far end of the field.

I find Taryn at the edge of the lake, engaged in conversation with a group of centaurs. His pets sit around him in a circle like something out of a children's fairy tale. Three of the centaurs I recognize as Thannis, Daimun, and Sylvie, but the other I haven't met. He has gray fur and matching braids, much older than the other three. His torso is covered in tattoos, and he gives off an air of power and wisdom.

They all look in my direction as I approach, and it feels like I'm intruding.

I lift my hands to apologize. If Taryn doesn't want me around right now, I understand. "Sorry, I can come back later if I'm interrupting."

Taryn is the one to answer. "Nah, it's all good. We just finished up. I was actually about to come track you down to see how your spear throwing was going."

"Uh—" His casual tone catches me off guard, leaving me speechless for a moment. "Let's just say I did the trolls proud."

He says good-bye to the others and stands by my side. "There's something I wanted to talk to you about."

I'm not sure why, but it makes me nervous. After waving to the others, I follow Taryn a few paces away.

When we stop, he just stares at me, eyes focused like he's trying to find the words, but the uncomfortable silence wins out, forcing me to speak.

"So, what'd you ge—"

He wraps his arms around me and squeezes. I'm not sure what's happening or where this is coming from, but I return the gesture, gently patting him on the back until he releases.

"We're good. I just wanted to let you know." He lets go and wipes his eyes, unleashing a deep breath as he pulls down his tunic to show me the tattoo. "What do you think?"

A massive grin spreads across my face, and Taryn mirrors my expression. "Nice."

A bright orange carrot rests over his heart. The black outline is thick and pronounced, while there are fine details accented with blue and green ink.

"It looks amazing. Did it hurt?"

His smile spreads even wider, revealing his pearly white teeth. It's the most genuine smile I've seen from him in a while. "It hurt, but it was one of the most amazing experiences of my life."

We grab a drink and walk around the perimeter of the lake while he tells me about the tattoo and the potion that reconnected him with Stompy. "It was hard to watch, but Stompy forced me to. In the end, I think it helped."

I offer him a half-smile. "I know I can't relate to what you're going through, but I'm glad you were able to find some semblance of closure. He was a great pet."

"That he was." Taryn takes a long swig, leaving beads of mead in his mustache when he's done. "But now it's time to focus on the present, clearing the forest and finding our way back to a big city. Maybe finding some adventure that doesn't revolve around psychopaths trying to kill us."

"I second that. Let's try to pry Limery away from his new friends and get some rest. I have a feeling tomorrow is going to be a hell of a day."

The next morning, I wake up to the squawk of some demonic-sounding birds. Their shrill call cuts through my restful sleep like a jagged blade. Sunlight spills through the open roof in streaks between the tall canopy.

Limery sits up on my chest, one eye still shut and the other halfway open.

"Good morning, party animal." I grin, scooping him up and setting him on the ground. "You enjoyed yourself last night."

Taryn peeks out from beneath his cloak, dreadlocks concealing most of his face. "Let's be real, Limery enjoys himself every night."

Limery shakes his head, and his body goes molten for half a second. Pieces of hay catch fire, but the imp looks as fresh as ever.

That's one way to cure a hangover.

I pat the flames and quickly extinguish them. "Let's not burn the village down before we leave."

He rubs his belly. "Limmy hungries."

We quickly gather ourselves and set out, the smell of roasted meat luring us through the village until we find a group of centaurs eating breakfast. Half a dozen fairies cook over several small fires. One pan crackles with what looks like bacon. Vegetables roast in another. A fairy cracks open a green speckled egg, and a matching green yolk falls into the pan.

Berry hovers too close to the fire, drool dripping from his mouth. Ruby sits on the bear's back, and Jordy clings to Taryn's side.

There's a chime as one of the fairies brings over a plate loaded with food and hands it to Limery.

Taryn throws up his hands. "What about the rest of us?"

Deep laughter comes from behind us. "Someone has made himself a friend of the fairies." Swift smiles as an equally big plate is handed to him. "How did you all sleep?"

I stretch my arms overhead and my back cracks audibly. "Surprisingly well, though your alarm isn't the most pleasant."

He laughs again. "Ah yes, the screeching pheasants can be... intense on the ears. But they lay the most delicious eggs." He stabs at the green eggs with a two-pronged fork before taking a bite. "I hope you are well-rested for your quest."

I say thanks to the fairy as it hands me a plate, and I take a seat on the ground. "We're excited to see what we can do to help."

The eggs are surprisingly good. There's a spice I can't quite place that's somewhat sweet and savory at the same time. The eggs give me a Wisdom bonus for one hour, but the real delight is the warthog bacon, which gives me a nice Constitution bonus.

Item. Screeching Pheasant Eggs. *+1 Wisdom for one hour.*

Item. Warthog Bacon. *+1 Constitution for one hour.*

Not a bad buff just for eating breakfast. The fairies must be doing something to give the food the added bonuses.

After breakfast, Taryn shows off his tattoo to Swift and some of the others. After seeing so many centaurs at the lake last night, the village feels almost empty this morning. Even though it's surrounded by a wall of fog, the village has to stretch further into the forest than I imagined with its sprawling fields, tall trees, and lush vegetation. I'm not even a hundred percent sure that this is the only village within the boundary.

Before we head out, Swift meets us back in our stable as we gather our belongings. "Before you leave, I have a final gift to help you on your quest. I do not share this information with just anyone, so use this knowledge wisely."

I wait anxiously as he touches me on the temple. There's a flutter of energy from his fingers, much the same as when Chief Rizza gave me my first quest, and then dozens of dots populate on the map in the corner of my vision.

He touches Taryn in the same manner. "These are the holes we have discovered. They spread by the day, but this should give you a starting point."

I rub my hands together in excitement. This is a game-changer.

I zoom in on the map until it takes up the majority of my vision. Where before, only brief sections of the forest were visible, it's now as detailed as a blueprint. The entirety of the hidden village, the lake, and all of the herd's outposts are marked all the way to the forest boundary. There are also veins that stretch out from the lake marked in a light blue. They snake throughout the forest but are most concentrated within the village. Those must be the channels of life aura.

"Wow." Taryn's eyes are distant and unfocused. "This will be super helpful."

I hear hoofbeats down the path outside before Thannis pokes his head in. "I must be heading off soon to scout our boundaries, but I wanted to offer you a parting gift while you complete the quest. I believe you will gain more use from it than we will currently."

He pulls the amulet he used in the forest from his satchel and hands it to me. It's surprisingly heavy for being so small. The yellow stone glows gently in the center of the bronze starburst.

Item. Amulet of Sight. *An amulet capable of revealing surroundings for thirty yards in all directions for a total of two hours per day, however, it is incapable of bypassing celestial or infernal obstructions. Remaining Sight: 120 minutes.*

I place the amulet around my neck and feel its warmth against my chest. "Thank you, Thannis. I'm sure this will prove valuable with our quest."

"I wish you all good fortune." His tail flicks as he turns around. "I must be going now. The work never ends."

On our way to the boundary of the village, we make a quick stop by the lake. Smoke continues to bubble and plume from the center of the lake, where the faint green aura can still be seen surrounding the raft containing the dragon egg. I count eight centaurs standing sentry around the edge of the lake, spears or bows held at their sides.

Swift heads to the wall of fog. "Do not worry, the egg will be well-guarded while you are away."

When we step through the barrier, I understand what he means. Every hundred yards along the boundary, a centaur stands guard. There is no way anyone or anything is making it into the village without them noticing.

I raise my brow. "All of this for a dragon egg?"

Swift's face goes stern. "A dragon can turn the tide of any battle. They can lay siege to castles and have been the rise and fall of kingdoms. Do not forget that. Good luck with your quest. The fate of Wandermere lies with you all."

There's nothing to say to that. With a final look at the centaur and the fog, we set out in the direction of the closest marked hole.

CHAPTER 8
WHAT LIES BENEATH

I PULL UP THE MAP, focusing on the locations Swift has marked while Taryn does the same. "You seeing what I'm seeing?"

The longer I stare at it, the more confident I am that there's a pattern to the hole formations. There's a sizable gap from the portal to the first set of holes, which I can't quite explain, but then they spread out in an arc. After the initial holes, they all seem to be expanding in the direction of the Hidden Lake, almost like a triangle. There are a few sections that break off midway as if they weren't sure which way to go, but then the trend continues toward the village.

The distant look fades from Taryn's eyes, and he focuses on me. "Yeah, it looks like they're expanding in our direction."

I run my finger over my tusk as I ponder on what might have caused this to happen. "I'm guessing that once the centaurs retreated from their outposts, the shadow monsters could sense the movement. Either that or they're being drawn to the life aura of the lake."

Taryn strokes his beard, the clasps jingling slightly. "Makes sense. Regardless of the reason, I say we meet them head-on. If we can manage to push them back, I think it will be a lot easier."

I equip Destroyer and give it a twirl in my palm. "Sounds like a plan. Want to hit us with a little druid speed boost?"

Taryn raises his staff and a moment later, Strong Wind takes effect, increasing our speed as we travel through the foggy forest. I cast Spirit Guide and allow it to lead the way, clearing our sight for at least a few extra feet in front of us. With only two hours of visibility from the Amulet of Sight each day, it seems smarter to save it for when we might really need it.

As long as we stay focused, traveling is easy, but taking my eye off the path for even a moment results in a surprise branch to the face more than once.

I keep a full army of horrors ready just to be safe, summoning replacements as soon as they expire. Limery disappears occasionally, soaring into the treetops after an unfortunate bird. Knowing where most of the holes are, I'm not as worried about him now, especially if he keeps to the air—not to mention I think he'd be pretty spicy for anything bold enough to try and eat him.

After a couple of hours, we arrive at the first hole. It has the same impenetrable darkness as the ones Thannis showed us. I'm careful not to lean too close over this one and risk French kissing whatever waits inside. About fifty feet behind it, there are two more.

Once we check the surroundings, I send a Horror of Finesse down into the hole. Being the smallest of the three horrors, it should have the easiest time exploring. It's inside for about two seconds before its presence vanishes entirely.

"Something's definitely in there." No sooner have I finished the sentence before a puff of smoke wafts out.

"What happened?" Taryn holds his staff at the ready in case something climbs out.

I shrug. "No idea. My horror was in there, and then it vanished."

"Hmm. So do we want to try to lure it out or kill it inside?"

I take a quick peek into the hole and then step back. "We don't even know what we're dealing with or how many might be in each hole. I think we've got to lure it out in order to know for sure."

He raises his eyebrows. "And how exactly do you propose we do that?"

The twitching leaves on Taryn's Sapling Staff give me an idea. "Do you think you can send the vines on your staff in there and get a gauge of how deep the hole goes?"

"Ugh, it's a good idea, but I don't like it." Taryn frowns. "Playing tug of war with a giant tongue trying to steal my staff doesn't sound like a good time."

I shudder at the memory of the tongue. "I have a feeling we might be doing a lot of things we don't like before this quest is completed."

Taryn climbs down from Berry and gets into position about six feet from the edge of the hole. He takes a deep breath, then the vines on his staff slowly extend into the darkness.

After about thirty seconds, the vines quit growing. "That's as far as they will go. Either the holes are connected or that hole is at least thirty feet deep. Whatever's in there doesn't seem to care about inanimate objects, though." The vines begin to retract back into his staff.

I walk over to the other two holes and look inside. They're just as dark and ominous as the first.

I summon more horrors. "Alright, let's see if we can flush it out. Can you summon your fungus around the other two holes to alert us if anything exits? If these holes are connected, we don't want to be attacked unaware."

A minute later, Taryn gives me the go-ahead and I send my ten oldest horrors into the hole. The first one vanishes from my awareness. As soon as it does, I cast Kamikaze on the rest. The ground vibrates for a second before the entrance to the hole collapses on itself from the horrors' explosion.

For a moment, the forest is quiet, and then I hear the gassy release of Taryn's poisonous mushrooms.

"Get ready, both holes just activated," Taryn yells.

"That's what she said!" This isn't the time for crude humor, but the opportunity was too good to pass up.

I send my horrors out into the fog surrounding the other two holes, and several of them vanish immediately.

"We need visibility now, Chod!" Taryn shouts.

I don't hesitate, activating the Amulet of Sight. A gust of wind rushes out from me, pushing back the fog for thirty feet in all directions. Leaves and dirt blow away, but there are no monsters in our immediate vicinity.

"To the other holes." Taryn urges Berry forward, and I follow beside him. The fog pushes back with each step I take.

I can hear whispers up ahead, the same ones I heard at the first hole when the tongue attacked me. Gripping Destroyer tightly, I press forward until a shadowy presence comes into view at the boundary of the amulet.

Three giant orbs of smoke hover in the air.

My heart beats faster as I take another step. The amulet pushes back the smoke surrounding the monsters, revealing them in all their grotesque glory. The core of the monsters are veiny, jelly-like sacks composed of nothing more than a mouth and claws. Each mouth is full of razor-sharp teeth and a long black tongue that nearly drags against the ground.

"Oh noes," Limery whispers.

Berry's low growl echoes the sentiment, and I completely agree. Goosebumps prickle along my arms.

Mesmer Wisp. *Level 24. Molded in the depths of the shadowlands, these wisps are far more deadly than their light-based counterparts. Mesmer wisps lure enemies with enticing whispers, putting them into a trancelike state before absorbing them into their amorphous bodies. After reaching peak size, wisps split in two, forming a collective with a hive mind. Underneath their shadowy silhouette, these wisps sport powerful claws used for digging interconnected burrows and a long, powerful tongue capable of subduing victims until they are ingested.*

The whispers call to me, and my grip on Destroyer slackens. The wisps aren't fast, but they approach with ominous intent. I take a step toward them. Distantly, Limery and Taryn call to me.

With each step, drool drips from the wisps' monstrous mouths, their veiny bodies pulsing like some alien spawn.

Lightning crashes between them, and their bodies glow with electricity for a moment before the whispers fade and my mind suddenly clears. I step back, sending my horrors at the creatures.

"Chod, what the hell?" Concern radiates from Taryn.

I shake my head to fully clear my mind. "It's some kind of enchantment. Don't get too close to them."

The mesmer wisps pluck my horrors with their tongues like frogs catching a fly. I cast Kamikaze on the rest of my horrors before they are devoured, but it has little effect on the wisps. Limery hurls fireballs that are slightly more effective, taking out their health in minuscule chunks.

Taryn casts Moonbeam, and the stream of silver light coats one of the wisps. Its jelly-like orb of a body sizzles upon contact, and an ear-splitting shriek leaves my ears ringing.

When I'm able to focus again, I notice the wisp that took the blow lost a third of its health from that one attack. Its once-pulsing body now seems shrunken and drained.

My spirit guide stands by my side, its pupilless eyes radiating cold anger as it paws at the ground. Streams of ethereal energy blast from its nostrils.

My ears quit ringing and I take a fighting stance, ready to smash these wisps into jelly. "Your Moonbeam must be extra effective on them."

Enraged by the attack, the wisps press forward, but they halt when they enter the radius of my spirit guide's light, hissing at the goat before retreating.

The three wisps disappear into the fog, but we don't pursue. We need to regroup and plan now that we have more information.

"Holy shit." I crouch and take a deep breath. "Those things were creepy."

Limery frowns in the direction of the retreating wisps. "Oh yes, Limmy no likes the scary monsties. They whispers for Limmy to come play, but Limmy no wants to."

Taryn grimaces. "That's probably a good idea, little man. How do those things even float in the air? The tongue is bigger than the body."

I shrug. "I have no idea, but your Moonbeam seemed to be the only thing that did any real damage."

He scrunches his brow for a moment, deep in thought. "They seemed wary of your spirit guide, too. Do you think they count as undead? That would explain the extra damage my attack did. Too bad it's not night, or I would get an even bigger bonus."

That's right, Moonbeam deals double damage to undead and fifty percent additional damage at night. "You think there's any way we can use that to our advantage?"

"Probably, but then that means we're fighting these bastards at night, where they probably have some advantages of their own." He looks up as if tracking the daylight left, even though the sun barely breaches the dense canopy.

"Right, we still have a lot of day left. Let's see what we can find out about their burrows." I stand and walk over to the two holes we didn't destroy, deactivating the amulet to conserve its power. With the wisps gone, I can see directly into the tunnels with no issues for the first time. "Limery, want to go on an adventure?"

Limery's bulbous yellow eyes flash with excitement. "Oh yes, Limmy loves adventures."

His grin fades when he finds out what the adventure entails.

I send him down into the holes to figure out how far they go and if there are any offshoot tunnels that connect to more of the mesmer wisps. After a couple of minutes, Limery pops out of the second hole covered in dirt.

He coughs before going molten and burning the dirt and debris from his skin.

"What'd you see?" I ask.

"The tunnelses only has two holeses. Limmy thinks theys was three but Chods exploded its."

"Good job." I turn to Taryn. "If all of the tunnels aren't connected, just the ones close to one another, then they likely travel in pods. If we can figure out how to hurt them, we can take them out one pod at a time."

Taryn nods. "I like it. A lot less dangerous than trying to fight too many at once."

We make our way to the next closest set of holes. Once again, there are three within a relatively close vicinity, and I can't help but wonder if there is some significance to that.

I take a quick peek into the hole, where the same impenetrable darkness stares back at me. Soft whispers call to me before I take a step back. "They're definitely in there. Whether they're the ones from before or a whole new batch, there's no telling."

Using the amulet for only a moment, I activate it to push back the fog and leaves. When I deactivate it, there's about a thirty-second break before the fog comes rushing back in. It's a good way to get a look at the area without wasting much power.

I point to the holes in the back. "If there was a way to block off those two back holes, then we could try to flush the wisps out of the front entrance."

Taryn climbs down from Berry and walks over to the two furthest holes. He moves his fingers through the air as if measuring something out. Then a mischievous grin spreads underneath his mustache, curling it up at the edges. "I think I've got a plan."

CHAPTER 9

WHISPERS

I SEND a horror into each of the furthest two holes from where we approached, keeping a careful perception on their presence as they crawl into the tunnels. It doesn't take long before one vanishes, soon followed by the other. I wait a moment before testing again. This time, I have the horrors wait just inside the entrance. They sit there undisturbed until I instruct them to go deeper into the holes. Each time, the horrors vanish once they go deeper, but the wisps never attack those at the edge.

Only when I approach the holes do the wisps seem to move closer to the entrance. It's as if they can sense my body but aren't attracted to the horrors.

I step back to where I believe the wisps can't sense me. "Looks like the wisps are hanging out about ten feet from the entrance to each hole."

Taryn summons a ring of poisonous mushrooms inside the first tunnel and then moves to the next. Once the cooldown is up, he summons mushrooms inside the second hole, rotating between the two until fungi surround all edges of both entrances.

While he does this, I equip Forlorn Scepter. I used it with great success back in the troll forest when we were fighting Glenn. The weapon's passive ability gives me fifty percent increased range for summoning.

It allows me to summon horrors inside the tunnels just out of reach of Taryn's mushrooms and far enough away not to disturb the wisps.

Taryn casts Stonewall over one entrance and then the other, leaving the front entrance as the only viable exit. The rest of the group—spirit guide included—all stand guard at the one open hole. I continue summoning horrors but only make it to four in each tunnel before I feel one of them vanish.

"Showtime!" I call to the others as a chain reaction of disappearing horrors goes down each tunnel.

I cast Kamikaze on the last remaining horror in each tunnel. The ground shakes slightly and purple gas seeps around the edges of Taryn's walls as his mushrooms activate. I run back to the others, equipping Destroyer just as a loud shriek echoes underground.

A thick ball of smoke emerges from the tunnel, and I quickly activate the Amulet of Sight. A gust of wind pours out, ripping the smoke from around the monstrous jelly being. It snarls before lashing its tongue at Limery.

Jordy charges, ramming into the wisp just as the dangerous tongue whips inches from Limery's face. The wisp barely budges as Jordy slams into it. Instead, its jelly exterior wraps around the frost goat. Ripples surge through the wisp's body, burying Jordy's head and neck inside its gelatinous membrane while the goat's hind legs thrash.

Taryn yells as Moonbeam cuts almost silently through the air, hitting the wisp dead on. Its translucent skin sizzles under the silver beam and its health plummets, forcing it to release Jordy as its mouth contorts with a violent scream.

My ears ring from the wisp's anguished cries. I take a step forward and bring Destroyer down on the wisp, expecting it to explode like a water balloon. The warhammer has little effect, lodging inside the gelatinous blob. The monster's tongue snakes down the handle of the weapon and up my arm before I have a chance to let go, gripping me with surprising strength. It continues to writhe up my arm, wrapping around my shoulder as I try to free myself. Pain flares along my arm and hundreds of needles stab me all at once.

Limery's yelling sounds distant as he peppers the wisp in fire. I lose focus as whispers surround me and two more mesmer wisps emerge from the tunnel.

A second tongue wraps around my neck as I continue to struggle with the first. It squeezes, cutting off my air supply until my vision darkens at the edges. I dig the claws of my left hand into the tongue but it only clenches tighter, while my right arm has gone completely numb. Sharp pain pierces my side as claws rake against my ribs, then a cold substance spreads over my hand and along my midsection. Panic flares through me as I realize that the second wisp is trying to absorb me into its body.

The more I struggle, the weaker I feel. The pain in my ribs grows more intense, but there is nothing I can do. It's like I'm trapped in a riptide, unable to escape.

Then, the pressure suddenly fades, and the tongue releases me from its embrace. I fall to the ground, gasping for air.

Limery hovers next to me, completely covered in silver goo. His bulbous eyes are full of worry, but his mouth is set in firm determination. He says something, but my ears are still ringing.

Two tongues lay motionless on the ground next to me, and the final wisp snarls at Taryn between lashes. My spirit guide steps forward, and the wisp unleashes another ear-splitting screech. Limery turns, body going molten as he darts into the wisp's open mouth. A Moonbeam hits the wisp at the same time as Limery flies down its throat. The jelly-like surface of the wisp erupts into boils, and a second later, it explodes.

I collapse to the ground, and pain pulses along my ribs while the ringing in my ears slowly fades.

A warm tongue licks me on the cheek, and I open my eyes to see Berry hovering over my head.

Taryn finishes casting Restoration on Jordy and then kneels beside me, examining my arm. "Are you okay? Those things really got a hold of you."

I sit up, and Limery perches on my shoulder, examining the dozens of tiny puncture marks that run up and down my right arm where the wisp's tongue was wrapped around me. Gashes cover my tender midsection.

Limery frowns. "Chods needs to bes more careful."

I gently press against my ribs before downing a health potion. "I'll be fine. I think Jordy and I both learned that we aren't going to power our way through this. How did you two manage to kill them, anyhow?"

Taryn kicks one of the tongues and it curls in on itself like a dead snake. "Moonbeam hits them like a knife through warm butter. The only problem is the cooldown. Limery's fireballs aren't that effective against their outsides, but he basically boiled them alive from inside, so I'm guessing they have some kind of magical resistance to their exteriors. I'm not sure what the deal is with your spirit guide, but whenever it gets close to them, it's like the wisps are in pain. They lose focus on whatever they are attacking until they are out of its range."

I cancel Amulet of Sight and crouch next to one of the tongues. Upon closer inspection, each tongue is covered in suction cups, almost like an octopus tentacle, except the edges are serrated. That explains the stabbing sensation. If these creatures are able to consume living beings by absorbing them through their bodies and can also drain them directly using their tongues, then they're even more deadly than I originally thought. It's like their entire purpose is to feed.

Jordy and I are lucky to be alive right now. If not for Taryn, Limery, and my spirit guide, we might not be. They're going to be integral to completing this quest.

I shiver at the memory of the tongue entangled around my neck. "Maybe we can find a way to use the spirit guide to our advantage. Once I'm healed enough, let's take what we learned and use it on the next pod, since we've still got a couple hours of daylight left. I'll be sure to stand far enough back next time."

While my wounds heal, I summon more horrors. By the time we arrive at the next set of holes, I have thirty horrors ready to go. The holes are spread out in the same triangle pattern. They remind me of a beehive with the way they all seem perfectly positioned to one another.

I send ten horrors into each hole. Once the first one vanishes, I explode the other nine in each tunnel. The tunnels collapse, blocking the exits and trapping the wisps in the center until they use their claws to dig straight to the surface.

The ground caves in near the center, and two claws poke through. Taryn catches the first wisp with a sustained Moonbeam as it squeezes through the small hole, killing it before it ever completely emerges. The cooldown allows the other two time to crawl out. They slowly climb through Limery's Firewall but only lose a fraction of their health. My spirit guide flanks the wisps, keeping enough distance to scare them away but close enough to prevent them from escaping into the fog.

The wisps screech and snarl when they get too close to my

spirit guide, but they refocus on us as I feed the wisps horrors to keep them engaged until Moonbeam is ready to go again. It's a game of patience but eventually, we take them all out.

We try several tactics over the next few hours, with some having more success than others. For my horrors, Kamikaze is the only attack that deals any damage, and it's the least effective of our party's magical attacks. I switch to Petrified Staff and use the gnarled staff's passive ability to shoot ranged physical attacks, but it's about as effective as flies attacking a crocodile.

Limery's fireballs and Firewall do minimal damage to the wisps' exteriors, but attacks to an open mouth are effective. These creatures have an insane magical resistance and their jelly-like bodies combined with a lack of internal organs make physical attacks almost useless. Any physical attacks to their bodies lodge inside like they are trapped in quicksand. Even removing a tongue from a wisp does little to hamper it because they can still absorb my horrors through their bodies.

For the first time, Taryn seems to be the strongest one in the group. His Lightning Bolt is more effective than Limery's fire, but Moonbeam is the star of the show. However, the cooldown on Moonbeam forces us to kite the wisps for far too long each time.

And then there's my spirit guide. It doesn't directly damage the wisps, but something about it causes them to retreat. Maybe because it's the antithesis of their shadowy nature. We lose several wisps to the depths of the forest due to my spirit guide getting too close, but anytime we're on the verge of losing, I'm able to call it in to save our asses.

Wherever the runaway wisps go, we're unable to track them. There are never more than three wisps in each pod, so they have to be going somewhere. I get the uneasy feeling that they'll all catch up to us again at some point.

We manage to clear ten pods before nightfall, but there are

still dozens more spread across the forest. As we make camp for the night, settling inside a fortress made from Taryn's Stonewalls, one thing I notice is the distinct lack of animal noise in the area. Far away, owls hoot and wolves howl, but there's nothing in our immediate vicinity aside from the whispering leaves.

I point it out to Taryn as I lean against the cool stone. "Strange, right?"

He rests against Berry, using the bear's belly as a pillow. "Either the animals are staying away from the wisps, or they've all been absorbed."

I grimace at the thought. "Do you have to put it like that? Absorbed. The mental image is enough to give me the creeps."

His expression mirrors my own. "I'll be glad when we're done with this. I don't want to be the token Black guy from every horror movie that dies to the monsters in the woods. Get me to an inn with crackling bacon and flowing drinks."

"Limmy wants drinks and bacons." Limery rubs his hands together.

The thought of bacon and drinks has me salivating as well. Not to mention a comfortable bed. We can make do in the wilderness, but there's something about the city's amenities that makes life much more interesting.

I take the first watch while the others sleep. My spirit guide is extra bright in the enclosed space, so I cancel it for the time being to keep from waking the others.

Limery snores softly in the crook of my arm, a large snot bubble inflating with each breath. His demonic features look peaceful as he slumbers.

Leaves hiss as they rub against one another in the night breeze, and then I hear something else. Whispers. They're soft at first, but they grow louder until they surround us on all sides of our small fortress.

My pulse quickens, but I stay still. The walls are high enough to keep the wisps at bay. They might hover in the air, but I've yet to see one fly higher than a few feet off the ground. That doesn't mean it's not possible, so I keep my focus overhead.

For hours, the wisps call to me, whispering words I can't quite make out. But this time, it feels different. Maybe it's the wall that separates us, but I don't feel the same compulsive urge to join them.

The night drags on, and the whispers multiply until it's almost torturous. How many are out there, waiting for an opportunity to strike? Even though they aren't luring me the same as before, their whispers are causing a different reaction. I'm weary and on edge. I don't know if it's an effect from the wisps or if listening to half-formed words for several hours is slowly driving me insane.

At this point, I'm not sure how long they've been outside, but I don't know how much more I can handle. I lay Limery to the side without jostling him and crawl over to wake Taryn.

I tap him on the shoulder at the same time as one of the walls expires. Fog floods through the opening and conceals everything in sight, all the while the whispers grow louder, luring me out into the forest.

CHAPTER 10

ONE STEP FORWARD, TWO STEPS BACK

Everything is distant and dark as I crawl through the opening where the wall used to be. Right now, the only thing that matters are the whispers calling to me, beckoning me into the comfort of darkness.

"Chod, snap out of it!" Taryn shouts.

A firm hand smacks me on the side of the head, bringing me back to my senses. I activate Amulet of Sight and both light and wind explode from my chest, revealing more wisps than I can count lurking outside our camp. Dozens of long tongues and spindly claws lash out, their grotesque bodies pulsing with dull energy.

The whispers call to me again, but they're cut off abruptly as Moonbeam hits a cluster of wisps and fireballs sail past my shoulder. Berry growls ferociously behind me.

In the moment of respite, I summon my spirit guide. Shrieks immediately echo across the forest from all directions as the wisps scatter into the darkness.

A second wall fades before Taryn has replaced the first, leaving us boxed in.

Limery and I stand guard in front of Taryn's pets. I summon more horrors in front of us, not that they can do much damage, and Limery hovers next to me, two fireballs in his palms.

We're still protected on two sides, but Taryn needs to get his walls up fast. My spirit guide circles our enclosure, a sentry of light, while Taryn replaces the walls one by one.

Limery's warm body presses against my shoulder. He grimaces. "Limmy no likes the monsties."

Taryn leans against the wall once he's finished and shudders. "There were so many of them. What the hell have we gotten ourselves into?"

I clap him on the shoulder. "Just another day in paradise."

"If this is paradise, I'm ready for the vacation to be over." Taryn shakes his head. "You need to rest, though."

"There's no way I'm sleeping after that."

"Take this." He grins as he pulls a vial of dull pink dust and tosses it to me.

Sleep Dust.

I laugh. "I guess that's one way to do it. I'll pass on the Dream Dust considering what's fresh on my mind."

"Look at you. Maybe there are some brains in that giant skull of yours." He winks as he strokes Ruby. "Limery and I will keep watch." He points a stubby finger in my direction. "You, get some sleep. I'm sure our new friends will be waiting for us in the morning."

This time, I leave the spirit guide outside our camp. I doubt the wisps will come anywhere near us with it around. I just wish I knew why they hated it so much.

All it takes is a pinch of the Sleep Dust, and I'm out like a light.

When I wake up, the walls are gone and I'm sprawled across the forest floor, groggier than I can ever remember being in-game.

"Chods is ups!" Limery calls from the tree above me.

A moment later, Taryn appears. "Might want to go easy on the Sleep Dust next time. There's no waking you up until it wears off. You don't even want to know the things we tried to get you up." He smirks.

Limery hovers in the air next to me. "Oh, yes. Chods had a big sleeps."

I stretch my arms and try to clear my head. The after-effects of too much Sleep Dust feel about the same as when I would get too much sleep back in the real world. My dad called it a sleep hang-over, and he said it was a luxury of having too little ambition.

After a quick breakfast consisting of dried meat and bread from the Hidden Village, we head back toward the wisp burrows to start the day's work. The lack of animals in the area does have me slightly concerned about what we'll eat when our rations run out. The forest is still certainly full of life, but the question is how far will we have to travel in order to hunt?

Taryn curses, bringing Berry to a halt.

"Something wrong?" I ask.

He has a distant look in his eyes. "Pull up your map."

I look over the map carefully, double-checking to make sure my mind isn't playing tricks on me. "You've got to be shitting me."

Yesterday, we took out ten pods over the course of the day. A few wisps managed to escape due to my spirit guide's overbearing presence, but we cleared ten burrows. After they were cleared, a red X replaced the circles that had marked them on the map.

Looking at it now, half of the Xs are gone.

I turn to Taryn. "How is that possible?"

He shrugs. "I don't know, but we need to check it out."

He casts Strong Wind, boosting our speed, and we arrive

where we were supposed to start today's work a short while later. A dark haze shrouds the entrance to the burrow, where the wisps wait inside.

We follow the path back to the previous burrow, the one that should be empty. When we arrive, the upturned earth and destruction from our battle remain, but not even twenty feet away, a new burrow has formed.

"Fuck." I kick a loose stone and it tumbles into the fog.

Taryn presses his fists to his eyes. "Could this be any more annoying? We spend half the day clearing these bastards out and they retake half their land back overnight. This is some grade-A bullshit."

Limery leaps from my shoulder, clenching his fist as he hovers in the air. "Yeah, this is somes grade-A bullshits."

Taryn looks up, a wide grin plastered on his face, but he doesn't say anything. He just gives me a knowing look.

I shrug. What's a curse word in the grand scheme of things? Limery drinks like a sailor and is fire made flesh. I just hope Lillith doesn't blame me for his bad behavior when all is said and done. I do not want to be on Limery's mother's bad side.

"I guess we go back and clear it all again. We've got a better understanding of how to deal with them this time. Plus, I've got an idea for the Sleep Dust."

By noon, we've retaken the lost ground, but we still have very little understanding of where these new wisps came from. We stop for lunch in a clearing, my spirit guide pushing back the fog for several feet in all directions.

Taryn rips off a piece of bread and gestures with it while he talks. "It's strange. If the wisps aren't leaving any of the burrows empty as they advance, and none of the ones we've cleared have had more than three wisps, then it means they're only expanding once they have new wisps. We know they are all connected, and their description said they split at peak size, but what does that really mean? Can they split at will or did they go out for a massive feast last night?"

I wish I knew the answer, but I think the only way we'd find out is if we're out in the open when they do their midnight marauding. So, with each wisp we defeat and burrow we clear, I keep my mind on the end goal, the reason we're out here to begin with—hatching a dragon.

After lunch, we get back to work. I pull up my inventory to see how many vials of Sleep Dust and Dream Dust I have.

I take one of each and display them in the air, shaking them in front of Taryn. "I've got ten vials of each, how about you?"

In addition, I also have several elixirs and potions, but I doubt their liquid state would work for what I have planned.

Taryn's eyes go vacant for a second before he answers. "Eleven vials of Dream Dust. Nine vials of Sleep Dust. What'd you have in mind?"

"I've got a few crazy ideas. We don't have the stock to use them at every hole, but if they work, it will be good to have them in our bag of tricks."

Taryn grins. "Alright, magic man. I'm sure this will be interesting."

I summon a Horror of Finesse and hand it an uncorked vial of Sleep Dust. I position it tilted in the horror's hand so that a small trail of dust falls out as it moves, then I send the horror into the tunnel.

Once my horror vanishes, I turn to Limery. "Will you do the honors?"

He summons a small fireball in his palm and tosses it at the trail of Sleep Dust. The line of dull pink glitter crackles to life, sending a streak of flame into the tunnel, followed soon after by an explosion that shakes the ground. A notification flashes in my vision, but I ignore it for now.

Two wisps emerge from the far holes, but the third is nowhere to be found. We finish them off much quicker than when we faced three at a time.

Now that the fight is over, I pull up the notification.

Congratulations! You have unlocked the skill 'Demolition.' You are now a level 1 Demolitionist (Novice). Increase your skill and learn advanced techniques for demolition by finding an advanced demolitionist (Apprentice or above). Crafting Ranks: Novice, Apprentice, Journeyman, Expert, Artisan, Master, Grandmaster.

Now that's a cool skill to have. I wonder what techniques I could learn at the higher levels.

At the next burrow, I do the same thing but use the Dream Dust.

Limery sets the glittery purple dust ablaze, and the explosion is twice as loud as the first. It's powerful enough to cave in the area around the explosion and send purple smoke pluming out of the other tunnels. Only one wisp survives this time, and Taryn quickly dispatches it with Moonbeam. I receive a second notification telling me I've leveled up my demolition skill again.

Taryn looks at me with wide eyes. "Bro, that was awesome. How'd you come up with that?"

"After you gave me the Sleep Dust last night, I remembered the fireworks display Limery and the fairies put on at the lake party. I figured it was pretty flammable, and it turns out I was right. I even unlocked a new skill for blowing shit up. We're saving this for emergencies, though."

Over the course of the day, we clear twenty-one burrows, more than double the previous day. Five of them we cleared for a second time, which feels like wasted progress, but at least I didn't get wrapped in killer tongues today.

When we make camp for the night, I station my spirit guide outside our enclosure to keep the mesmer wisps away. Taryn takes first watch, allowing him to replace his walls before waking me for my shift.

"Any whispers?" I ask as I rub the sleep from my eyes.

"Barely. Your spirit guide seems to be doing the trick. I can hear them out there, but they sound way more distant than last night." He snuggles in next to a snoring Berry. "By the way, you should really come up with a name for it. It's kept us safe enough to earn one."

"Heh, you might be right. I'll give it some thought."

He pulls his hood down over his eyes. "Glowy has a nice ring to it."

I roll my eyes. "Dude, go to sleep."

In a matter of minutes, Taryn is snoring in rhythm with Berry. Ruby lies curled up in his lap, and Jordy has his legs folded so compactly that he looks like he could be stuffed in a box and shipped.

Limery lies sprawled out along Berry's side, oblivious to the world.

Despite all of the pain and hardships of the last few weeks, I can't help but feel incredibly lucky to be here. The longer I get away from the real world, the less desire I have to ever go back. Mythos has plenty of challenges, but it has become my home, and everyone within these four walls are a part of my family.

I will do whatever it takes to protect that.

A gust of wind blows overhead, snapping a branch that crashes to the ground outside of our camp. Limery stirs and his bulbous yellow eyes squint open.

For a moment, I'm not sure if he's actually awake, but then he wipes his eyes and flies over to my shoulder.

"Time for watches," he grumbles.

"You can go back to sleep if you want. I think I can handle it tonight."

He looks up at me. "It's okays. Limmy likes to stays up with Chods."

"Good, I like staying up with you, too." I gently poke him in the stomach. "Can I ask you something, little man?"

He nods. "What is its?"

"When this is all over—when we've fought all the bad guys and things go back to normal—what do you want to do?"

He scrunches his brow while he thinks, tapping his lips with a sharp claw. "Hmm, Limmy likes adventures. He wants more adventures with Taryns and Chods."

"Don't you miss your family? Your mom and dad and brother."

"Oh yes." He clasps his hands together. "Limmy misses thems very much. Maybe one day Leo will comes on adventures with Limmy."

My mind wanders back to my earliest days in Mythos, back when I spent some time with Limery's family in their burrow. Leo had a fiery personality, that much I recall, but by the time Limery and I had returned from my quest, Leo had set off on his own grand adventure. I wonder what he's up to now.

"The world better watch out the day that happens." I laugh, and Limery grins. "Taryn thinks I need to come up with a name for my spirit guide. What do you think about that?"

"Limmy thinks the spirit guides needs a names. What does Chods want to names hims?"

"That is the question." I lean back against the wall.

Anything but Glowy.

Limery flies to the top of the wall and looks down at what I assume is my spirit guide. He scratches his chin before rejoining me. "Limmy doesn't knows what to names hims."

I wish I had Taryn's confidence to create the dumbest name

and just roll with it. Back when I used to stream, picking a name at character creation was always the hardest part. I'd spend twice as long deciding on a name as I did picking out every minute feature on my character because I wanted the name to mean something. Meanwhile, Taryn would play a paladin named Pete. His most popular character was a cleric named Bert McHealy.

For my spirit guide, I can finally make up for the fact that I had no say when the AI named me Chod.

I rack my brain thinking of names that conjure meanings of light or ghosts, from mythological names like Apollos and Hades to more quaint names like Aurora or Raiden. There are so many options, but in the end, one stands out above them all.

In school, I was a bit of a history nerd. I remember when our class studied the Seven Wonders of the Ancient World. Students gave presentations in front of the class about the Great Pyramid of Giza, the famous Hanging Gardens of Babylon, the Statue of Zeus, the Temple of Artemis, the Mausoleum at Halicarnassus, and the Colossus of Rhodes.

I was the final presentation that week. With a cracking voice and shaky hands, I told the class about the seventh wonder of the world. A lighthouse in Alexandria that served as a beacon to guide ships along the Mediterranean Sea. For centuries, it was one of the tallest man-made structures in the world. The lighthouse itself was located on a small island called Pharos, where the structure became so well-known that the name of the island was now synonymous with beacon or lighthouse.

And that's what my spirit guide is: a beacon of hope in dark times. A guiding force that can always lead us back home.

"Pharos," I whisper. "I'll call him Pharos."

CHAPTER 11
FORGOTTEN QUESTS

"I STILL LIKE GLOWY BETTER." Taryn crosses his arms, and after a moment, he smirks. "But this beats hearing you say 'spirit guide' a hundred times a day."

I roll my eyes at him and then pull up my map as we follow Pharos through the fog. Just as we anticipated, nearly half of the burrows we cleared yesterday have been retaken by the wisps. At this rate, we'll spend half of our time retaking lost ground.

We're three days in, and I can't help but wonder if there's been any progress with the dragon egg back at the Hidden Lake. The prospect of having my very own green dragon excites me every time I think about it. Isn't it every nerd's dream to have a pet dragon? And I might actually make it happen.

Strong Wind passes over me, and my legs move a little faster. A few streaks of light break through the treetops, like golden arrows piercing the dim underbelly. We make our way to the beginning of the reclaimed burrows so that we can eliminate those first. We want to keep the wisps as far away from the

Hidden Village as possible, and if that means retaking lost ground every morning, then so be it.

At least the wisps are sticking to a predictable pattern. They never leave more than a hundred yards between burrows, and they never skip ahead to retake what they lost. We just need to clear the burrows faster than they can spread.

Over the course of the day, we manage to clear twenty-five burrows. Each day, we get a little better and quicker at eliminating the creepy monsters. Once we find a decent routine, it's all about kiting the wisps and keeping them engaged so that Taryn and Limery can damage them while also preventing them from retreating into the fog.

This time, we only manage to lose one wisp due to Pharos' getting too close.

Each day feels like a grind, but we make steady progress until we are clearing thirty burrows a day. After over a week, the end seems like it's finally in sight.

When we make camp for the night, I check the map again. "With a little luck, we might clear the last of them tomorrow."

Taryn shakes his head and the clasps in his beard jingle. "There's about thirty burrows left, not to mention that we'll have at least a dozen or so retaken by morning. I think we're looking at at least two more days, and then we can all get the hell out of here."

"Yeah, thens we's can gets the hells out of here," Limery echoes.

"Not without a dragon." I grin.

"Oh, yes. Limmy wants to play with the baby dragons. We can makes fires and fly high in the trees and chase all the birdses." His bulbous eyes flare with excitement.

"Ha, whatever you say, little man." I lean back against Taryn's wall once our camp is set for the night. "You guys get some sleep. I'll take first watch tonight."

The nights have gotten more peaceful since our first encounter with the wisps that wanted to cuddle us in the dark. Thanks to Pharos's nightly patrol around the encampment, the whispers sound further away than ever. Soon, they'll be gone altogether.

My mind wanders as I watch the others sleep until a loud scream carries across the forest.

"Help!" a deep voice yells. "Spawn of the shadowlands! Oh, gods, help! Heee—"

The words cut off, leaving the forest in silence aside from the pounding in my ears.

I crawl over and shake Taryn awake as fast as I can. "Get up, there's someone out there that needs our help. It sounded like they were attacked."

He gives me a confused look. "What are you talking about?"

I grab Taryn by the shoulders and shake him until the sleep fades from his eyes, waking up all of his pets and Limery in the process. "Listen to me. I heard a man screaming for help. I don't know why they would be out here at this hour, but I can't stand by and do nothing. Cancel your walls so that we can go check on him." The memory of my body entangled in the wisps sends chills down my spine. "If the wisps have him then we don't have much time."

Limery must sense my urgency because small flames sprout along his body.

"That way!" I point in the direction I heard the screaming. "Fly ahead with Pharos. We'll be right behind you."

Limery and Pharos take off into the fog, and Taryn and I follow close behind. Branches smack me across the chest as I run blindly through the forest.

"You sure this isn't a trick by the wisps?" he asks.

After getting entranced by the wisps on more than one occasion, I'm far from certain. But if there is someone out there, we have to help, so I keep my doubts to myself. "I'm sure. There was definitely someone out there."

"Chods! I found hims," Limery calls from up ahead.

He hovers high in the air next to a green cloak that's crumpled on the ground. Two large clouds of fog surround the lump, long tongues wrapped around it like snakes constricting the life from a mouse.

Pharos charges into the wisps, his ethereal body passing through them and dispersing the smoke that conceals them. Blood-curdling shrieks claw at my ears, but the wisps release their victim and disappear deeper into the fog.

Pharos stands protectively over the unmoving figure, his eyes glaring intensely where the wisps vanished.

With so much fog, even my night vision is unable to penetrate across the forest. I activate Amulet of Sight to clear the area, and wind and light pour out from me. At the edge of the boundary, the amulet reveals the grotesque features of a half-dozen wisps. Their tongues lash and claws grasp in our direction.

Pharos charges a few steps, and screams rip through the night as the wisps vanish into the darkness.

"Ungh." There's movement under the cloak and a large red head pokes out with a braided beard that drapes across the ground.

Emrak Stonebraid

Level ???

Ivory Dwarf

First Ranger of Seascape

The ivory dwarf's clothing is in tatters, and scrapes and scratches run along his arms and neck from the wisps. His leather armor is caked with blood from where the wisps raked their claws across his midsection. Strands of hair escape what I imagine is normally an immaculately-kept beard, and there's dirt smudged across his brow and clothing. He grunts as he stumbles to his feet, face stricken with worry.

"Oh, gods," Emrak says weakly, looking back over his shoulder.

Taryn climbs down from Berry and pulls a health potion from his satchel. "Here, take this." He hands the vibrant red potion to the dwarven ranger. "What the hell is a dwarf doing in Wandermere? You're a long way from home."

Emrak's eyes go wide when he notices Taryn, then he gulps down the potion. "Gods, you're a tough lot to catch. I've been tracking you all the way from Goldspire."

"What for?" I ask.

"I've a message from the king." He looks over his shoulder. "What in the dwarven hell are those things doing in Wandermere? I thought these lands were protected by the centaurs. Those monsters nearly sucked the life out of me." He shivers as he finishes the potion.

Taryn takes the empty vial and stuffs it back in his satchel. "Those monsters were mesmer wisps. They lure their victims with whispers and then drain the life from them. From what we've heard, shadow monsters are appearing through various portals all across Mythos. These wisps have spread across Wandermere like a parasite, and we're on a quest to eliminate them."

I pat the dwarf on the back and shoulders, wiping some of the dirt from his cloak. "I had a pretty close encounter myself not too long ago. The potion should heal the wounds from their tongues in no time."

He squints as he takes me in, his eyes lingering on my horns. "You've changed quite a bit since you were in Seascape. I hope it wasn't something you ate."

I don't remember meeting Emrak personally while I was in Seascape, but there were more dwarves than I could count in the city for the king's quest. Being First Ranger, he might have even been in the castle.

I decide to have a little fun with him regardless, so I reach up and touch my horns, gasping as if I didn't know they were there. "Where did these come from? It must be a side-effect from the wisps."

His eyes look like they are about to bulge out of his head before Taryn and I burst into laughter.

"I'm kidding. You said you had a message from the king?"

He scowls at both of us as he pulls a piece of rolled parchment from inside his cloak. "As First Ranger for King Orso, I am often sent abroad to deliver messages to those who don't want to be found. Before the portals opened, that meant the lands below the Greystone Mountains. In light of recent events, my skills have been tested further." He turns from me to Taryn. "No offense to our dwarven hero, but this message pertains to Chod, Hero of the Forest Trolls."

"Ands the mountains and arctics trolls," adds Limery.

"Very well," acknowledges Emrak. He hands me the scroll.

A wax seal depicting an axe and warhammer crossed over one another remains intact. I break it and unroll the parchment, wondering what kind of message the king could have for me but not Taryn.

Chod,

I hope your adventures find you well. There has been barely a moment to catch my breath since the portal opened in Seascape Square. Your actions in opening the portal are precisely why I have sent my most trusted ranger, Emrak Stonebraid, to hand-deliver this message.

In the ensuing chaos of the portal's reopening, certain promises and rewards have remained unfulfilled. I promised a dwarven keep and all attendant lands to whoever managed to complete the quest to open the portal. You held up your end of the quest, and it is high time I did the same. Therefore, I am awarding Chod, Hero of the Forest and Mountain Trolls, the keep at Tawdrybluff.

Traditionally, one would be granted dominion over all attended lands within its borders, answering to Seascape in stately and legal matters. You would be responsible for taxes, and to provide those of fighting ability in times of war. However, you are not a dwarven citizen and these are not normal times.

In your absence, a large force of forest and mountain trolls now reside in Seascape as we make preparation for what is coming. If you accept, I would propose that they be given Tawdrybluff Keep to rule in your stead as a sovereign nation until you return. This will cement an official alliance between dwarves and trolls, and allow the trolls to have a societal outpost in the north. Chief Rizza and her council have given their consent, but the final word is yours. Please give your response to First Ranger Emrak with haste.

-King Orso Brightgaze

A notification flashes in the corner of my vision, but I read the letter three times before acknowledging it. I'd completely forgotten about the reward for King Orso's quest. Hell, I thought since I activated it accidentally that I wouldn't receive anything at all. It wasn't like I thought jumping into the portal would trigger the forest troll's blessing and open the whole thing up. It was pure dumb luck.

I pass the letter to Taryn and pull up my notification.

Quest Alert. *You have completed the quest "Open the Portal."*

Reward: *Dwarven keep and all attendant lands.*

Please return to Seascape to claim your reward from King Orso Brightgaze.

As Taryn reads through the letter, his eyes get wider and wider. When he's done, he stares at me, his mouth hanging open.

"He gave you a castle," he says dryly.

"Well, technically, it's a keep." I grin.

"Don't give me that. The keep is the heart of a castle, and you get all the attendant lands. That means lands necessary to keep it functioning. So unless there is a keep out in the middle of nowhere with no walls and no buildings inside those walls, then you are getting a fucking castle." He rubs his fingers through his dreadlocks and sighs. "How are you this damned lucky? It's like you're the protagonist in a fantasy novel."

I gently pat him on the back. "Don't worry, bud. Your time will come."

He pushes me in the side. "So, you gonna do it?"

I stare off into the darkness as I ponder his question. When I first logged in, the forest trolls were on the verge of extinction. They were hunted on sight and never left the boundary of the forest. And now here we are, being offered a castle and an alliance with the dwarves. How could I possibly turn that down?

"Yeah, I'm going to do it." I turn to Emrak. "You can tell King Orso I accept his proposal, but I would advise you to camp with us tonight for your own safety."

CHAPTER 12

MONEY CAN'T BUY HAPPINESS, BUT IT CAN BUY ITEMS

I HAVE a hard time falling asleep once we set up camp again. My head is filled with visions of a castle where a massive dragon perches on the watchtower. Calling it excitement would be an understatement. Things are definitely looking up for old Choddy-boy.

Will my new achievements open up more opportunities or will it put an even bigger target on my back?

If I'm able to give out quests, then maybe I could use it as a recruitment base to gather more heroes. Only time will tell.

Pressley the Death Knight briefly crosses my mind. He wanted a castle so bad that he partnered with that shady cleric to get one. I wonder what he's up to right now. Is he still in Goldspire, or has he set his sights on treasure elsewhere? Wherever he is, he's going to be jealous once he discovers I got a castle before him.

I open my eyes and notice Emrak is having a hard time sleeping as well. It probably has something to do with the ordeal he just went through, so I offer him a pinch of Sleep Dust. I take one for myself and in a matter of seconds, it's lights out.

When we wake up, Taryn has a small fire going with eggs roasting in a pan. Considering I don't feel as groggy this morning, I think I did a much better job with the Sleep Dust.

Taryn waves his spatula at me. "Limery thought you all deserved a proper breakfast. He flew deep enough into the forest to find some eggs."

"I'm in your debt." Emrak bows slightly. "I've been eating nothing but bread, cheese, and dried meat for the past week."

Taryn laughs. "Must be a hard life."

Emrak smiles. "I know I sound like a spoiled elf." He takes a seat around the fire. "No one tells you that you get used to the finer things in life. You become soft and you forget what it took for you to get there to begin with. I might be stronger and more accomplished than I ever was, but in my younger days, I traveled far and wide. My reputation was forged in the fires of adventure. Every meal I hunted with my own hands." He balls his hand into a fist and squeezes. "I drank swill with the common folk, not from barrels that cost more than they'd ever hope to earn in their lives. I would have killed for a block of cheese and stale bread on some of those trips, and now here I am complaining about it."

Taryn hands him a plate with a fried egg. "Awareness is half the battle."

He shrugs. "Doesn't make it any less true. If you want my advice, don't settle down just because you have a castle now. It'll be waiting for you when you're old. There's far too much of the world out there waiting to be adventured. There's a reason politics are an old man's game."

I take a seat next to him, and Limery brings me a plate of food. I offer my thanks before returning to Emrak's conversation. "I'll keep that in mind. Don't be too hard on yourself. If you worked for everything you have, then you have a right to enjoy it. No one is promised tomorrow."

Emrak bursts out laughing and pieces of egg fall into his beard.

"What's so funny?" I ask.

"Wise words coming from a hero. You lot have more lives than an alley cat. How many times have you died now?"

His words catch me off guard. Of course, it's not the same for me. I might come back, but every death takes me further from my objectives. Being here in Wandermere has made that even more apparent. How long would it have taken the wisps to overtake the entire forest had we not shown up when we did? The centaurs and fairies could have possibly fortified the Hidden Village, but how long could that hold when access to the portal would be closed off? By the time they would have formed a plan to fight back, it'd be too late.

Threats like this are why heroes exist.

I suddenly lose my appetite. "I've died too many times already, and I can't afford to die another."

Emrak eats the rest of his meal in silence. When he's finished, Taryn takes the plate.

"Don't mind him. Sometimes he needs to brood." He lets Berry lick the plate before stuffing it in his bag.

True to Taryn's words, I do sit and brood. I give myself five minutes to dwell on how impossible this all seems, and then I put it to the back of my mind. Those thoughts will always be there, but I can't let them control my every moment.

As Emrak is packing up his things, I'm struck with an idea. One that might help us clear the last of the wisps before nightfall.

"Hey, Emrak. How would you like to get a little payback on those wisps before you go? I'd love to see the First Ranger of Seascape in action."

He looks up from his pack, grinning. "I don't see why you lot should have all the fun."

Emrak digs into his satchel, pulling out a change of clothing and more leather armor, as well as a variety of weapons and vials of brightly-colored liquids.

After changing from his tattered clothing, Emrak looks like a new dwarf. The greens and browns that he wore before are replaced with vibrant shades of red accented with silver. He wears a red tunic covered by a deep crimson leather armor. Two embroidered silver arrows cross over one another across his chest, and a maroon cloak drapes from his shoulders. Silver vambraces cover his forearms and a matching clasp engraved with runes dangles from the end of his fiery beard.

He definitely can pull off the look of a renowned ranger when he wants to.

Next, he pulls out an ornately-carved bow. The bow is made from a material as black as night, and the string glows a piercing silver even in the dull light of the forest. A warthog head is carved just above the grip, its tusks jutting outward and serving as the shelf for arrows to rest upon. A quiver hangs from his waist on one side, filled with a variety of arrows with different colored fletchings, and a dagger with a jeweled pommel rests on his other hip.

Taryn gawks at him with dwarven pride. "Badass!"

I step closer, taking in all of the small details on the bow. "Definitely badass, but just so you know, physical attacks aren't really effective against the wisps."

He winks as he taps his quiver. "That shouldn't be a problem. One doesn't become First Ranger without learning a few tricks."

I'm intrigued to see what the old dwarf has up his sleeve. Archard was a superb ranger and expert marksman, but he had no abilities outside of his own skills. I get the feeling that's not the case with Emrak. We fill him in on the wisps as we travel to the first burrow, explaining our strategy and how the wisps operate during the day versus at night. According to our map, there are forty-two burrows that we need to take out.

Emrak grumbles. "Those bastards might have caught me unaware in the darkness, but they'll have a much tougher time singing me to sleep while there's daylight."

At the first burrow, we show him our technique, using Stonewall combined with my exploding horrors, Taryn's Moonbeam and Lightning Bolt, and Limery's fire to make short order of the wisps.

"Not bad." Emrak nods approvingly. "You all fight as one. That is a crucial advantage in most situations—the ability to rely on your party to cover your blind spots and act in predictable ways."

Taryn laughs. "That's only because we've been at this for a while. I don't want to say any names, but the big guy with the horns has a way of doing the unexpected."

I shrug. "What can I say? I'm a barbarian."

Emrak scouts the next burrow, examining each hole and surveying the surrounding area. He mumbles to himself as he walks around, occasionally tapping one of the arrows in his quiver.

When he's finished, he returns to where we are waiting. "There are several options I could take, but after last night, I feel I should take a little pride in myself. Could you be so kind as to lure the wisps out into the open?"

We do as he says, blocking off the two furthest entrances with Stonewall. Then, I have Pharos approach from between them, and though it doesn't deal any damage, his presence alone penetrates through the ground, funneling the wisps out of the lone exit.

Violent shrieks pour out of the tunnel as they try to escape.

When the first wisp emerges, its tongue lashes out, and drool flings across the forest. I activate Amulet of Sight, and its smoky shroud rips away.

Emrak grunts as he nocks an alabaster arrow with a golden tip and matching fletching. It contrasts starkly against the dark-colored bow. As he pulls it back, the arrow floods with white energy, and the warthog's obsidian eyes flare a deep red. White energy swirls around the shaft as he takes aim. A second and third wisp emerge, and then he releases.

Melodic notes sing from the arrow, and sunlight pierces through the treetops as it sails. A beam of light follows the projectile as it soars across the forest. The blinding white arrow penetrates the first wisp, tearing through its flesh. The gelatinous exterior explodes like a water balloon captured in slow-motion. The skin rips apart, curling into ribbons as fluid bursts forth. Light continues to follow the arrow as it punctures and gashes through the final two in a similar fashion.

In a matter of seconds, all that remains are three writhing tongues and a puddle of liquid.

"Holy shit!" Taryn and I say in unison, both of our eyes wide with shock.

"No." Emrak smirks. "Holy arrows."

"Whatever it was, it was awesome." I kick one of the tongues back into the hole. "With abilities like that, we'll have this cleared in no time."

He shakes his head. "That was a combination of an ability and a very rare item. Blessed arrows take a cleric a month just to enchant one arrow. They are incredibly time-consuming to create and equally expensive to purchase, but as you can see, they wreak havoc on dark-aligned creatures. I don't have enough Blessed Arrows for all of the burrows, I'm afraid." He taps his quiver. "Though I do have quite the arsenal."

"We wouldn't want you wasting something so precious out here anyways. The wisps are dangerous, but not worth that kind of expenditure." Taryn purses his lips. "Do you have any spells, or do you rely only on enchanted arrows?"

"A little of both. Most of my abilities enhance my tracking and fighting prowess. Though I'll be honest, my buffs are mostly geared toward fighting monsters that pose a physical threat, not those from the shadow realms. I can move through the forest quieter than a fox, and my senses are on par with your bear companion. My supply of arrows makes up for any deficiencies I may have."

"What happens when you run out of arrows?" I ask.

He grins. "I'll let you know if it ever happens. Here, take a look at this."

He takes off his quiver so I can analyze it.

Item. Quiver of Holding. *A quiver capable of holding an enormous supply of arrows. Simply focus on the arrows you desire, and they will appear in the quiver. Quiver of Holding can be linked to other expandable items for even greater inventory.*

"Wow, that's impressive." Taryn looks on in astonishment. "So, if your quiver's inventory is full, you can have it pull arrows from an expandable satchel? Talk about an unlimited ammo cheat."

Emrak slings his bow across his back. "Not unlimited, but I'll perish before I ever pull from an empty quiver. I have arrows for all occasions, some much more valuable than others, as you have seen."

I pat him on the back and head toward the next burrow. "No point in waiting around all day. Let's see what else you've got in your bag of tricks."

While nothing is as devastating as the Blessed Arrow, the variety of arrows in Emrak's arsenal is incredibly impressive. He has arrows that explode, tracking arrows, arrows tipped with small vials of holy water, electric arrows, and many more.

We learn the effect of ice against the wisps when he hits one with a frozen arrow. The gelatinous wisp freezes solid, falling to the ground with a thunk. Jordy rams into it with his powerful horns, shattering the wisp into hundreds of shards.

The day winds on and we make amazing progress, but as dusk approaches, there are still ten burrows left. Emrak could make the portal by nightfall, but not with the wisps still about.

"Taryn, do you still have your Dream Dust?" I ask.

His eyes go distant as he checks his inventory. "Eleven vials. What are you thinking?"

"We can restock when we head back to the village." I flash him a devilish expression that would make Limery proud. "I say we use everything we've got and go scorched earth on their slimy, jelly asses."

"Dream Dust?" Emrak raises his eyebrows. "Back in my younger days...Well, let's just say I liked to experiment. Some of the parties King Orso threw, he'd kill me if I told you." He smiles mischievously at the memory. "How exactly do you plan on killing a wisp with that stuff?"

My grin matches his own. "Not *a* wisp. All of them."

CHAPTER 13

TICK TICK BOOM

Between Taryn and I, we have twenty vials of Dream Dust and seventeen vials of Sleep Dust to use among the ten remaining burrows.

I plan to use every last one of them.

Taryn looks up from the pile on the ground. "This is never going to work. The burrows are too far apart, and there's no way to ignite all of the vials at once even if you do manage to get them inside each tunnel. Let's just take them out one at a time."

"Dude, aren't you tired of doing this day in and day out? I'm going to rip my horns off if I have to spend another day twiddling my thumbs while I watch you and Limery do all the work. If we play this right, then we can be back in the Hidden Village tomorrow." I turn to Limery. "Limery, you used to build contraptions back home. Do you know any way we can rig together a fuse of some kind? We don't have enough dust to make a trail like we did last time. Not from burrow to burrow."

Limery scratches his chin. "Limmy will thinks on it."

After a few minutes of silent pondering, he leaps into the air with excitement and hovers as his words spill out a mile a minute. "When Limmy was littles, he liked to make bombses, but when Limmy blows ups the kitchen tables, Mommy doesn't let Limmy make bombses anymore. Limmy still remembers, though. If we has strings and waxes, then we can use the Sleeps Dusts to make the fuses."

I search through my inventory, where I have about twenty feet of rope, but that's not nearly enough for what we would need. "I've got about twenty feet of climbing rope, but I think it's too thick for what we want. What about you two?"

Taryn shakes his head. "Climbing rope, but that's it, sorry."

Emrak laughs to himself as he digs in his satchel. "I guess you lot are lucky I showed up after all. Not only do I have rope, I have string. A good ranger never leaves home without it."

I clap my hands together, startling Ruby who is curled up near a tree trunk. "Awesome, how much do you have?"

"A good ranger is always prepared for the unexpected." He grins even wider. "But me, I'm a great ranger. I have enough that I'll never even need to think about buying string again."

Taryn pumps his fist in the air. "If you weren't so ugly, I'd kiss you, old dwarf."

"Dammit!" I curse as a new realization dawns on me, killing my excitement as quickly as it came. "We still need wax, and I have no idea how we're supposed to find it. Do you have any candles in that bag of yours?"

Emrak pulls out a large spool of string from his satchel. "I'm sure myself or the bear could track down a beehive if need be, but lucky for you, my bowstring is already waxed. It protects it from the elements and keeps it from snapping as easily. A little heat and it should melt enough for you to do whatever it is you need to do."

What else does he have hidden away in his expandable satchel?

My hands tingle with anticipation. We just might pull this off. "Alright then, we don't have much time. Let's get to work."

By the time everything is in place, twilight can't be more than twenty minutes away. A heavy silence settles across the forest. If this doesn't work, then the time we spent setting all of this up has probably added an extra day to our quest.

A slew of fuses stretch out before us, thirty in total. Limery used his natural body heat to soften the waxed string without melting it, then we coated the string in Sleep Dust. It took seven vials to coat thirty strings in enough dust to make a working fuse.

Each fuse runs to a separate entrance at one of the ten remaining burrows, where a horror stands ready and waiting with a vial of Boom Dust. One vial of Dream Dust was enough to explode an entire burrow by itself. For this, we elected for overkill. By mixing the twenty vials of Dream Dust with the remaining Sleep Dust, each burrow is about to be hit with more than double the explosive power as last time. My hard work creating the mixture manages to gain me an extra level in Potion-making during the process.

I double-check with my horrors one last time, making sure they're all in position.

"We ready?" I ask the group.

Taryn and Emrak nod.

"Readies." Limery summons a fireball in his open palm.

"Once the fuse is lit, cover your ears and open your mouth until it's over. The explosion will be big, and we don't want anyone bursting their ear drums." I give Limery the go-ahead, and he lights the fuses.

The strings ignite like sparklers on the Fourth of July, quickly burning away into the fog. Once they're out of sight, I pray that the fuses stay lit as I send my horrors descending into the burrows, a trail of Boom Dust spilling out with each step. A moment later, their presences begin to vanish.

And then we wait.

We're at least fifty yards from the first burrow when it explodes. The ground shakes and dirt erupts into the sky like a volcanic blast. Fog is pushed out of the way like a tidal wave, revealing a pink-and-purple mushroom cloud pluming into the trees. A heartbeat later, a shockwave hits me like a sledgehammer, flinging me into a tree as debris peppers me like a shotgun blast. My entire body burns and aches as my vision darkens at the edges.

I crawl across the forest floor, trying to regain my bearings enough to find the others when the explosion cracks like a sonic boom, reverberating in my chest and nearly crippling me. A second explosion follows, trailed quickly by a third and then a fourth. Over the course of ten seconds, all our homemade bombs detonate.

I search for the others, coughing as debris rains down around us. Between falling dirt and the dissipating smoke, I can't see more than a foot in front of me. Notifications flash in the corner of my vision, but I push them away.

"Is everyone okay?" I shout.

I bump into Berry, and he grunts his annoyance. The fog is gone for the moment, but a heavy layer of dust hangs in its wake, making it equally impossible to see.

"Ungh, we're okay. A little bruised, but otherwise fine," Taryn answers from the other side of Berry. "Limery? Emrak?"

"Limmy is okays."

"I'll live. Gods, remind me to never piss the three of you off." A hand grabs me by the side as Emrak steadies himself. "Oh, there you are. I haven't seen an explosion like that since Brannia Bravefall, a powerful young pyromancer mage, went mad and tried to explode Seascape portal many years ago."

By the time the smoke and dust clear enough for us to see in our immediate vicinity, it's well-past nightfall. We're all covered in so much dust from the explosion that we look like we stepped out of a sepia photograph.

Luckily, I have enough juice left in the Amulet of Sight for us to survey the damage.

Taryn grimaces as the amulet reveals the area. "We're going to be in so much trouble."

A crater the size of a house sits where the burrow once was. The damage is so extensive that the amulet can't reveal it all within its radius. As we walk to the next burrow, the edge of the first crater overlaps the second. The trees that surrounded the burrow are gone, and there's a gaping hole through the canopy from the explosion, revealing a full moon among the starry sky.

When all is said and done, our explosion has formed a crater big enough to be a small lake. The hair on the back of my neck stands on end. We're lucky to be alive. If we had been any closer, we might not be.

"Yep, we're so screwed." I sigh. I just hope this doesn't affect the deal we made with Swift.

"So screweds," murmurs Limery.

Emrak pats me on the lower back. "Don't sweat it. They asked you to eliminate the wisps. Unless they specifically said to not blow up a large portion of the forest, I think you'll be okay. Just tell them to request a water mage from King Orso, and they can call this the 'Not-So-Hidden Lake'."

Taryn grins. "You'd make a good lawyer."

"There's no need for lawyers when there is a king. His

majesty's word is the law. Speaking of which, now that I've delivered the king's message and you've fulfilled your quest, I'll be taking my leave come morning."

I extend my arm, and we shake. "You have our thanks. There's no way we could have done this without you."

"Maybe not this." He nods toward the giant crater. "But you would have cleared the forest of wisps just fine. I'm glad to have played a small part. This will be a story worth telling over a large mug of ale when I return."

"I remember ale." Taryn groans. "Let it know that its sweet taste still lingers on my lips."

"Okay, Casanova." I squeeze Taryn on the shoulder. "How about you summon some shelter for us and then you can dream about your frothy mistress without creeping the rest of us out."

We make camp near the crater, and even though the wisps are gone, we still use Taryn's walls for safety. I elect to leave Pharos outside as well, just in case. After the past week, a little peace of mind goes a long way.

As I rest against the wall, taking first watch, I finally pull up my notifications from earlier.

Quest Alert: You have completed the quest "Tit for Tat." Mesmer wisps haunt the forest no more, and soon peace shall return to Wandermere.

Reward: Increased favor with Swift Thundercrest and the Wandermere Herd.

Bonus: In exchange for your efforts, Swift Thundercrest has agreed to help you through the process of hatching a green dragon egg.

Please return to the Hidden Village to claim your reward from Swift Thundercrest.

Congratulations! You have reached level 26. +1 stat point to distribute. +1 Strength and Constitution racial bonus.

Not bad. A quest completion and a new level. I also get three more levels in my Demolition skill from the epic blast, putting me close to becoming an apprentice. It feels like I leveled up much quicker than I have been the past few weeks, but I guess we did a lot of fighting, especially by clearing most of the burrows more than once. Maybe I got some kind of bonus for taking out so many in one go last night. Either way, I'll take it. It puts me even closer to level thirty and the exclusive Warforged class Jegaar told me about.

With this newest stat point, I now have seven that I haven't distributed. I'm anxious holding onto them when they could be benefiting me, but I keep waiting for something to offer guidance on how best to allocate them. My racial bonus makes it a waste to put them in Strength or Constitution. Dexterity makes the most sense to keep my speed matched with my power and toughness, especially now that I deal splash damage with each attack thanks to the Ram Rage passive from my Spirit of the Beast path. But there's no telling what leveling up Intelligence or Wisdom could do for my summoning abilities.

The one thing I know is that I don't want it in Charisma. I still don't understand why that particular stat works so much more differently than it does in other games, but I've done just fine without it and don't want to ever feel that reckless again while I'm in Mythos. There's too much on the line.

I analyze the others while they're sleeping. It seems everyone leveled up from the quest, but it's impossible to tell with Emrak. With his level hidden, there's no telling how strong he actually is. Judging by his attacks, he's definitely stronger than us.

Taryn and I are both level twenty-six now. Limery is close behind at twenty-five. Jordy is twenty-three, Berry twenty-two, and Ruby eighteen. It's been so long since we ran into any other heroes outside of Glenn and Jude that I'm not sure where we stand in comparison. Sometimes I feel like Taryn and I are the only ones trying to make a difference in this world while everyone else is out there having fun.

When my watch is over, I nudge Taryn on the shoulder. "Wake up. It's your turn to take watch."

He grunts as he sits up. "I can't wait to be back in a city where we can get a full night's sleep again."

"You and me both, buddy. Looks like we all leveled up today. You think Limery unlocked anything like we did for hitting level twenty-five?"

Taryn shrugs. "He didn't say anything. But he never said anything when he unlocked his molten form either. Maybe it's not the same for imps. He doesn't exactly have a class, does he?"

It's my turn to shrug. "Who knows? I'm still not one hundred percent sure how things are different between us and the NPCs. Anywho, I'm beat." A yawn overtakes me as I lie down. "See you in the morning."

After such a long day, I'm asleep as soon as my head hits the ground.

I wake up to the sound of birds chirping. With the wisps gone, it doesn't take long for nature to return to the area.

"Sleeping Ugly has arisen," Taryn jokes as he prepares breakfast.

"Mornings, Chods!" Limery perches on my shoulder as I sit up. "Do we gets to sees the baby dragons today?"

His excitement warms my heart. "If we're lucky. I have no idea how long it takes to hatch a dragon." I look to Emrak, but he just shrugs.

"I can't recall the last time a green dragon was hatched." He shifts his gaze to the forest. "But I can't think of a more potent location for life aura."

After a quick breakfast, we pack up our things. In the daylight, the devastation our bombs left behind is even more apparent. Without the tree cover, the sunlight spills through, pushing back the fog in the immediate area. The tree branches cling to debris like an overzealous spiderweb, and a thick layer of dirt covers limbs and bushes. We really did a number on this section of the forest.

"What's next for you all?" Emrak asks as he tosses his satchel over his shoulder.

"We were planning to go to Pruxford, but now that I have a castle, I guess we should probably head back to Seascape once we're finished in the Hidden Village and check in with King Orso. With the arctic trolls joining the forest and mountain tribes, I should probably help them get settled as well."

"What did I tell you? The castle will be waiting when you return." Emrak narrows his eyes. "Do you not trust Chief Rizza to maintain the peace and hold order until then?"

I lower my head like a scolded child. "I do."

"Then go and explore Pruxford. The gnomish council supports King Orso's efforts against the dark wizard, but they are not as concerned as they ought be. Their annual tournament still stands, and some of the greatest warriors across Mythos will try to showcase their skill." He grabs me firmly by the arm. "It is said that the council showers the winner in favors. King Orso has sent messengers to the council time and again, but they are not concerned with the mounting threats. You may have better luck yourself. Win and you will have an opportunity to speak to the council directly. If you truly want to make a difference, that is the way."

I ponder on his comments for a moment. Competing in a tournament could give us the platform we need to bring in more powerful allies. If other heroes have been sticking to major cities, they've likely heard about it. This might be the best chance we have to meet other heroes. There are still a great many we haven't met, and if they are looking for gold and glory, then my castle can wait. I trust that Chief Rizza can manage until I get back.

"What kind of tournament?" asks Taryn.

"I can't say for sure. The last time a Seascape dwarf competed was before the portals closed. We can't afford to part with our strongest warriors with times being as they are, but King Orso and King Favian have encouraged heroes to enter. Pruxford is known as the City of Glass, named for the Crystal Palace and its amazing arena carved from towering gemstones. It's primarily gnomish, but many races live among one another in relative peace. Our histories from before the portals closed describe wondrous battles between warriors and mages in their tournaments. Heroes competed against one another in ancient times. From what I recall, a field of combatants eliminate one another in single combat until a lone victor remains." He makes eye contact with Taryn and me in turn. "If my time among you is any indication, then either of you have a shot."

Taryn and I exchange glances, but his face gives away nothing.

Taryn runs his fingers through his beard, making the clasps jingle slightly. "I don't want this to come across the wrong way, because I know how important your relationship with the trolls is, but if Chief Rizza has shown us anything, it's that she's a great leader. Even Kronan has given up his own power to follow her lead. Chief Laojin is a wise leader as well. Between the three of them, they can run a castle until you return." He nods at Emrak. "Emrak is right, and I think you know it. This is an opportunity not only for us to test ourselves against some of the greatest warriors across Mythos, but I'm sure there will be other heroes there. Heroes we can recruit. To save the trolls and the dwarves, we will need every ally we can get."

"Yeah, I think you're right. This is too good of an opportunity to pass up." I wink at Taryn. "Besides, finally getting to go all out against one another might be pretty fun."

He flexes a short stubby arm. "Maybe you haven't noticed, but I can carry my own weight nowadays."

"Believe me, I've noticed." I'm reminded of how useless I've felt for most of this quest. We're long past the days of mindlessly farming just so he can catch up on experience. With his pets and new abilities, Taryn is a formidable opponent.

We say our good-byes to Emrak, and the ranger disappears into the foggy depths of the forest. Pruxford awaits, but first, we have a dragon to hatch.

CHAPTER 14

THE WAITING GAME

THE FOREST SEEMS livelier than ever with the wisps gone. Birds chirp overhead, and Limery disappears among the trees several times over the course of the journey. There's constant movement in the underbrush, even though the source of the disturbance is often concealed by the fog.

I can't help but feel a sense of pride that we did all of this.

I share those sentiments with Taryn. "It's pretty crazy what we've been able to accomplish as a group. Between Limery, your pets, and my horrors, we've become a pretty formidable party. I think we could hold our own against a group of four or five heroes no problem."

Taryn scoffs. "I'd rather not test out that theory any time soon. I'm all for adventure, but nothing good ever comes of meeting other heroes."

"That's not true," I say flatly.

He narrows his eyes. "Hmm, let's see. Glenn and Jude? Murderhobos. The warlock and his posse we met in Lynchton? Servants of the dark wizard. The cleric? Trouble follows him like a baby duck. Not to mention the run-ins you told me about before I got here."

"Oh, come on. It's not that bad. What about Pressley? Or Jon? They both turned out alright."

He laughs dryly. "Key word is 'turned out.' They were a headache to begin with, too."

I shake my head. "Who peed in your mushroom soup this morning? You're the one who said we should go to Pruxford."

He sighs. "I know. I know. It's just... Ugh, I don't know. Everywhere we go, you've got a target on your back, and by extension, I have one on mine. That means my pets do as well. It's one thing to know going to this tournament is the smart decision. It's another thing to think about what it might cost us."

I slow my pace, and Berry does as well. "Believe me, I know. But we can't stop fighting for what's right. I made a promise to the trolls. We both made a promise to King Orso. We're in the thick of this. Maybe back in the re—" I catch myself before I say 'real world.' "Maybe back home, we don't have the power to affect great change, but here, we do. And you know what they say about great power."

He chuckles at the reference. "Yeah, yeah. With great power comes a high electric bill."

I shove him in the arm a little too hard, and he nearly falls off Berry's back before catching himself on the saddle. After that, Taryn's shoulders relax, and he seems more at ease. I never really thought about it much before coming to Mythos, mostly because I always kept everything bottled inside until it finally erupted into a rage-fueled tirade, but sometimes just talking about your worries can make them feel less oppressive. Funny how it took me embodying a raging monster to find a little inner peace.

Even with Strong Wind buffing our speed, it takes us most of the day to make it back to the Hidden Village. Thanks to Pharos, we don't need to use our maps, and his passive ability guides us back without issue.

A dark-colored stallion stands sentry at the village boundary, holding a spear in his powerful arm. He looks around as if making sure the coast is clear before disappearing into the fog.

Taryn casts me an uncertain look as we approach.

Something definitely feels off, so I cancel Pharos and we advance quietly. After a short moment, the centaur returns. A minute later, he looks around before disappearing into the fog barrier once again. This happens twice more as we watch from behind a large bush.

"Everything okay?" I call out once he returns.

The young stallion nearly jumps out of his skin at my words.

He raises his spear but lowers it once he identifies us. "Gods, you startled me. I'd be grateful if you didn't tell Swift," he pleads, looking at me sheepishly. "I'm on guard duty tonight, but this is a once-in-a-lifetime event. I don't want to miss it."

"Miss what exactly?" I raise my eyebrow.

His front hooves tap against the earth in his excitement. "You should really see for yourselves. I don't want to spoil the surprise."

I shrug at his vague answer and step through the fog barrier.

On the other side, I stop in my tracks. The village looks nothing like it did when we left. An eerie green glow stretches across the village, covering everything in a spectral radiance. Hundreds of centaurs stand around the Hidden Lake as it pulses ominously. Fairies zoom across the evening sky, their chimes ringing through the air. Toxic-looking bubbles burst around the altar in the middle of the lake, spewing ghastly fog into the sky. The aura from the altar is brighter than ever, a dense chartreuse that's almost sinister in its brightness. In the center, the dragon egg shimmers, nearly double the size it was when we left.

Limery gasps in awe above my shoulder, and a chill runs down my spine. How is it possible that the egg has grown bigger?

Taryn gulps. "This is creepy as hell. What have we gotten ourselves into?"

"I don't know." My hands tingle, and I clench my fists several times until the feeling fades. "Let's go find Swift and see what the deal is."

The eerie silence as we make our way down to the lake has my skin crawling with goosebumps. Aside from the chiming of fairies, and the gentle bubbling in the lake, the otherwise quiet is unsettling.

Every centaur is focused on the lake. It's almost like they are in a trance as we squeeze between their massive frames. I spot Swift down by the water's edge next to Thannis and Sylvie. His silver hair reflects the bright glow of the lake.

He doesn't so much as turn in my direction when he speaks. "Forgive us for not showing you a hero's welcome, but as you can see, we've been a bit preoccupied."

I glance around, wondering if I'm missing something. A hidden reason as to why the centaurs are behaving so weird. "What exactly is going on?"

His tail swishes, but he still doesn't look away. "Can you not feel it? That gentle pull at your being? We are witnessing a historic moment."

Maybe they got into a little too much fairy dust while we were away. "I have no idea what you are talking about."

Swift takes a deep breath, and then finally turns to face us. For a moment, he looks annoyed, and then his face softens. "You may be from the forest, but you still have much to learn." He rests a hand on my shoulder. "Close your eyes, all of you."

I do as he says, and my sense of hearing slowly expands, honing in on the chimes of fairies, the gentle bubbling of the lake, and the occasional crunch of the earth as a centaur repositions their hooves.

"Now focus within yourself." His voice is relaxed, soothing. "Life aura runs through the forest, and it beats within your heart. Just like the mana that powers your heroic abilities, life aura flows within your being. Focus on your center, on your own life aura."

It feels a bit silly, but I do it anyway. As I try to look inward, the world softens around me. The sounds of the village become distant. Like some hippie meditating in Central Park, I try to find my center, but all I hear is my own breathing.

"Limmy feels it!" the imp shouts excitedly. "Limmy feels its, Chods."

I try to dig deeper, searching for anything out of the ordinary, but nothing happens.

"I feel it, too," Taryn whispers. "Wow. You'd never notice otherwise, but it's like it's pulling a trickle of energy from me."

"Precisely." Swift's voice is calm. "The egg is growing, drawing life aura from its surroundings until it is ready to hatch. Over the past three days, a change has come upon the village. When the egg has gathered enough aura, it will begin to hatch."

I open my eyes to find Swift once again gazing upon the egg. "Are you telling me that you've all been out here for three days?"

He nods. "I agreed to help you hatch the egg. The more life aura it gathers, the quicker it will hatch. By gathering our herd around the lake, we are speeding up the process."

"I'm sure that's not necess—"

He turns on me in a flash, eyes flaring with intensity. "When the histories are written, it will not be said that the centaurs did not play a part."

I raise my hands defensively, startled by his outburst. "Sorry, I didn't mean to offend you. I just thought you might have better things you could be doing."

"Our forest is overrun with creatures we cannot fight, while darkness gathers in the shadowlands. Right now, there is nothing better for my people to be doing. A dragon has the power to balance the scales once again."

Taryn nudges me in the side. "You really have a way with authority."

I ignore his comment and try to ease the tension. "You're right, Swift. It's not my place to question you. We've cleared the forest of the mesmer wisps, and it's once again safe for the herd to move about the forest." Swift is clearly on edge, so I leave out the part about the giant crater for now.

"I had no doubts you would succeed. Once the dragon is hatched, we will return to our outposts once again."

"Since we're back, is there anything we can do to help?"

He shakes his head. "For now, we stand strong and we wait. You may come and go as you please. You are an honored guest while you are here, and the fairies will see to anything you need."

"That's very kind of you." I bow slightly. "Do you all not need to sleep?"

He laughs. "The herd can sleep while standing when needed."

I wave to get Taryn's attention and nod in the direction of the village buildings. We make our way through the herd to where we can speak freely.

I crouch near a tree once we are far enough away. "This is weird. Did you actually feel something back there?"

Taryn raises an eyebrow. "You didn't? I guess I shouldn't be surprised that someone whose first option is to punch things isn't in touch with the natural world. If you can't tell by looking, there's definitely something going on here."

I frown. That much is evident. "So what, we just wait? Our maid always said a watched pot never boils."

"Your maid..." He rolls his eyes. "You'll be right at home in your new castle." He mumbles the words, but I still manage to make them out. "After we eat, I'm going back down to the lake. They've piqued my curiosity, and I definitely want to be there when something happens."

I don't have anything better to do, so after eating, I join Taryn and the others at the lake. As much as I try, I can't seem to feel whatever is happening with the life aura. Maybe it has something to do with my rapid regeneration or high Constitution.

Over the next two days, the centaurs barely move or eat unless they're switching guard duty around the village. Two days of doing nothing, and I still haven't been able to talk with Swift or any of the others about how we cleared the forest.

The aura becomes denser by the day, and the egg continues to grow until it's as big as Limery, but nothing else happens. I have no idea how large the egg is supposed to get. Dragon's are huge, so if it hatches at the size of Jordy or Berry, we could be waiting a while. What I wouldn't give for a pair of headphones and some music as I sit around doing nothing.

I take a deep breath and lie on my back. As boring as this is, it could always be worse. At least I'm not in prison.

I close my eyes, once again trying to find my center so that I can feel this mysterious force supposedly draining my life. The world fades away, and my breathing takes center stage, in and out like a rising tide.

There's a dull rumble in my chest, and I think that maybe I'm close to breaking through. But then the rumble spreads, and I realize it's not coming from within, but from beneath.

My eyes snap open, and the ground continues to quake violently. The silent centaurs bump into one another as they search for balance. Voices suddenly fill the air. Next to me, Taryn attempts to calm his pets as they pace in alarm. Limery hovers in the air, searching for unseen threats.

Leaves fall from the trees, and waves crash along the shore. I crawl to my feet on wobbly legs, and as quickly as the earthquake came, it stops.

Murmured chatter stretches in every direction.

I push my way through the crowd until I find Swift, grabbing him on the shoulder. "What the hell was that?"

His eyes burn brighter than ever. "Verdaria is stirring."

Cold dread weighs on me like an avalanche, and I turn my eyes to the lake. I signed up to hatch a baby dragon, not wake a sleeping adult. "Stirring how?"

The last thing we need is an ancient dragon wreaking havoc through the village while the egg is still hatching.

A loud bang echoes from the middle of the lake, amplified by the turbulent waves. The aura around the altar blazes with power, flaring some twenty feet in the air. My heartbeat thunders in my ears and for the life of me, I can't look away.

The egg wobbles on the altar, and the shell cracks down the side.

CHAPTER 15

HOW TO TRAIN YOUR DRAGON

THE CRACK SPLINTERS along the egg like an arc of lightning. Pieces of jade eggshell flake off as it continues to shake against the altar. The ground quits quaking, and the green glow of the lake fades slightly. Turbulent waters continue to toss the raft, but the aura surrounding the items on the altar shrinks to its original size.

Minutes pass before the water stills, and the egg's movement ceases.

All eyes focus on the altar. The village sits in an eerie silence aside from the chiming of fairies overhead.

A low growl, almost like a puppy learning to bark for the first time, comes muffled from within the egg. It wobbles slightly, then a small green claw pokes through the crack, breaking off more of the shell. The claw wiggles before disappearing back inside.

The intake of breath around me is so pronounced that it could have come from the forest itself.

"Thannis, pull the altar to shore," orders Swift.

Thannis wades into the water and grabs the rope, pulling the altar toward the expectant crowd.

135

"Chod!" Swift shouts as if he's unaware that I'm right behind him. "Come down!"

"I'm right here." My chest is tight, and my hands tingle with excitement. Whatever is about to happen, this is the reason we came here.

Swift grips me firmly on the shoulder. "When the altar is ashore, take the egg and go deeper into the forest. Sit with the egg until it hatches. This will produce the strongest bond with the young dragon."

I have a million questions running through my mind, and Thannis has already pulled the raft halfway to the shore. "And then what? Should I try to help it free itself?"

His gaze is penetrating as he speaks calmly. "Wait for it to hatch. A dragon will bond strongly with the first being it sees. While it's not a permanent bond, this is your best chance of laying the groundwork for such a connection. Afterward, return to the village."

By the time he finishes, Thannis has lugged the altar onto dry land. Swift steps aside, gesturing for me to approach.

The crowd parts as I go to the altar. I hesitate for a moment, as muffled growls continue inside the egg and a tiny claw pokes in and out of the crack.

Alright, little dragon, come to papa.

Taking a deep breath, I pick up the egg. It's hot to the touch. If not for my tough troll skin, I'm certain it would be blistering right now. There's a hiss, and a second claw pokes through the crack, breaking off more of the shell.

"I'll be back soon," I tell Limery and Taryn as I walk carefully through the crowd. The last thing I want to do is trip and fall, crushing the poor creature before it's even hatched.

I walk deeper in the forest, away from the village and the hundreds of eyes following my every movement. The green aura of the forest has already faded dramatically by the time I reach a small clearing next to a towering tree.

Taking a seat on the ground in front of the tree, I cradle the egg in my palms. Three claws have managed to break through the shell. The talons grate against the exterior scales as it continues its struggle to break free.

The egg's warmth reminds me of the cold winters when I would sit on the balcony overlooking the city with a cup of hot chocolate. The toasty mug would keep the frigid cold at bay, steam trailing into the cool air of the bustling city.

A piece of shell breaks off, and the first full paw reaches through. The tiny leg is the color of freshly-mown grass, vibrant and untarnished by the world. It grasps at the air, and more cracks form along the egg as the dragon maneuvers inside.

Another large section breaks off and a snout presses through the opening. It sniffs at the air, and then a wisp of green smoke puffs out.

There's a tingle in my chest that I can't quite explain. Maybe it's the fact that I'm witnessing something that anyone back in the village would kill for. It's a once-in-a-lifetime—hell, once-in-several-lifetimes—event that could shake the world of Mythos as we know it. And I'm seeing it all by myself.

I shift the weight of the egg, cradling it in my left hand as I stroke the dragon's nose with my right index finger. The dragon lets out the most adorable snarl I've ever heard and snorts out another small plume of smoke.

"You can do it, little guy. You're almost there." I offer my best encouragement.

The egg shakes as the dragon applies pressure from within. For a moment, I consider whether or not I should help it, but then I remember Swift's directions to wait for it to hatch.

After about an hour of grumbling and growling, a piece of egg breaks off, leaving a hole big enough for the dragon's head to fit through. At this size, it looks more like a large lizard than a powerful dragon. Two nubby horns stick out from the top of its head like a young deer. Big, round, golden eyes blink rapidly as a milky fluid drips down its face.

I lift the egg to where our heads are at eye level. The dragon snaps at me, its jaws clacking from the powerful bite. Not even an hour old and it could probably draw blood.

"Easy there." I put my finger up, and the dragon quiets as its golden eyes follow my every movement.

"Trolls are friends, not food." I use the most soothing voice I can. "I'm gonna pet you. Do not bite me."

An inch at a time, I lower my finger until it rests on the dragon's head. The scales are smooth and covered in a layer of slime. Gently, I stroke the slick scales of its forehead, and the dragon closes its eyes. It growls, but this time, it sounds more like a purr than a warning.

I quit petting the dragon, and its eyes lock onto mine.

"Alright, you've got this. Show that egg what you're made of."

It struggles, writhing one shoulder through the opening and then creating another crack as it forces the other. Once its midsection is through, it uses its paws to slither the rest of its body out of the opening, plopping onto the ground with a thick, gelatinous sheen covering its body.

The hatchling shakes like a wet dog, flinging egg fluid in all directions, and a set of leathery wings unfurl from its back. The motion sends it tumbling to the ground, and with a grumble, it rises back up on unsteady feet. Standing at its full height, the dragon is about the size of a house cat.

Green Dragon. *Unique Monster. Level 1. Green dragons rule with impunity over the forests they inhabit. They are the most territorial of all dragon species, and capable of spewing toxic gas in lieu of* *flames. Wherever a green dragon calls home, a dense fog is said to follow.*

"Level one. We're going to need to change that pretty quick." I extend a hand, and the dragon walks awkwardly in my direction. It nuzzles against my palm, its cool scales a stark contrast to the earlier heat of the egg. "You're gonna need a name." I pick the creature up and it curls around my hand, sharp claws gripping me firmly. "Are you a boy or a girl?"

I look underneath its belly, but I have no idea how to distinguish a male from a female. Maybe Swift will have more answers.

"I guess we'll save the naming for later." I place him gently on the ground. "Just remind me not to ask Taryn for suggestions."

I take the time to enjoy the moment alone with the baby dragon. It's likely the only time we'll be truly alone for the foreseeable future.

Reaching into my satchel, I pull out a piece of jerky. The dragon immediately focuses on the strip of dried warthog.

"You must have a pretty good sense of smell."

It jumps into my lap, jaws snapping as it tries to bite the jerky from my hand. I grab the dragon by the midsection and place it on the ground.

"No," I scold. "We're going to need to teach you some manners. Now, sit." I hold the piece of meat over the dragon's head.

Its head tilts up as it eyes the jerky, forcing its hind legs to the ground. With the task completed, I drop the jerky into its mouth. It snatches the jerky out of the air, swallowing it after only a few bites.

"Are you hungry?" I ask, pulling out another piece of jerky.

The dragon jumps on its hind legs, trying once again to take the snack from me.

"No." I wag a finger. "Sit."

The dragon huffs and a trickle of green smoke erupts from its nostrils.

"Sit," I say more firmly.

It jumps in the air, nearly reaching the jerky, but I pull it away at the last second.

"No. Sit."

The dragon growls but then places its rear on the ground.

"Good job!" I excitedly drop the jerky into its mouth.

I've never had a pet before, but the pride from teaching it to sit has me understanding Taryn's bond with his own pets a little better than before.

"Alright, little dude. Time to show you off to the village and see if they have a copy of *Raising Dragons for Dummies* lying around anywhere."

When we return, the centaurs are no longer huddled around the lake, but it's clear that the majority of them are waiting around to see the dragon.

It walks by my side, easily distracted by the slightest movement or sound in the underbrush. Several times it pounces on a pile of leaves, growling and pawing at the earth.

"Chods!" Limery calls out as he zooms in our direction followed by a troop of fairies. "Did yous hatch the dragonses?"

He lets out a delighted squeal when he notices the small dragon catching up to me. Limery flies to the ground a couple of feet in front of the creature, and chimes fill the air as the fairies gossip and point. In the distance, the clop of hooves announces centaurs on the move.

The dragon backs away, its back arched as it stays close to my leg, unsure of Limery.

I kneel beside it, stroking between its wings. "It's okay. Limery is a friend."

Limery reaches his own tiny hand out. "It's okays. Limmy is yous friends."

"Here, give him this." I toss Limery my last piece of jerky.

Limery feeds the dragon, and its demeanor immediately changes. It nuzzles against the imp's belly, and Limery wraps his arms around it. Looks like the two of them have something in common already.

Swift and many centaurs trot over, followed by Taryn and his pets.

"I can already tell those two are going to be trouble." Taryn grins. "I can't believe it's moving around so well this quickly."

Swift watches the dragon and imp interact with wonder, as do the centaurs behind him. "If the tales hold true, young dragons are full of mischief. It will be your duty to raise it with honor, lest it becomes a terror in its own right."

They ogle over the newborn dragon, but Swift's words weigh heavily on me. The idea of having a pet dragon was so enticing that I never thought about the responsibility that would come with it.

Am I ready to take care of a pet this powerful? I probably should have considered that before going through all this trouble.

What if I can't control it and it grows into a monster capable of destroying villages and towns?

I'm so caught in my own thoughts that I don't even notice Taryn standing beside me until he taps me on the back.

"It's gonna be fine." Taryn offers me a kind smile. He must be able to tell I'm freaking out. "I say this from experience, but you figure it out as you go."

"I hope you're right." I don't point out the fact that all of his pets were full-grown when he bonded with them. Or that they have an actual bond due to his Tame ability.

For the next hour, we talk with Swift while the herd cycles through, giving each of the centaurs an opportunity to see the dragon. The solemn faces that greeted us upon our first arrival are filled with something else now. Hope, maybe? With the wisps gone and the forest free of threats, the centaurs can finally return to their way of life.

The fairies are particularly enamored with the dragon, filling him up with roasted meat. The little dragon turns out to be a quick learner and highly motivated by food. Limery and the fairies teach it several tricks using only hand motions, and pretty soon, it knows how to stay, lie down, and can do this weird little gliding hop by flapping its wings as it jumps.

"It is strong to be so small." Swift hardly ever takes his eyes off the dragon, even when he is talking to me directly. "I imagine it will be flying in no time."

"Will it learn on its own?" I rub my jaw as I think, unsure how I could possibly teach it to fly.

"It is said that the instincts of a dragon are superior to all creatures. It may need guidance, but you can see it is already learning the motions of flight."

"One more thing..." I hesitate before asking. "How am I supposed to know if it's a male or female?"

He laughs so loud, it takes me by surprise. "Dragons make their own destiny. You won't truly know until it is time for it to mature. Male green dragons will develop a scaled beard. The females do not. Though you may learn more from its nature as it continues to grow."

"Is one more powerful than the other?" Taryn runs his fingers through his beard.

He turns to Taryn, expression as placid as can be. "Is fire more powerful than water? Both have the power to preserve life. Both have the ability to wreak great havoc. A dragon is a dragon, no matter the sex."

Eventually, all the centaurs have their moment with the dragon and return to their duties. Swift invites us to join him for dinner so that we can finally discuss the quests with the wisps.

The fairies prepare us a table down by the water's edge. A platter of roasted vegetables sits in the center next to several pitchers of mead, and a warthog roasts over a spit to the side.

The village has finally returned to normal, with the lake a pristine blue and the green aura completely gone. Many centaurs remain, but a majority have returned to their normal duties, dispersed throughout the village and the forest of Wandermere.

Limery and the dragon play in the lush grass, wrestling and chasing each other. Occasionally, Limery flies into the air, and the dragon tries to follow. When its wings are unable to fully support it, the dragon roars and blows streams of smoke from its nostrils.

Swift carves a platter of sliced meat from the warthog and places it on the table before pouring us all a glass of mead. Limery abandons his playtime to join us at the table, leaving the dragon to play with Taryn's pets, who are not nearly as enthusiastic about the experience as it jumps and nips at them like a rowdy puppy.

Swift raises his mug. "A toast to Mythos's finest heroes, for saving the forest and hatching the first dragon in hundreds of years."

I tap my mug to his. "None of it would have been possible without your help."

"In the end, it's better to walk together than alone." He smiles. "Now, tell me. How did you manage to clear the wisps from the forest?"

The mead is a little too sweet for my taste, but it's plenty strong. Over several glasses, Taryn and I fill him in on our adventure in the forest, from our first encounter with the wisp to the grand finale.

He stares at us with wide eyes when I finish. "The lot of you are lucky to be alive. The forest will heal, but you—" He pauses, as if only just remembering we are heroes. "Well, maybe not you, but them—" He gestures toward Limery and then Taryn's pets. "—they are not so lucky. Not to mention the danger to an envoy from King Orso."

"Believe me, we know. The size of the explosion was a surprise to us as well." Taryn grimaces and runs a hand through his beard. "Pretty sure I singed a few hairs."

Swift sighs. "At least you survived. What is next for you all?"

I wipe mead from my chin before answering. "Emrak told us of a tournament in Pruxford. We plan to check it out before returning to Seascape."

A wide grin spreads across his face. "Draydon was fond of the tournaments. You must seek out his sculpture while you are there."

I lean forward. I completely forgot that Swift's brother used to compete. Maybe he will have insight into what awaits. "We definitely will. Do you happen to know what the tournaments are like?"

He shrugs. "Each tournament is different. I didn't make it to many, but Draydon loved to boast of his victories when he returned home. They were thrilling tales. Some were battle royales, where they fought to the last man. Some were duels where the victor advanced. Some even pitted multiple warriors against monsters or other threats. There is no telling what awaits you, but I have faith you will make a name for yourselves."

By the time we are done with dinner, Limery is swaying back and forth as he stands on the table. The baby dragon is mesmerized by the fireballs Limery casts and tries to bite each one as the imp juggles them.

I'm feeling a little intoxicated myself as I wrap an arm around Swift. "I'm not sure when the tournament starts, but I don't want to miss it. We appreciate all of your hospitality, but I'm afraid tomorrow we must set out."

"I figured as much." He glances up to the village. "Come with me. I have a parting gift for the two of you."

Our drunken fellowship stumbles up to the main structures of the village, pets and dragon in tow, and we follow Swift through a maze of buildings until he leads us down a long corridor. At the end is a room filled with several chests. Its roof is open-air like the majority of the buildings, and a large tree towers over us from the middle of the room.

He turns around to face us. "Thanks to you all, the forest is free once more. We can finally return to our outposts across Wandermere."

He opens the chest in the far back, pulling out a dull gray shield and leaning it against the tree trunk. It's the same shield used to create the aura on the raft. Then, he removes the matching spear topped with an emerald spearhead, and finally, the stone etched with an ancient rune.

He extends the spear to me. "These items belonged to my brother. I hope that they will bring you the same fortune that they brought him."

"You don't have to do this." I try to hand the spear back to him, but he refuses, pressing it against my chest. "Hatching the dragon was more than enough payment."

He shakes his head. "This isn't about repayment. This is an investment in your future. In Mythos's future. Take it."

"Thank you." I take the items, and as soon as they are all equipped, I receive a notification.

Notice! Complete Set: Regeneration Triad. *While wearing all three pieces of the Regeneration Triad, user will be granted a ten-foot aura that provides 20% increased regeneration for companions within its radius.*

I look over the items one more time.

Item. Renewal Spear. *Capable of holding life aura equivalent to 500 HP. The Renewal Spear gathers aura passively while equipped and can steal health from enemies during battle. Life aura may be absorbed by the wielder at any time.* ***Bonus:*** *When paired with Regeneration Stone and Shield of Vigor, user will be granted a ten-foot aura that provides 20% increased regeneration for companions within its radius.*

    Item. Shield of Vigor. *Increases HP by 30%.* ***Bonus:*** *When paired with Regeneration Stone and Renewal Spear, user will be granted a ten-foot aura that provides 20% increased regeneration for companions within its radius.*

    Item. Regeneration Stone. *Increases health regeneration by 20%.* ***Bonus:*** *When paired with Shield of Vigor and Renewal Spear, user will be granted a ten-foot aura that provides 20% increased regeneration for companions within its radius.*

The fact that I get this bonus without needing to wear any additional armor makes it a perfect complement to my playstyle. The shield is a little heavier than I would like, but it opens a lot of possibilities for tanking the brunt of the damage.

"And for you, master dwarf. This item has sat in our troves for far too long." Swift kneels, reaching deep within the chest and pulling out a leather thong with a brass key hanging from it. It's a slender skeleton key, but both the bow and the bit of the key have tiny gears and pistons. Even the shaft appears to be made of several rotating barrels. "Draydon won this item during one of his tournaments where each combatant wagered a powerful item as their buy-in to compete. After defeating a rather troublesome halfling rogue, he won the Nimble Key. Aside from these chests, there are no locks throughout the Hidden Village, so it has sat here unused.

Item. *Nimble Key.* *When placed in a keyhole, the gears of the Nimble Key begin to turn, revolving and shifting to fit the dimensions of the lock. After one minute, even the toughest locks will open. Note: The Nimble Key is not effective against magical or enchanted locks.*

Taryn takes the key and flicks the bow with his finger. The gears spin and the bit undulates as metal teeth rise and fall from the end of the key.

"Now, that is cool." He flicks it again. "This can pick any lock?"

"As long as it's not magically protected."

"Nice." Taryn grins mischievously. "With my cloak and boots, I wouldn't be a half-bad rogue myself. And if I put my next ability point into Shadow Cloak, I'd be a ninja at night."

Swift frowns. "I'm not sure what a ninja is, but if they are stealthy, then indeed you would be a ninja."

I chuckle at that, but there is some truth to Taryn's words. With boots that leave no tracks and a cloak that conceals the sounds of his movement, he could definitely come in handy. Too bad dungeon doors are magically sealed, or we'd be speed-running through every one we could find.

"What do yous haves for Limmy?" The imp clasps his hands together like a starving orphan begging for scraps of food.

The dragon paws at Limery's leg, annoyed that his playmate has diverted his attention.

Swift grins. "For you, we have something extra special."

He whistles, and a moment later, several fairies fly in from the open roof. Two of them hold the ends of a silver necklace with a tiny vial of purple dust as the charm.

"They wanted you to have something to remember us by. Plus, if your antics in the forest are any indication, then it might come in handy if you're ever in a pinch."

The fairies chime as the two holding the necklace surround Limery on each side, draping the necklace around his neck.

The imp beams as they close the clasp and holds the vial in his hand like it is some precious jewel. "Limmy loves its."

The fairies giggle in response before disappearing back into the forest, leaving a glittery trail in their wake.

Swift closes the lid to the chest and faces us. "We are a simple people, but I hope these gifts will aid you in the future. We must first secure our borders, but I will send an envoy to King Orso in the coming days. If the centaurs are needed in battle, the herd will ride."

Taryn holds up the key, giving it a final spin before placing it in his satchel. "We're grateful for your generosity, and all of the help you've provided."

Likewise, I put my new items in my expandable satchel, even the mighty shield fits without much noticeable weight added. "I don't know that we would have had the patience to hatch the egg without your help. Thank you."

We take our leave, spending the night in one of the empty stables, where it turns out the dragon is a bit of a night owl. It runs around the room chasing its tail, growling, and pouncing on piles of hay while we all try to get some rest. Swift has the fairies bring it food almost hourly so that we can get a full night's sleep while we're still here.

At some point, I'm awakened as it climbs up next to Limery, curling in a ball on my chest.

CHAPTER 16

ON THE ROAD AGAIN

I WAKE to the sound of the dragon wrestling with Berry against the far wall. The massive umber bear lies on his back, pawing at the young dragon as it tries to bite through Berry's thick fur. A powerful but playful paw sends the dragon tumbling into a pile of hay.

Above us, the forest is alive with chirping birds, rustling tree leaves, and the distant chiming of fairies. For a moment, I simply lay there, feeling Limery's warm body in the crook of my arm. I'm surprised he's not awake and part of the mischief.

My moment of peace quickly fades when I notice the message icon flashing in the corner of my vision. Since Taryn is still asleep next to me, that can only mean one thing.

I take a deep breath and focus on the icon. Two messages appear as a scroll across my vision. The first is from the admin, and the second is from Valery herself.

Incoming Message (Admin): *Greetings, Heroes! The time has come for your regularly scheduled break. In three days' time, you will be logged out of Mythos while your avatar sleeps. Please make safe accommodations for yourself, preferably within a safehouse establishment such as an inn or castle. Failure to do so will result in automatic extraction and may result in loss of levels or items during your absence if your avatar is attacked while you are logged out.*

Incoming Message (Admin): *Chod, you continue to surprise us with the connections and the quest lines you have unlocked. The world is moving faster than we ever anticipated, and hatching a dragon will certainly have ramifications across Mythos going forward.*

There have been some new developments regarding our understanding of the AI and the effect your presence has within the system. I would like to discuss further once you're out. -Valery

New developments? What could that possibly mean? Have they finally figured out why the system is only bugged when I log out?

Taryn stirs next to me, and Ruby yawns as she pokes her head out from beneath his cloak. She stretches her front legs out, hindquarters sticking proudly in the air before lying on her belly.

I poke Taryn in the shoulder, making sure he doesn't fall back asleep. "Check your messages."

Limery's bulbous yellow eyes flutter awake, and he grumbles something that sounds like jumbled words.

Taryn's eyes glaze over as he reads the message. I feed the dragon a few pieces of jerky, and it gobbles them up. Limery stares at me, drool dribbling down his chin, so I give him one as well.

"Three days, huh?" Taryn shakes the straw off his cloak and

drapes it over his shoulders. "That's not a lot of time to get out of the forest. Guess we better get moving."

"No kidding. It'll take us close to two days just to get back to the portal with nothing slowing us down. Assuming there's an inn near the Pruxford portal, that's only a day of wiggle room."

We pack our things and find Swift with a handful of centaurs talking over breakfast. There's no sign of Thannis, Sylvie, or Daimun, so I assume they're back to patrolling the forest. I use the opportunity to ask Swift about the Pruxford portal.

He sets down a half-eaten roasted carrot and wipes his mouth with the back of his hand. "The portal empties into the heart of Pruxford. The main market will offer everything you could possibly need to resupply and prepare for the tournament. But don't fear, we will send you on your way with food and provisions."

The other centaurs abandon their breakfasts entirely to spend a few final moments with the young dragon, feeding it scraps and reinforcing the commands it already knows. The expression each of them share is so far removed from our first meeting.

The dragon eats the scraps from all of their plates and still begs for more. I'm not sure if my eyes are playing tricks on me or if it has already grown bigger in less than a day since hatching. Something tells me we're either going to be doing a lot of hunting or spending a fortune on food in the near future.

After a quick breakfast and a stop by the market to resupply with potions, fairy dust, and provisions for the road, we set out once again.

Swift walks us to the edge of the village, and the guards outside the wall of fog bid us farewell. While fog still heavily coats the forest floor, it has a different feel than previously. The forest feels more alive, more peaceful, and less ominous. I'm sure we could spend weeks exploring its vastness if we had time.

Travel is slow-going with a baby dragon, and it hates being carried unless by its own choice. Still, we make steady progress, and Limery enjoys putting his bird hunting skills to use to feed the small creature.

Pharos leads the way, using its passive ability to guide us back to the portal. Jordy walks beside my spirit guide, and the two frost goats hold their heads high as they parade through the forest. Next to me, Taryn rides Berry, with Ruby in her usual position curled between his legs.

I equip the Renewal Spear while we walk, using it as a walking staff. The end of the dull gray weapon sinks into the soft earth with each step. I can feel a change in the weapon as it fills its reserves with life aura. A faint glow surrounds the spear's emerald tip, rising as the weapon stores aura within. If I focus on it, I can see a gauge similar to a health bar that shows how much aura it has gathered.

While Limery is off hunting, I use the time to talk to Taryn about the messages we received. "Valery says she has an update about the system that she wants to talk about in person. I wonder if they've finally figured out what's causing the crash."

"Who knows?" Taryn shrugs. "She did say I'd be able to video chat with my family this time, so I'm looking forward to that."

"That's awesome! I'm sure that'll be nice. Make sure to tell them I said 'hello.'"

"Will do. It feels like it's been forever since we last logged out. It'll be nice to check in with everyone." His smile fades. "Think you'll hear from your parents?"

I scoff at the idea. "If so, that'll be the most surprising thing to happen since I've been in Mythos."

A solemn silence passes over us as we walk. I'm happy for Taryn. He misses his family, and they undoubtedly miss him too, but the only people waiting for me when I log out will be Valery and the technicians. Not that I'm complaining. I'll hear what she has to say, do my check-ups, and then gratefully log back in. One thing I've noticed is that the more time I spend here, the less I think about my problems in the real world.

Most of our day is spent traveling slowly and feeding the dragon. It eats almost hourly, and it never seems to be satiated. If I thought Limery was a bottomless pit, this dragon puts him to shame. I wonder if it will eat less frequently once it has matured.

We pass several centaur outposts on our journey. Once again, they are staffed and operating, usually with a single centaur. They're simple structures, with a stable and some supplies, mainly used for patrolling the forest and offering assistance to those who may need it. Though, hearing them tell it, the latter is much less frequent than it used to be. Given the appearance of the wisps, it's more important than ever to be vigilant.

We pass through a dense section of towering oaks when Pharos suddenly comes to a halt. Jordy bleats and lowers his horns at a boulder in the middle of the path.

The boulder is about the size of Jordy. I'm about to make a joke when I notice that the giant rock is actually a level-twelve golem. It looks like nothing more than a boulder surrounded by stacks of smaller rocks, but then the rocks shift as the golem moves.

The dragon runs up next to Jordy, growling at the monster and snapping its jaws.

I flash Taryn a devious smile. "Want to let the kids play?"

Normally, we wouldn't even bother fighting something so weak, but this could be a good opportunity to get the dragon some fighting experience. The golem out-levels it greatly, but Taryn's pets have enough of an advantage that they can protect the dragon.

He climbs down from Berry. "No reason we should have all the fun. Get him, squad!"

Jordy charges at the rock golem, horns smashing into the large boulder that forms its core and sending it into a nearby tree. Pieces of rock break off upon impact, scattering into the fog as the golem falls to the ground. The single attack took out a quarter of the golem's health.

The golem groans, and pieces of dirt and rubble roll across the forest floor toward the monster, replacing the damaged areas. At its full height, the golem isn't much taller than Taryn, but it's still a fearsome-looking opponent.

The dragon roars like a lion cub, gnashing its teeth and taking a step forward followed quickly by a step back.

"Try to pin it to the ground," Taryn calls to Berry.

The bear stands on its back feet, towering over the rock monster. The golem punches at Berry, but he absorbs the blow and lunges at the creature, tackling it to the ground.

The end of Taryn's staff glows as he casts Imbue on the dragon, doubling its size and giving us a preview of how big it will soon be.

Emboldened by its new size, the dragon pounces on the golem. Its sharp claws rake against the golem's body, leaving gashes in the stone. Even though it's only level one, the claws still manage to do slivers of damage.

The golem struggles against Berry's weight, but it's no match for the bear. The dragon continues its attack, learning with each strike until eventually, the golem crumbles to pieces as its HP reaches zero.

"Good job!" I reward the dragon with a treat. "You're going to be mighty strong one day."

"And it gained a level. Nice!" Taryn pumps his fist. "That's what I'm talking about."

There aren't a whole lot of low-level monsters in Wandermere, so Berry and Jordy do most of the work. Ruby isn't a fighter, so she sits around with Taryn watching the others battle it out. The dragon's instincts are excellent, especially on animals like warthogs and wolves. It's as if it knows it's the apex predator, and with each fight, we witness more of its potential.

"Gets its!" Limery shouts as he zooms through the air over the fight, offering encouragement as Berry and Jordy take turns assaulting a large warthog.

The imp is a great cheerleader, and nearly as entertaining as the action itself.

Jordy rams into the warthog, and it wobbles in place. The imbued dragon pounces on the stunned warthog's back, tearing through flesh and sinking its teeth into the beast's neck. By the time the stun wears off, it's too late.

Even with breaks for fighting and constantly feeding the dragon, we make good progress. By the end of the day, the dragon is already level four and nearly fifty percent bigger than it was this morning. Where it was the same size as Limery, it's now about as big as a medium-sized dog. Even the little nubs on its head have started to blossom into branchlike horns.

We sit around a campfire for dinner, roasting some of the meat from the animals we slaughtered. It smells delicious, and a little bit of Gherhardt's famous spice flavors the meat perfectly.

Taryn takes a bite of boar leg and juices explode into his beard. "All we need to do is find some super strong allies, and they can power-level us the same way. We'll be ready for the dark wizard in no time."

I laugh at the idea. "Good luck with that. I think they've all got better things to do than babysit heroes. Besides, I've already power-leveled you once. Can't have you going soft on us. Grinding builds character."

He throws a piece of meat over my head and the dragon pounces, snatching it out of the air. It can jump way higher than before, and the little flutter it used to do is now more of a glide.

After dinner, we spend the rest of the evening training the spunky creature. Once it's annoyed with the constant commands, it darts off and climbs up a tree like a cat, staring at us menacingly.

"Alright, fine." I shoo it away. "Go have some fun. Limery, keep an eye on him, please."

Taryn burst out laughing.

I frown. "What?"

"My mom used to tell me the same thing when I was watching my sisters. You're officially a parent."

I roll my eyes. "Oh, shut it."

I toss a bone in Taryn's direction, but he swats it away—to Berry's delight. The umber bear picks it off the ground and carries it away to munch on.

Taryn's joking, but that doesn't mean there's no truth to it. He's always had a great deal of responsibility. Growing up, his time with me was his escape. For me, this is the most responsibility I've ever had in my life, the first time I've really felt like what I did mattered.

It's a good feeling.

CHAPTER 17
NAME DROPPING

THE DRAGON'S sharp claw rips open the chest of a large buck, advancing the dragon to level five and providing us with enough venison to feed the growing monster for most of the day.

It turns back to me and preens, proud of its accomplishment. A green aura flares from its body for a few seconds, and the young dragon begins hacking and coughing.

I rush to its side, patting it on the back to no avail. I'm not sure if it's choking on deer flesh or managed to eat something bad while I wasn't looking.

The dragon wheezes and a jet of dark green smoke pours from its mouth. The smoke flows into a nearby bush, withering the leaves and gnarling the branches before dissipating. There's a hiss as the bark constricts and splinters before the entire bush shrivels into wispy tendrils.

The hair on my arms stands on end. I forgot green dragons can shoot toxic gas instead of flames. If it can damage a plant like that, I can't imagine what it will do to an enemy.

After a few more hacking coughs, the dragon regains control

of itself. Limery stands beside it, gently petting the creature and whispering, "It's okays. It's okays, little dragons."

Taryn gawks at the damage. "That's going to be dangerous."

"No shit." I scratch the dragon under the chin, and its eyes close to slits. "We're going to need to get that under control ASAP."

Not long after, we witness just how dangerous the toxic gas can be under the wrong circumstances.

While Taryn's passive, Nature's Bulwark, keeps him from being attacked unless provoked, it doesn't keep me from triggering a Wandering Creeper growing along the edge of the path.

The sentient bush has limbs covered in brambles capable of tearing flesh. It wraps one around my arm and cuts sting as it rips into my tough skin.

Jordy rams into the creeper, and it releases its grasp on my arm. I take a step back, and Berry pins it to the ground. The dragon pounces, ripping branches with its mouth and tearing through leaves with its claws. It roars before unleashing its new attack. Toxic gas pours from its mouth like a thick fog, covering both Berry and the tree.

Berry howls in pain from the burning gas, releasing the bush and running several yards to safety before licking his scorched paws.

The toxic gas finishes off the low-level bush, and Taryn casts Restoration on his injured pet.

I pull the dragon aside after the fight. "Look, you're going to have to be more careful. That's a powerful ability, and you can't go spewing toxic gas on your party members, got it?"

A dragon's intelligence is supposed to be incredibly high, so I speak to it like I would Limery. The dragon just stares at me, occasionally blinking.

"Got it?" I put my hand on my hips and ask again.

The dragon huffs, and a tiny puff of smoke plumes from its nostrils. Then it lowers its head and nuzzles my shins.

Taryn laughs. "I think he's got it."

I raise an eyebrow. "What makes you think it's a boy?"

He squints, looking over the dragon once more. "Maybe I'm wrong, but that's the feeling I get."

That's more of a feeling than I get, so I shrug. "You are a druid, so who am I to argue? I need to give it—or him—a name soon."

Taryn grins, and his eyes go wide. "Hear me out—"

I shake my head. "Nope. Absolutely not. Won't even consider it."

"Bro, come on." He puts his hands together like he's praying. "Just one suggestion."

I close my eyes, massaging my forehead in preparation for the headache I know is coming. "One suggestion. If it's shit, you're permanently banned from suggesting names ever again."

"Alright, hear me out. While Scaley would be the obvious choice—" He raises his hands in the air defensively before I have a chance to lose my cool. "—if he were mine, I think Caustic is a fitting name that inspires fear and terror in the hearts of enemies."

"Caustic. Huh?" I look at the dragon that's not so little anymore. Surprisingly, the name fits. Maybe not for a baby dragon, but he'll grow into it. The way his gas destroys anything it touches is the definition of the word. "Let's try it out."

I kneel in front of the dragon, scratching it on the head between its branchlike horns. "How do you feel about the name Caustic?"

He purrs, nuzzling his head against my hand to reach that perfect spot that makes his tail waggle.

"I knew it." Taryn smirks. "I am the king of names."

"You're a real wordsmith," I tease. "Let's get moving."

The trick to traveling fast with a baby dragon is to outsmart it. Luckily for us, Little Caustic's stomach far outweighs his stubbornness. We've taken to calling him Little Caustic while he's still small. Kind of like calling a baby Steve, it just doesn't sound right to call him Caustic until he grows a little bigger.

Judging by his current rate of growth, it won't be long before he earns his true name.

Limery flies in front of the dragon, dangling a piece of venison from a string while Taryn buffs us with Strong Wind. For minutes at a time, Little Caustic chases the meat at incredible speeds, teeth snapping as he avoids the temptation to pounce on monsters and follow every sound in the forest.

Taryn calls for us to halt as we come upon the massive crater left behind from our run-in with the wisps. This section of the forest already looks like a different place, and it's only been a week.

The life aura has healed the bark of damaged trees, those that weren't completely demolished in the explosion, and tiny limbs sprout from broken branches. New saplings grow from the deadfalls, and birds chirp in the treetops. The bottom of the crater has pooled with water from the thunderstorm we heard a few days prior. If the centaurs can manage to divert a creek or stream to this location, then maybe it could be a lake one day soon.

Out of the corner of my eye, I catch the glint of metal at the far end of the new pool. A massive boulder sits at the bottom of the crater, a sword halfway buried in the stone. Sunlight spills through the open canopy, hitting the protruding sword of the Wanderer and casting a kaleidoscope of colors from the jewel-encrusted hilt upon the nearby trees.

The sword-wielding stone has made a new home in the ruins

of our battle. A deep rut runs along the embankment from where the enchanted creature slid down into the crater. Its massive boulder of a body stirs gently in the fading sun.

As the faceless golem stands, Little Caustic lets out a low growl, but the Wanderer is either oblivious or ambivalent to our presence. It takes a few steps into deeper water and sits again.

I crouch beside the dragon and take in the majesty of the Wanderer one last time. "That's not a fight even you want to take, little guy."

Defeating it would be an accomplishment, but I'm not sure we have the time to fight something forged from life aura and still make it to Pruxford in time to log out.

"Pretty swords." Limery eyes the shining weapon greedily.

I tap him on the back of the head. "Don't even think about it."

We leave the Wanderer in peace and set our sights on the portal once more. About an hour later, the sun dips below the treetops, casting the forest in the shade of twilight. Limery sits on Jordy's horns at the front of our party, and Pharos burns like a beacon against the darkness. As we come upon another centaur outpost, we're greeted by a familiar trio.

Sylvie absolutely beams when she sees the dragon, and Pharos's glow ignites her alabaster skin, setting her blue tattoos ablaze. She kneels, and Caustic totters toward her.

"Nice to see you again." Taryn blushes as he tries to make eye contact and avoid her bare chest.

She scratches Caustic behind the horns. "And you as well. The forest is better for your time in it."

Thannis strokes his forked beard, and even his stern demeanor is softened by the dragon's presence. "I agree. It is good to run free once again."

"We're glad. Have you seen the damage we left behind?" I gesture over my shoulder in the direction of the lake.

Daimun laughs. "Quite the destruction, I must say, but the forest will heal. With a little work, it will make a fine watering hole."

Taryn closes his eyes and shakes his head, as if clearing his mind, causing the clasps in his beard to jingle. "Just watch out for your friend, the Wanderer. It has made itself a home in the bottom of the pit."

"We are not so foolish to attack the Wanderer." Thannis smirks at Taryn. "Are you hoping to pass through the portal tonight?"

Taryn glances at me, and I pull up my map. We've still got a ways to go, but it would be nice to settle into an inn this evening.

"What do you think?" I ask Taryn.

"With Strong Wind buffing us, we could probably make it within a few hours."

Thannis nods. "Be careful. The wisps may be gone, but there are still dangers within the forest. Would you like an escort?"

I shake my head, summoning a Horror of Power as I do. "We appreciate the offer, but I think we'll be fine. If we don't get Taryn an ale soon, he'll turn into a real diva."

"Hey—" Taryn starts to argue, but Sylvie cuts him off.

"It is an attractive quality to know what one wants in life. I hope you find your ale." She winks at Taryn, and I'm surprised he doesn't fall from Berry's back.

He opens his mouth a few times, but all that comes out is a croak.

I pat Taryn on the back and bow my head to the others. "I think that's our cue to leave. I hope we meet again someday."

As we're leaving, I remember that I still have something that belongs to Thannis. I pull the Amulet of Sight from around my neck and hold it out to him. The stone in its center glows a dull yellow. "I almost forgot, but I believe this belongs to you. We never would have cleared the forest without it."

He takes it, rubbing his finger over the amulet. "I'm glad to have played a small part. Safe travels to you all."

Taryn waves at Sylvie as we leave, then mumbles, "She said I was attractive."

"Okay, playboy." I let Taryn have his moment and don't point out that she said it was an attractive quality.

When he finally returns to his senses, we're buffed with Strong Wind and follow Pharos as he prances through the forest. This is our first time actually traveling at night, and though the fog conceals most of what lies in the depths of the forest, green and red eyes stare down at us from the treetops.

Taking Thannis's warning to heart, I keep a steady supply of horrors just in case we come upon anything.

Much to his protest, I carry Caustic over my shoulder in order to make better time. For now, I'm much stronger than the dragon and he eventually tires of struggling against me. His scales feel cool against my skin as he holds on tight.

On my other shoulder, Limery perches quietly, his warm body a sharp contrast to the dragon's.

We travel quickly through the forest, and I almost feel bad that we're speeding through such picturesque scenery. Everything is so lush and full of life from the towering trees to the bats and nocturnal birds that swoop through the fog after some small creature on the ground.

Limery sighs. "Chods, is we's there yets? Limmy is ready to sees the cities."

"It shouldn't be too long, buddy. We'll be there before you know it."

Soon after, the glow of the portal shimmers in the distance.

Something large rises from the fog, casting a silhouette in front of the silvery swirl of the arch.

Pharos halts, and we all gather behind the spirit guide. The shadow of a giant with harsh edges and jagged limbs blocks the portal. The shadow doesn't move, frozen like a statue.

I send my spirit guide closer, parting the fog until his light reveals the monster blocking our exit.

I let out a sigh of relief when it's nothing more than charred bark, moss, and lichen. "It's a dead tree. Any idea what it means?"

He shakes his head. "Never seen anything like it. I don't think it was here when we came through the portal, though. Let's approach with caution."

I set Caustic back on the ground and equip my warhammer just in case. This could be a trap, or it could be a dead tree that wasn't quite so spooky in the daylight.

Pharos and my horrors take the lead. With each step, the spirit guide pushes away more fog.

Taryn curses next to me, and a moment later, I understand why.

"What the shit is this?" I ask no one in particular.

A ring of giant mushrooms surrounds the portal on all sides, interspersed with three more creepy dead trees. These definitely weren't here when we came through the portal. I try to analyze them with my herbalism skill, but I get nothing. Large, bulbous mushrooms circle the platform to the portal, ranging in size from a small houseplant to some as big as Taryn. The three other trees are equally as unsettling as the first, but about three-fourths of the size.

I grip Destroyer tightly in my palm. This whole situation has my skin crawling. "Is this some weird forest magic to keep people out of Wandermere? Or is it meant to keep us from leaving?"

He frowns. "No idea. Whatever they are, I can't identify them."

At first, I thought it was my low-level herbalism skill, but if Taryn can't identify the creatures, something is definitely up.

I send my horrors closer to inspect, thirty of them bunched close together around Pharos while thirty more hang back with us.

I'm not sure what I expect to happen, but red eyes blazing to life behind a moss-covered face isn't it. A bone-chilling scream tears through the bark as it splinters into a monstrous mouth. In a quick and fluid motion, the tree steps forward, its trunk cracking as it splits into two legs. It swipes a massive limb through half of the horrors, exploding them and tossing others like bowling pins. The wooden fist passes through Pharos, dissipating the spirit guide for half a second before it reforms. The tree swings again and more horrors explode upon impact, and the rest are tossed back into the fog while the creature continues its assault, stomping and smashing in quick succession.

"Those aren't plants, they're monsters!" Taryn shouts.

"No shit, Sherlock." I take a step back and try to figure out how the hell we are going to deal with this monster when the surrounding mushrooms unroot themselves from the earth. Now that they're moving, I'm suddenly able to analyze them. I focus on the rampaging tree.

Woodland Horror. Level 20. *Born of the remains of once sentient trees, woodland horrors are bitter protectors of the forest. As life aura infuses the dead matter, they become watchful guardians, remembering the eons they lived before, but cut off from the web of roots that connects the forest and unable to communicate with the shared consciousness of the ancient trees.*

A fungi army surrounds the horror, composed of mushrooms in different shapes, sizes, and colors. One is purple and bulbous. Another is black with strings of black goo dripping from the edges of its cap. Some of them shriek at the night, while others emit poisonous gas. They walk on ghoulish feet of translucent roots, marching toward us.

In a matter of seconds, my horrors are obliterated. The monstrous plants seem unaffected by Pharos's presence, making it unlikely that they are from the shadow realms. They're still a threat, and unfortunately, they're standing in the way of us and a soft bed.

A bolt of lightning crashes into the charging mushrooms, ripping through the soft tissue of several and charring a few more. A squat green mushroom explodes, its innards raining down like jelly. Limery's claws dig into my shoulder as he takes flight and peppers the mob with fireballs. The skin of the mushrooms curls like wax paper against the heat of his attacks. Another fireball hits a woodland horror, setting its moss ablaze, and making the burning tree even more intimidating.

I kneel in front of Caustic, looking the dragon directly in the eyes. "Stay put. This is too dangerous for you."

I say it with as much authority as I can muster, but with the monsters approaching, there's no time to wait and see if he listens. I ready Destroyer and charge into the fray, summoning extra horrors as I do.

Ahead of me, Moonbeam streaks through the night in a silvery beam, way less effective than it had been on the wisps. Taryn stands back, Ruby hiding behind his legs as he casts spells as they become available. An imbued Jordy rams into a puffball mushroom, punting it into the fog like a soccer ball, and Berry's claws rip through mushrooms like butter. Poisonous gas and goo cover everything as the mushrooms explode, slowly ticking down the pets' health, but the real threats are the trees.

I smash Destroyer into one of their legs, and a shockwave of energy passes through, knocking down mushrooms in an arc behind the woodland horror. The splash damage from Ram's

Rage doesn't disappoint. Red flares through my weapon as it gains a stack of inferno, and I swing again. This time, wood splinters, and the horror tumbles to the ground. My own horrors rush the downed monster, and Berry pries his claws between the scraps of wood that make up its shoulder, trying to rip it apart.

I flip the warhammer over, bringing the piercing end down on the tree's chest. There's a nasty crunch as wood splinters at the impact. Its jagged mouth opens, and a scream pours from the void, setting my hair on end. I press my foot against its midsection and pull Destroyer free before a well-placed fireball snuffs out the creature's remaining life.

The mushrooms fall quickly, leaving the three remaining trees in various stages of health. Two are half-dead, and one is nearly done for. A flame wall between two of them sets the monsters ablaze and their flailing arms light up the night. Taryn's lightning bolt hits the weakest of the three, stunning it in place while Destroyer finishes it off.

A flaming punch catches me unaware, hitting me in the jaw and knocking me to the ground. Stars dance in my vision as I try to sit up. There's a throaty growl as Caustic pounces on me, staring down the woodland horror that towers above us.

The scales on Caustic's neck stand on edge and he roars again, this time breathing toxic gas on the monster. The gas hits its flaming body like gasoline on a fire, erupting into a ten-foot blaze. The monster stumbles around for a few seconds before its charred flesh crashes to the ground.

Holy shit! His gas is flammable.

The flames on the final woodland horror are doused as it wrestles with Berry on the ground.

"Call him off!" I shout as I climb to my feet. "I want to try something."

Taryn calls for Berry, but the horror has no intention of giving up the fight. It lunges at the bear as he runs away.

I point at the woodland horror. "Caustic, hit it with your gas."

The young dragon obeys, snarling as it covers a small area in dense green smoke. The horror steps into the gas, which does very little damage by itself due to the gap in their levels.

"Limery, hit it with a fireball."

"Limmy's on it!"

He darts into position and a fireball erupts in his palm. He throws it, hitting the gas as the horror steps into the center of the cloud. An explosion engulfs the horror. Warm air assaults my face, and the monster falls to the ground, body sizzling and smoke rising from the corpse.

Taryn and I stare at each other for a moment in disbelief. The look on his face says he's just as surprised as I am. We've discovered a whole new level of devastation.

He casts Restoration on his pets while I survey the damage. Caustic gnaws on a piece of charred wood that used to belong to the woodland horror. The smell of burnt wood and dead fish linger in the air, and the ground is speckled with debris and fleshy pieces of mushroom. The scene looks like someone tossed colored chalk on the set of a horror movie.

Berry and Caustic gain a level from the fight, bringing the dragon up to level six.

When Taryn is done healing Jordy, he joins me among the wreckage. "That was weird. I guess the forest wasn't ready for us to leave." He chuckles.

"Maybe so. We should probably head through the portal before any other crazy monsters try to say good-bye."

He whistles, and his pets walk over. Even Caustic abandons his chew toy. "No shit. After that, I definitely need a beer."

With Caustic at my side and Limery on my shoulder, I focus on the rune for Pruxford and step through the swirling vortex.

CHAPTER 18

PRUXFORD

EVEN AT NIGHT, the city of Pruxford is one of the most beautiful places I've ever seen. As soon as we step through the portal, the glass palace shimmers at the far end of the city. It reminds me of the northern lights with the way streaks of emerald and amethyst fluctuate through the building.

Limery gasps. "Pretties."

While the palace is the focal point of the Pruxford, the rest of the city is just as beautiful. Glass sculptures are spread through the courtyard around the portal, reminding me that we need to go see Draydon's at some point.

A notification flashes in the corner of my vision, and I pull it up.

Regional Event Alert! *Welcome to Pruxford, the City of Glass! The Quincentennial Tournament of Champions is only a week away. The coming week will be filled with parties, parades, and celebrations honoring all of those who help make Pruxford the most amazing city in Mythos.*

Looks like we arrived just in time. A week of partying is exactly what the doctor ordered.

Behind us, thick glass walls wrap around the city. On the other side, sprawling fields of sunflowers take on the silver glow of moonlight. The walls must be enchanted to offer any sort of real protection, but their beauty is unmatched.

People traipse through the city. Gnomes, dwarves, humans, halflings, and beast-people in all shapes and colors. The only race I don't see are elves. Magical streetlights line the cobblestone streets, each one filled with dancing yellow lights. Aside from Sandholde, I don't know if I have ever seen such immaculate streets.

I can't quite explain it, but it feels like society has progressed quicker here than on Isle of Mythos while the portals were closed. The Pruxford gnomes are widely known as master tinkerers, but I didn't expect this. The contraptions and lights are far beyond anything I've seen so far. Signs on buildings rotate. Enchanted gemstones flash on each storefront, mimicking the effects of neon lights and igniting the window displays in an array of colors. The sign on a pub called The Brazen Swordsman has a wooden arm that slashes up and down. This is like being in a fantasy version of Times Square.

The city stretches out in all directions, with the Crystal Palace towering above it all. Seascape and Vanaria are massive cities, but Pruxford easily dwarfs them both by comparison. Most of the shops have shut down for the evening, but the inns, taverns, and restaurants bustle with activity. Minstrels play in the streets, and the porches are filled with laughter and conversation. A gnome wearing stilts clatters through the streets as he catches coins in a top hat.

Taryn takes a deep breath, breathing in the city. "This is what

I'm talking about. Let's get the pets to a stable and find a place to stay for the evening."

"Good evening, sirs." An older gnome approaches us. He has shaggy blonde hair, a short blue beard, two golden hoops in each ear, and a rich purple tunic covered in a starburst of yellow and orange sequins. He eyes Caustic, licking his lips greedily, but shows no hesitation at the sight of the rest of our party.

He flashes us a brilliant white smile and bows. "Bildri Quilldrip, master travel guide, at your service. The city is a maze of fantastic shops and luxurious inns. It can be quite over-whelming to those unfamiliar. For a small fee, I will help you navigate the abundance of options before you." He holds a notepad in one hand and a feather quill hovers in the air next to him. "Oh, my, is that a dragon? And so young!"

Taryn urges Berry forward between the gnome and Caustic, forcing Bildri to step out of the way. "We appreciate the offer, but we'll be fine exploring on our own, thanks."

Bildri adjusts his robes and straightens his posture. "But, sirs, the city can be overwhelming for outsiders such as yourselves. Please allow me to—"

"I said we're fine," Taryn snaps, and Berry lets out a low growl.

"Very well." The gnome huffs before skittering to the next group that steps through the portal—a human couple wearing fine linens followed by a halfling in rags pulling a cart piled with luggage.

Taryn scratches Berry behind the ears. "Good boy."

I narrow my eyes at Taryn. "What was that all about? Don't you think it would be smart to have someone help us through the city? It's already late, and we don't know anything about this place."

Taryn laughs. "Rich people. That guy was going to hustle us.

Did you see the way he was eyeing Caustic? He'd recommend us to places that are putting the most coin in his pocket and over-charge us for everything. If you want to find the best places in the city, you find a native, and one who isn't a salesman."

"I see. We're the prince and the pauper now." I laugh. "Alright, wow me with your street smarts."

"Hey, you!" Taryn waves down a young gnome in tattered clothing.

The kid reminds me of Brock, the orphan from the Underground Circus.

"Yes?" He eyes Taryn with suspicion.

Taryn pulls out a silver coin and flips it in the air. "Want to make a quick coin? Where's the best stable in the area?"

The kid grins. "That depends. The New Dawn has the nicer stables, but Farryn is an ass. The Rusty Bucket might not look like much, but Ms. Breebis has a way with the animals."

Taryn tosses the coin to the kid. "The Rusty Bucket it is. Which way?"

After a short trek, we arrive at the Rusty Bucket. True to the kid's word, it doesn't look like much. Compared to the fancy buildings with stained glass and elegant architecture on both sides, the stable looks like it belongs back in Lynchton. There's nothing off-putting about it, but it's rustic and out of place and I can see why people might pass it by.

The stables are quiet, minus the occasional bleat of sheep or grunt of some animal we can't see. A hammock gently swings across the pillars of the entry.

"Hello?" Taryn calls. "Anyone here?"

There's movement in the hammock, and then a mossy green head peeks over the edge. Deep red eyes look us over from beneath a large bun of dark green hair.

"Howdy," she says.

"Are you Ms. Breebis? We were hoping to house our pets for the night. You come highly recommended."

She swings her legs over the side of the hammock but doesn't climb down. "Is that so? We don't get many of your type around here."

"Dwarves?" Taryn asks.

I clench my fist. This was supposed to be a city where different races lived in peace, but here we are being judged by a three-foot-tall bean sprout.

"Foreigners." She slides off the hammock and lands softly on the ground.

She walks up to Caustic without fear, stroking him beneath the chin. To my surprise, he lets her, a soft purr rumbling within. She moves to each of the pets in turn, pulling a carrot from her pocket and feeding it to Jordy, and then scratching Berry behind the ear until he groans in pleasure. She even has a bite-sized treat for Ruby that she uses to make the jackal stand on its hind legs.

Taryn is enamored, and I must say, I'm impressed.

"Beautiful lot you have here. I'd be honored to watch over them for you. With me, you don't pay for the location, you pay for the service. They'll be fed. They'll be bathed and brushed. We have mind-building exercises in the morning and social time in the afternoon. Everyone gets a bedtime story at night, and my crew all sleep in hammocks from the rafters. There's no better place for your pets in all of Pruxford."

She's managed to put all of my concerns at ease. "I'm sold, but can I ask you something?"

She crosses her arms and leans against the wooden beam. "What is it, big guy?"

"If your place is so good, why are you hidden away like this?"

She scoffs, tossing her arms up. "Look around you. Pruxford is a city of glamor, but it's only skin deep. If you pull back the curtain, you'll see things aren't as great as they seem. The rich stick together, making each other richer, and the poor get swept under the rug. My family has owned this building for nine generations. Nine! We've always cared about quality over everything. We invest our gold in training, in quality food, and in workers with the right temperament to handle any creature. If anyone in the outer boroughs needs a stable, they come here."

"Then why aren't you more popular?" asks Taryn.

She laughs, but there's no mirth to it. "We're not a part of the 'in' crowd. The other stables can't compete with our quality, so they trash us with advertising and spread rumors. Farryn has friends on the advertising council, and they reject our requests and deny our appeals. Eventually, my father gave up the fight. You won't see our promotions in the market or plastered around town, but we don't lose customers. Their word of mouth keeps the torches burning."

"Damn, I'm sorry to hear that." Taryn hands her the reins to Berry. "I wish there was something we could do."

She smiles. "Your business is more than enough."

After we check in our pets, Breebis gives us directions to an inn she recommends. With only Limery joining us, our party feels unnaturally small.

Along the way, I take in the beautiful architecture and manicured streets of the city. There are specialized shops for just about everything, from toy stores to spice emporiums and several guild headquarters. Mixed in between them are houses and apartments.

A carriage passes us by, pulled by goats and loaded with boys about the same age as the one who gave us directions. The carriage stops next to an overturned trashcan, and the boys jump out, brooms in hand. They sweep up the trash in under a minute, and the carriage is clattering down the street once again.

I can't help thinking about what Breebis said. "You think it's true? About the city not being as great as it seems?"

Taryn nods. "Do you think your dad made all his money by treating his competitors nice? People are obviously doing well for themselves here, at least some of them. But I guarantee you there are more stories like Breebis's. There's no king here, so the power has to go somewhere."

I stare at my oversized feet, wondering how much truth there is to his statement. "Everyone has always said my dad was a shrewd businessman. I just assumed it was from making good decisions and not backing down, but I'm sure someone had to fail so that he could succeed."

"It's the American way. And maybe the gnomish way too." Taryn shrugs.

We stop in front of an inn called The Puzzling Peacock. There's a giant peacock sign above the porch. The peacock holds a magnifying glass over one of its eyes, making it much larger than the other. The tailfeathers of the sign glow with green and purple light. They must have a lot of enchanters in order to keep so many signs going all the time. Or maybe they're permanent or rechargeable enchantments. Either way, it has to be a lot of work for someone.

Limery claps his hands. "Pretties. Limmy likes the peacocks."

Inside, the inn is bustling. Only a few tables remain empty, and two bartenders work the bar, one gnome and one ivory dwarf, slinging frothy mugs of ale. A human woman rushes around, delivering giant mugs six at a time. There's a stage in the back, where a duo performs. A gnome with spiked blue hair plays a lute while one with pink pigtails sings a song of battle.

Taryn eyes the woman carrying beer greedily. "You see the size of those mugs? This is my type of place alright."

"Yeah, this is Limmy's types of place, too." He wipes a string of drool from his chin.

I squeeze in between a gnome and human at the bar, but it takes a minute for one of the bartenders to make their way over.

"What can I get fer ye?" The dwarven bartender places his palms down on the bar and leans forward like a bulldog.

"We need two rooms and three strong drinks."

"Aye, have a seat and I'll have Lissa bring 'em out for ye."

We claim one of the few open tables by a window. Here, no one seems to think we're out of place. No one stares at us. Even as a giant blue troll with horns sprouting from my head, people acknowledge me and look away.

This must really be a melting pot. About two-thirds of the patrons are gnomes, and they come in a wide array of skin tones and hair colors. The only thing they all have in common is their short stature and pointy ears. Scattered among them are a few dwarves, blue-skinned lizardfolk, a couple of catfolk, and a group of rowdy humans in the far back corner. In the midst of the humans, a tall, one-eyed giant holds a mug in each hand. His massive eye takes up most of his face, and when he laughs, it reveals a mouth full of sharp pointed teeth. I try to analyze him without staring.

Arty

Level 29

Warrior

Cyclops

"Bro." I tap Taryn on the arm. "It's a cyclops. Look at the size of him."

Taryn looks over his shoulder and quickly turns around. "Whoa, that's a big mother—"

"Forgive me for the wait." Lissa places three frothing mugs of amber ale on the table. "The city is packed for the tournament, so consider yourselves lucky that you got our last two rooms." She reaches in her apron and hands Taryn and me each a key with a colorful rope lanyard. "The key matches the color of the door to your room. If you need anything else, wave me down."

We lift our mugs, Limery with two hands, and clink them together.

"To civilization." I tilt the mug up and let the malty goodness wash over me.

"That's the stuff." Taryn finishes his first mug in a matter of seconds and already has his hand waving after Lissa. He holds up two fingers when she acknowledges him.

Limery closes his eyes after the first sip, and he couldn't look more blissful if he tried. "Oh, yes! That's the stuffs, Taryns."

As soon as Lissa returns with our second round, Taryn orders a third. The drinks flow freely until the inn is roaring with laughter, conversation, and music. A queue forms in front of Arty as he arm-wrestles one challenger after another. One of the catfolk joins the two gnomes on the stage, and her powerful voice has the crowd going wild as she belts out some heroic fighter's victory over an orc chieftain.

Taryn slams an empty mug on the table and slurs his words as his head sways back and forth. "Lemme tell you, Limery and Caustic, those two're gonna be a scary combination when he gets older."

I turn back my mug and savor the last drops of my ale. I've paced myself better than Taryn, but my vision is still swimming.

Limery, on the other hand, has his arms wrapped around the mug with his head resting on top. His eyes flutter as he fights sleep.

"I agree, bro. I can't wait to see what they're capable of."

A loud thud behind us startles Limery for a moment before he drifts back to sleep. I turn around to see the cyclops smirking as the human across from him rubs his arm. The cyclops puts his elbow on the table and clenches his fist.

"Will no one else challenge the mighty Arty?" He makes eye contact with me, holding my gaze for several seconds. "A hundred gold to anyone who can best me."

The music softens and murmurs snake around the inn. A hundred gold is a massive amount of money to wager on an arm-wrestling match.

I wave down Lissa. "Who is this guy?"

She smiles as she glances in his direction. "That's Arty, one of Pruxford's most famous adventurers. He might look mean, but he has a heart of gold."

"Really? He looks like he could rip someone's arm off without breaking a sweat."

She laughs. "And you don't, Mr. Troll? He's a good man. One of the best to come out of the outer borough. A human family found him crying and all alone while hunting in the dark forest. He was so small back then, now look at him. He's made us all proud. That's for sure."

I watch Arty for a moment as he waits for a challenger, laughing and joking with those at his table. He sits back and wraps his muscled arms around the two closest to him. The dude couldn't look any more monstrous, and yet he's earned the respect of not only his friends but the barmaid as well.

If he truly is as good as she says, then I want him on our side.

I equip Forlorn Scepter, holding it beneath the table. When I stand, the inn goes quiet, even the gnome playing the lute softens his music. My chair grates as it slides across the wooden floor, and I feel every eye lingering on me.

"A hundred gold? I'll take that challenge."

I point the scepter toward the floor, concealing the flash of green below the table as I summon a Horror of Power outside the window. The weapon's passive allows me to increase the range of summoned creatures by fifty percent. If this guy is competing in the tournament, then I want to keep as many surprises up my sleeve as possible. Not to mention the chaos summoning horrors in the middle of a crowd of drunks could cause. I quickly summon a Horror of Finesse and Vitality as well.

Arty stands, smiling dangerously. He's a few inches taller than me and every bit as muscled. I'm not sure about the perks that come with being a cyclops, but I have to imagine he has a pretty high Strength and Constitution build. Being a level twenty-nine warrior, he definitely has an advantage over me. Even if it's minor, he would win out in a test of pure strength.

He extends his hand. "You don't look anything like the troll paintings in the museums."

I grip his hand firmly in mine and squeeze. "I'm not your average troll."

"Hmm. It appears so." His massive eyelid blinks. "There have been stories of a troll hero making waves on the isle. Might there be some truth to those stories?"

I summon three more horrors outside as we continue our standoff. "There might be."

He sits down. "Then it will be an honor to test your strength."

Lissa was right. This guy looks like a one-eyed asshole, but he seems nice as can be. I take a seat across from him, draping my scepter across my knees.

I make small talk so that I can hopefully get in a few more

horrors before the match begins. "So, you're planning on entering the tournament?"

He tilts back his head and laughs. "It wouldn't be a tournament without Arty. I've already won two tournaments this year, but this one is special. It's the quincentenary of Pruxford's first Battle of Champions. Five hundred years since heroes and powerful fighters fought one another for glory before a crowd. I expect a real challenge for this one." He places his elbow down on the table. "Are you ready?"

I plant my elbow and grip his hand. "Ready."

His fingers clench around mine and his strength clashes with my own. For a moment, we're in a stalemate, neither one of us giving way. His massive eye bores into me, but his face remains placid. My veins enlarge as I channel my strength against him with all my might, but damn, he's strong.

Slowly, he starts to gain leverage, pushing my arm toward the table a millimeter at a time. I cast another round of horrors, bringing my total to twelve, and use Sacrifice. They vanish outside the window, and four points flood into my Strength, Dexterity, and Constitution. My bicep bulges, and his arm starts to move in the other direction.

Arty's giant eye widens. "So, we're playing that way, eh?" He grins.

A red aura surrounds his arm, and he slams my wrist against the table with such force that the wood splinters. Pain flares from my wrist to my shoulder. I grimace as I clench my fist to make sure it still works.

Arty bursts out laughing and slaps the table. "That was good. For someone so big, you're a sneaky little goblin."

There's a brief round of applause before the music resumes and it's like the match never happened.

I shake out my sore arm. "What the hell was that?"

He leans forward. "I could ask you the same thing."

I laugh as the pain fades from my arm. "I can't reveal my cards before the hand is over." I glance over at the table, where both Taryn and Limery are dead to the world. "I should probably help get these two into bed. Thanks for the challenge."

He flashes a dangerously-toothy grin. "See you in the arena, Chod of the forest trolls."

I can't help but like this guy. "I'll be looking forward to it."

CHAPTER 19

NO ONE SAID THERE WOULD BE A TEST

A KNOCK outside my room wakes me from a blissful sleep. When I open the door, Taryn is bright-eyed and bushy-tailed, with no lingering effects from the exorbitant amount of alcohol he drank the previous night.

"Dude, have you heard of sleeping in? It's our first night back in a city." I stumble back to the bed and lie down, where Limery continues to snore.

"Exactly!" He rips the covers off the bed and tosses them to the floor. "All the more reason to get up. Pruxford is huge! We need to register for the tournament, and then I want to get some shopping in. Now, get up, you two."

"Limmy is sleepies." The imp tucks his head in the crook of my arm.

"Yeah, just give us a few more minutes." I place the pillow over my face to block out the light from the windows.

Taryn taps his foot against the floor, and I imagine him standing there with his hands on his hips. "There's breakfast downstairs."

The magic words.

Limery's head pops up like a meerkat. "Oh yes, Limmy is hungries." He pulls the pillow from my face and presses his bulbous eyes inches from my own. "Wakes up, Chods. Times to eats."

"Goddammit, Taryn." I throw the pillow across the room at him, but he just grins mischievously.

Once the food arrives, I'm glad that we didn't skip out on breakfast. A lilac-skinned gnome wearing a chef's hat sets a platter down in the center of the table. There's bread with an assortment of jams, crispy bacon and sausage links, and speckled baby blue eggs the size of a softball.

I bite into one of the sausages, and the juices explode in my mouth. Juicy, fatty, savory deliciousness. Limery holds a piece of thick-cut bacon in one hand and a sausage in the other, alternating between the two.

For the first few minutes, we devour the food in silence.

I wipe some of the grease from my chin with a napkin and fill in the others on what they missed the night before. "While you two were passed out at the table last night, I spent a little time with Arty. He's crazy strong, and I think he could be a good ally."

Taryn shoves a piece of bread slathered with butter into his mouth. "The scary-looking cyclops?"

Heavy footsteps clank down the stairs. "Master dwarf, I am wounded by your comments."

Arty smiles, revealing his sharp teeth, and it's difficult to judge the expression of his single large eye.

Taryn gulps. "Sorry, I just meant you're an intimidating presence. Kind of like Chod here."

Arty laughs. "I'm only kidding. I know what I am." He flexes his arms, posing like a bodybuilder. "A terrible, frightening warrior who abducts children and uses their bones as toothpicks after I'm done stripping the flesh from their bodies."

Limery's eyes go even wider than normal.

One of the barmaids pushes Arty in the side. "Oh, stop that. You're nothing of the sort." She turns to us. "Don't you listen to a word he says."

"If you say so." He shrugs. "Anyways, there's much to do. Have a good day, gentlemen."

I call out to the cyclops as he makes for the door. "Arty, hold up. Will you be staying here all week?"

"Until the tournament is over."

"I'd love to talk sometime. I've got a proposition for you."

His single eyebrow raises. "Consider me intrigued. I'll see you around, Chod."

Once Arty is out the door, Taryn massages his forehead. "If I mysteriously disappear, check his toothpick container for my bones."

After breakfast, we stop by the stables to check on our pets. Breebis is in the middle of training Ruby when we arrive. She taps her shoulder, and the jackal leaps high into the air, landing on the gnome with surprising finesse. The gnome feeds Ruby a small treat, and the jackal jumps back to the ground.

"She's a quick learner." Breebis grins. "They all are."

Taryn kneels, and Ruby rushes over to him. "Now I just need a mouse to climb on her shoulder and we can join the circus."

Breebis tucks a loose strand of green hair behind her ear. "How can I help you, gentlemen?"

Taryn scratches Ruby behind the ears and pulls her against his chest. "We just wanted to check in before we explore the city."

"Thanks for the recommendation for the inn, by the way. It was a great spot." I stand on my tip-toes to look deeper into the stable, where a pink elephant-type creature is munching on a pile of rainbow-colored hay. "I think I'm going to take Caustic with me today. We're still bonding, so I think it's good to spend as much time together as possible."

"Absolutely." She claps her hands together. "Let me grab him for you. Follow me."

She leads us through the maze of stables. There are traditional mounts like horses and oxen for pulling wagons, but also a camel and a large beetle with a metallic carapace. We pass Jordy's enclosure, where he practices his charging against a gnome covered in padding. The gnome holds a padded shield similar to the ones boxers practice with. Jordy slams into the gnome, rocketing it against the wall of the stable.

"That's my boy." Taryn puffs out his chest, preening like a dad whose kid just scored the winning goal.

Berry groans at us as we peek into his enclosure, where his fur is being brushed with a bone brush.

Taryn climbs on the railing. "Don't get too spoiled in there."

In the far back, we finally find Caustic. The trainer plays a game with him where she hides a treat under one of three metal cups. She then rearranges them all in a quick motion before Caustic chooses which one contains the treat. Three times in a row, he gets it on the first try.

Breebis turns to me. "I was surprised to learn that Caustic is a true green dragon. A lot of people try to pass off their winged lizards as dragons, but you can always tell by how stupid they are. Dragons are intelligent creatures, even lesser dragons like wyrms or wyverns. A true dragon is a rarity, but a young green dragon like this, I doubt even my father had the pleasure to see one in person. They must be challenged mentally or they'll grow restless, especially as they grow stronger. I'll give you a list of common training exercises before you all check out."

"Thanks, I appreciate it." I reach my arm over the railing, and Caustic licks my fingers. "Want to go explore the city, little guy?"

He leaps up to the wooden railing, his leathery wings now bigger than ever. His growth rate hasn't slowed, and he's easily the size of a large dog at this point. When he flutters down on the other side, Limery hops on the dragon's back and uses the growing antlers as handlebars.

"We'll have him back in time for dinner." I wink.

After a quick lecture on how to behave in a crowd and a stern warning that he'll never see the light of day if even a plume of toxic gas makes its way into the city, we step out into the street. Like any young child, Caustic is fascinated by all the people. He sniffs at stray dogs, pounces toward pigeons eating crumbs off the ground near a food cart, and continuously looks over his shoulder to make sure we're still following.

A wagon pulls to a stop beside us, and a group of hesitant young gnomes asks us to move out of the way so they can clean up a half-eaten sandwich off the ground.

After stopping for a few meat kabobs, we find a street vendor selling maps of the city for only five silver. Normally, I'd pass on the offer, but Pruxford is so big, we'd never explore the entire city on our own.

Once the map is in my inventory, it populates across my vision. Every shop in the city shows up with a directory separating them by the items they sell. There's a multitude of stores selling everything from armor to trinkets, clothing, and food. Every inn is listed, along with statues, public buildings, guilds, temples, and any public location someone would need. Personal quarters aren't listed, but everything else is. The only thing it doesn't have is a review system.

The sheer scope is overwhelming.

"Why doesn't every city have one of these?" Taryn holds the map spread out before him. "They could make a fortune."

I spread my arms, gesturing at how big the city is. "Most cities don't have this scale of commerce. They only need a public directory at the city or town hall. I'm glad we bought these, though. Best five silver I've ever spent."

I pull the map back up and find the closest notice board. Luckily, it's at the end of the street, and it'll be our best bet for finding info on the tournament without having to track down a city official.

Onlookers point at Caustic as we head down the street. For the first time since entering Mythos, I'm the least-interesting member of our party.

The notice board is filled with flyers and posters. There are non-guild quests, notices for clubs and guilds, concerts, events, and so much more. Underneath the new posters, there are faded pictures of missing children. Glenn crosses my mind, but there's no way he would risk being captured in a city like this. In the middle, there's a massive poster for the tournament. It has an image of the stadium and several silhouettes in the center with the slogan, "Who will reign supreme?" At the bottom, there's a row of fine print.

Notice: *Those who wish to compete in the Quincentennial Tournament of Champions must register with the Department of Entertainment and Events no less than three days prior to the tournament. Prospective combatants will be given a placement test prior to acceptance. Not everyone who enters will qualify. Adventurers and Heroes welcome.*

"Placement test? What do you think that is all about?" I ask.

Taryn shrugs, his eyes focused on another flyer. "They probably want to make sure no one gets accidentally killed."

I lean over his shoulder. "What has you so fascinated that you don't even care about the tournament?"

"Oh, I care. I just thought this was rather interesting." He rips the flyer off the board and hands it to me.

For One Week Only!

All The Way From The Isle Of Mythos

The Underground Circus!

Experience a Show Unlike Any Other!

I read over it several times to make sure there's not some mistake, but sure enough, the flyer is stamped with the black lion logo of the Underground Circus. They were in Sandholde last we saw, but I guess Hawkin set his eyes on more fruitful pastures. I'm glad he took my advice to heart. The circus has come a long way from performing in the streets of Vanaria and from the looks of it, they could be a hit all over Mythos.

"Good for them. We'll definitely have to stop by one night and say hello." I tack the flyer back on the board. "Let's get the boring part over with, shall we?"

We find the Department of Entertainment and Events located inside City Hall, along with dozens of other departments responsible for everything from cleaning the city streets to enforcing the amount of magical meat imported by local restaurants.

The foyer of the building has jaw-dropping architecture. Marble floors gleam from the light that passes through the crystal walls of the entryway. The entire front of the building is a mixture of crystal and stained glass. There's a central fountain with a gnome holding a staff overhead. Water shoots out from the staff, arcing across a glass bridge and splashing in a smaller pool some twenty yards away, where colorful fish dart through the water.

People hurry about like office workers in Manhattan, carrying scrolls from one department to another. This city feels more and more like New York every day.

We find the office we are looking for on the fourth floor. Caustic's claws clack against the marble with each step. We catch a lot of looks, but no one says anything. To the untrained eye, he looks no different than a large reptile someone might keep as a pet. Only a handful of people actually inspect him enough to recognize that he's a dragon.

The inside of the D.E.E. office reminds me of a whimsical clerk's office with colorfully-dressed gnomes sitting behind counters. Some wear monocles while others use magnifying glasses to examine documents. Feather quills hover in the air next to them, jotting down notes onto scrolls. Their conversations with those in line are somehow magically muted from the rest of us, because I can see their lips moving but no sound is coming out.

The walls are covered in giant paintings depicting the advertising campaigns of previous events.

"That looks like fun." I point to one showing a gnome riding some catlike creature as it races against a human on a horse. They race through the streets of Pruxford, the Crystal Palace towering in the background with *Pruxford Grand Prix* in giant red letters at the top.

"For sure. Imagine blazing through the city using Strong Wind with no pedestrians to slow us down. I bet Jordy could give any of those mounts a run for their money. Get a load of this one." He points to a painting of some gnome bard. Only instead of playing in a dimly-lit tavern, she's singing on a stage surrounded by thousands of people. Fireworks explode behind her underneath the words *Cecily Vanderpants* written in an elegant script.

"This city really does have everything."

After taking in our surroundings, my focus shifts to the others waiting in line. Some of these people look like average citizens, but many look like adventurers. I'm only now keenly aware of how few adventurers there were on Isle of Mythos. Here, it seems like there are enough that it must be a stable form of income. Either that or they've come from all over to enter the tournament.

A tall, female human wearing leather armor stands in front of us. She holds a spear in one hand that is a foot taller than she is. In front of her, a panda beast-person with broad shoulders blocks my view of whoever stands in front. The panda wears a wide-brimmed straw hat, silver bracers, and a loin cloth, but nothing else.

I catch a lizardfolk with golden scales watching us from the farthest line, his eyes fixated on Caustic. He wears finely-embroidered clothing with a well-tailored long coat in a regal plum color. Several golden amulets dangle from his neck. The gnome at the counter calls for the next-in-line and he heads over. Both the woman and the lizardfolk have their stats concealed, so I'm unable to gain much aside from their appearance. They both look like formidable opponents.

As we watch those go through the line before us, I get an idea of how the whole process works. Each gnome working the counter has an enchanted orb that scans each applicant. Some people are turned away on the spot. If they pass the scan, then the gnomes fill out a bunch of notes. I have no idea what the questions are, but the hovering pen writes rapidly. Once that portion is done, the applicant is either turned away or sent through another door to where I assume the next part of the test is administered.

After the female human goes through the mystery door, it's my turn. I step up to the counter with Limery on my shoulder and Caustic beside me.

A gnome with bright orange hair trimmed into a bob looks up from her stack of parchment. "One at a time, please."

I place a hand on the counter. "We're actually together."

She blinks a few times, staring at me like I'm some kind of idiot. "Are either of these beings a pet or summoned being?"

"Well, the dragon and I haven't permanently bonded yet. And Limery, the imp, he's—"

"Then one at a time, please." She stares at me blankly, waiting for one of us to leave the counter. When I don't immediately leave, she raises a hand. "Security!"

"Oh, for fuck's sake, lady! Give me a second." I turn to Limery, on the verge of losing my cool. "Hey, bud, I guess we have to do this one at a time. Will you wait with Caustic until I'm done?"

Limery frowns before hopping to the floor beside Caustic. "Okays. Caustics, come with Limmy."

I take a deep breath and return to the counter. "Happy?"

She doesn't say anything as she lifts a dark blue orb in front of me. Energy swirls within the orb and then there's a pulse as it scans me. A strange sensation passes through me, and just as quickly, it's gone.

The quill jots something down on the paper. The gnome reads it, and then looks up, no emotion on her face. "You are of satisfactory level to compete."

She then rattles off several questions in quick succession.

"Race?"

"Forest troll."

She raises an eyebrow. "Class?"

"I'm a dual-class barbarian summoner."

"Where are you from?"

"Isle of Mythos."

"Answer the next questions with your base stats only. Strength?"

"Forty-three."

"Dexterity?"

"Twenty-four."

"Constitution?"

"Forty-four."

"Intelligence."

"Ten."

She pauses for a second, coughing before asking for my Wisdom stat. I'm pretty sure this is her attempt to keep from laughing.

I give her my best fake smile. "Fifteen."

"Charisma?"

"Six."

"Any notable victories or accomplishments you would like the judges to be aware of?"

"Let's see. I completed a regional quest, defeating a mana-infused wyrm. I've cleared a faerie dungeon, a marsh dungeon, and a salt dungeon, defeated the leader of the mountain trolls in single combat, made peace with King Favian of Vanaria on behalf of the forest trolls, and fought the gladiators of Goldspire in order to deliver a message for King Orso of Seascape. I've fought a behemoth, cleared Wandermere of mesmer wisps, and hatched the first green dragon in hundreds of years. Oh, and I'm a hero."

Her expression never changes, as she's thoroughly unimpressed with my accolades. "That will be all. Please step through the door to your right and wait for your turn."

I take Caustic and wish Limery luck before heading to the other door.

I pass by Taryn, who's waving his arms animatedly as he tells a story to the clerk. The chubby gnome with purple curled hair tilts her head back, laughing at whatever he just said. Why couldn't I get the fun one?

A gnome wearing an orange sherbert-colored uniform waits by the door holding a notepad in her hand. "Name?"

"Chod."

"You'll have to leave the li—" She pauses, tilting her head as her eyes fix on Caustic. "Er, dragon, outside while you finish the test. I can arrange to have him delivered to you upon completion."

These guys are making this way too difficult.

I take a deep breath and sigh. "Fine."

Reaching inside my satchel, I pull out some rope and fashion it into a makeshift leash.

I place it around Caustic's neck and kneel beside him. "Please don't bite or burn anyone."

After handing the gnome the leash, she allows me to enter. I step into an empty room with three closed doors against the far wall. Each door has a different colored gemstone set in its center. Red, blue, and yellow. The door behind me shuts, leaving me in a dim room aside from the gentle glow of the three gems.

A soft voice speaks from all around me. "You have been judged worthy of competition. Ready your weapon and prepare to be tested. You may use any weapons in your inventory and all of your abilities, but the use of elixirs, potions, or other items will end the test."

The yellow gemstone in the door on the right lights up, and the door opens. I equip Destroyer and summon three horrors as I step into the next room.

The room is similar to the previous in its aesthetic but much bigger, about the size of a basketball court. In the center, rows of neatly-lined statues take up a quarter of the space. Warriors holding swords and spears make up the first two rows, each one kneeling with their weapon beside them. Behind them, there are two rows of mages wearing long, flowing robes that stand with outstretched hands. In the furthest two rows, archers point their bows toward the heavens. All in all, I count twenty-four statues.

Depending on how strong the statues are, I'm guessing the test is either how long I can survive before certain parameters are hit or how quickly I can defeat them all.

I eye them warily out of my peripheral as I take in the rest of my surroundings. Each wall has two torches, casting the room with a forest of shadows. The flickering flames give the statues a lifelike quality. The walls, ceiling, and floor are all a dull gray, which is a stark contrast to every other building in Pruxford—but it gives the statues an even more menacing presence. There are no other entrances and no obstacles to use for defensive positioning.

I keep my distance with the three horrors in front of me, summoning more and readying Destroyer for whatever comes next. I'm not practiced enough with my new weapons and there's no telling what these gnomes are going to throw at me.

The grumbling of my horrors is overshadowed by stone grating against stone as the first row of statues comes to life. Dust falls from their joints as they stand with clunky movements, reminding me of those humanoid robots that move in effective but unnatural motions. I try to analyze them, but their stats are concealed.

Gnomish Stoneguards. *Level ???*

Great. I guess I'll have to get punched before I know how strong they are.

With each step, their movements become more fluid until they swing swords and spin spears like seasoned warriors. I take a few steps forward, giving myself some space in case I need to retreat. The closest stone swordsman charges, weapon held over his shoulder. I order my horrors to the back wall and meet the attacker head-on. Destroyer clashes with his sword, shattering the stone weapon and sending broken shards clattering around the room.

A second swordsman slashes to my right, but I move quicker, spinning around and hitting him square in the chest. Energy from Ram's Rage ripples through the air in a cone, hitting the two spearmen behind him. Stone explodes in all directions, and a spear rips through my braid, narrowly avoiding my throat. All around the room, more statues begin to move. I dodge another spear jab and spot the glowing hands of the stone mages out of the corner of my eye.

I smash a stone spearman into oblivion, but an arrow catches me in the shoulder, sending white-hot pain flaring from the impact. With a grunt, I rip the arrow out and toss it to the ground. Then I equip the Halite Shield, using its translucent properties like a riot shield so I can formulate a plan while fending off two swordsmen and a barrage of arrows.

There's no way I'm taking down all of these guys, so I can only imagine this is a test to see how long I survive. Losing a level to qualify for this tournament is a shit gamble, but the payoff could open opportunities that are otherwise impossible.

A fireball explodes against the shield, and heat flows around all four edges. My eyes water, and the attack leaves a black residue on the outside of the shield, obscuring my vision as arrows continue to rain down around me. I push forward with all my might, but the stone warriors seem anchored to the floor.

I summon a horror in front of the soldier and cast Kamikaze, but the attack has little effect on the stone armor.

A second mage attack hits my shield, and this time, ice spreads around from the impact. I drop the shield just before frost creeps onto my hand. A second later, wind rips through the room, tossing shards of broken stone like shrapnel and peppering my body with damage.

Each of the mages must have a different elemental attack. If I keep playing this passively, I'm going to get backed into a corner. I'm so used to fighting alongside Taryn and Limery that I haven't had a need to go at it alone. The days of running headfirst into battle have been few and far between as of late.

I need to take this on the offensive if I'm going to have a chance.

The few Horrors of Vitality I have charge by my side, their passives slowing the stone warriors enough to give me a slight movement advantage. The pointed end of Destroyer shatters a swordsman. It flashes red from a stack of Inferno, and I spin, bringing the hammer in an upward swing that explodes the head of another statue. The other spearmen stab through my horrors in seconds, and a blast of water hits me like a firehose, knocking me off balance as three arrows tear into my chest.

I don't have time to pull them out before a spear jabs at my throat. I parry the attack, but a fireball catches me in the ribs. The smell of burning flesh is nothing compared to the searing pain that accompanies every movement.

A stone fist slams into my side, cracking ribs and bringing me to my knees.

"Fuck this!" I shout as I roll out of the way just as another fist crashes into the floor inches from my head.

I activate Berserker Rage and sacrifice all of my remaining horrors, boosting my stats by a few more points. My vision goes red, and the pain of my injuries becomes a distant memory as my muscles bulge with increased power and speed. Thanks to Ram's Rage, not only do I deal splash damage, but my barbarian rage now lasts twice as long. My wounds stitch themselves together thanks to my increased healing, and I jump to my feet.

Destroyer crushes the head of the closest swordsman, and I duck as an ice projectile soars by, smashing against the wall.

Spells and arrows continue to assault me, but the stone warriors take some friendly fire from the attacks. If I can find a way to get past them then I can do some damage to those at the back.

I cast Champion and a mesmer wisp forms in the center of the room. Smoke pours from the creature, making for poor visibility, but the mages and archers immediately focus on the new target. Its tongue whips in and out of the smoke, and I use the momentary distraction to summon another Horror of Vitality. I make my move as the horror slows the spearman pursuing me.

I smash three archers with a fully-stacked Destroyer, the blazing heat from Inferno turning the stone black with each hit. The wisp shrieks as it dies, and the attention falls on me once again. A lightning bolt hits me, but thanks to my rage the stun is ineffective. I power through their attacks, my health dropping in chunks and climbing back as I smash through statue after statue. Nearly half of them are destroyed by the time my rage ends, leaving me a steaming pile of tattered blue meat.

Destroyer suddenly feels incredibly heavy, and as I raise it over my head, an arrow lodges in my throat. The warhammer falls from my hand, and the last thing I see is a fireball hurling at my head before everything goes black.

CHAPTER 20
A DASH OF CHAOS

I come to inside of a plain room similar to the one I was just in, only this one is much smaller and there are no statues trying to kill me. A single door beckons from across the room, and a notification flashes in the corner of my vision.

Placement test complete. *Please await further instructions.*

I check over my stats, expecting to have lost a level, but whatever happened, I was brought here before I actually died. There must have been some kind of enchantment protecting me from death while inside the training room. Even Destroyer and the Halite Shield have returned to my inventory.

The door clicks, and Caustic runs into the room, tongue hanging from his open mouth while he pulls a worried-looking gnome by the leash.

"Here's your dr-dragon, s-sir," the gnome stammers as he hands me the leash. "You'll be notified of your placement when entries lock in two days."

I want to ask him more questions, but Caustic jumps on my leg like an excited puppy. With his sharp claws, we're going to need to nip that in the bud right away. I pull a piece of jerky from my satchel and hold it in front of the excited dragon.

"Sit," I say firmly. When he obeys, I toss him the treat. "Good boy! We can't have you crushing people when you become an excited thirty-foot-tall dragon, now can we?"

We exit the room into the same hallway where the D.E.E. is located. I send Taryn a quick message, telling him I'll be waiting downstairs for them when they are done. I wonder how Taryn will do without having his pets there. He's not exactly a master of hand-to-hand combat, and those statues sure pack a punch.

I sit next to the fountain in the foyer, watching the colorful fish dart underneath the bridge. Among the patter of feet and constant chatter, the bubble of the fountain is calming and the fish entrancing. Caustic chases the fish around the pond excitedly, and I have to scold him several times not to jump in as he paws at the water.

I'm not sure how much time passes before Limery perches on the ledge next to me.

"Ooh, pretties." He leans forward, dipping a finger into the water.

"How'd you guys do?" I fist-bump Limery before turning to Taryn. "Had to be pretty tough without your pets? Those stone warriors were pretty resistant to magical attacks, too."

Taryn frowns. "Stone warriors? I fought these demonic creatures. They popped in and out of shadows. What about you, Limery?"

The imp puffs out his chest proudly. "I fought scary plantses. The gnomes saids Limmy did goods."

"I bet you did." I hold up my hand, and he slaps his against mine. "There were three doors when I entered, so I guess they tested our strengths. How'd yours go, T?"

Taryn grins. "I think I did alright. I had to get creative, but I took out a few. Not bad considering my pets are my strongest advantage, and I didn't have any with me. Once I found out they liked to hide in the shadows, I cast Endless Night and went scorched earth on their asses. But I guess we'll know in two days. Want to get out of here and grab a bite to eat? The clerk at the D.E.E. was telling me about this great gnomish restaurant run by tinkerers where all of the food is served on little contraptions."

My stomach rumbles, and I realize just how hungry I am. Fighting always works up my appetite. "Yeah, that sounds go—"

"Well, I'll be damned," a familiar voice calls from over my shoulder. "Of all the town halls in all the cities..."

"You've got to be fucking kidding me," I mumble before I turn around.

The cleric standing before me has upgraded his robe since the last time we ran into him, but there's no mistaking the blue eyes, chiseled jawline, and blond hair of Richard Hummel—the cleric who serves the god of chaos. Everywhere he goes, trouble follows.

"Nice threads." I gesture at his chest, where his old robes had a hole from where Pressley stabbed him. His new ones are a dark gray, embroidered with silver. He still wears a thick, black chain around his neck. "Surprised no one has stabbed you again."

"Believe me, they've tried." He smirks. "I'm digging the new look, by the way. The horns are very menacing."

I sigh, massaging my temples just beneath my horns. He is one of the last people I wanted to see today. "Do I want to know what you're doing here?"

His smile broadens and he winks. "Just waiting on a friend to finish upstairs."

I cross my arms. "You're entering the tournament?"

"Me?" He laughs. "Gods no."

"Well, whatever it is you're doing, I want no part in it. Trouble follows you everywhere you go."

He shrugs. "I could say the same thing about you."

Taryn snickers beside me, and I scowl at him.

"What?" He throws his hands up. "It's true."

There's a splash as Caustic jumps into the pond. A moment later, he crawls out with a shiny purple fish in his jaws.

"Goddammit. Caustic, no!" I point my finger at Richard. "You're bad luck, dude."

He waves at us as a gnome security guard escorts us out of the building. "Good seeing you!"

Once we're out in the street, I clench my fists and fight the urge to punch something. "God, he's an asshole."

Taryn cackles beside me.

"What's so funny?" I snap.

He fights back a grin and his lip quivers. "Bro, you've got such a rage-boner for this guy, but what has he actually ever done to you?"

I'm keenly aware of Limery sitting quietly on my shoulder. Maybe I'm not being the best role model at the moment, so I take a deep breath and try to calmly explain my issues with the cleric.

"Look, he serves the god of chaos. So, if he's around, then shit is going to hit the fan. He tried to get me to trade him one of my gifts from Chief Rizza in exchange for information about Jude when I was in Vanaria. He got Pressley killed in Seascape. He's the reason Pressley is a death knight now instead of an actual knight."

Taryn stares at me blankly. "And?"

"What do you mean 'And'? Is that not enough?"

He purses his lips before speaking. "It sounds to me like he hasn't done anything to you directly. And if you recall, he paid a price for what happened to Pressley. So what if he serves the god of chaos? Whoever said chaos has to be a bad thing?"

"Whoever said chaos has to be a bad thing?" I mock him,

rolling my eyes. "I just don't trust him, okay? If he'd ruin Pressley's life like that, then he's capable of anything."

Taryn shrugs. "Maybe. Maybe not."

"Whatever, let's just get some food."

The gnomish restaurant we stop at for lunch reminds me of one of those Japanese restaurants where you pick your food off little conveyor belts. Only this one has a tiny track that we all sit around, where little mana-powered contraptions deliver plates of food upon their backs.

We devour a plethora of meat-filled dumplings and drink exotic teas until our stomachs bulge.

On our way to the arena, we stop by a shop named Tinker Time. On the other side of the warped glass windows, gnomish apparatuses move of their own accord.

Limery presses his nose to the glass. "Cans we go looks, Chods?"

I'm sure everything in there is super expensive and easily breakable, but in the end, his excitement wins out over my hesitation. "Just promise not to break anything." I turn to Taryn. "Do you mind watching Caustic while we go in?"

He holds his hand out for the leash. "I'd be more worried about your big head knocking something over if I were you."

Inside, I feel like a bull in a china shop. Everything is packed so close together, I have to focus to not accidentally bump into a table. Spinning mobiles hang from the ceiling, and clockwork toys hop around the floor. After a close call nearly toppling a figurine that plays music as it spins, I decide to stand in a corner and take in the room from a distance.

Limery presses the button on a tiny red box. The box ticks

rhythmically for about thirty seconds before a loud chime goes off.

He cackles at the noise before disappearing deeper into the store, where an older gnome with a long purple beard chats him up.

This place is full of interesting oddities and contraptions, most of which I'm not even sure what they do. The table in front of me has a flask that can purify water up to three times before it breaks. Next to it, there's a bowl of glittery ball bearings, but I'm unable to analyze them. There's also a pair of gloves with small hooks embedded in them that claim to make climbing easier. The whole place has the feel of one of those "As Seen On TV" stores at the mall. After a while, Limery returns carrying a small package.

"What'd you get?" I ask.

He grins mischievously. "Its is a surprise."

I narrow my eyes. "As long as you paid for it."

After the tinkerer shop, we walk over to the arena to get a lay of the land. Where the arena in Goldspire was rustic like the coliseum of Ancient Rome, the arena in Pruxford could be a modern attraction anywhere in the real world. If not for the imposing stature of the Crystal Palace next door, the arena would be the crown jewel of Pruxford in its own right.

A myriad of vibrant gemstones jut nearly a hundred feet into the air, giving the exterior of the arena the appearance of a crystalline bird nest. The towering prismatic structure sparkles in the sun with a variety of hues. The entry gates are closed for now, but a beautiful walkway wraps around the arena spotted with dozens of crystal statues of past champions. A towering centaur holds a spear tucked under one arm just outside the front entrance.

I grab Taryn by the arm and pull him over. "That must be Draydon."

The statue resembles Swift a great deal, minus the beard. A

myriad of blue-shaded crystals make up the statue, from a sapphire lower half to an aquamarine upper body, indigo hooves, and intricate detailing of everything from the spear tip to the braids draping down his back.

"That's some amazing craftsmanship." Taryn traces his fingers along Draydon's hoof.

Limery flies over and perches on the spear, tugging at the spearhead.

"Don't even think about it unless you want to spend the night in jail," I warn, and he looks at me sheepishly. "Look at this." I point to a bronze plaque set a few feet in front of the statue.

Draydon Thundercrest

One of the greatest champions to ever come out of Wandermere, Draydon was a behemoth on the battlefield. Whether facing monsters or dueling against other adventurers, it was always said that the mighty centaur put on a show.

In an unfortunate accident, Draydon perished after an injury obtained during a duel where he was not given the customary protection spell. Through this statue, his legacy lives on.

"Protection spell? What do you think that is?" I wonder if that is what kept me from dying during the placement test.

Taryn strokes his beard. "No idea. Maybe it's something that keeps those competing from actually killing each other?"

We walk the perimeter of the arena, taking in the sculptures and the beauty of the architecture. Taryn and I sit on a bench while Limery and Caustic chase each other through the courtyard.

Something feels off as I watch the multitude of tourists admiring the Pruxford landmark. Then it hits me: there's not a single phone or camera in hand, just people enjoying life. They read the plaques and appreciate the statues, not for some meaningless internet points, but because they want to be here.

"What are you grinning about?" asks Taryn.

"Ha, is it that noticeable? I was just thinking about how no one has a phone or camera."

He frowns as he looks over the crowd. "Wow, it's a little unsettling, isn't it? Back home, there would be a handful of families and a dozen chicks posing in front of each statue."

"I think it's nice. The more I think about it, I don't know if I could ever go back to streaming after being here. It all just seems so pointless. I doubt another game could ever compare to this place."

Taryn nods. "You can say that again. Still, it has to end sometime, right?"

My focus wanes, and though I can still hear Taryn rambling in the background, my thoughts are on tonight. On logging out and discovering what updates Valery might have for me. Is it wrong for me to hope they don't have a solution? Rooting for the failure of the most immersive and advanced game there is just so it benefits me staying here?

Yeah, it's selfish, but aren't we all entitled to be a little selfish sometimes? It's not like I'm actively sabotaging their research.

The day passes quicker than expected, and after exploring some of the shops and boutiques, we drop off Caustic before heading back to The Puzzling Peacock.

We have time for a couple of drinks before bed, so we grab a table near the stairs. I scour the room for him, but Arty is nowhere to be seen. A band on the stage plays tranquil music.

"Much more calm than last night." Taryn takes a swig of his ale, and a thick layer of foam coats his mustache.

Limery laughs, not realizing he's sporting one of his own. When I point it out to him, he cackles even harder. "Limmy is an old mans."

Once we're on our second ale, I decide to broach the subject of Richard again. "So, who do you think the cleric was with? We should have stayed around to find out."

Taryn shakes his head. "Bro, you're starting to sound obsessed. I know he's sketchy, but that doesn't mean he's always plotting."

I cross my arms and sit back in my chair. "Honestly, I can't believe you aren't more concerned. It'd be one thing running into him in some small town like last time, but this is one of the biggest events on Mythos. If he's completing some quest for his mysterious god, then it's bad news for everyone here."

We go in circles for a while, with Taryn telling me I'm overreacting and me telling him he's not worried enough, until it's time for us to head upstairs.

I open the door to the room, and Limery stumbles inside.

Taryn stops me before I step through the doorway. "I appreciate that you're a little more concerned about this situation after everything that happened with Stompy, but you can't go searching for a boogieman around every corner or you'll live your whole life in fear." He taps me on the arm. "Something to think about."

Maybe he's right. It's possible I am just being overly paranoid after everything that has happened.

I squeeze him on the shoulder. "Say 'hey' to your folks for me."

CHAPTER 21
FAMILY MATTERS

Taryn stared at his reflection on the tablet as he waited for it to connect for the video chat. The face that stared back at him was his, yet it wasn't. He'd grown accustomed to the round face, the larger nose, and the beard of his dwarven body. Still, this felt right too, like the opposite of a split personality.

He grabbed a few strands of hair from his afro and tugged. "I'd look good with dreads."

The dull melody of the tablet connecting ended, and then his family appeared on the screen. They sat on the sectional sofa and seeing their smiles instantly warmed his heart. Two of his sisters, Jada and Laila, sat sandwiched between his mother and father, but the oldest of the three wasn't there.

"Where's Dez?" Taryn asked.

"She's at a sleepover," Jada, the youngest, answered, crossing her arms. "When do I get to go stay the night with my friends?"

"How about when you learn to keep your room clean and do your chores?" Their father gave Jada a knowing look and she groaned, slamming her body back into the oversized pillow.

"You know how it is, Taryn. She's at that age." Taryn's mom leaned forward. "How's your testing going? Are they feeding you well?"

"Judging by the checks they're sending, I bet he's eating like a fat cat." Taryn's dad grinned.

"Oh, Peter. Don't be tacky." She gave her husband the side-eye Taryn had seen a million times.

"What?" Peter feigned innocence. His dad has always been one to speak exactly what was on his mind.

"I like the beard, dad." His father's normally clean-shaven face was now covered with a full beard. Streaks of gray ran throughout. "I didn't realize you were getting so old."

"I think it looks sophisticated." He carefully stroked the outer edges of the beard. "Your mother, however, said it made me look like a... What was it, dear?"

"A bum." She narrowed her eyes. "You have such a distinct jawline, and you want to cover it with that gutter trash."

"Trash? Woman, those are my follicles you're talking about." He mirrored his wife's expression. Their banter had been the highlight of many family dinners. "So, how is it? Still everything you hoped?"

Taryn grinned at his father. "You know I can't talk about the game. They made me sign an NDA, remember?"

"Right, right." He nodded. "So why are you here then?" His dad burst out laughing.

"Oh, you know, just wanted to see your ugly face and make sure you hadn't drowned Jada and Laila with attention since you don't have me to pick on." Taryn winked at his sisters. "Is he bugging you two to death yet?"

Both girls giggled, but Laila answered. "Daddy's been helping me with my homework since you've been gone." She looked at her father out of the corner of her eye, a spitting image of her mother's expression. "I'm not sure I trust him, though."

Peter laughed. "I'm not sure I trust me either. Who knew they could change how math works? I feel like I'm the one who needs a tutor for some of this fourth-grade math."

Taryn raised his eyebrows. "Maybe if you'd studied more in school instead of chasing mom around."

He tilted his head, sharing some secret look with his wife. "You ain't wrong there. How's Chad doing? He heard from his folks at all?"

Taryn shrugged. "I'm not sure. We won't see each other until we're back in the game. He said to tell you hi, though."

"You give him our best." His mother offered a sympathetic smile. "Tell him that we're praying for him."

Peter shook his head. "This is something else, I tell ya. The kid gets in trouble, and it turns out to be the best thing to ever happen to this family."

"Peter!" Taryn's mom scolded her husband. "Children."

"Sorry, what I mean is that the system is something else. You think Taryn would be in this situation if he'd been the one to get in trouble? Chad did his time, and I respect that, even if the charge was BS. My point is that I guess you never really know what connections you'll make in this life."

"Yeah, I think about that a lot." Taryn sighed. "We owe a lot to him. So, how's everything with you all?"

Peter tapped Jada on the leg. "Why don't you girls say good-bye to Taryn, and then head upstairs to get ready for bed. It's way past your bedtimes already."

"What time is it there?" asked Taryn.

"Here?" His dad laughed again. "We're in the same time zone, son."

"Yeah, there's just no clocks where I'm at."

"It's almost midnight." His mother tapped Laila's leg in a similar manner as her husband. "You heard your father. Go get yourselves cleaned up. We'll be up to tuck you in shortly."

The two girls said their good-byes, and then sulked their way up the stairs.

Peter watched them go before turning back to the camera. "They're going to be hell to get out of bed in the morning, but they'd be worse if they found out they'd missed seeing you."

"That's the truth," his mother echoed.

As much fun as he'd been having, Taryn had missed his sisters as well. They were growing up faster by the day, and he was sad to miss that.

His dad had a serious expression, and it put Taryn on edge. His father was normally a cheerful guy. He always had a smile on his face, but right now, he looked dead serious.

Taryn's chest tightened. "What's going on, Dad?"

His father took a deep breath. "Son, I owe you an apology. I know I always said that playing these games so much was a waste of time, that they'd never take you anywhere. But thanks to you, we finally feel like a family again. Thanks to the money from Mythos Gaming, I was able to quit the second shift at the factory. I can spend more time with the girls, and your mother isn't picking up extra shifts anymore. We missed a lot of moments just trying to keep a roof over our heads and food on the table. A lot of your special moments. And when it came to the girls, you picked up so much of the slack. Now, we can give your sisters more of what you deserved. I'm just sorry you aren't around here to experience it, too."

Taryn's eyes suddenly blurred, and his face flushed with heat.

"Oh, Taryn, don't cry." His mother's voice shook. "You're going to make me cry."

He wiped his eyes. "I'm just happy I can help. You guys always did everything you could to make sure that we had all of our needs met. We might not have had the newest shoes or cable TV, but every field trip, every extracurricular, everything we needed, you made it happen. You deserve a break."

Peter blinked rapidly, and Taryn could tell he was fighting back tears of his own. "You're a good son, Taryn. We're lucky you were the first born."

Valery stuck her head through the doorway and tapped her watch. Time was almost up.

"Alright, alright." Taryn wiped his eyes again. "Enough of the sappiness. I've got to get back in, but it was great seeing everyone. Tell Dez I miss her."

"We will." Taryn's mom blew a kiss at the camera. "We love you."

"Love you, too." Taryn tapped the end-call button and sat back against the chair. After a few sniffles, he took a deep breath and stood, clapping his hands together. "Let's go, baby. Time to shine!"

CHAPTER 22
CHANGES

Beyond the haze of blue, two shadowy figures loom over me as I awake in the pod. I sit up, coughing as the nanites flow out of my lungs. It's a strange feeling, completely different from choking on water when it goes down the wrong pipe. No hacking, just a smooth stream as the nanites exit my body like a string of jelly being pulled from my throat.

Valery's eyes dart between me and the tablet she's holding while several technicians check readings on the display. Aside from them, the laboratory is pretty peaceful.

"Welcome back, Chad." Valery taps the tablet and then hands it to one of the technicians. "Or do you prefer Chod these days? How are you feeling?"

My gaze lingers on the technicians, waiting for any indications that the AI is acting up again. When one of them makes eye contact with me, I remember that Valery asked me a question.

"Uh, I'm good. Chad is fine." I'm not exactly in the mood for small talk at the moment. Too much is still up in the air.

"Good. Good." She smiles. "Hop on out. There are a few things we need to discuss, but first, let's get you out of the pod."

As I crawl out of the pod, I'm stunned by how defined my abs look. Valery said the nanites would be taking better care of me than I did myself, but I had no idea I was this muscular underneath my layer of skinny fat. Even my forearms look larger than I remember. And my quads, wow. Has being in Mythos for so long changed how I perceive myself or is this all thanks to a well-balanced and nutrient-rich diet?

I can feel Valery's gaze lingering on me, and I'm not sure if she is expecting me to say something or not. Once I'm out, she hands me a robe and leads me down the hallway to her office.

She gestures for me to sit and takes a seat across from me behind the desk. "We'll do your physical and psychological evaluations shortly, but there's something I need to tell you."

My stomach tightens. Is this where she tells me they've fixed the bug and it's time for me to log out? My fingers dig into the hard plastic of the chair.

Something is definitely off. Valery's normal alluring confidence is gone, replaced by something else. Nervousness? What could she possibly have to be nervous about?

She takes a deep breath. "I'm going to be straight with you. We've isolated the incident that caused the AI to believe that you were part of the system. We still don't know how the error happened or if it can be replicated. To put it plainly, the AI for the system and the nanites are supposed to work separately from one another. The nanites keep the body in stasis, and the system interacts with the mind. In your case, when you jumped into that mana pit, somehow the AI and the nanites were able to communicate with one another. Our working hypothesis is that it was a perfect storm of your race, class, and current active abilities that kept the system from respawning you. Most other races would have died instantly, but you survived, and now the nanites in your pod interact with the system."

The lump in my throat makes it difficult to speak. "So, what does that mean exactly?"

"It means that the nanites are responding to the AI when it comes to your body. And that there have been... changes."

My heartbeat pounds in my chest as I wait for the hammer to drop. "Changes, what do you mean?"

She stands from the desk and walks over to the door, shutting it. A full-length mirror stretches the length of the door. "Come here."

I don't know why, but I touch my temples, half expecting to feel a pair of massive horns curling around my head. My fingertips graze my hair, and I laugh at my absurdity.

When I step next to Valery in front of the mirror, my jaw drops. She's a slender woman. Curvy, yes, but I don't think it would have been a stretch to say that she and I were a similar size when I first logged in. The person staring back at me is almost unrecognizable. After the nanites cleared up my acne and stripped some of my body fat after my first couple of weeks in the game, I thought it was pretty impressive.

This... This should be impossible.

I look like a fucking athlete. My hair is the same jet black, greasy-looking mess it has always been, and my eyes and nose are clearly mine, but the body, it could belong to a stranger. Even my jawline is more defined.

I open the robe, admiring my broad chest and defined midsection. Even my legs look bigger.

I stare at my reflection with wide eyes. "How is this possible?"

She sighs. "I wish I knew. But as your avatar grows stronger in the game, your body is responding to the same stimuli. This is the result."

I flex my arm, admiring the bulging muscles of my bicep that I've never seen before. "And this is only happening to me?"

"Correct. I understand that you may be a little freaked out right now, but I assure you, all of your vitals are completely normal. We aren't seeing any adverse effects, so there is no need to worry about—"

"Worry?" I look myself over in the mirror once again. "Why would I be worried? This is incredible."

Valery's shoulders relax and her frown fades. "Well, good. There's still a lot we don't know, but for now, we'd like to continue as usual. If there's any cause for concern, you will be informed immediately. Obviously, we would reward your efforts with a substantial pay increase."

"Give it to Taryn. As far as I'm concerned, he and I are in this together."

"I'm sure we can make that happen." All traces of her nerves have disappeared.

I get the feeling that she has been dreading this talk for a while. For me, I don't care about the money. I never have. I just want to continue playing Isle of Mythos, but I know that this kind of money could change Taryn's life.

Besides, I might not be able to get a phone call from the bastard, but I know that if anything bad happens to me, I can count on my father to sue this place into oblivion. I'm sure they know that, too.

In the mirror's reflection, Valery leans against the edge of her desk and crosses her arms. "We heard from your mother."

The words catch me off guard like a punch to the chest. I turn to face Valery, my furrowed brow narrowing my vision. "I'm sorry, what?"

"Your mother called last week." She purses her lips before continuing. "My father thought it would be a good idea to give your parents my direct number for some reason. She wanted to know when you would be able to talk."

I'm suddenly aware that my fingernails are digging into my palm. "And?"

She sits behind her desk once again. "I had to explain to her that you were no longer serving your sentence, but that you had volunteered to keep testing the program. I gave her the date and time of your next scheduled logout, but when we followed up earlier today, she apologized that they wouldn't be able to make it since they would be on a flight. I'm sorry."

I scoff. "Typical. At least I can count on dad to have the decency to be a shitty father from a distance. It was always mom who would get my hopes up. A day out together here, followed by twenty promises that got broken or canceled. Rinse and repeat. Somehow those always hurt worse." I fight the urge to slam my fist into the wall. "I'm sorry, I don't know why I'm telling you this."

"Hey, you have nothing to be sorry for." She gives me an apologetic smile. "If it's any consolation, I'm glad that you're here. It might have been under unfortunate circumstances, but this technology has the power to change the world. And thanks to you, maybe in ways we didn't even imagine."

After our talk, the doctor performs a physical, though I'm not sure why it's needed when the nanites monitor my every spec. When I point this out to him, he frowns, asking me how many years the nanites went to medical school.

The psychological assessment is more boring than the physical. I only half pay attention to the questions, constantly expecting a frantic technician to bust into the room and tell me that the system is crashing again. To my surprise, the system seems back to normal.

While they might not need me to keep the game running now,

I'm essentially patient zero of the super-soldier program, so I think my time in Mythos is secured for now.

Before I climb back into the pod, I walk past some of the other players, wondering how many of them might be in Pruxford for the tournament. They're tucked away in various rooms across Mythos—all except for Jude and Glenn, who share a run-down shack with hobgoblins standing guard at the door.

Just looking at them sends my blood boiling. They'll get theirs in time.

Valery's heels clack against the floor as she returns to the lab, telling me my time is up.

I remove my robe, and with a final glance at my new body, I climb into the pod. "Game on."

CHAPTER 23

THE CRYSTAL PALACE

LIMERY AND I meet Taryn downstairs for breakfast. He already has a pile of food on the table and a mixture of eggs and syrup coating his beard. Limery flies over, taking a seat and sneaking a piece of sausage from Taryn's plate.

"Didn't want to beat down our door this morning?" I wink when he looks up from his food.

He returns my jibe with a grin. "You look chipper this morning. I'm guessing things went well?"

I sit across from him and lean in. "There's no way you're going to believe me. I'll fill you in later. How was yours?"

"Bro, it was just what I needed." He takes a bite out of a pink, hard-boiled egg. "I'm ready to grab this tournament by the balls!"

Limery takes an egg and tosses the whole thing in his mouth. "Yeah! Limmy is ready to grabs this tournaments by the ballses!"

I bury my head in my hands to keep from laughing.

After breakfast, we head out into the streets. The city is alive as the tournament festival begins in full force. There are street performers, minstrels, and many fanciful costumes of people dressed as monsters or fantastical heroes.

A young gnome races by in a red dragon costume, complete with a long tail that drags along the street as he chases behind a group of performers that hold up dancing fabric monsters on long poles. The monsters soar over the crowd, with glowing eyes and moving jaws, like something out of a Chinese parade.

We take in the excitement for a few minutes before heading to the stables to grab Caustic. In the end, Taryn decides to bring all of his pets into the city for the day. It turns out to be a good thing, because on Berry's back, Taryn can see over most of the crowd.

"If you asked nicely, I could have let you sit on my shoulder in your bird form," I tease.

"Hardy-har-har." Taryn rolls his eyes. "Maybe I'll perch on one of your horns and poop on your shoulder."

We take some of the outer streets that are less crowded as we make our way to the Crystal Palace. Since we still have two days before the tournament contestants are revealed, we decide to use today to try to speak with the gnomish council. If all goes well, we can make some headway with them before the tournament begins.

Jordy leads our little procession, followed by Caustic, who has put on a few more pounds since yesterday. Breebis must be feeding him well. The little nubby horns have started to split into full-blown antlers. Limery rides on the dragon's back, perched between the crest of his wings.

"So, how'd it go?" Taryn leans toward me so that he can speak over the crowd.

"You first. Mine is pretty big news. How's the family?"

He frowns for a second before his face lights up. "They're doing great, man. Mom and Dad have both cut back on their hours, and they're spending so much time with my sisters. Honestly, I'll never be able to repay you for this."

I slow my pace and look him in the eye. "You don't owe me anything. Mythos would not be the same without you in it. Oh, and you're getting a raise."

He jerks Berry to a halt, his face set in stone. "Dude, don't play with me like that. Are you serious?"

"Dead serious." I point toward Jordy and Caustic, who haven't slowed down. "Now, catch up with them, and I'll tell you all about it."

Berry grunts as he hurries to catch up with the others. We pass an interesting-looking building for the Cartographers Guild with a sign on the window stating 'Local Dungeon Maps for Sale.' I make a mental note to stop by if we have time to do any dungeon diving while we're in the city.

"If you drag this out any longer, I'll be old and gray," Taryn mumbles.

"Okay, okay." Even though I could send him a message, I feel like saying this out loud. It gives it more weight. I lean in close so that I can't be overheard. "They found out what was causing the system to crash when I logged out."

His eyes widen. "And?"

"Even though the nanites that keep us in stasis and the AI that is running the system are both groundbreaking technology, they're designed to work independently of one another. The nanites are a conduit for our brains to interact with the game world, but that's it. All of the bodily processes are independent of the AI. Somehow when I jumped into that mana pit, that changed, and my nanites have been responding to stimulus from the system."

His brow furrows as he processes the information. "What the hell does that even mean?"

"It means it's not just my mind being affected by the system. My body is growing outside of the game based on what I do in here. I've put on twenty pounds of muscle since I've been in here."

Taryn snorts, and then his face falls flat. "Oh, wait, you're serious? Is this happening to everyone?"

"No, just me." I shake my head. "Valery said it was the perfect storm of coincidences. I'm guessing that there's some connection between the AI and the ley lines. And when I didn't die in that mana pit, a switch that they didn't know could turn on got flipped. So they offered me a raise to keep playing—I guess kind of like hazard pay—but I told them to give it to you."

"You didn't have to do that." He looks at me with a worried expression. "Are you sure this is safe?"

"I jumped into that mana pit months ago. If something was wrong, I feel like they'd know by now. When I got out, I felt fine."

His frown deepens.

"What's up?" I give his shoulder a light squeeze. "Are you having second thoughts?"

He shakes his head. "Even if I were, it wouldn't matter. After seeing what this extra money has done for my family, there's no way I would back out even if it were a risk. You and I, we're in this together." He stares at me with a quizzical expression. "Twenty pounds, huh? What is that, like, half your body weight?"

"How the tables have turned." I shove him in the shoulder, laughing. "Seriously, though, I feel like this changes things big time. If they are able to replicate what is happening to me, imagine what kind of news that would be. You lay down in a pod for a few months and come out in peak physical health."

"Unfortunately, I agree. Nobody seems to care about mental health these days." Taryn sighs. "People sympathize with a broken body, but if you show an ounce of weakness when it comes to your mind then you're a pariah." His eyes narrow, and I see a glimpse of Taryn that very rarely comes out. "My dad, when he got hurt playing football, everyone showed up to support him. They brought balloons and flowers, celebrating the fact that he'd gotten hurt doing the thing he loved. As long as he pretended everything was fine, people wanted to be around him. But losing his passion took its toll, and when the rehab and the depression replaced his happy-go-lucky personality, people stopped coming. He was alone. It's fucked up, but that's how the world works."

"Damn, I'm sorry." Every time I was ever around Taryn's father, he was caring and funny. I can't even imagine him any other way.

"It all worked out." He winks, and his mustache twitches at the edges. "Eventually, he met my mother, and the rest is history."

The Crystal Palace has its own stable where we check our pets in while we visit. Each stall has translucent crystal walls, thick enough that I can't see through them, but I can still make out the silhouettes of the animals on the other side. We pay for a stall big enough to house all of our pets together. In spite of being twice the cost, it doesn't come with the amenities that Breebis offers, but we should only be gone for a couple of hours.

There must be a hundred stairs that make up the palace entrance, each one carved from dusty pink or lilac marble. Every third stair is made of clear crystal, allowing visitors to view a stream that flows beneath and runs through the city. Every so often, a bright-colored fish will flash by.

At the top of the stairs, several dozen guards, all wearing pearlescent armor that swirls with countless hues, stand sentry. The mixture of races has them all at varying heights from as short as three feet to a few that are taller than me. Each one holds a golden spear tipped with a sapphire.

Once inside the palace, it appears more like a tourist attraction than an actual government building. Statues line the outskirts of the hall, with one in central prominence of a gnome wearing a crown that towers above us all. The arched ceilings are painted with beautiful works of art, depicting great moments from Pruxford's history. There's a slew of gnomes scattered around, all wearing burgundy robes and black biretta hats, complete with fluffy poms similar to clergy.

One of them approaches us, bowing slightly before he speaks. "Greetings, gentlefolk, and welcome to the Crystal Palace, home to Pruxford's illustrious gnomish council. I am Pipten, one of the many palace guides. Tours are conducted every thirty minutes, and tickets can be purchased from the ticketmaster on the far left side. The gift shop is to the right, next to the famous Libation Station and Eatery that serves some of the most exquisite food and drinks in all of Mythos. What can I help you with today?"

I step forward, looming over the small gnome. "We'd actually like to speak with the council. We come on behalf of King Orso Brightgaze of Seascape."

"Oh, that is most unfortunate. The council does not take audiences without an appointment. I'd advise you to take your message to the borough office of your choice. However, if you are adamant about an audience with the council, you may accompany me to the administration corridor, where we can schedule you a meeting."

"Borough office." Taryn scoffs. "Why is it always the government that hires a dozen people to do the job of one?"

We make our way through the crowd, following Pipten across the entrance hall. Next to the ticketmaster, he brushes his hand beneath a painting of a hazy blue mountain range. Limery gasps as the painting elongates, stretching to the floor and opening into a secret entrance. We walk down a narrow hallway where my head nearly scrapes the ceiling. When the hallway forks, we go to the left and through an unmarked door so small that I have to crouch to enter, forcing Limery to abandon his perch on my shoulder. After going through the door, we descend a long spiral staircase that comes to an abrupt halt at an empty alcove.

Taryn and I cast each other uncertain glances as the gnome pulls the torch from the wall and uses it to light the shadowy area next to the stairwell. The word 'appointments' is engraved into one of the bricks. The gnome presses it, and a grating sound fills the alcove as bricks shift out of position to form a door.

This all seems a bit odd just to schedule a meeting, and I can't imagine it's very practical to make this journey several times a day, but maybe that's the point.

Inside, an old gray gnome wearing a teal outfit in the same style as Pipten sits at a table with a roll of parchment and vials of ink spread out in front of him. Behind purple spectacles, the gnome is fast asleep.

Pipten clears his throat. "Bertrand."

The old gnome stirs, mumbling something incomprehensible.

"Bertrand," our guide says more forcefully. "These fine guests would like to schedule an audience with the council."

Bertrand wipes his eyes and looks us over, frowning. "Yes, yes, let me see." He pushes around sheets of parchment, tracing their contents with a long finger. "Hmm. Let's see. Our next available appointment is on the fifth of Rineholm."

I'm suddenly aware I have no idea how days, weeks, or months function in this world. So far, I've never needed to know. My cheeks go hot. "Uh, when is that?"

"Nine months and two days."

"Are you fucking kidding me?" My voice echoes around the

chamber. "What kind of racket is this? You hide away deep below the castle in an inaccessible room, making it nearly impossible to book an appointment, and then tell me the next one is in nine months. This is bullshit."

"Ah yes," the guide answers this time. "It is most unfortunate, but the council is busy with matters of the city. It is not prudent to waste their time with the day-to-day complaints of the realm. That is what the borough offices are for."

I clench my fist, ready to give these two an even bigger piece of my mind, when Taryn grabs me by the forearm.

"Hey, it's not worth it. There are other ways to get a meeting with the council. Let's just stick to the plan."

"Fine," I snarl, staring daggers at the two gnomes. "Let's get the hell out of here."

The long walk back is filled with silence, but by the time we reach the entrance hall again, I'm calm enough to have a conversation without yelling. "What is it with the government always giving you the runaround? It doesn't matter where you go."

"Some things are universal." Taryn gazes out across the crowd. "As long as we're here, we might as well take the tour. You never know what we might learn."

"Okay, but we're not going with that asshole." I point at Pipten, who just wasted a half-hour of our time.

After spending another half-hour in line to secure tickets, we have fifteen minutes to kill before the tour begins so we stop by the Libation Station for a quick drink. The pub is as eccentric as the rest of Pruxford, with crystal tables and chairs, and laughter ringing all around us. Their special for the day is called the Jester's Delight, so we order three.

The drinks arrive in prompt order, served in a chilled tulip-shaped glass. The cocktail is bright pink with baby blue fog that spills over the edges before dissipating.

"Pretties." Limery's bulbous eyes flash with greed as he lifts the drink.

Taryn holds up a hand between the glass and the imp's mouth. "Have you no manners?" He cocks his head and puffs out his chest as he mimics nobility before lifting his glass. "Cheers."

We clink our glasses, and I take a large sip. The drink is sweet and tangy, reminiscent of strawberry and cotton candy with just a hint of cream. As it works its way down my throat, a sense of elation passes through me.

Limery giggles and a moment later, Taryn joins in. My cheeks grow tight as an uncontrollable urge to smile comes over me. When I open my mouth, laughter pours out.

Taryn tilts his head back, his beard jingling as he unleashes a boisterous laugh.

Limery points at me, gasping for air as he fights through a fit himself.

Twenty seconds later, the urge fades but the sense of mirth remains.

"What the hell was that?" I ask, still unable to stop smiling.

"I think it was the drink." Taryn taps his finger against the glass, grinning.

Item. Jester's Delight. *This gnomish concoction is capable of bringing joy to even the most somber of occasions. One sip will ensure twenty seconds of uncontrollable delight and is a staple at comedy shows around Pruxford.*

We spend the rest of our time at the pub drinking and laughing until our cheeks hurt.

A loud gong signals the start of the next round of tours. Our tickets say to locate our tour guide next to the statue of King Prism, the last king of Pruxford. In the center of the entrance hall, an odd assortment of tourists stands before a gnome wearing the standard guide uniform.

She does a quick headcount before speaking. "Now that everyone is here, my name is Maripol, and I'll be your guide through the Crystal Palace today. Over the course of the tour, you will learn about the history and see the many wonders of the palace. As you can see, the other groups are gathering at various statues, each with its own piece of Pruxford's history, but none are more prominent than the statue before you. King Prism was the last king of Pruxford and the architect behind what this great city has become. Now, if you'll follow me, we'll begin our journey through the great hall."

Maripol leads us through a massive set of double-doors into a long room filled with magnificent tables, each one topped with the most elegant place settings I've ever seen. The tables shimmer and sparkle with a mixture of precious metals and gemstones. Along the walls hang elaborate tapestries and paintings that make the room even more imposing. At the front of the room, perpendicular to the other long tables, is the host table set a few feet off the ground so that they can look down on their guests.

My parents forced me to go to some amazing dinners in my day, but none of them compare to this. This is like something out of a fairytale, elegant and mesmerizing. I lose myself in the grandeur of it all, missing half of Maripol's speech.

"...and some of the greatest feasts in Mythos have been held in this room. After dinner, guests would then head over to the grand ballroom for a night of dancing and socializing. Follow me."

Taryn nudges me in the ribs. "So, you gonna have a fancy shindig like this when you get your castle set up?"

I laugh. "I doubt I could afford a place setting this nice for the three of us, let alone an entire keep. We'll have cheap drinks, and lots of it."

"Oh, yes!" Limery clasps his hands together, pulling them to his chin. "Limmy loves to parties."

Over the next hour, we tour what I imagine is only a small fraction of the actual palace. Maripol shows us an indoor pool with bubbling enchantments that make it a giant hot tub, an indoor garden full of glass flowers and mechanical birds, a library with thousands of books, scrolls, and artifacts, a picture gallery of famous Pruxfordians, and a music room with instruments that play themselves.

After ascending another staircase onto an open landing, Maripol comes to a stop, pointing at a closed door. The arched door is carved with intricate designs of birds and flowers, and the translucent crystal is set with hundreds of colorful gemstones. A beautiful mosaic covers the floor with a painting of the same mosaic along the vaulted ceilings.

"Once upon a time, this was the throne room for the royalty of Pruxford, until the day that King Prism turned over the governing of the city to the council. Since then, it has been known as the Grand Council Room. This historic date changed the fate of Pruxford from a fledgling kingdom into the most illustrious city in Mythos. The council room is not a part of the tour, but if you will follow me this way, we will take the Palace Chute down to the gardens. But first, we will stop at the viewing panel overlooking the city."

"Palace Chute, that sounds like fun." I get in line behind the others when Taryn grabs me by the arm.

He holds a finger over his lips, signaling me to be quiet.

I don't know what he's up to, but I follow him anyway as the group disappears around the corner.

Once they're out of sight, I break the silence. "What's going on?"

He grins mischievously, holding up the Nimble Key he got from Swift. "We're going to put this bad boy to use."

CHAPTER 24

A LACK OF COUNCIL

ONCE THE COAST is clear and we're sure Maripol hasn't noticed our disappearance from the group, we head to the door of the council room with caution. Taryn's Cloak of Silence muffles his every step, and I do my best to walk gingerly behind him, but my claws tap against the marble floors with each step I take. My paranoia amplifies every clack like a gunshot even though there's no one around to hear. I'd take the soft muffle of earth over this any day of the week.

The door to the council room is a work of art, with the keyhole hidden within an elaborate display of gemstone flowers. I give the handle a tug, but it doesn't budge.

Every sound puts me on edge, so I turn to Limery. "Keep a lookout on the hallway while Taryn picks the lock."

The imp zooms away, hovering around the corner to watch the hallway.

Taryn grins as he raises the Nimble Key to the door. He flicks the bow, and the tiny pistons and gears on the skeleton key spin to life. The key bit resizes itself as he presses it into the keyhole.

"Open sesame," he whispers, releasing the key.

The key whirs as it works its magic, gears spinning, barrel rotating, and pistons undulating. After a minute, the gears stop spinning and an audible click comes from inside the lock as the door cracks open.

I pat Taryn on the back. "Well done."

He pulls the door open and gestures for me to enter. I snap my fingers, and Limery rejoins us. Inside, massive pillars run along both sides of the room. A set of rainbow-colored stairs ascend to a platform where I imagine a throne used to sit. Now, there's a jeweled cornucopia that must weigh several tons. At the bottom of the stairs, a single gnome sits at a hexagonal table with his head buried between hands covered with jeweled rings. Aside from him, the council room is empty. I focus on the lone gnome.

Felston Boonspan

    Level ???

    Gnome

    Pruxford Councilmember

The gnome looks up as we enter, eyes wide over his bulbous nose, and I recognize him as one of the envoys from King Orso's council meeting. "You can't be in here. Guar—"

I hold up a hand, cutting him off. "Please, we just need to talk. My name is Chod. I was at the council meeting in Seascape."

He sighs. "I know who you are, even with the new additions." He gestures to the sides of his head. "But breaking and entering is a crime, even for heroes."

"I'm sorry. It's just that we needed to speak to the council. There are urgent matters to discuss."

He sighs. "I'm sure I know why you are here, but trust me when I tell you that there is nothing you can say that hasn't already been said."

Taryn steps up beside me. "Where is the rest of the council?"

The gnome sits back against his chair, abandoning his protest over our entrance. "Out and about for the festival. It seems you have wasted whatever effort it took to unlock the council room door."

I step closer until I'm across from him at the table. "We need to speak to them. There have been more attacks. Wandermere was nearly overrun with mesmer wisps."

He scratches his chin contemplatively. "Your words will fall on deaf ears. Even with my report of the happenings at Seascape, the rest of the council are reluctant to believe it. 'The portals have been reopening for the last century,' they will say. 'It is not a cause for concern.'"

I slam my palms against the table. "Then how do you explain the monsters appearing from the shadowlands? You were there when the behemoth came through Seascape's portal. You promised that Pruxford would stand with us. Does your word mean nothing?"

The gnome's eyes narrow, and there is venom when he speaks. "My word is everything, but in case you haven't noticed, this is a council table and not a throne room. One person does not make decisions for the realm." He closes his eyes and just sits there for a moment. When he speaks again, it's calmer. "Pruxford will help if there is a direct attack on Seascape, but the council will not approve action based simply on roaming monsters, no matter their origin."

"Dammit!" My voice echoes around the room. "There has to be something we can do."

"I would advise against breaking into a government building. You will find that the other councilmembers are not so slow to serve justice as I am, and the dungeon of Pruxford goes very deep. If you want a chance to speak before the council, then win the tournament. In addition to the rewards, it will grant you an audience with the council."

My hand wraps around the back of the chair before me, and I'm sure I could crush it if I tried. "So, that's it? All our hope comes down to this tournament?"

He nods. "The wheels of government turn slowly, even for you. But if it means anything, I wish you luck."

"We'll take all the luck we can get."

By the time we drop the pets off at Breebis's stable and make it back to The Puzzling Peacock, it's nearly nightfall. We grab a quick dinner and some drinks before we head out to the Underground Circus for the night. After the disappointment at the palace, some entertainment sounds like exactly what we need.

I'm polishing off the last of my ale, belly full, when the door opens and Arty walks in with his adopted human brothers. They're all covered in dirt and blood, but they laugh and carouse as they stomp toward a table in the back.

Arty stops by our table, flashing us a smile that reveals his sharp teeth. "Getting a head start?" The cyclops's massive eye makes it hard to read his expression, but his tone is friendly.

"Grabbing a bite to eat before heading to the circus." I set the empty mug on the table. "You all look like you've been through hell."

He looks down at his filthy tunic, wiping away a patch of

either dried mud or blood. "Me and the boys went dungeon diving. I was planning on going by myself tomorrow, but if you'd like to join, the dungeon is where bonds are built. You can tell me all about that proposition of yours."

I turn to Taryn. "What do you say? Up for a little action?"

Taryn nods, mouth full of bread.

I stand up and offer Arty my hand, only coming up to the cyclops's chin. "Sounds good to us."

His grip is firm. "Excellent, see you at sunrise."

Arty takes a seat among his brothers, and Taryn, Limery, and I leave the inn with a slight buzz.

Without Berry to carry him, Taryn walks speedily beside me. "You sure that's a good idea?"

"Sure, he's a giant teddy bear." I laugh.

He rolls his eyes. "Tell that to the remnants of whatever he killed on his tunic."

I poke him in the shoulder. "What, are you scared of dungeon diving all of a sudden?"

"No, it's just an awfully convenient way to eliminate a few competitors from the tournament." Taryn frowns, staring off into the distance as we walk. "He has to know you're one of his biggest threats."

"When did you become so cynical? I'd say there are very few people in Pruxford who even know I exist."

Taryn stops in the middle of the street, turning to face me. "I'm not being cynical. It's just that we have a lot riding on this tournament, assuming we even get to compete. I don't want to blow our shot."

I sigh as I struggle between my instincts and Taryn's concern. The last thing I want to do is dismiss him after everything that's happened. "I hear you, I really do, but that sounds like all the more reason why we should gain experience while we can. I trust him, and I hope you trust me."

He sighs. "You know I do."

"Good, now hurry up before all the good seats are gone."

CHAPTER 25

THE WHOLE WORLD A CIRCUS

THE COBBLED STREETS are packed as we make our way toward the entertainment district. A steady stream of people travel alongside us in the same direction, and street performers line the alleyways, trying to make a few coins off those going out for the evening.

Once inside Millimoo Square, named after the gnomish actor, Taryn stops in front of the entrance to the Amazing Hydro Park. Streams of water form an arched entryway, and the nearby mist creates dozens of rainbows. The sign boasts that the venue is a water park run by one of Pruxford's famous water mages.

Taryn touches the stream of water and it splashes into a fine mist. Droplets cling to his beard. "This is cool. We could spend a week just visiting all of the attractions here."

He's not wrong. Some of the most popular attractions in all of Pruxford are located in this square. There are museums, theaters, a maze, menageries, and gardens—enough to keep anyone busy. In the heart of the square, there's a stage where a gnomish band is currently performing folksy music.

They sound pretty good, and I consider stopping for a song

236

before I spot the black flag of the circus waving at the far end of the square. I suppress a laugh at the sight of the circus tent. It has changed shape and color once again, somehow able to morph to fit within the space provided. In Sandholde, the tent was wide and striped with an assortment of colors. Now, the pavilion can't be any wider than a small house, but it rises three or four stories into the air, towering above the other establishments. Red-and-white stripes run from top to bottom, further elongating its appearance. It looks like a strong gust of wind could topple it over, but the enchanted tent holds firm. People continue to funnel into the whimsical pavilion.

Atop the slender tent, the black flag emblazoned with the red lion logo of the Underground Circus whips in the wind. A line stretches from the entrance, hundreds deep even as they continue to disappear inside. The group in front of us talks in excited voices, and I overhear an older gnome telling a beastkin that he's been to the circus every evening since it arrived.

"They must be doing well for themselves." Taryn tilts his head back, looking up at the towering tent.

"Good news tends to travel fast. I wonder if they have any new acts since the last time we saw them." It feels like a lifetime ago that we saw the circus perform in Sandholde—back before Seascape, before the portals opened, before everything carried such weight.

"Limmy likes the bubble drinks." He grins with delight at the memory of the magical drinks that had everyone blowing bubbles from their mouths.

The line moves quickly, and soon we're inside where a large man stands sentry to the inner pavilion, taking coins from the circus goers. He wears a black tunic adorned with a red lion head, and I recognize his dual-colored eyes—one brown eye and one blue—from my very first encounter with the circus.

I pull out a gold coin and wait for him to let us enter.

He pushes my hand down. "A friend of the circus is always welcome." He winks and gestures us inside. "You're on the list."

I turn to Taryn, brow scrunched. "List?" I mouth. Did Hawkin somehow know that I would be here?

Taryn pushes me in the back. "We're VIP. Don't question it."

We step through the crease in the canvas into a world of the fantastic.

"Holy shit," I whisper, jaw hanging wide as I take it all in.

Taryn and Limery have the same reaction. Overhead, a night sky stretches on forever where the tent should be. Galaxies spin, distant planets twinkle, and stars shoot across the brilliant expanse. Gentle instrumental music plays in the background. It reminds me of the planetarium, only more detailed and majestic.

The smell of candied popcorn and exquisite delights assault us from every direction. Twinkling gemstones glow softly along the floor, marking aisles and seating, while glowbugs flicker through the air.

The inside of the tent is much bigger than it was in Sandholde. That one fit hundreds. This one looks like it can hold thousands. They must have some kind of enchantment that resizes it to each audience, making it always seem full.

Circusgoers fill the stands, and the magical concessions are showcased in all their glory. An elephant beastkin blows bubbles from its trunk while a young gnome pops them. Steam shoots from the ears of another gnome, while a dwarf blows smoke from her nostrils.

"This is amazing." Taryn walks past me. "Let's go find a seat."

"Mr. Troll! Mr. Troll!" an excited young voice calls from down below.

A kid with glowing face paint rushes up the aisle. He wears a red tunic with the circus emblem in black.

"Brock, is that you?" I recognize the black hair of the young boy who snuck into my room at the castle in Vanaria.

"Yes, sir, Mr. Troll. Me and Neville got us official circus uniforms and everything." He beams as he presses his palm against the tunic, which is a far cry from the tattered clothes he used to wear on the streets of Vanaria. "We saved you a special seat in the front row."

"How'd you know we were coming?"

He does an animated shrug, bringing his hands parallel with his shoulders. "I don't know, but Mr. Hawkin said he had a feeling you'd be stopping by."

Brock leads us to three seats in the front row. I offer him a coin for his trouble, but he declines.

"Can't take it, Mr. Troll. I'm official now." He puffs out his chest. "Have a seat and Neville will be by with some refreshments for ya." He tips an invisible cap and disappears back up the aisle.

A moment later, Neville shows up with a tray of concessions. With the circus uniform and face paint, he looks almost identical to Brock, except his fiery red hair. "I knew we'd see ya again, Mr. Troll. I tell ya, our lives certainly have changed since you came to town. Pick whatever you'd like, it's on the house."

There's popcorn and an assortment of candies on his concession tray, along with half a dozen drinks in the back row. Limery dives in, filling his hands with as many snacks as he can and stuffing them in his seat. Then he grabs a cup filled with a bright yellow liquid.

"Thankses!"

He takes a sip and immediately gasps as tiny bolts of electricity form along his fingertips. He stares at his hands with wonder, and when he moves them closer together, the bolts from each hand connect to one another with a crack. After about ten seconds, the energy fades, and Limery takes another drink.

"That's pretty cool." I lean forward, examining the other beverages. "What do these other ones do?"

Neville grins. "You'll have to find out for yourself, Mr. Troll."

I take a lavender drink with a thick fog floating on the top, and Taryn grabs a green one that fades from neon at the top to forest green at the bottom.

"I think Limery got enough snacks for all of us. Tell Hawkin I said thanks, Neville."

"Will do. Enjoy the show!"

I lift my drink and tap it against Taryn's. "Cheers!"

We both take a hearty swig as Limery continues to shoot lightning from one finger to the other, laughing maniacally as the electricity pops.

My drink is smooth and incredibly creamy. As it settles in my stomach, a feeling of calm washes over me and my arms feel almost weightless.

"Woah." The word warbles like a long piece of tin hit with a hammer, reverberating inside my mouth.

As my head swims without a care in the world, I analyze the drink.

Item. Tonic of Bliss. *This calming drink puts worries at ease and will have you feeling as if you were laying on a pillow of clouds. Spatial distortion may occur, but any effects are not permanent.*

"Dude, you've gotta try this." I offer my drink to Taryn and notice the effects of his own drink for the first time.

Vibrant flowers have bloomed along his dreadlocks and beard, with neon butterflies fluttering in the air around him.

A butterfly lands on his outstretched finger, and Taryn's eyes go wide. "Bro, I need more of this. It fits my aesthetic perfectly. I would honestly waste all my money just to walk around like Father Earth all day."

He takes a sip of my drink, but I decide to leave the bugs and foliage in the forest where they belong. Beside us, Limery pops candies and popcorn into his mouth like a crazed demon. I snatch a box filled with various colored candies from between our seats and toss a yellow one in my mouth. I bite into it, and a tiny jolt stuns my mouth shut. A red jelly causes smoke to plume from my nose, and the light blue candy sends chills down my body.

The candies are called Snickety Snelly's Mysterious Jellies, and there's a spinning wheel on the outside of the box in a rainbow of colors. Apparently, each of the jelly candies has a different flavor.

We continue sampling the snacks and drinks as more people flow into the pavilion. A gaudy-looking gnome couple wearing robes made of sequins sits beside us. The lady holds a pair of miniature binoculars with a long slender handle attached to one of the frames. She lifts the binoculars over her eyes and gazes at the night sky.

Soon after, the music swells and the universe overhead dims. The torches around the pavilion extinguish, and the bright stars and galaxies above fade to black until we're in complete darkness.

A single star flares overhead, a tiny dot in the blackness. Around it, several more flash to life, pulsing gently. Some burn brighter than others, and a constellation begins to form. Lines of light connect between the stars, painting the outline of a lion as the universe continues to reform itself in the background.

More lines connect, further detailing the lion until it looks almost realistic. The music dies, and the stars shift as the constellation roars so loud that a few children in the audience scream. The lion pounces from the stars and everyone gasps.

The lion plummets from the cosmos to the circus ring, galaxies swirling within its eyes. When it hits the ground, braziers roar to life around the ring, casting the circus in light as a warm breeze passes over us. Just as quickly, the fires fade, and a starry night reigns once more. The crowd applauds, and a spotlight falls in the center of the ring in a single beam, burning steadily. I look up but can't find its source.

A moment later, Hawkin steps into the spotlight. He wears his jester's clothing—a black-and-red-striped tunic, billowing pants, and fanciful red shoes that curl up at the end. His face is painted white, with a red clover painted over one eye and a black diamond over the other.

His voice is amplified when he speaks. "Tonight, you will enter a land of whimsy, where anything is possible if you only believe. You will see things that shouldn't be possible, things that are not possible, but for tonight, they will be. Welcome to the Underground Circus!"

The braziers erupt again, and the circus roars to life. The crowd applauds, and men on stilts emerge from the darkness, towering over us and juggling as they walk. Soon, there are fire breathers and sword swallowers. Glowing trapeze artists fly through the air while dancers contort themselves on the ground. There's so much action that it's impossible to follow it all at the same time.

Hours fly by and when the black lion returns to the stage, I know it's almost over. The lion jumps through a flaming hoop, and its red mane bursts into flame while extinguishing the fire of every torch and brazier around the stage. The lion leaps onto a platform at center stage, roaring at the crowd. When the fire fades from its mane, we're in darkness once again.

The blackness is impenetrable even to my night vision, and whispers murmur around us. The strum of a lute quiets the crowd, and glowing musical notes shoot across the ring from where the lion once stood. A silhouette begins to take shape in the darkness, outlined by the glowing melody. Hawkin's face appears, glowing with the same face paint as Brock and Neville—a heart and a diamond over his eyes. He strums again and musical notes shoot high in the air, exploding like fireworks and adding an echo to the song he plays.

The crowd oohs and ahhs at the spectacular display as the melody transforms into wispy animals that run overhead. A giant bird swoops over the audience, and a school of fish dart through the crowd, dissipating into our bodies.

The melody changes, and the glowing notes congregate over Hawkin's head. At first, they form a ball, but ever-so-slightly, it expands until a neon dragon flaps its massive wings. It circles around the circus, musical notes spewing from its mouth in lieu of fire.

Then the dragon dives for the crowd, exploding into a firework finale fit for the Fourth of July. Sparks rush into my body, and the circus goes dark for a final time. When the torches reignite, the stage is empty.

The crowd gives the performers a standing ovation, and a new notification flashes in the corner of my vision.

You have been targeted with Luck of the Dragon. The odds will move in your favor for the next twenty-four hours.

Wow! Hawkin has really stepped up his game since last time. Twenty-four hours of good fortune could change a lot.

"I can't believe he just gave us a luck buff." Taryn claps even harder. "No wonder people keep coming back."

"I know, right? And for a full day. That was a hell of a show."

Beside me, Limery lies passed out in his seat with empty candy wrappers all around him. His fingers are stained with chocolate, and drool runs down his chin.

I leave him be as the crowd funnels toward the exit, and we

wait for Hawkin. After a few minutes, he pokes his head through the curtain.

"Enjoy the show?" He winks with his heart-painted eye.

I step down into the ring and shake his hand. "It was amazing. As hard as it is to believe, you outdid your last performance. How'd you know we'd be here, anyhow?"

He smiles mischievously. "I can't be giving away circus secrets, now can I?"

"I suppose not. We're grateful for the experience." I point over my shoulder to Limery. "He certainly enjoyed himself."

"The little ones do enjoy the treats." Hawkin's smile widens as he looks at Limery, and then it fades, suddenly serious. "We owe you a debt that a lifetime of shows could not repay, Chod."

"That's not—" I start to argue, but he holds up a hand, silencing me before continuing.

"No, it's true. Before you came to Vanaria, we simply survived. I guided the circus as best I could, and we held close to one another, outcasts of society. Many of us performed in the streets, making enough to get by and sharing what extra we may have among those less fortunate. We called ourselves the Underground Circus because that was the only place where we truly felt safe." He lifts his arms, gesturing to the pavilion around us. "It was your vision that inspired this. You believed there was a better life out there for us if we only believed in ourselves. Through all of that, the people of Mythos somehow came to believe in us. Our show has grown beyond my wildest dreams, and we are no longer simply surviving. We are living. And for that, I thank you. We all do."

"I—" My throat catches, and I take a moment to regain my composure, clearing my throat before continuing. "I'm glad for all your success, but I only gave you an idea. You made it happen. All of you."

He squeezes my arm, grinning again. "So modest for a troll."

"That was quite the buff you gave everyone." Taryn changes the subject, for which I'm grateful. "You better watch out or the gamblers will come hunting for you."

Hawkin laughs. "Fear not, that was a one-time buff for a friend. I hope it pays good dividends to your party."

The curtain at the back of the ring ripples, and a woman with flowing blonde hair pokes her head through. Leona. She and I shared a drink together at the Underground Circus in Vanaria.

She waves. "We're about to head to the Rocky Rooster for after-show drinks. You all are more than welcome to join us."

I return the gesture. "Any other night we would, but we've got a date with a dungeon bright and early tomorrow." I glance over my shoulder at Limery. "Plus, this guy is out like a candle."

"See you around then." She winks. "And good luck tomorrow."

As we say good-bye to Hawkin, I get the feeling we've already got all the luck we need.

CHAPTER 26

THE ADVENTURERS' GUILD

EVEN THOUGH WE WAKE EARLY, Arty is already waiting for us downstairs the next morning. He sits alone at a table with enough food to feed half a dozen people.

"Dig in." He gestures at the massive spread before him. "Don't want to try and clear a dungeon on an empty stomach."

"You don't have to tell me twice." Taryn takes a seat and shovels bacon and sausage onto his plate.

Limery rubs his stomach. "Yums. Limmy is hungries."

"Eat your fill, little one." Arty stabs a massive sausage with his fork and rips into it with pointed teeth.

I take a seat next to him and pile a plate for myself. "Thanks for the food. So, what kind of dungeon are we headed to today?"

He talks with his mouth full, his massive eye focused on me. "There are plenty to choose from. Did you know that Pruxford has some of the most popular dungeons in all of Mythos? We're one of the few cities where one can make a living as a full-time adventurer."

I look at him quizzically. "I had no idea. How's that work?"

"Adventuring is practically an economy in itself. Some of the dungeons are ancient dungeons and some are mob dungeons. The ancient dungeons are filled with relics, but the mob dungeons are how most adventurers earn their living. In the same way that hunters keep the animal populations in check, the council offers rewards for killing dungeon mobs once they start spilling out of the dungeon. It keeps the monsters from attacking the unprotected towns and villages outside of the kingdom. Plus, we get to bring back any items or materials we find to sell or trade at the market."

"That's interesting." Taryn takes a swig of juice before continuing. "What's the difference between an ancient dungeon and a mob dungeon?"

He took the words right out of my mouth. We've explored our fair share of dungeons, but this is the first time I've heard these terms.

Arty's eye sparkles with excitement as he speaks. "Ancient dungeons are far more dangerous than mob dungeons. They're sapient, and they usually form around areas dense with magical energy, whether it be a ley line or something else. They offer better loot because their goal is to try and kill you, and they've built their troves by taking the items of failed adventurers. They also spawn items created from the remains of fallen monsters."

"Hold up." Taryn's brow furrows. "So, you're telling me that these dungeons are alive?"

"In a manner of speaking."

"And what about mob dungeons?"

Arty grins. "They're just areas where monsters naturally congregate. Sometimes they're the ruins of ancient dungeons."

I take the last bite of my food and push my plate forward. "It sounds like every dungeon we've explored has been an ancient dungeon."

Arty slides his chair back, signaling that it's time to go. "For a hero, I don't doubt it."

A blue rooster struts through the Rusty Bucket stable when we arrive, crowing loudly. The thing is twice the size of a normal rooster with a purple mohawk that flares with each crow. The stable-hands are already hard at work for the day.

Breebis approaches from the back, her dark green hair pulled up in a messy bun as she shoos the rooster out of the way. "Go on now, the whole neighborhood is up."

Caustic trails behind her, slightly bigger than the day before. He nips at the rooster, sending it fluttering to the rafters. When he notices me, he leaps toward me, his wings flapping like leathery sails a few times as he closes the distance.

I cup my hands around his head, and he licks me with a sandpapery tongue. "Did you miss me? We're going to have some fun today."

"By the gods, is that a dragon?" Arty sounds impressed as he moves closer, extending a hand. "May I?"

"Don't blame me if you lose a limb." I wink as I step out of the way.

He carefully inches closer until he places the back of his hand on Caustic's head. "So young. He can't be more than a few weeks old."

I laugh. "You're a good judge."

"Arty used to be obsessed with dragons as a kid." Breebis smiles and nudges the cyclops in the leg. "It was practically all he talked about."

He shows no shame in the comment, still focused on Caustic. "Part of the reason I became an adventurer, actually. They're such majestic creatures. I've only ever seen one in the wild, though."

Breebis scratches the dragon behind the horns, and he leans into her. "He's taken to following me around everywhere I go. Keeps the other animals in check." She laughs, turning to Taryn. "Taking the full squad out today?"

"Yes, ma'am." Taryn nods. "We're clearing a dungeon with Arty and need all paws and hooves on deck."

After Breebis brings us Taryn's pets, we're ready to hit the road. This early in the morning, the streets are as sparse as I've seen them, only filled with those preparing to take on their work for the day.

Taryn climbs atop Berry and sets off in the direction of the outer gate.

"It'd take us all day to reach the dungeons on foot," Arty calls from behind us, pointing the opposite way. "Follow me, and I'll show you how we adventurers do it."

Caustic catches a lot more curious looks this early in the morning, and I begin to understand why. During the day, he doesn't seem out of place among the costumes and celebrations of the festival. We've seen so many dragon costumes that I'm sure most people don't even think he's an actual dragon. But no one is partying this early in the morning, and people take notice, especially when he's traveling with a cyclops and a blue-skinned troll.

Limery rides Caustic as Arty leads us through a few alleys and across cobbled streets. Jordy's hooves clack against the stone as he keeps next to Arty, always wanting to lead the way.

The Adventurers' Guild is rather plain compared to some of the other buildings in the area. A shield crossed with a bow and a sword hangs over the porch, with "Adventurers' Guildhall" engraved in an elegant script. The double doors are wide enough that we can fit Berry through without issue.

Inside, a grizzled old man sits behind a counter with his feet propped up. His gray beard is dense like a lumberjack's, with a thick walrus mustache. He smokes a pipe, blowing smoke rings that slowly rise before dissipating against the ceiling.

There are a few chairs around the room, and a notice board pinned with quests.

He sits up when we enter, eyeing us all with intrigue. "Arty! You're in rare company. And a dragon! What are you up to, my boy? Are these new recruits?"

Arty leans against the counter. "Just taking a few new friends out for a little dungeon therapy."

"You put the rest of us to shame." He inhales from his pipe and blows another large smoke ring. "If you all have an interest in joining the guild, you look like you'd make a good fit."

"I bet the life of a hero is more exciting than anything we could throw their way." Arty gently taps his fist on the counter before heading deeper into the guild. "No rest for the wicked. See you around, old man."

The old man lets out a hearty laugh. "To be young and spry. Give the new recruits a little hell for me on your way out."

We follow Arty down the hall, and it turns out the guildhall is even bigger than I imagined. The building is a giant square, with an open area in the center for training. We pass by a mess hall filled with long tables and a bar on the far end. On one side of the room, seasoned adventurers chat and laugh as they eat their breakfast. On the opposite side, the recruits eat in silence.

Arty stops by the recruits' table and narrows his lone eye at them. "Here I am about to hit the dungeons, and you lot haven't even finished your breakfast. Soft, I tell you. I used to be in the training pit at daybreak."

Laughter rings out from the adventurers at the far end as the recruits shovel their food faster.

Arty grins in our direction. "They'll be fine in time. It's the duty of us old-hands to give them a hard time. After a year of training, they'll be fit to test the world themselves."

Next, we pass the armory and the barracks before entering the open air of the training area. A veranda stretches around the perimeter. In the center, there's a sandpit and various stations dedicated to different styles of training. At the far back, there are five large boulders, each one painted a different color. A party of two gnomes, a human, and a lizardfolk stand around the purple boulder.

I stop in my tracks as the two gnomes touch the boulder and vanish into thin air.

"What the hell is that?" I ask as the lizardfolk disappears in the same manner.

"Portstones. They're very old magic used to travel short distances. They're not as powerful as a portal but accomplish the same goal on a shorter scale. Some of the guilds have one or two, but the Adventurers' Guild is the only place in Pruxford that has five. Their counterparts are scattered outside the city walls, allowing us to travel to the dungeons in a fraction of the time."

With a nod to Arty, the human touches the stone and vanishes.

Caustic jerks on his leash, pulling toward the stone, but I hold him firm. "How do they work?"

Arty laughs. "Don't worry. You won't accidentally port anywhere. They require a guildstone to activate, but if we're touching one another, we can port as a group."

We're a sight to behold as we gather around the yellow stone. Limery sits on my shoulder, and I hold Caustic by the tail. Beside me, Taryn and Ruby sit atop Berry. The bear has one paw on Jordy's back, and I grip Taryn on the leg. When we're ready, Arty grabs Taryn's forearm from the other side, and space distorts around me as the world goes black.

CHAPTER 27
LUCK OF THE DRAGON

THERE'S A SLIGHT POP, and we appear in a glade surrounded by trees on all sides. Limery's claws dig into my shoulder, and my stomach churns. I look to the trees overhead, taking steady breaths until the feeling passes.

"I think I'm gonna be sick." Taryn groans, followed by a splatter that I try not to picture.

Caustic seems unaffected as he jumps up and down excitedly. Apparently, he enjoyed the trip.

"The first time is always the worst." Arty grins as he pats Taryn on the back. "You'll get used to it."

Jordy prances around the lush meadow, and Caustic takes off in pursuit of the frost goat. A yellow boulder matching the one in the guildhall sits in the center of the clearing. Three well-trodden paths branch out from the portstone in different directions.

Arty points toward two of the trails. "Both of these lead to mob dungeons. Either one should do fine for us."

"What about the other one?" I nod toward the path leading in the opposite direction. After Hawkin's buff, I'd rather tackle a dungeon that provides some actual loot.

"That one is an ancient dungeon. We rarely tackle those, and the guild usually recommends a party of at least five. Even then it can be a struggle." He turns back to face the direction of the mob dungeons. "Not worth the risk."

Between Taryn's pets, my horrors, Caustic, and Limery, we're way stronger than the typical five-man party.

"I think we'll be alright." I summon a horror and smirk. "Taryn and I are feeling pretty lucky."

Arty reluctantly agrees to let us try the ancient dungeon on the condition that we retreat if things get too tough. The Pruxford countryside is as odd as the city itself, filled with rolling hills, giant mushrooms, and cartoonish trees with branches that curl and twist at odd angles. Some of them even grow hair instead of leaves. Massive gemstones sprout from the earth in clusters, making it evident how the city was able to build such lustrous crystal structures.

I summon horrors as we walk, and we fill Arty in on our playstyle and abilities. We keep a few of our abilities a secret, like my Champion summon and Taryn's Endless Night, just so he doesn't learn all of the tools in our toolbox. He shares his skills with us, but I'm sure he keeps a few hidden as well. As a warrior, Arty only has physical abilities, but they seem pretty formidable by his description.

While we follow the dirt path, I let Caustic roam without his leash. Breebis has definitely had a good effect on him, because he stays with us for the most part—only breaking off when he sees a creature or movement in the grass. I'm forced to give him a healing potion after he takes a bite out of a toxic ooze basking in the sun on the side of the trail.

Even with the portstone, we end up walking almost an hour to the ancient dungeon. For such a supposedly dangerous location, it doesn't look the part.

An arched cluster of gemstones forms the entrance, and an opalescent door with no handle blocks our entry. Speckled mushrooms line the path as we get closer, starting small and increasing in size until those by the entrance are several feet taller than me and Arty. As far as dungeons go, it seems pretty welcoming.

Arty stops at the entrance, his posture stiff. "Don't let the look of it fool you. She's out to kill you as much as the rest."

"She?" Taryn holds back a laugh from atop Berry.

The cyclops nods. "I always thought of dungeons as female. They're tough as nails and capable of ending you, but worth the effort if you treat them with respect and give them your all."

His answer takes me by surprise. It's a romantic thought for someone looking so brutish.

"I'll be honest, you act nothing like how I imagined you would based on your appearance." I pat Arty on the back and equip Destroyer. I'm not ready to reveal the weapons and armor I got from Wandermere quite yet, considering he could be an opponent if we qualify for the tournament. I do equip the Regeneration Stone in one of Destroyer's sockets, increasing my health regeneration by twenty percent. "Let's find out what Lady Luck has in store for us today."

Arty reaches into the satchel around his waist and pulls out a sword. The pommel is fitted with a polished emerald, with two more set at each end of the guard. The blade is beautiful, with dark gray swirls within the metal, and wider than anything I've ever seen, easily as wide as the cyclops's massive head. It seems never-ending as he pulls the weapon from the satchel.

I keep expecting to see the tip, but he continues to pull. When he finally frees it from his bag, the sword is nearly as tall as he is. He rests the flat of the blade against his broad shoulder, and it's almost comical.

"Damn! How do you fight with that thing?" I ask, still in awe.

He smirks, holding the sword in front of his body like it weighs nothing. "These muscles aren't for show."

"Sure you aren't overcompensating?" Taryn grins beneath his beard.

Arty laughs. "That's quite the insight from a dwarf who chooses to ride a bear. Were all the ponies taken by your kin?"

Taryn's cheeks flush with color. "Always with the short jokes."

I burst out laughing. "Let me get this straight. Everybody in Pruxford adores you. You're strong, perceptive, and quick-witted. How are you not married?"

Arty tosses the sword back over his shoulder and raises his lone eyebrow suggestively. "Why, are you interested?"

"Funny, too." Taryn joins in the laughter now that Arty's quick wit is at my expense. "This is going to be a fun day."

Arty digs a few more items from his satchel—a full set of studded leather armor and matching helm. We corral the animals and approach the dungeon entrance, where the door bars our entry. The opalescent door shimmers in the sun like oil on a water. Streaks of pastel blue and green seem like they are swirling within the stone. When I focus on it, a prompt appears.

Curio Dungeon. *Would you like to enter?*

I accept, and the door slides into the earth. The doorway expands, revealing a set of spiraling stairs that lead underground. Instead of torches, gemstones protrude from the wall, casting light in an array of colors. I send my horrors in first, all sixty of them. I might have overdone it, because it feels crowded as we make our way down. I follow the horrors, and Limery rides on

Caustic's back behind me, holding onto the dragon's horns for balance. Taryn and his pets are next, and Arty brings up the rear.

Once we're all inside, the door rises and locks us inside.

"So you've really never beat this dungeon?" Taryn asks Arty as we follow the spiraling stairs.

Arty shakes his head. "No, I've only been to a few ancient dungeons, and it's always been a challenge just making it back out after our first few fights. It's like I said, as adventurers, we do the jobs no one else wants or can do. We track down bounties, return stolen property, things that would take the guards away from their duty to protect the city. When the mob dungeons start to overflow, we deal with that, but ancient dungeons are a different beast. They're old magic, back from the time of heroes. Or I guess I should say the old age of heroes. Occasionally, a young adventurer will enter one to try and prove his toughness. But the truth is that if we don't bother them, they don't bother us."

All that to say we have no idea what we're up against. Which is no different than any other dungeon we've faced, and we managed to squeak out a victory time and time again.

Out of my sight, some of my horrors begin to lose health faster than normal. I ready Destroyer, and the rest of the party follows my lead. The monsters' grumbles sound louder than normal in the stairwell.

The horrors charge forward, and Caustic follows them. The air crackles as Limery summons a fireball in one hand while hanging onto the dragon's horn like a cowboy with the other.

"Keep him to the outskirts of the fight, Limery! I'm counting on you," I shout over the chaos.

"Limmy's on it."

I turn the final curve of the stairwell and empty into a room shaped like a massive halfpipe. Across the way, there's a door.

Clusters of gemstones hang from vaulted ceilings like stalactites, twenty to thirty feet off the ground.

A dozen furry balls about the size of a beachball roll from one side to the halfpipe to the other like bowling balls, crashing into and crushing my horrors, leaving a glittery trail in their wake. When they hit the other side, the balls rocket into the air, nearly touching the ceiling before gravity sends them plummeting back to the halfpipe to repeat the motion on the other side. Horrors that take a hit head-on explode on impact, and more lose their health in the dust that each ball leaves behind.

I focus on one of them to try and get an idea of what we're up against.

Floofer. Level 25. With bulbous blue eyes, and dainty paws as soft as silk, floofers may look cute and innocent, but these monsters have a vicious streak. Underneath their fluffy exterior sits an armored shell that can curl into a ball capable of wreaking immense havoc. While in ball form, their entire bodies remain protected, and they can generate enough force to self-propel, capable of escaping or wrecking anything unlucky enough to get caught in their path. Their fur contains a poisonous dust used in many death potions.

Shit, these things are going to be tough to stop.

Limery hits one of the floofers with a fireball. There's a small explosion as the fire interacts with the dust, burning away all of the hair but leaving the creature unaffected. Without the fur, it looks even more dangerous as it pummels through more horrors with its metallic shell.

One of the balls barrels toward Caustic out of the corner of my eye. I drop Destroyer without hesitating and pull him by the tail, saving him from death by only inches.

"Stay," I order, letting out a sigh of relief. "This is not your fight."

My horrors continue to drop left and right as they try to attack the floofers. Nearly a quarter of them are already gone, and the passive slow from the Horrors of Vitality is having no effect. "We've got to find a way to slow these things down. Taryn, can you summon a wall?"

He joins me at the edge of the stairwell, making it even more cramped as he lifts his staff. A twenty-foot-wide wall appears down the centerline of the room. There are several loud crashes in quick succession, and pieces of rubble rocket across the room.

A few of the floofers slow, only going a fraction of their normal height when they hit the ramp, but on the return, they self-propel, regaining their momentum in full. It only takes seconds for the wall to be reduced to rubble.

Taryn frowns as his wall comes crumbling down. "Dammit. The cooldown is too long for the walls to be useful."

"Any other ideas?" I look between Taryn and Arty.

Arty scratches his chin. "If we can get the floofers to open up, their underbelly is soft. We'll be able to kill them, no problem."

"I've got it!" Taryn shouts. "If we want to stop them, we just need to hit them with an equal force."

"And how do you plan on doing that?" I watch helplessly as more horrors vanish. I've pulled those I can onto the stairs, but more die by the minute as they try to play Frogger to return to the stairs.

"Not me, this is up to you two." He points at me and Arty. "Get out there and do what you do best. Smash."

"Say no more." I turn to Arty. "Ready to put those muscles to use?"

He stuffs the giant sword in his satchel and pulls out a dual-sided warhammer, slate gray with black runes etched along the handle. He snarls. "Let's do it!"

I sacrifice the remaining horrors that are stuck in the halfpipe of doom, flooding my body with increased Strength, Constitution, and Dexterity for the moment.

When the closest floofer comes rolling in my direction, I hit it with the flat end of Destroyer. The impact reverberates up my arm, shaking me to my core, but it works. The floofer unrolls, sitting dazed and confused in front of me. Bubbly blue eyes stare at nothing, and its dainty arms keep it from falling over. It's cute, I'll give it that, but it doesn't stop me from twisting the warhammer and bringing the pointed end down on the poor creature.

Behind me, Arty's arms take on a bluish aura as he swings his hammer. His arms don't so much as quiver from the impact.

"We're gonna hit them. The rest of you, finish them—" I jump over a speeding floofer that nearly takes out my legs, and the wrecking ball barrels toward the ramp on the other side. "—off."

The rest comes easy. Arty and I stun the creatures with our warhammers, and our party kills the floofers as they wobble with dazed expressions. Out of the corner of my eye, Caustic finishes off the last one, his muzzle covered in blood.

I kneel and he runs over to me, tail thrashing against rubble and dead floofers.

"What a good boy." I scratch him underneath the chin, and he groans with pleasure. He managed to gain two levels from the fight, bringing him up to eight.

Arty opens and closes his fist, his arm no longer glowing with the aura, reminding me of my own sore muscles.

I admire his weapon. "Those things sure packed a punch. You're pretty good with a warhammer."

He lifts it and gives the handle a spin against his palm. "There's not a weapon that exists that I can't wield."

"Ha! So much for being modest." Taryn strokes Ruby who sits on his lap.

The floor shakes, and a grating sound comes from behind us as one of the tiles in the center of the room sinks. A few seconds later, it emerges with a glowing chest.

"That's odd." Arty's lone brow furrows.

"What's odd?" I ask.

"Dungeons don't normally drop treasure in the first room."

Taryn hops down from Berry and runs over. "Must be our lucky day."

Thank you, Hawkin. The chest is smaller than most that we've found, but the magical aura is undeniable.

We gather around Taryn as he opens the lid, fighting against Jordy and Berry to see what's inside. Taryn pulls out a silver necklace with a black teardrop pendant. Gray smoke swirls within.

__Item. Whispers of the Damned. +3 Constitution.__ Infused with the last breaths of the dying, when this pendant is activated, the haunting voices of the dead will cast confusion upon their mark. For every kill accrued while wearing this necklace, Whispers of the Damned will gain a charge (Max. 3). Charges may be released to cast confusion on an enemy for up to five seconds. (Max. 3 charges per day)

Taryn holds the necklace up. "How should we divvy this up?"

Arty holds up a hand. "That's a little too sinister for my taste."

"Yeah, it's pretty fucking creepy." I consider taking it, but before I do, Limery flies over, plucking the necklace from Taryn's hand and draping it around his neck.

"Limmy wants its!" The necklace automatically resizes to his tiny neck. He holds the pendant between his fingers, admiring it.

"That's settled." I walk across to the room to where the other door has opened. It leads to a similar stairwell as the one we entered through. "Who's ready to see what's next?"

CHAPTER 28

LIGHTNING IN A BOTTLE

The stairwell spirals downward, nearly identical to the one we entered through. After a short descent, the floors and walls shake, and a loud grating noise comes from below. Jordy bleats at the sudden disturbance, and Caustic growls by my side. Ruby stands alert on Berry's back, staring intently down the stairs.

When the dungeon quits shaking, we all share a look of uncertainty.

"What the hell was that?" I pet Caustic reassuringly, his scales cool and smooth to the touch.

Taryn strokes Ruby, who hasn't looked away. "No idea, but something's up if Ruby is on alert. You know anything about this, Arty?"

"No idea." He shakes his head. "We can always turn back."

I squeeze his shoulder. "Come on, big guy. Where's the fun in that?"

He stares at me deadpan. "The fun is in the not dying. Lest you forget, I don't come back from death."

I give him my most heartfelt smile. "You're a world-class

adventurer. I trust you can handle anything that comes at us. Plus, we're stocked on potions and elixirs. You'll be fine."

He grunts affirmation, and Taryn and his pets lead the way as we continue downward until the stairs empty into the next level. Even though the others block my view, I can see fresh grass growing along the floor beyond the bottom step.

"Bunnies!" Limery pulls his hands to his chest as he gushes.

Caustic, sensing prey, takes off running down the stairwell before I have a chance to inspect the room.

"Stop!" I yell, but he's already out of reach, claws clicking against each stair as he races downward.

A wall appears in front of the stairwell, and Caustic crashes into it.

"You're welcome." Taryn gives me a knowing look, his staff pointed in front of him.

Thank goodness for Stonewall. I let out a sigh of relief and grab Caustic, putting the leash on him.

"I hope that didn't use up all our luck." I kneel, looking into the dragon's golden eyes. "Do not go running off like that again."

He huffs and bites at the leash.

Tiny thuds sound against the other side of the wall, similar to darts hitting a board.

"Did anyone get a good look at what was in there? Everything happened so fast that I didn't see more than the grass."

"There was bunnies with hornses." Limery's bulbous eyes flash with excitement.

No one else got a good look aside from Limery. The thuds grow less and less until they stop altogether. The enemy aggro must have disappeared once they could no longer see us.

I summon a few more horrors while we try to come up with a game plan. "How many did you see?"

Limery hovers in the air, waving his arms wildly as he speaks. "Oh, theres was lots of bunnies. Lots and lots."

"Alright, once Taryn cancels his wall, we fan out into the room and try to get an idea of what we're dealing with. I think we've lost their aggro, but the ones at the entry point will lock onto us pretty fast. We take them out first. Taryn, do you think you can use Imbue on Caustic once we're inside? Whatever these things are might be a little more hesitant to attack him if he's bigger."

Taryn nods. "Not a problem."

Arty trades out his warhammer for the giant sword once again. I'm actually excited to see it in action.

After I summon another set of horrors, I face the others. "We ready?"

They all confirm, and Taryn cancels Stonewall.

Nearly a dozen bunnies fall to the ground as soon as the wall vanishes. They're all about the size of a large house cat, each one with speckled rainbow fur and a shimmering spiral horn that's about a foot long. The thuds must have been them lodging their horns in Taryn's wall.

My horrors swarm the bunnies, pinning them to the ground before they have a chance to attack. I cast Kamikaze, and the horrors explode, taking out nearly three-quarters of the bunnies' health.

"Caustic, gas them, then everyone get back," I order as I take cover up the stairwell.

He responds to my command, sending a stream of green gas that shrouds the bunnies.

Once we're out of range, Limery tosses a fireball and the gas ignites. Warm air rushes up the stairs, and we charge into the room.

I step over the charred remains and move to the left, quickly taking in our surroundings. This level is a similar size to the previous one but designed differently. It's all flat, with grass and boulders from end to end. The walls are made of polished stone and the ceiling glows with the light of gemstones. Close to two dozen more bunnies are scattered around the room, all standing on their hind legs, suddenly aware of our presence.

Bunnycorn. Level 25. *While they may look as cute as their non-horned counterparts, bunnycorns are deadly and tenacious. The vampiric bunnies travel in packs, hunting prey three to four times their size and using their horns to impale enemies before draining them of their blood.*

Vampiric bunnies? You have got to be shitting me.

Taryn casts Imbue on Caustic, just as a bunnycorn launches itself in my direction. Its powerful hind legs propel it like it was shot out of a cannon. I duck out of the way, and the creature snarls at me as it flies past until its horn clatters against the smooth stone of the wall. Whatever the dungeon walls are made of is a lot harder than Taryn's wall, because the horn just bounces off it.

Next to me, Caustic has doubled in size, taking on the appearance of a formidable dragon and giving me a glimpse into what the future holds. He breathes his toxic gas, and it spreads across the floor like fog. It doesn't do much damage, draining barely a sliver of HP at a time. But when Limery's fire hits it, bunnycorns explode across the room.

A sharp pain flares through my left shoulder, and I lose my grip on Destroyer, dropping it to the floor. I look down to see a bunnycorn horn buried in my chest all the way to the creature's head. The demonic bunny digs its claws into me as it tries to pry itself free. Every movement sends pain like hot iron through my chest and back, and I'm pretty sure it has pierced me all the way through.

I wrap my good hand around the bunny and squeeze until

bones crack. In a quick and painful motion, I rip the horn free and throw the bunny against the wall with everything I can muster. It hits the wall and falls motionless to the ground. The wound suddenly feels icy, and I lose my breath for a moment.

"Fuck." I grunt as I pick up Destroyer. The pain starts to subside as my increased healing takes effect.

Fire and lightning rage around the room as Taryn and Limery wreak havoc. Taryn has used his Sapling Staff to form a protective cage out of vines on Berry's back, preventing the bunnycorns from attacking him. Two of them dangle from the cage with their horns stuck between the vines. Jordy prances around the room, ramming anything that gets too close to him.

At the far side, Arty's sword cuts through two bunnies with a powerful slash as they jump through the air, sending a stream of blood along the wall. He spins, moving the massive blade like a trained dancer, decapitating another.

Caustic rips a bunny to shreds with his claws, but he doesn't notice a second one running toward him from his side. The bunny sets its feet and launches at the dragon.

I call out to him, trying to get his attention to the blindside attack, but he doesn't hear me. There's no way he'll react in time, and I'm too far away to do anything helpful. I ready a health potion, cursing myself for bringing him here before he was ready and hoping that it will be enough to save him.

The bunnycorn horn aims for Caustic's throat, and my heart sinks. Then it bounces off of his body like it hit a metal wall and falls to the ground. Caustic turns, annoyed, and snatches the bunny in his teeth, tossing it in the air and swallowing it whole.

Tension releases from my entire body. Even a level-eight dragon is a dangerous enemy. I've been babying him for nothing.

"Good jo—"

Pain tears me from the moment as a second bunnycorn

impales me, this time in the ribs. I pry it out, rage battling against the pain as I throw it to the ground and stomp its body with a sickening crunch.

"Fucking bunnies!" I shout as I activate Berserker Rage. "I've had enough of these motherfucking bunnies in this motherfucking dungeon!"

My vision goes red as I unleash a roar, and my healing kicks into overdrive. I swing my warhammer like a madman. It flares red with stacks of Inferno, splattering scorched bunnycorn corpses against the wall and floor. In this moment, I want nothing more than to kill every last one of these annoying little fuckers. Steam radiates from my skin as sweat mixes with bunny blood. Thanks to my Spirit of the Beast path, my rage lasts twice as long as it used to. When Berserker Rage finally wears off, I stand there heaving.

Arty and Taryn both look at me with a mixture of shock and amusement, while Limery tries to pry the horn off a dead bunnycorn.

Taryn stares, his mouth halfway open stuck between a smile and gaping wonder. "You alright, bro?"

"Did no one else get impaled?" I toss my hands up in frustration. "The little fuckers got me twice."

Arty bursts out laughing. "We've got lots of potions and elixirs. You'll be fine."

I just shake my head. "Famous last words, right?"

Taryn and Limery join in the laughter, and pretty soon, I do too.

"Your barbarian rage is impressive," Arty says as he stows his weapon.

Taryn climbs down from Berry. "Yeah, he's got anger issues. It's kind of his thing."

I roll my eyes. "It is not my *thing*. I don't have a thing."

The dungeon groans, interrupting our banter, and a chest appears in the center of the room, similar to the one before. We gather around it, and Taryn flips the latch. Inside, there's a steel blue helm with an open face and cheek guards. A crest of silver feathers with blue tips lines the top of the helm like a mohawk.

Item. Helm of Resolution. +3 Dexterity. *While equipped, consecutive attacks within two seconds of one another increase the user's attack speed by 1%, stackable up to 25%.*

"Nice," Arty whispers.

"That's a nice helm. A twenty-five percent bonus is pretty damn good." I grab it from the chest, admiring the craftsmanship, then I hand it to Arty. "Here, you deserve it."

He hesitates before taking it. "Are you sure?"

I point to my head. "I think I'm well beyond headgear at this point, and you more than earned it. I saw you slashing bunnycorns to pieces while I was becoming a Chod-kabab." I instinctively touch my shoulder where the first bunnycorn impaled me. "Besides, we wouldn't even be here without you. Put it to good use."

He removes his current helm and puts on the Helm of Resolution. It fits perfectly above his massive eye. "There is something strange going on with this dungeon. I can feel it."

"Maybe we're just lucky." I flash him a mischievous grin.

While we get ready for the next floor, Taryn heals a few minor wounds on Berry and Jordy, and I take a moment with Caustic while I summon more horrors.

With his imbued size, I'm able to look him in the eye while standing. "You did a good job during that last fight, and I think it's time I quit treating you like a baby. You're growing up fast. You're a strong and powerful dragon, and it's time I let you show it. You have my back and I'll have yours, got it?"

He licks me with his forked tongue, and I chuckle.

"Yeah, you've got it. And you gained another level, too, look at you." At level nine, he's catching up fast.

By the time we're ready to move on, Imbue has worn off, and Caustic has returned to his normal size.

Taryn approaches me and Caustic. "I'm gonna use Imbue on him again if you don't mind. It was pretty cool having a big-ass dragon fighting beside us."

"Go for it. He's an intimidating presence, that's for sure. And I think it's time to see what he's really capable of, because I had no idea his scales were that tough."

"I'm sure he's full of secrets." Taryn reaches out and pets Caustic. "We ready to get moving?"

Midway through our next descent, the dungeon shakes again, and I get the feeling that the rooms are somehow shifting into place. Maybe randomly, or possibly they are being influenced by our increased luck.

The next room is a plain slate gray on all sides, and the gemstones along the ceiling are dimmer than in the other rooms. Clusters of oddly-shaped mushrooms grow from cracks in the floor.

There are giant snails scattered around the room, along with slimy iridescent trails that follow them along the floor, walls, and ceiling. The snails' translucent shells reveal their colorful organs. Two long tentacles stretch from their pastel bodies, each one tipped with a giant bloodshot eyeball encased in a cluster of crystals.

Flail Snail. Level 25. Don't let their fragile appearance fool you. Though they move at a snail's pace on unslimed terrain, flail snails can travel with amazing speed along the slick paths they leave behind. Their tentacled eyestalks are capable of elongating, and when closed, they can be used as weapons. Once prey is subdued, the snail will devour it with the thousands of teeth hidden within its mouth flaps.

I shiver after reading the last line. Just what we wanted, snails with weapons for eyes, thousands of teeth, and probably a tough ass shell to go with it. This will be fun.

The snails move incredibly slow as they cling to the walls and ceiling, but as soon as we enter the room, their tentacles stiffen, and close to fifty eyes turn in our direction. Their sludgy mouths flap like a flag in the wind as they make a sound like blowing a raspberry. I'm guessing it's supposed to be a hiss or a growl of some kind, but it's not at all intimidating.

Until I see the vortex of teeth that looks like something from a horror movie.

The area around the entryway is clear of their slime trail, which doesn't start until about thirty feet from where we stand. There's no immediate danger of them speeding over, so we have a little time to formulate a plan.

"This'll be interesting." I ready Destroyer as the first snails start crawling over. "Limery, see if you can burn away the slime trail."

"Limmy's on it!" He flies over, summoning a firewall on a patch of slime. It sizzles beneath the flames, taking a good ten seconds to burn away.

It works, but not quick enough.

Caustic blows his toxic gas, and it settles around the snails in the center of the room. They immediately retract into their shells, taking no damage from the poisonous smoke once inside. Limery throws a fireball, and the explosion rockets them in all directions but they still don't take any damage while hidden within their shells.

When the snails hit the floor, their gelatinous bodies emerge, clinging to the stone and flipping the shells upright. One of them at the far back hits a slick of slime and zooms to the middle with blazing speed, coming to an abrupt halt once it reaches the unmarked flooring.

"Holy shit!" Taryn's eyes go wide. "Stay out of their slime trails. Those things travel faster than the floofers."

Several more connect to the slime trails, and pretty soon there are half a dozen looming ever closer. I summon more horrors and get ready to smash the snails across the room with Destroyer.

The closest group of snails all stop except for two that move in separate directions. One heads toward Arty on the far end, and the other toward me and Caustic. After a short distance, they quit advancing as well.

The snails close their eyes, turning their tentacles into crystal-tipped flails, and whip them in a circle like a cowboy readying a lasso. With each rotation, the tentacles grow longer, until they are spinning in a blur only a few feet from where Caustic and I are standing.

They suddenly seem a lot more menacing. The snail flails whir as they spin, and I prepare to take a swing.

I urge Caustic to back away and swing with all my might. Destroyer hits the flailing eyes with a clank. I expect the change in momentum to carry the snail to the back wall, but its body suctions to the floor and the flails circle back around, hitting me in the back. Jagged crystal rips into my spine with enough force that I drop to my knees.

All around the room, snails flap their gelatinous mouths at my pain. Somewhere nearby, Limery voices his concern.

The snail retracts its dangling eyes and whips them at me again. Caustic pounces on the snail, wrapping his mouth around its shell as he flutters by and causing the flails to smash against the wall. When his feet hit the ground, he slips in the slime trail, and his legs shoot out from under him. He falls on his back with a thud, and the snail retracts its eyes to a shorter length, pummeling the dragon with its flails.

There's a flash of red, and Limery is by my side. He activates Whispers of the Damned, and a silvery wisp shoots from the pendant. It hits the snail in the face, wispy tendrils dissipating into the creature's body, and the flails go limp as the snail wobbles in place.

The confusion won't last long, so I try to crawl to my feet. Out of the corner of my eye, Arty leaps across the room. His massive sword trails behind him like some badass action hero, and the plumage on his new helm ruffles as he covers nearly twenty feet in a single bound.

He lands inches from the slime trail, bringing his sword around in a blur and severing the snail's tentacles. The blade stops inches from slicing me in half in an amazing display of strength and control. The snail screeches as its eyes clatter to the floor, and Arty kicks the snail with enough force that it bounces off a mushroom near the back wall before crawling blindly away.

Arty offers me a hand. "New plan. Chod and I cut off their eyes, then they'll be easier to deal with. The rest of you try to find a way to kill the slimy bastards."

Limery, Taryn, and the others gather by the stairwell as more snails approach from across the room. I search through my inventory for anything sharp, but all I have are magical staffs, a spear, and a trident. Nothing with a sharp blade.

"You don't happen to have an extra sword, do you?"

"An adventurer is always prepared." Arty grins as he reaches in his satchel, pulling out a short sword. "You break it, you bought it."

Item. Brightblade. +2 Strength. *With every consecutive attack, the enchanted metal within Brightblade grows brighter. Once out of combat, the blade will dim 1% every minute.*

Sounds like a weird weapon, but it's better than nothing. I equip my Halite Shield in one hand and Brightblade in the other, avoiding the slime trail as Arty and I press the attack. The translucent shield allows me to see exactly where I'm going while using it as a riot shield to block their flails.

The closest snails whip their tentacles at our approach, and in seconds, the flails are whirring through the air.

I extend the shield and the flails bounce off, wiggling on the ground as the snail tries to retract them.

"Not so fast." I swing down with Brightblade and sever both tentacles.

The blade takes on a dull glow as the snail retracts into its shell. Arty has blinded his as well, so we press forward again.

Arty takes a more direct approach, using the length of his blade to his advantage and chopping the tentacles from a safe distance.

"Kick them back here," Taryn calls from behind. "I've got an idea."

As I pass the blinded snail retracted into its shell, I kick it backward to Taryn.

It rattles against the floor as the shell bumps along. Taryn climbs down from Berry and equips his Shadow Daggers. The shadowy blades pass through the shell without issue, capable of draining the life force from the snail without having to actually break through the tough exterior.

He says something to Limery, and the imp presses molten hands onto the next shell Arty kicks. His molten form is far hotter than his normal fire, causing steam to pour from the shell's opening as the snail shrivels at the intense heat.

Something splats beside me, and I turn to see a flail snail has fallen from the ceiling. It attacks me with its flails but only manages a few hits before I sever both spiked tentacles.

Arty and I stay close together, pressing forward and severing tentacles while kicking them back to Taryn and Limery to finish off. More snails fall from the ceiling, but now that we know to expect them, we respond quickly. By the time the room is clear, Brightblade shines so bright that it's almost blinding to look directly at it.

"That's some blade." I hand it back to Arty.

"That she is." He slides the blade into his satchel. "Not the most practical in many situations, but perfect for clearing mobs in a dark cave."

"I can imagine." I raise my arms overhead, stretching out the stiffness from the beating I just took. "That was great teamwork, everybody. The way everyone fell into position and adapted when things went south, I don't think we could have planned it any better."

When the room groans, we already know what to expect. We head to the center of the room, where a chest rises from the sunken tile.

Taryn opens it, pulling out a glass bottle topped with metal prongs.

"Hell yeah!" He looks at the bottle with admiration.

When I analyze it, I see why he's so excited.

Item. Lightning in a Bottle. *This one-time use item is capable of holding up to five charges of electricity. When the bottle is broken, charges will release, damaging up to five enemies within a 50-foot radius with a 50% chance to stun. To store a charge, simply leave the bottle outside during a lightning storm and the prongs will attract lightning bolts.*

Not bad at all. "Assuming you can use your spell to charge it, that has your name written all over it."

"Only one way to find out." Taryn places the bottle on the ground. "Everybody stand back."

He casts Lightning Bolt, and an arc of lightning shoots from above, striking the bottle. Once my ears quit ringing, I notice that there are bolts of electricity jumping throughout the bottle.

Taryn picks it up, admiring the miniature storm within. "With it being a one-time use, I'll need to make sure not to waste it, but it's essentially five Lightning Bolts at once without having to wait for the cooldown. A fifty-percent chance to stun isn't bad either."

We stay a little longer than normal before heading to the next level so that Taryn can fully charge the item, just in case we need it. I use the time to summon more horrors. Even though Caustic didn't play a major role on this floor, he still managed to gain another level, bringing him up to level ten.

In between our ability cooldowns, we ask Arty what he knows about the tournament.

He shrugs. "With this being the quincentennial tournament, it's hard to know what to expect. There are tournaments in most of the bigger cities, some big and some small, but Pruxford's is the most prestigious. Usually, the Pruxford tournament is invitation only, with the field consisting of either eight or twelve of the best fighters from across Mythos. This year, they added qualifiers, so there's a chance that a dark horse could make a name for themselves. I even saw a few farmhands entering," he says, grinning. "It was five hundred years ago that four heroes battled one another to be crowned the first champion. I think it's fitting that heroes might once again compete. But don't expect us to take it easy on you."

Limery perches on my shoulder, holding his pendant with one hand. "And we's won't takes it easy on yous, either." He crosses his arms, looking intimidating before ruining his bravado with laughter.

Arty grins. "That's the spirit, little one."

The dungeon shakes as we descend to the next level, where we fight a group of Rattling Ferretsnakes. The poisonous furry creatures have the head and tail of a rattlesnake with a six-legged body of a ferret. Taryn makes a point of letting us all know that a group of ferrets is called a business. I don't want to go anywhere near the rabbit hole of how he knows that information.

For the first time in this dungeon, we show them the business, destroying them with overwhelming force.

The chest on this level gives us a Nullification Bomb, which completely disables magical abilities for thirty minutes for anyone or anything caught within its blast radius. I put it in my inventory, but I have a feeling the best is yet to come.

On the next level, we face Armor Golems. The sentient plate armor is heavy and thick, but once I get full stacks of Inferno, the armor dents with every blow. Taryn uses Stonewall to separate one from the group, and the rest of our party focuses on distracting the others as I work my way through them one at a time, hammering away until the armor is nothing more than a pile of warped metal.

The dungeon drops a Vapor Elixir, which allows the user's body to take on a gaseous form for up to an hour. I hand it to Arty, and he tries to refuse.

He pushes the bottle of gray liquid back to me. "The helm was more than enough. I'm sure this will be more useful to you on one of your heroic adventures."

"Actually, that's what we were hoping to talk to you about." I hold out the elixir again. "Consider it a gift for listening to our proposition."

He reluctantly takes the bottle and stuffs it in his satchel. "Alright, let's hear it."

I sit on one of the crumpled pieces of armor, taking a drink of cool water from my Brimming Tankard before passing it around. "What do you know about Valmar Worren?"

"The elvish necromancer? Every child learns about the atrocities of the dark elves in school." He furrows his brow. "Why, what does that have to do with you?"

I look him straight in the eye, leaving no room for misinterpretation. "We believe he's still out there."

He starts to laugh, but then he frowns. "Oh, you're serious. What makes you think that?"

"King Orso believes he's still alive," Taryn answers. "He was never killed, and dark elves can live for centuries." Arty starts to argue, but Taryn holds up a hand, continuing. "It's not just that. A behemoth came through the Seascape Portal. Mesmer wisps threatened to overtake Wandermere. Another hero has made a pact with some dark god or being, with the goal of stopping us from gaining allies. There is movement from the shadowlands, and we don't know when or where, but an attack is imminent."

Arty stares at the ground. I can imagine it's a lot to take in.

After a long moment, he removes the helm and rubs his head. "Say I do believe you. Say there are forces gathering in the shadowlands. What does that have to do with me?"

I stand up, and there's a tightness in my chest that I can't shake. "If Valmar is out there, do you think he's waited hundreds of years to launch a half-assed attack? I don't. I think he's testing us slowly, sending monsters in a few at a time and sealing the portals until he's ready. If he brings an army through those portals, it will be with the intention of taking everything you and I and everyone else in this world holds dear. I don't—" My voice cracks, and I take a breath. "No, I can't lose that. Not any of it. So, when the time comes, we want you on our side."

"Shit." He sighs.

"Yeah, shit."

His eye narrows to a slit. "Why have we not heard about any of this?"

My grip tightens around Destroyer as our conversation with Felston replays in my mind. "Because only one of the councilmembers was in Seascape when the behemoth attacked, and even though he believes the threat is real, the rest of the council do not. They think King Orso is overreacting because Seascape is the newest portal to open."

Arty grunts. "Pruxford has one of the largest standing armies in Mythos. Without them..."

He leaves the rest unsaid. Without them, we are fucked.

Taryn pours water from the Brimming Tankard into a bowl for his pets, and they all flock around it. "This is the real reason why we entered the tournament. If we win, then we can speak to the council directly."

Arty's mouth tightens, and I can tell he's deep in thought. "If I win, I will let you speak to them in my place. And I will do all within my power to sway the Adventurers' Guild to your cause, with or without Pruxford." He extends a hand, and I grab it. "Though I may live to regret it."

I squeeze his hand firmly before letting go. "The barmaid was right about you. You are a good man."

He tosses his sword over his shoulder. "Enough of that. Let's go kill some shit."

My shoulders relax, and the tension fades from my chest as we prepare for the next level. If Arty can somehow convince the Adventurers' Guild to join the fight, they're the next best things to heroes.

"That went better than expected," Taryn whispers.

I nod. "Yeah, but I have a feeling he would have said yes even without the increased luck."

The extra time on this level allowed me to summon a full army of horrors, and sixty of them pack into the stairwell before us.

"Alright, everyone, ready up!" I call to the group and they all gather behind us.

Jordy lowers his head, forcing his way through my horrors until he's at the front. A Horror of Finesse climbs on the frost goat's back, holding on to his horns. We push forward, and a moment later, the dungeon shudders.

Lush green grass covers the floor of the next level. We fan out as we enter the room, with me and Caustic to the far right. Taryn and his pets are in the center, and Arty and Limery are to the left. On the far end, a group of small, blue-horned, pink minotaurs with big heads lie sleeping in the grass. They stir as we enter, standing and crossing their arms.

Mini Manataur. Level 26. *Small and mighty, until they're not. The manataur's name is derived from its ability to drain mana directly from opponents' bodies using its horns. The more mana a manataur consumes, the larger, more powerful, and more self-obsessed it becomes.*

Self-obsessed? I have no idea what that means. They're like cute little chibi versions of Dakota, the minotaur gladiator we fought to enter Goldspire.

Taryn snickers. "This has to be a joke, right?"

"Don't let their appearance fool you. If they're in this dungeon, then these are dangerous enemies." Arty readies his sword.

My horrors charge in, and the manataurs move in unison, planting one leg behind them and bending the other in front while they tilt their giant heads forward. Their horns point at the approaching wave of horrors.

This must be some kind of defensive stance, but my horrors should bowl them over with overwhelming numbers.

The Horrors of Finesse lead the way, sprinting through the grass on spindly legs slightly ahead of the others. As they're about to swarm the manataurs, I experience a strange sensation as my connection to their normally steady presence wavers. Usually, I can tell exactly where they are at all times, even if I can't see them. Their presence only vanishes when they die. This feels different. Something is definitely off.

And then I see why. The horrors grow wispy at the edges, their bodies turning to smoke that funnels into the tips of the manataurs' horns. As the smoke gets sucked into the horns, the manataurs grow, muscles bulging and limbs elongating. In a matter of seconds, the Horrors of Finesse are nothing more than a memory.

The Horrors of Power are not far behind, their powerful legs propelling them forward like a lion on the hunt.

I call them off, but it's too late. Their rear legs dig into the ground in an attempt to stop, but their momentum carries them sliding across the grass. Half of the horrors are already dissipating, their tusks and massive heads wisping away and funneling into the manataurs' horns like ships caught in a whirlpool. More horrors slam into one another and suffer the same fate.

Only a few manage to turn tail and retreat, along with the Horrors of Vitality.

"Chod, what the hell just happened?" Taryn watches with a confused expression.

"I guess my horrors are made of mana? I don't fucking know."

The manataurs continue to morph until they're nearly six feet tall and their bodies finally match their disproportionate heads.

"Jesus, man." Taryn grimaces. "You just gave them a fucking buffet."

I cast Sacrifice on the remaining horrors, boosting my Constitution and adding a few points to Strength. I'd rather use them now than lose more to the manataurs. "Any idea how we beat these guys when we can't get near them?"

The manataurs are easily twice as big as they were before.

They stand across the room flexing their muscles and shooting steam out of their nostrils like furry bodybuilders. Maybe that's what the description meant by self-obsessed.

Arty growls as he reaches into his inventory, pulling out a glowing silver potion. "I didn't want to use this, but it might be our only option. Do you have any throwables?"

"Yes!" Taryn's eyes light up. "The Boom Dust!"

"Boom Dust?" Arty scrunches his brow. "Never heard of it, but if it does damage, we can make it work. This is a Frozen Earth potion. It will freeze the manataurs in place for ten seconds. If you can summon a wall and leave a little space at the top to throw your items, it should amplify the damage in an enclosed space."

"Dammit," Taryn says, frowning. "We don't have time to make a fuse, though."

"We don't need a fuse if we shatter the vials against the wall. Summon the wall after I toss the bomb, and Limery can hit it with a fireball." I pull out a vial of Boom Dust from my inventory. You'd never know the power of the pinkish-purple substance just by looking at it. I show the vial to Arty. "These are no joke. When they go off, we'll need to be in the stairwell."

"Alright, then let's hurry." Arty makes sure we're ready, and then he tosses the Frozen Earth potion.

A yellow aura surrounds Arty's body as he throws the potion, and it rockets across the room with the force of a major league pitcher. The bottle hits one of the manataurs and shatters, its contents exploding in all directions. Icy tendrils stretch out rapidly, covering the posing manataurs in a layer of frost and freezing them in place. The way they stand there posing reminds me of a renaissance painting.

I don't waste any time, equipping a half-dozen vials of Boom Dust and chucking them toward the far wall. They shatter upon impact, raining glitter on the frozen manataurs. I grab Caustic's attention, and we run for the stairs. Taryn's staff glows and Stonewall activates, summoning a wall with about a two-foot gap at the top.

"Now, Limery!" I shout.

The imp throws a fireball, then he zooms to the stairwell. Taryn and his pets are barely ahead of me, and Arty is already out of sight. A second later, there's a massive explosion.

The floor shakes, and a tidal wave of hot air rushes past us, followed by searing pain as flames kiss my back, peeling away layers of flesh.

I fall forward onto Caustic, and his scales sizzle against my skin like a hot iron as they scorch my frontside. The fire disappears as quickly as it came, but everything burns, even with my phoenix feather negating some of the damage. A notification flashes in the corner of my vision, but all I can focus on is the stinging sensation as my body begins to heal itself. I pop a health potion to speed up the process and check on the others.

Caustic nuzzles his head against me and licks at my peeling skin. His tongue is like sandpaper, but I appreciate the affection.

"Is yous okay, Chods?" Limery pats my head, his bulbous eyes full of concern.

"I'll be fine. How's everyone else?"

There's a loud groan, and I stand up to see Taryn with a golden aura as he hovers over Berry. His eyes are focused as he casts Restoration. The umber bear's backside is hairless and inflamed, but the others are fine. He must have shielded them with his massive frame. Berry whines as his flesh returns to its normal coloring and hair sprouts along his back.

Jordy licks Berry's forehead, matting the bear's fur while Ruby tries to tend to his wounds.

Arty peeks his head around the stairwell. "You weren't kidding, were you? That was something else."

By the time Taryn's finished healing Berry, my own skin is nearly back to normal.

Taryn pets Berry affectionately, and the bear nuzzles against his chest. "I think we might have overdone it a bit."

"Yeah, that was definitely overkill. One to two vials might have been enough."

When we return to the room, it's nothing more than scorched earth and charred remains. Every single manataur is burnt to a crisp.

The floor shakes, and a pristine chest rises to the surface. I'm the first one there, so I open the chest. At the bottom, there's a dark purple stone with a bright red center.

*Item. **Effect Stone.** Effect: Return to Sender. When activated, the item equipped with this effect stone will automatically return to user. Cooldown: 1 hour.*

This is an awesome stone, and I really want it, but I didn't clear this room by myself. I hold the stone between my thumb and index finger, showing it to the others.

"Do you have any weapons that hold enchanted stones?" I ask Arty.

He grins. "Those weapons are hard to come by, even for adventurers. It's all yours."

"Yeah, take it, bro," Taryn chimes in. "I can't count the number of times you lost your weapon during battle."

He has a point. I pull out Destroyer, and when I hold the stone to my weapon, a notification appears.

Effect Stone. Would you like to equip effect stone to Destroyer? 1/3 slots filled.

I accept, and the purple stone fits perfectly into the socket beneath the Mana Stone. Enchanted stones have been hard to come by, but I still have one slot left if I find another. They aren't permanently bonded to the weapon, but it takes time to unpair the stone and attach it to another weapon, so I'm not exactly switching them out mid-battle.

Having this new ability means I can use Destroyer in a variety of new ways, even throwing it. The effect might only work once per hour, but that doesn't mean it won't be invaluable.

Another notification flashes in the corner of my vision, and I remember that I never checked the ones from after the fight.

I hold up a finger. "Give me a second while I check my notifications."

Congratulations! You have reached level 27. +1 stat point to distribute. +1 Strength and Constitution racial bonus. +1 ability point to distribute.

Alert! *Luck of the Dragon has ended.*

When I focus on the others, both Taryn and Arty gained a level after the last fight. Those manataurs must have been packing a lot of experience.

Caustic is now up to level fourteen, and Limery is only one level behind me. Damn, we definitely put that buff to good use.

I have an ability point to use, and I can finally unlock the final stage of my Spirit Path. Even though I trust Arty, I don't want to give away any secrets before the tournament. I send Taryn a message.

Message (Chod): *Let's wait until we're back at the inn to allocate our stats. I'd like to keep any new abilities a secret for now.*

Incoming message (Taryn): *Lol. Why do you think I didn't say anything?*

Taryn looks at me and rolls his eyes. "I think we've grinded about as much as we can today. You gents ready to head back to town?"

"This was an experience, I'll tell you that." Arty takes a deep breath, exaggerating it as he exhales. "Arty is going to sleep like a log tonight."

"We couldn't have done it without you." I pat him on the back. "I'm sure the guild will want to hear all about it."

"Ha, they won't believe a word of it."

With that, we head back up the stairs toward the exit.

CHAPTER 29
STATS ON STATS

WHEN WE MAKE it out of the dungeon, it's nearly nightfall. Only a sliver of sunlight peeks over the mountains in the distance. My hands tingle with excitement at the prospect of unlocking a new ability, and I'm constantly pulling up my character sheet as we walk. I'm equally excited to see what Taryn picks.

I'm analyzing how best to allocate the eight stat points I have saved up when I bump into Berry's backside.

The bear grunts, and I close out the interface. "What's going on?"

Taryn shrugs. "Not sure. Something is in the path."

Both Caustic and Jordy are gathered around a small, translucent green blob in the middle of the trail. Caustic sniffs at the blob and a gooey appendage reaches out and smacks him before the entire thing goes bouncing down the road like a slinky.

"It's a slime!" Taryn claps his hands excitedly and urges Berry forward. "I've always wanted one. Don't let it escape."

Limery zooms ahead and casts a flame wall across the road. "Stop it, slimesies."

The slime stops in front of the flame wall and slinks to the right, where Caustic is waiting. It jumps back to the left, but Jordy has it pinned. The slime shrinks in on itself, trembling.

As it sits there, terrified to move, I notice there are small objects inside of the slime. Some pebbles and leaves that it must have absorbed while traveling. Two pebbles move to the top, and its body morphs into the shape of a miniature cartoon ghost. The pebbles form eyes, and the area just beneath shifts into what looks like a mouth, then a cartoonish scream pours out.

"I'm sorry, dude. This will only hurt for a minute." Taryn leaps off Berry with a Shadow Dagger in one hand, landing in front of the slime.

The ghastly slime vibrates in what I assume is sheer terror as Taryn plunges the dagger into its midsection. Its health drops quickly, and Taryn removes the shadowy blade once it hits five percent, picking up the gelatinous creature and cradling it in his arms.

When he activates Tame, a tendril of yellow energy flows from Taryn's hand to the critically-injured slime. Once the bond is complete, the slime's health starts to rise and it congeals back into a denser version.

Taryn looks down on the cradled slime like an adoring parent. "There we go. Nothing to worry about, little guy. Welcome to the family."

The slime gurgles, a much happier sound than before, and it slinks up Taryn's arm, settling on his shoulder. I've got no idea what Taryn plans to do with a slime that's smaller than his own head, but if it makes him happy, I'm all for it.

Taryn grins from ear to ear. "I've got the perfect thing for him."

He reaches in his satchel and pulls out a large potion bottle and some rope. He holds the bottle up to his shoulder, and the slime jumps in, morphing to fit the shape of the bottle. A small bit of slime peeks above the top, two pebbly eyes looking out.

Taryn takes the rope and ties each side beneath the lip of the bottle, making a sling that fits over his shoulder. "This will do until I have a chance to buy something better." He turns to the rest of us. "Isn't he cute?"

Limery hovers in the air, bulbous eyes watching the slime as it moves within the bottle. "The slimesies is so cutes."

The slime container rests against Taryn's side like a purse as he climbs onto Berry. Once he's situated, Ruby sniffs at the bottle and then taps the glass curiously. A slender slimy hand reaches from the bottle, tapping Ruby on the head.

Taryn chuckles. "Look, they're friends already."

"A slime?" Arty steps beside Berry, frowning as he inspects the creature. "Why in the world would you want a pet slime?"

"Hey, slimes need love, too." Taryn holds a finger above the bottle, and the slime surrounds the stumpy digit in a green casing.

Arty shrugs. "If you say so."

"Let me guess, you're gonna name him Slimey?" I ask.

"Actually, I was thinking of calling him Flubs."

"Of course you were."

Now that Flubs is bottled up, I take a second to analyze him.

Forest Slime. Level 9. Pet. *The forest slime is a subspecies of ooze. Though they do not possess a toxic exterior, forest slimes are still capable of trapping creatures and devouring them within their gelatinous bodies. It's not uncommon to see a forest slime with the skeleton of its victims still inside.*

That's both cool and creepy, but at level nine, I'm not sure how useful the creature will be in a fight. Then again, Ruby has made herself invaluable without needing to engage in actual combat. I trust Taryn to maximize the slime's capabilities, whatever they may be.

The rest of the journey to the portstone is uneventful. Porting through the stone is even a little easier the second time around.

We say our good-byes to Arty as he heads back to the inn, while we go to the stable to drop off the pets. Limery perches on my shoulder, somehow managing to stay upright as he drifts off to sleep.

I understand the feeling. It was a long day for all of us.

When we arrive at Breebis's, Taryn's pets head for the gate, but Caustic hangs back, sticking near my side as the other animals enter the stable.

Breebis closes the gate behind them and comes out into the street, where Caustic now stands a few heads taller than the gnome. I didn't notice at the time because of how frequently Taryn used Imbue on him, but gaining so many levels in one day has accelerated the dragon's growth. His antler-horns are more defined, with pointy tips instead of nubs. His wings have greater width, the small spikes along his spine and tail are longer and more rigid, and a scaly beard has started to come in around his jawline. He looks more fearsome than ever.

"You all must have been busy today." Breebis smiles as she looks up at the dragon. "And it seems your bond has grown stronger. Very good." She looks over to Taryn, who still has his slime in the bottle around his neck. "Will this one be joining me as well?"

Taryn shakes his head. "I think I'll keep him with me tonight. Have you ever kept a slime before?"

"We've seen all kinds of oddities in Pruxford over the years. Slimes are not common pets, but they aren't unheard of either." She turns back to Caustic. "You ready, big guy?"

Caustic looks at me, and his bright golden eyes are more intense than ever.

"Go on. You're gonna have to get used to stables, you're much too big to fit through the doors of an inn now. Don't worry, we'll be back around tomorrow." I scratch him under the chin, and when I stop, he follows Breebis into the stable.

***

Back at The Puzzling Peacock, a band plays in the tavern. Several of Arty's brothers sit at the back table, but the cyclops is nowhere to be found. If I had to put money on it, he's fast asleep already.

We already ate while on the road, so we head straight upstairs. I put Limery to bed, and then go to Taryn's room so we can allocate our stats.

He sets the sling on the bed, and the slime slithers out. It travels like a slinky, flipping end over end as it inspects the room, looking under the bed and pulling out dresser drawers.

"Alright, you ready to do this?" I ask.

Taryn nods. "You go first."

I have eight stat points to use, but the priority is the ability point, so I pull up my available abilities.

Available Abilities (*1 ability point to unlock*):

Massive Bite. *Deals double damage. Cost: 20 rage.*

Claws. *Swipe at opponent with both hands, dealing extra damage. Cost: 10 rage.*

Multi Attack. *Bite and Claw at the same time. Cost: 20 rage.*

Iron Will. *Immune to slows and stuns for 30 seconds. Cost: 50 rage. 180 second cooldown.*

Perception. *For 10 minutes, gain increased awareness of your* *surroundings. Spot hidden objects, as well as unusual sounds, odors, and tastes. Cooldown: 6 hours.*

__Cleave.__ Your next attack causes bleed damage, dealing 1% of opponent's health per second for 5 seconds. Cost: 10 rage.

__Battle Cry.__ You let out a ferocious roar, increasing rage by 20. No cost. 60 second cooldown.

__Subclass:__

__Spirit of the Beast.__ The Spirit of the Beast path is composed of five phases. (Phase 1-4 complete)

__Phase 5: Spirit Power.__ The path of the beast is not for the faint of heart, and those who complete all five stages are blessed with a mighty power from their spirit beast. Gain a new active ability based on your spirit beast.

__Completion:__ Unlock using one ability point and the Spirit of the Beast path will be complete.

__Class Advancements.__ Upon reaching level twenty-five, you have unlocked a class advancement. You may only advance one class at a time. A second class may not be advanced until completion of primary advancement.

__Subclass:__

Summoner Advancement.

Dreadbeasts. Unlock for further details.
Dual Subclass. Unlock for further details

Honestly, it's not that difficult of a decision. I can't wait to unlock Dreadbeasts and see what that is all about, but it's not even an option until I finish the Spirit of the Beast path. The older abilities just aren't as useful as they once would have been, especially since unlocking my summoner class. I use weapons so often that my rage abilities rarely come into play aside from Berserker Rage, so there's little reason to put a point into any of them when levels are so hard to come by now.

The only reason we're doing this at the inn now instead of the dungeon earlier is in case some kind of change comes over me like it did with the horns. I trust Arty, and I'm glad he'll give us his meeting with the council if he wins, but I still want to win on my own merit. Until the tournament is over, it's best to keep some things close to my chest.

I put my ability point into Spirit Power and receive another notification.

Alert! *Spirit of the Beast Phase Five: Spirit Power complete. New ability available.*

Ability: (New)

Concussive Force: *Physical attacks can be imbued with concussive force, knocking opponents back with a chance to stun them. Cost: 100 mana.*

Alert! *Spirit of the Beast path complete.*

That's awesome! There's no cooldown, and for only a hundred mana, I can knock opponents back no matter what weapon I'm using. A jab with Sea Scorpion would create even more distance. On top of that, the attack has a chance to stun.

I fill Taryn in on the details, and he nods approvingly.

"Nice!" Taryn pets Flubs, who has returned to his lap. The slime is somehow both firm and gelatinous at the same time, kind of like Jell-o. "We're starting to get a lot better crowd control abilities than we used to have. And you'll be able to use that a lot more often than my Lightning Bolt!"

"Now what about you? What are you going to spend your point on?"

Taryn's eyes glaze over as he pulls up his character sheet.

He talks me through his choices. "Let's see. I've got Barkskin and Stoneskin, but I'm not really feeling either one of those. Insect Plague is pretty cool, it lets me summon all of the insects within a fifty-yard radius to attack a target. That one could be OP in the right environment, but useless if there are no insects around.

"Then there's Conceal, but I've made it this far without hiding my level, so I don't see any point in starting now. I don't need Perception when I have Ruby. And then there's all of the newer abilities from my Shadow Druid class. Scry, which lets me locate a target on my map as long as I have one of their personal items." His fist clenches as he reads off the ability, and I know he's thinking about using it on Glenn and Jude. He still has the glove that he took during the fight where Stompy died.

"Mind Warp is cool. It makes an enemy attack their allies for thirty seconds, but it has a thirty-minute cooldown. That one could be pretty useful, though I'm not sure if it would be a great choice for the tournament. Tidal Wave lets me summon a wave from a nearby body of water, but it's just as limited as Insect Plague, maybe even more so. Shooting Stars is like Moonbeam, except it's a barrage instead of a single beam. Good if we want more burst damage. And then there's Shadow Cloak, which gives me increased stealth at night or in the shadows. With my cloak, boots, and daggers, I'd be as sneaky as a rogue."

The glazed look fades, and he looks me in the eye. "So, what do you think?"

I know this isn't going to be what he wants to hear, but I have to tell him the hard truth. Unlocking Scry right now would be wasting an ability point.

Taking a deep breath, I prepare to take whatever lashing he gives me and tell him what I think. "I know you want to unlock Scry and go after Glenn and Jude for what they did to Stompy, but I don't think it's the right move. Not right now. We have a chance to possibly make a difference with the fate of Mythos if we can win this tournament, and I don't see how Scry helps us win now."

I know I didn't answer his question, but it needed to be said before we even discuss the other options.

Taryn pulls down the collar of his tunic, revealing the carrot tattoo over his heart. His hand rests over it, and he closes his eyes for a moment.

God, I'm an asshole. If something had happened to Limery, I doubt there would be anything Taryn could say to keep me from moving heaven and earth to make those responsible pay. And here I am asking him to postpone his vengeance.

He opens his mossy green eyes, his hand still resting over the tattoo. "I've made my peace with losing Stompy. You best believe that those motherfuckers are going to get what's coming for them —I guarantee it—but I know that it's not today. We can't lose sight of what's in front of us, because if we do, then what did

Stompy die for? So, I'll ask you again, what do you think I should spend my point on?"

His response is so stoic that I'm not sure how to respond. So, I don't. Instead, I answer his question. "You're right that Insect Plague and Tidal Wave are situational, but I think Insect Plague could be a good play. Maybe not for the tournament, but for our everyday lives—especially considering how much time we spend traveling. Having a swarm of high-level insect monsters suddenly on our side could be deadly, and at the very least, low-level insects would be annoying. But I also like Mind Warp considering how much people seem to want to gang up on us."

He nods. "I'd narrowed it down to those two as well. My gut is telling me to go with Mind Warp. The cooldown is longer, but it creates more chaos. It's like taking two enemies off the board at once. Because if their ally is attacking them, then they're going to have to defend and possibly injure whoever is under the spell."

"Sounds like a good plan then. I'm still not sure what to do with my stat points."

He shrugs. "I'm splitting mine between Intelligence and Wisdom."

I grimace as I think it over. "Part of me thinks I should get mine up as well. It could help with my Kamikaze ability."

"Bro, come on. You're not a mage. You're definitely not an Einstein. You have, what, one ability that does magical damage? Kamikaze. And half the time that you use it, most of your horrors are already dead." He narrows his eyes. "You are the bruiser. You deal damage and take a beating while doing it. Your horrors even build off of your Strength and Constitution. The only thing you're lacking is speed. Be the dumb strong brute you were always meant to be."

"Damn, T. Tell me how you really feel." I laugh at his brutal honesty. I can't believe I was the one worried about telling him the hard truth. "Sure you don't want to chop my balls off while you're at it?"

He grins. "You know I'm right."

My lip curls at the edge. "Maybe."

I put all eight points into Dexterity, bringing me up to thirty-two. Immediately, I feel more responsive to my body's movements, the same feeling that happens when I cast Sacrifice on my Horrors of Finesse.

Oh, yeah. This is gonna be good.

CHAPTER 30

ROLL CALL

"CHODS! CHODS!" Limery shakes me awake. "We dids it! We dids it!"

He's so excited that tears well up in his giant yellow eyes. I groan as I sit up, and he releases me, hovering in the air.

"What are you talking about? What did we do?"

"We's gots in the tournament!" He does a backflip in the air and plops onto the bed. "We's dids it."

"We what?" But then I notice the notification in the corner of my vision.

I focus on it, and a wall of text fills my vision.

Alert! *You have qualified for the Quincentennial Champion's Tournament!*

Regional Alert! *Over one thousand challengers took part in the qualification round of the Quincentennial Champion's Tournament.*

Hailing from all across Mythos, forty have been judged worthy to compete in this historic event. This is the most competitors appearing in one tournament since the three-hundred-and-twelfth tournament. With over a dozen heroes competing, this is destined to be one for the ages!

Beneath the regional alert is a list of all the challengers. The first thing I do is search for mine, Limery, and Taryn's names. Somehow, all three of us made it.

I scroll down the list, searching for the names of other heroes. They're easy to pick out, as every challenger has their home kingdom listed next to their name. I'm assuming that's so everyone who received the regional alert will know who they're up against.

Jason Montoya *(Vanaria)*
    Lester Hobbes *(Vanaria)*
    Randy Billson *(Vanaria)*
    Don Othello *(Vanaria)*
    Otis Wiggins *(Vanaria)*
    Ethan French *(Vanaria)*
    Kevin Harris *(Vanaria)*
    Michael Didato *(Vanaria)*
    Troy Malloy *(Vanaria)*
    Tommy Sullivan *(Vanaria)*
    Scotty Heyden *(Vanaria)*
    Sam Taylor *(Vanaria)*
    Bridger Phillips *(Vanaria)*

Taryn Jones *(Seascape)*

I clench my fist as I read through some of the names. Out of the fourteen heroes, I've had a run-in with nearly half of them at some point.

I fought Jason Montoya and Lester Hobbes south of the troll forest. I can still remember the look on Lester's face when he ordered the hired soldier to slit Ismora's throat.

Randy Billson and Don Othello nearly found me and Limery on our way back from slaying the mana-infused wyrm. That was before the trolls had peace, and if not for my Camouflage ability, they probably would have killed me then and there.

None spark my ire greater than Otis, Ethan, and Kevin. Those three laid a trap for us after we left The Dancing Donkey. If not for the timely arrival of Limery and the trolls, they would have killed us and Taryn's pets. Those three are working for Valmar—if not directly, then on behalf of some being with the same goal. The fact that they didn't want us to ally with other heroes means their presence here may be more disturbing than the cleric's.

Michael Didato had the sense to abandon his partnership with Jude, but that doesn't mean he doesn't want to put a blade in my back, especially after our encounter outside the dungeon.

Of the remaining names, I recall seeing Troy Malloy and Tommy Sullivan's names when they killed a mana-infused wyrm. The other three, I've never heard of or met. Maybe I can use this as an opportunity to win them over if they aren't murderous assholes.

I guess Richard the cleric was telling the truth when he said he didn't enter. Either that or he didn't qualify, which wouldn't surprise me. His damage has always been done by utilizing others.

I'm a little surprised that Pressley isn't on the list, but the last time I saw the death knight, he was in Goldspire. If he's managed to clear any of those high-tiered dungeons, he could be stronger than all of us. I count it as a blessing that we won't be facing him.

Jon the enchanter is probably still training in Vanaria if I had to guess. Hopefully, his skills are leveled up when we need them most.

Aside from Jude and Glenn, who are probably still in Frostmoor, there's only one other hero that I know of that's not on the list—Percy Mcdonnell, who slew a mana-infused wyrm. Though I know nothing about him aside from his name.

When I count them all up, that's eighteen heroes I'm aware of. That means that somewhere out there, there are still six heroes I've never come across.

I scan through the list again finding one more name that I recognize. It seems Arty made the cut as well. The other challengers are all a mystery, though their location gives some clue to their race. Goldspire, Frostmoor, and Wandermere are not represented at all, and there are several kingdoms represented that we haven't visited. A few of the names stand out because of how different they sound, even by troll and gnomish standards.

Drizz'rt (*Ellynmylly*)
  Lanxkuri (*Antedale*)
  Tozzet Girok (*Mistville*)

I remember Jegaar telling us that Ellynmylly was the largest kingdom in Mythos, and so diverse that they called it the Melting Pot. There's no telling what race their challengers are. With six challengers, they're only outnumbered by Vanaria and Pruxford.

There's no surprise that a kingdom so big would have such a large presence, even in a foreign tournament. Antedale has three challengers, and Mistville has two. Antedale is the home of the catfolk. If I remember correctly, they are known for their healers. I recall Mistville as the land of the merfolk.

With thirteen competitors from Pruxford, I have to think that there was some hometown favoritism involved in the selection process. Either that or not that many outsiders entered.

After I finish looking over the challengers, there's still one more notification.

Alert! *As a qualifier for the Quincentennial Challenger's Tournament, you have been invited to the Challenger's Ball. There is a strict "No Combat" policy at the Challenger's Ball. Anyone in violation of this policy will be removed from the tournament. Each challenger may bring one guest. Please arrive at the Crystal Palace tomorrow at sundown.*

I close out the notifications and just sit there for a moment. Limery continues to bounce around the room singing a song about how we're all going to the tournament.

There's so much to process. How in the hell am I going to make it through an evening with some of these assholes without fighting? Just the thought of Ethan and his goons sets my blood boiling.

Watching Limery, I wish I had his level of excitement, but all I see are threats and danger. I take a breath and try to steady myself. I can't concern myself with other heroes right now. This should be a moment of celebration. Because we did it. Out of all the people who entered, we made the cut. Along with Arty, we make up ten percent of the field. And now I have a dragon to go to battle with, a dragon that grows stronger by the day.

"We dids it! We dids it!" Limery sings as he zooms through the air.

"That we did." A smile finally overtakes me. "What do you say we go and tell Taryn the good news?"

We beat on Taryn's door for a solid minute before he opens it, dreadlocks askew and sporting a deep frown.

"I thought we were sleeping in?" he mumbles.

I push past him into the room. His slime sits perched on the windowsill overlooking the street. Limery sits on my shoulder, holding in the good news with both hands clasped over his mouth like he's about to explode.

"Limery has something he wants to tell you." I nod to Limery, and he erupts like a volcano.

"We dids it, Taryns!" He flutters through the air, alarming the slime, who slithers under the bed. "We dids it!"

Taryn raises an eyebrow. "What's he talking about?"

I grin, seeing the humor more now that Limery's antics aren't directed at me. "Check your notifications."

Taryn's eyes glaze over and after several minutes, he looks at me, wide awake. "We got in, but wow. That's a lot of heroes. Don't you have beef with some of them?"

I nod. "Want to talk through it all over breakfast?"

Downstairs, Arty is sitting at a table with his four brothers. He cheers when he sees us. "Fellow challengers! Congratulations."

Two of his brothers stand, both level twenty warriors with short brown hair and freckles. One wears a brown tunic, the other green. Honestly, all four of them look nearly identical.

The man in the green tunic extends a hand. "We haven't officially met. I'm Roddick, This is Reddick. We'll be seeing you in the tournament."

"I bet it was hell keeping the two of you straight growing up." I shake both of their hands in turn. "Three challengers from the same family, now that is impressive."

Reddick smiles. "Mom knows how to raise 'em, that's for sure. If not for all of the heroes, we might have gone four for four."

I share their laughter. "I don't doubt it. Good luck, and if we meet in the arena, I hope it's a hell of a fight."

"To hear Arty tell it, we're all competing for second place." Roddick shoves Arty in the shoulder, but the boulder of a man doesn't budge. "We were just about to head out to clear a mob dungeon today. You're more than welcome to come."

Taryn holds out his slime, who's nestled in his palm. "There are a few things I need to take care of around town for this guy. Some other time?"

The brothers scrunch their brows simultaneously at the appearance of the slime.

I hold back my laughter. "It's a no for me, too. I was planning to do some non-combat training with Caustic today. Thanks for the offer, though. But before you head out, I wanted to ask if you know anything about this Challenger's Ball?"

Arty pushes his plate forward, then stands. "It's just a little something they do before the tournament. The leaders of various kingdoms all gather to flaunt their wealth and feel important as they are surrounded by the best fighters across Mythos. For the challengers, it's an opportunity to get shitfaced on fine drinks for free and have two days to sober up before the fights."

That would be amazing any other time, talking about adventures and drinking. But now, with so many enemies that close together, it sounds like a recipe for disaster. "Isn't that a little dangerous considering the no-combat clause?"

He shrugs. "From what I hear, people usually find more creative ways of settling disagreements."

Somehow, I feel like attempted murder and the destruction of all that is good in the world aren't the type of disagreements settled over an arm-wrestling match. "Thanks for the info. Have fun at the dungeon."

After they leave, we take an open table and order our food. Taryn's slime slinks around the room, inspecting everything. It's a very curious creature. Maybe slimes are more intelligent than I thought.

Taryn leans forward. "Alright, I know about some of the heroes, but fill me in on the rest."

"Some of them we ran into very early on, so while I might know a little about them, they've probably progressed a lot since then. They might even have a second class or expanded their primary."

I pause my story when the barmaid comes over with a pitcher of milk, pouring us all a glass. Limery tilts his cup up, taking a massive drink, and when he's done, there's a thick milk mustache across his upper lip. He cackles when Taryn shows him his reflection in a knife.

"The first two I ran into were Randy Billson and Don Othello. Actually, we ran into them again at The Dancing Donkey. The rogue and the mage weren't half-bad the second time around. I almost forgot with everything that happened after leaving. I don't have a clue what type of mage he is, though."

Taryn nods along as I talk, only pausing when our food arrives.

"We saw Michael Didato, the paladin, in Seascape Square when he tried to unlock the portal, though I had a run-in with him long before that. Now that I think back on it, it was probably a shitty thing to do, but the trolls were on the cusp of extinction and my anger was running wild. We attacked him and Jude as they were leaving a dungeon south of the troll forest. I know he has a heal, some kind of buff that gives off a white aura, a holy light kind of similar to your Moonbeam, and then some other ability where light radiates from him, damaging everything nearby."

Taryn bites off a piece of sausage and points the rest of it at me. "So, you killed them for no reason? That explains a lot."

"Things were different then. The trolls didn't have peace with Vanaria. If they would have seen us first, they would have done the same thing."

He shrugs. "I guess we'll find out at the ball tomorrow night."

"On our way back to the forest after clearing a dungeon, we were ambushed by Jason Montoya and Lester Hobbes." As I tell this part, a scowl settles on Limery's face, and I'm sure the memory is still as vivid to him as it is to me. "Jason is a wizard, and he had these arcane chains that could hold an enemy in place. He also had this magical cube that he could hide inside and use as a shield. Lester is a ranger. He could shoot imbued arrows, but he also had an ability that allowed him to subdue other people's pets. He had to touch the pet to use the ability, but it could have evolved since then, so watch out for that if you're facing him. He's the one who ordered a soldier to kill Ismora. If not for Limery, she'd be dead now."

"That's good to know," he says with a full mouth. "I doubt he could subdue one of my pets without the others attacking, though."

"You already know about Otis the barbarian, Ethan the warlock, and Kevin the sorcerer. The other five, I don't have a clue."

Taryn sits back against his chair, his plate empty. "Sounds like we have our work cut out for us."

That's an understatement.

CHAPTER 31

PECULIAR ITEMS

While Chod left for Breebis's stable to train Caustic, Taryn had a few errands to run. He'd stop to see his other pets once he was finished. For now, he was enjoying the alone time with Flubs.

The slime was a curious creature, somehow intelligent despite being an amorphous blob. It had taken to using pebbles to represent eyes but would shift them from one side of its body to the other in seconds. Its appearance could change at the drop of a hat, sometimes appearing gooey, at other times slick and gelatinous.

Flubs might be a nontraditional pet, but Taryn was certain he'd only scratched the surface of its capabilities.

Pulling up the detailed map he'd bought for only five silver, he searched through the list of shops for the ones he had mentally marked earlier.

Grimward's Collection of Oddities and Eccentricities
  Titra's Formal Wear
  The Crystal Ball: Precious Stones and Jewelry

Bottles Galore

The four shops were scattered around the city, so it would take a while to get everything he needed. He formulated the most expedient route to hit all the shops without having to backtrack and set off to Bottles Galore.

Flubs peeked above the lip of the bottle draped by Taryn's side, taking in the sights and sounds of the city.

"Compared to the quiet of the forest, I bet this is a lot for you to take in, isn't it?" Taryn gently stroked the slime, and it gurgled.

The closer they got to the city center, the more congested the streets became. The tournament celebrations were in full force. After getting recognized by a stranger, Taryn pulled his hood up, concealing his face as he hurried along.

The door to Bottles Galore had a large slab of glass set within the wooden frame. The glass twisted in a swirling pattern, changing from lighter to darker colors the closer the swirls got to the center. It was mesmerizing. Taryn couldn't tell if the glass was actually moving or if it was some kind of optical illusion.

A chime rang out as he pushed open the door, and an elderly gnome with purple spectacles poked her head above the counter. Dozens of small bottles and vials lined the counter, sitting on small racks and hanging from spindles. The gnome's faded purple hair was pulled up into a bun with two glass rods holding it in place.

She hobbled around the counter. "Welcome, welcome. Come on in." She stopped in front of the counter, gesturing to the many shelves lined with bottles in all shapes, sizes, and colors.

The store was like a library of peculiar glass containers. Some were big enough that Taryn swore he could climb inside them.

"We have bottles for every occasion. If you can't find what you need here, you can't find it anywhere." Though she moved slowly, the gnome's words were practiced and true, like any good salesperson's.

"Excellent." Taryn pulled back his robe, revealing Flubs and the potion bottle he nestled within. "I'm looking for something to hold my pet slime. As you can see, this one is rather cumbersome to be wearing around my neck. Do you happen to have anything that's enchanted so that he can fit inside, but that's small enough that I can also wear it around my neck?"

"Of course, master dwarf. As I said, if you can't find it here, you can't find it anywhere. Just give me a moment to go search. We keep the enchanted bottles in the back."

Taryn grinned as the woman disappeared down an aisle filled with colorful orb-shaped vases. He stood in place, keeping Flubs inside the container. The last thing he needed was to accidentally knock something over. There was no telling how much some of these bottles might cost.

She returned holding her hands behind her back. Grinning, she presented Taryn with a vial not much bigger than her outstretched hands. It was shaped like a swirling vortex, spiraling to a pointed end. A small lip jutted out from the top, stuffed with a cork, and a silver necklace attached at both sides.

"Wow. It's beautiful." Taryn's eyes widened as he analyzed the bottle.

Item. Small Abyssal Vial. *Although small, this enchanted vial can hold a great deal of material. Similar to an expandable item, the abyssal vial can hold what the satchel cannot—namely liquid, viscous, or granular substances.*

She held it up, letting the vial dangle on the chain. "The inside will expand to fit the vial's contents, up to the volume of a large barrel. I don't know how big your slime will grow, but this will accommodate you for a very long time."

"How much?" Taryn asked.

"For you?" She gave him a warm smile. "Three gold."

"I'll take it."

Her smile shifted to a smirk. "Three gold...on the condition that should you win the tournament, you will thank Bottles Galore for outfitting you with all your bottling needs."

She was good. Very good.

"Deal." Taryn shook her hand and paid for the vial.

He uncorked the stopper and placed it in his satchel. With Flubs inside of the vial, there was no need for the cork. As the slime slithered from the large bottle to the tiny vial, its body bulged at the lip. Even though it appeared that he wouldn't fit, Flubs slid inside no differently than he had in the larger bottle. Once inside, the vial changed to a forest green.

Flubs emerged partway from the bottle. As he did so, the slime expanded to its normal size, with a wispy tendril that connected to the vial like some kind of genie.

The next stop was The Crystal Ball: Precious Stones and Jewelry, where Taryn purchased two small amethysts. He traded Flubs for the pebbles, and now the slime's makeshift eyes sparkled from within.

After that was Grimward's Collection of Oddities and Eccentricities. The entrance to Twilight Avenue was nearly concealed between two buildings, so far down the depths of the dark alleyway that he'd almost missed it. The alley funneled into a dead-end street with four buildings on each side and a brick wall at the far end.

Compared to the elegance of most of Pruxford, calling this place sketchy would be an understatement. Taryn gulped as he stepped out of the alley, and Flubs gurgled from around his neck.

Somehow, the light was dimmer, despite being as open to the sky as any other street. A heaviness settled on the street that he couldn't quite explain. The cobblestones were stained and faded, littered with trash that blew around in the wind, occasionally clinging to the steps of one of the buildings.

All of the windows were a cloudy gray, hiding the contents within, and the signs offered little description of what awaited inside. If not for the map, he'd be lost.

He took a deep breath and opened the door to Grimward's. It creaked as it opened, and somewhere in the depths of the shop, a cat meowed, followed by heavy footsteps.

The smell of incense lingered above all else. The floorboards were dusty and warped, and cobwebs clung to most of the inventory. Taryn shivered, hoping that the spiders kept to themselves, while Flubs retreated to the safety of the vial.

The shelves lived up to the store's name, filled with an assortment of oddities that set Taryn's hair on end. Jars stuffed with eyes preserved in a yellowish liquid. Dolls with porcelain faces and way too lifelike eyes. Skulls of various shapes and sizes. Taxidermies that he was certain were created from parts of more than one animal. A necklace made of black pearls gave off a sinister red aura as it rested on a faceless mannequin, and candles burned with green and purple flames.

There was something off about a painting of what looked like a haunted castle. When a face suddenly appeared behind one of the castle windows, Taryn nearly screamed.

"Can I help you?" a raspy voice asked as a gaunt man stepped from behind a shelf filled with books covered with suspiciously human skin-like leather.

The man was halfway to becoming a skeleton, with sunken cheeks and milky eyes that only offered the faintest glimpse of pupils within their depths. The man's hair was gone, save for a few strands that hung across his face. Taryn could only imagine the frail body hidden beneath the black robes.

He had the urge to run out the door screaming, but he swallowed hard and pressed on with what he'd come for. "I was hoping to buy a skeleton of a small animal. Someone told me you might have one for sale."

"You came to the right place," the man croaked. "Do you need it for a potion or reanimation?"

The man's smile was unsettling as it stretched across the bony face.

"Uhm, neither." He tapped on the vial for Flubs to come out, and the slime slithered into his palm. "I was hoping to use it for my slime."

The man stared at Flubs with intrigue, before disappearing down the aisle. He returned carrying a small canvas bag. It rattled as he turned it upside down and bones clattered against the floor.

The skeleton was small. Judging by the skull, it was probably half the size of Ruby. Taryn wasn't sure he wanted to know what had happened to the poor creature.

He released Flubs, and the slime surrounded the bones, absorbing them into his body. It was like a science video as the bones moved within and slowly assembled into a skeleton. When Flubs was done, a layer of slime surrounded the bones of what had most assuredly been a cat at one point. The two amethysts Taryn had purchased sat in the eye sockets, and the tail swished back and forth as Flubs walked around the room. Whether it was from the slime's abilities or natural instinct, the movements were almost identical to a real cat.

"That's amazing." Taryn watched in awe.

He could store the bones in his inventory when Flubs was in the vial, but this would allow the slime to take a more solid form. And truth be told, it looked exceptionally badass.

Taryn paid for the bones and left the store in short order.

Whether or not this purchase was entirely legal remained to be seen, and the less time spent in that shop the better.

With Flubs now walking alongside Taryn like a haughty housecat, the two made their way over to Titra's Formal Wear, where he purchased a set of emerald-green robes for the ball.

Chod might have no issue wearing a loincloth and flapping his junk in the wind for all the world to see, but this was Taryn's first time at a dignified event, and it warranted more than the clothing he wore in day in and day out.

The time had flown by exceptionally fast, and after picking up his formalwear, it was already early afternoon. He headed back to the stables. Flubs caught plenty of stares as they walked, and Taryn grinned underneath his hood.

When they arrived at Breebis's, Chod and Caustic were nowhere to be found.

Breebis stood on a stool, brushing Berry's dense coat in the outer pen. "Little Caustic—well, I guess he's not so little now—finally has the strength to keep himself aloft. Chod and Limery took him outside the city gates for some flight training. Less likely to cause a commotion that way." She frowned as she noticed Flubs arch his back and lean into Taryn. "Odd creatures, slimes."

Taryn gave her a devious smile. "Check this out. Flubs, release."

The skeleton within the slime detached, and the bones fell through Flub's body, clattering against the ground as he launched himself at Taryn's chest. He hit the vial, and in a flash, he was gone.

Breebis stared at Taryn with an open mouth, leaning from side to side to try and see where the slime had disappeared.

Taryn tapped the vial around his neck that was now a deep green, and Flubs peeked out. "Awesome, right? I could fit a dozen slimes inside this thing and still have room."

She nodded approvingly. "I must say, I've never seen that before."

They stood in silence for a moment. Breebis continued to brush the umber bear, and Taryn stared at the ground, gathering the courage to put himself out there.

A bead of sweat formed on his brow, and he cleared his throat. "Uh, there was actually something I was wanting to ask you."

Breebis looked up, one eyebrow raised. A strand of loose green hair fell across her forehead, and she blew it back in place. "What's up?"

"Well, uh..." Taryn's palms were suddenly so sweaty that he wiped them on his cloak. "Each of the challengers gets to bring a guest to the Challenger's Ball, and I was kind of hoping you'd want to go with me."

The tension was palpable as Breebis dropped the brush. It clanked against the stool, and Berry groaned, waggling his rear for more affection.

Taryn threw up his hands hurriedly. "But if you're busy, that's cool, too. I know you have a lot of animals to take care of."

"N-no." Breebis climbed down, picking up the brush with shaking hands and flushed cheeks. "It's not that. I was just surprised is all." She took a deep breath, and she seemed more herself. "I've never been to a ball, but I'd love to go with you."

Her cheeks grew even more rosy, and for a moment, they both just stood there awkwardly.

"I've never been to a ball either, so I guess we can figure it out together."

He smiled, and she did the same.

CHAPTER 32
CHALLENGER'S BALL

AFTER A LONG DAY of training with Caustic, Limery and I enter the Puzzling Peacock eager for a warm meal and strong drink. Taryn is already there, laughing with several gnomes while a bright-green-striped cat struts across the table.

"Don't tell me you've gotten another pet? Wait—" I do a double-take as I notice the gelatinous consistency of the cat's body and the skeleton that's clearly visible inside. "Is that Flubs?"

Taryn grins. "The one and only. What do you think?"

Limery flies over, poking the slime-cat with a pointy finger. It sinks into the slime's body up to his knuckle and the imp cackles.

How in the hell did it get bones? Honestly, I'm not sure if I want to know the answer to that.

I just shake my head. "Was this your special errand?"

"Part of it." His mustache twitches. "I hear Caustic can fly now."

Now, it's my turn to be proud. I can't help but stand a little taller as I brag about him. "He's getting stronger every day.

Watching his wings flap, and the power it takes to lift himself off the ground... I can't explain it."

"I know the feeling." Taryn pulls a chair over from a nearby table and pats for me to sit. "Tell me all about it."

We spend the next few hours drinking, laughing, and boasting to our new gnome friends about how special our pets are. For a little while at least, I forget about what waits for us tomorrow.

The next day, I get in some more solid training with Caustic before we have to get ready for the ball. Taryn insists that he needs to go back to the inn beforehand. When he knocks on my door, I see why.

His cloak, tunic, and antlered helm are all gone. Instead, he wears a slick, emerald-green robe. Some of his dreads are pulled together in a tail and the rest drape over his shoulders. The clasps in his beard are extra polished.

"Alright, T. You really went all out, didn't you?"

He looks me up and down. "Some of us had to. Where's Limery? I got him a little something."

Limery is on my shoulder in a second, eyes bulging. "You's gots a present for Limmy?"

Taryn pulls a ruffled white collar from behind his back. "Sure did, buddy. Try it on."

Limery buttons the collar around his small neck and preens., then he flies down and wraps his arms around Taryn. "Oh, Taryns. Thank yous."

After getting a look at these two, I don't want to appear like a complete savage, so I change into the leather kilt and vest that King Favian gave me when I visited Vanaria. The deep brown leather looks great against my blue skin.

With the spooky slime-cat in tow, we set out for the ball, but Taryn heads in the opposite direction.

"Wrong way, dude," I call after him, gesturing over my shoulder with my thumb. "Palace is that way."

He stops and turns around. "We need to stop by the stable first."

"Bro, you spent all day with your pets. I think it'll be fine if we attend the ball without them."

He frowns. "We're not going for my pets. We're picking up my date."

"What!" My jaw nearly hits the floor. "Why didn't you tell me you were getting a date?"

He shrugs. "I didn't think you cared."

"I didn't, I mean, I don't." I groan. "I just wish I would have known so I would have had the option."

Limery pats me on the back of the neck. "It's okays, Chods. Limmy will be yous date."

Date? Five gold says I'll be babysitting his little imp butt after he's had too much to eat and drink.

***

The sun hovers above the horizon as we ride toward the Crystal Palace. After picking up Breebis, Taryn insisted we take a cart. A young gnome pedals up front as we bump along the stone streets. He occasionally groans, probably regretting accepting my enormous weight. I'll make sure to tip him extra for his trouble.

Breebis and Taryn sit awkwardly beside each other. In all the years I've known him, this is the first time I've actually seen him go on a date. Not that he didn't have opportunities. Unlike me, Taryn had no problem getting girls' attention. There's just something about being six-feet of caramel man muscle that would turn them into puddles any time he walked by. The fact that he didn't seem interested probably made him that much more desirable.

Seeing him nervously tapping his leg as he sits next to someone that wouldn't come up to his waist in real life is kind of heart-warming.

Breebis is almost unrecognizable from the gnome we first met. Her normally messy bun is neatly brushed and falls around her shoulders with an emerald luster. The dirty work clothes are gone, replaced with a black-and-silver ball gown that accentuates her pale green skin. I don't know if she and Taryn planned it, but their color choices complement each other very well.

I catch them stealing glances at one another, and it brings back memories of Senzala. Now that I have Caustic, the arctic troll and I have more in common than ever, though I don't know if her bond with Nesira is the same as the one I'm trying to form with Caustic. I imagine there's a big difference between having a dragon as a totem versus a pet.

I wonder how she and the other arctic trolls are managing in Seascape. Hopefully, Chief Rizza has made them feel like a part of the tribe.

"Oh, you've got to be fucking kidding me." Taryn's outburst pulls me from my reminiscing.

His eyes narrow as he looks past my shoulder. I turn around, wondering what has him so upset.

Several carriages wait in line before us, emptying as guests arrive for the ball. One is made of green crystal, with a stagecoach directing two ponies adorned with gaudy gold harnesses. The couple that exit the carriage are equally ostentatious. Where Breebis's outfit is refined and elegant, these gnomes look like they're wearing every piece of jewelry they own. At my dad's business dinners, there were always a few older women who dressed the same way. Hopefully, the perfume on this couple is more subdued.

My gaze shifts to the dusty pink and lilac stairs that catch the glow of the moon, every third stair reveals the trickling stream underneath. Even at night, it's a sight to behold. Dozens of extravagantly-dressed guests make their way up the hundred-plus stairs toward the Crystal Palace.

Midway up, a group has gathered in a circle, and they aren't moving. I finally understand what has Taryn out of sorts, and I let out a stream of curses myself.

It's impossible to miss the warlock's shadowy wings that spread a good six feet on each side of him—Ethan, the ringleader of the jerks who tried to ambush us. His party stands in front of him—Otis, the bald, bearded barbarian, and Kevin, the sorcerer—with a group of bystanders surrounding them on all sides.

"What's the matter?" asks Breebis.

"Trouble." Taryn scowls at the three assholes.

Ethan stands behind the other two with his phantom wings outstretched while Otis mimics slashing with an axe and Kevin extends his hands in a blasting motion. The warlock's wings fade away, and all three start laughing, followed by those around them. They're too far away for me to analyze them.

Limery hovers next to me, and the air around him distorts as he stares at the trio like a dog ready to pounce.

"Easy, buddy. Remember the rules. If we fight, we're out of the tournament."

The air returns to normal as the imp sighs. "Limmy hates thems. Theys tried to hurt Chods and Taryns."

"Don't worry about them," Taryn speaks to him softly. "Tonight is about us. Come on, let's go enjoy the ball."

Our driver pulls to a stop at the bottom of the stairs. Around us, people and carriages continue to arrive. I catch several looks as

I climb down, first helping Breebis and then Taryn from the cart, before tossing a gold coin to the driver. His eyes go wide when he catches it.

"Thanks for the ride." I nod and turn toward the palace.

I set my face, showing no emotion, and Limery perches on my shoulder as we ascend the stairs. Taryn and Breebis take the lead, their short legs moving slowly toward the palace. Whoever designed the palace didn't want to make it easy for visitors, that's for sure, but as we pass each crystal stair, the view of fish swimming underneath makes it almost worth it.

Almost.

I can hear the loud voice of Otis as he tells the gathering crowd of some monster they killed, but I keep my eyes set in front of me. There's too much riding on this for me to get baited into a fight with these assholes.

"Would you look at that?" He abruptly changes the subject, and I can feel dozens of eyes staring in our direction. "Looks like Papa Smurf got a makeover."

I should have known they wouldn't let us pass without saying something. Limery's claws dig into my shoulder, and several people in the crowd laugh, but it's clear they're only mirroring the heroes' reactions.

"What's a smurf?" someone asks.

"Hey, blue balls! I'm talking to you."

I stop and look over to see Otis staring at us with a shit-eating grin. He's level twenty-nine now and has advanced his class to Berserker, but the other two both have their levels concealed. He wears a sleeveless black vest trimmed with white fur that cuts in a deep V over his hairy chest. The sorcerer mirrors his expression, wearing a long red cloak, absent the vials that he normally keeps strapped about his chest. The warlock watches us with a more intense gaze, his dreadlocks falling by his jawline and concealing some of the tattoos that cover his face. His only adornment is the purple amulet around his neck, hanging over a black robe with sleeves that cover more warlock tattoos.

Otis tucks his fingers in the V of his vest. "Ethan said if we waited long enough, you'd show your ugly face. You don't think you actually have a shot at this tournament, do you?" He smirks as he looks around the crowd for approval.

Some laugh, but more step away, putting plenty of space between us and the other heroes until there's an open line of sight between us.

"What's the matter, cat got your tongue?"

"Come on, Chod." Taryn grabs me by the arm, and I follow. "This clown isn't worth it."

"Yeah, that's right. Walk away, bitch."

I turn and roar. I can tell he wasn't expecting it because he flinches. Kevin jumps to his side, hand glowing with a toxic green aura. Ethan smirks, and several guests scream and more scatter up and down the stairs.

I smile, and it sets off a rage that burns behind the barbarian's eyes.

"When you tell your little stories, make sure you mention how you ambushed us and still managed to get yourselves killed. And don't forget the part where you squealed like a stuck pig."

Otis pulls an axe from his inventory and charges. He might be level twenty-nine, but he's still just a dumb brute. Fire crackles next to me as Limery summons a fireball.

"Enough!" Ethan's voice rings out, amplified by some dark power that reverberates within my chest.

Otis stops, letting his weapon fall to his side. It's no surprise who calls the shots in their crew.

"Now is not the time," Ethan says, his voice now normal. All amusement is gone from his face.

Limery puts away his fire, and I wink at Otis as we continue up the stairs.

Once we're far enough away, Taryn turns around, pointing a short stubby finger at me. "What the hell was that? What happened to playing it cool?" He's three stairs higher than me, so he pokes me in the chest. "New rule—we don't go anywhere near them for the rest of the night."

"Alright, alright. My bad." I force away my smile. "But you saw him jump, right?"

Taryn turns, but not before I can see the edge of his mouth curl up in a smile.

Breebis leans toward him. "Is there always this much drama among heroes?"

Taryn shakes his head. "Only when Chod's involved."

I roll my eyes. There's no way my reputation is that bad.

Several dozen guards wait at the top of the stairs, each one wearing gleaming armor with a rainbow of colors somehow infused within the metal. They stand sentry and don't so much as acknowledge us as we enter the palace.

In the lobby, the palace guides are here, but their burgundy robes are now a pale lilac. Lines form in front of each one. An orb hovers by their side, scanning people in a similar fashion to the qualifying line at the Department of Entertainment and Events.

"Guards!" one of the guides shouts at the far end before a gnomish couple are escorted down the steps.

The orb scans the three of us, and Taryn announces Breebis as his date, then we're allowed inside. Soon after, I receive a notification detailing the schedule of the night's events.

Welcome to the Challenger's Ball, a celebration of one of Pruxford's greatest traditions, the Champion's Tournament!

Schedule:
(To begin at dusk)

Social and Cocktail Hour
Opening Remarks
Dinner
Introduction of Regional Leaders
Introduction of Challengers
Dancing

"Well, that certainly saves a lot of paper." I close out the schedule and take in the ballroom.

Crystal chandeliers hang from the massive domed ceiling, which is painted with beautiful mosaic patterns. Bars are set up in at least eight different locations around the room serving vibrant cocktails, beer, and wine. There's a stage in the center, where minstrels play classical music as a distant backdrop to the chatter.

There have to be at least a few hundred people here. The majority of the attendees are gnomes, but I pick out an assortment of catfolk, merfolk, and humans. A giant of a woman towers above everyone, holding a mug of beer in each hand. She wears a tunic emblazoned with a silver teapot. I'm guessing she's from Ellynmylly.

Kazzandre Strongback
Level 28
Warrior

Giant

Turns out she's a literal giant.

I nudge Taryn in the shoulder. "Looks like this is what we're up against."

His eyes widen when he sees her. "The bigger they are, the harder they fall, right?"

"That is a saying of small men so they can sleep at night." Deep laughter rings out as Arty steps beside us, his firm hand grabbing me on the shoulder. "She's a good fighter, strong as they come."

His brothers, Roddick and Reddick, stand behind him. All three wear a similar leather tunic with the sword and shield of the Adventurers' Guild embroidered over the heart.

"It's nice to see a friendly face." I shake his hand.

He grins, showing his daggers for teeth. "It seems you've already made your presence known."

Taryn scoffs. "I told you. We can't take him anywhere."

Arty notices Breebis for the first time. "By the gods, I didn't recognize you, Breebis. You clean up nice."

She laughs. "You don't do half bad yourself. We've come a long way from nicking apples off passing carts in the borough. Some things never change, though, I can still smell you before I see you."

"Hey now." Arty frowns. "You know I can't help that."

They both burst out laughing, and Arty kneels to accept her hug since she barely comes past the cyclops's knees.

Over the next hour, people continue to filter into the ballroom. I'm increasingly thankful for Arty as he points out some of the challengers. Some he knows personally, while others he's only heard of. The most curious is a gnomish monk with a class called

Drunken Master. The gnome has a shaved head except for a single patch on his crown that grows a ponytail. He wears a tank top and harem pants, swaying as he walks, yet somehow never spills a drop of his drink. Being in the Adventurers' Guild, Arty's familiar with most of the action that happens in the region. He even introduces us to a few challengers.

In turn, we point out some of the other heroes. A group of them gather around Ethan and the others when they finally come inside. Jason Montoya and Lester Hobbes, the wizard and ranger I fought in the forest, cast menacing glances in our direction.

Michael Didato shows up in full-plate armor and has his own crowd of adoring fans gathered around him. Holy light follows him everywhere he goes, giving him his own personal spotlight. He seems in good spirits and even nods at me once. Maybe he's not so bad after all.

A few heroes either didn't show or are hidden among the crowd, but I do spot two new faces. Sam Taylor, another monk, walks barefoot among the elite, wearing simple green pants and a flowing shirt. Scotty Heyden, whose class is listed as sniper, stands beside the bar tossing back drinks left and right.

Before we've finished pointing out everyone, the music fades and the cocktail hour is over. We're ushered into the adjoining great hall, where the long tables have been replaced with a great number of smaller circular ones. Elegant crystal place settings sit on a silk tablecloth. A bouquet of glass flowers sparkles as the centerpiece, set in a vase where small brightly-colored fish dart within. A water mage walks from table to table, filling goblets with a wave of her hand.

At the far end of the hall, there's a raised platform with a long table that overlooks everything where the council will sit along with the leaders of the other kingdoms. Each challenger receives a notification with our table number among eight specially marked tables, each one seating five challengers and their guests. For the heroes who didn't bring guests, prominent citizens are offered the option to dine with the challengers.

Limery and I end up at a table with Randy Billson, Don Othello, and Drzz'rt, who, it turns out, is the golden lizardfolk that was in front of us at the D.E.E. He's the only one who brought a guest, another lizardfolk, so we're also sat with two wealthy catfolk from Antadale and two gnomes. I take a second to look over the other challengers' stats.

Randy Billson

Level 29

Rogue

Human

The dark-haired rogue has gained a couple of levels since our last meeting in Lynchton. He still wears the boiled leather emblazoned with the silver wolf and his silver gauntlets, but the weapons he normally keeps strapped across his chest and legs must be stored in his inventory. All ten fingers glimmer with rings.

Don Othello

Level 30

Void Mage

Human

The first thing I notice, aside from his new class, is the change in his eyes. The whites and pupils are gone and mesmerizing galaxies swirl within each eye. His robe is a fine purple, and a triangular amulet inset with a red and black eye hangs from his neck. His fingers are equally as adorned as his partner.

Drzz'rt

Level ???

Assassin

Lizardfolk

An assassin? If I had to guess, that must be a class upgrade for rogue. If there's any truth to it, he'll be an especially dangerous opponent. He dresses similarly to our encounter in the D.E.E., wearing finely-embroidered clothing, a royal blue long coat that pops against his golden scales, and several amulets around his neck.

"We were—"

I start to make conversation, but one of the councilmembers clinks his glass and the great hall goes quiet.

For the first time, I notice the councilmembers together and can't help but smile. I'm not sure if this is their formal attire or what, but each one wears a long pointy hat similar to a garden gnome. Well, if that garden gnome was purchased at an upscale boutique in Manhattan. Each gnome has a hat in a different pastel color, as well as a complimentary robe. If someone took a picture, they'd make a killing around Easter. The gnomes make up for their simple clothing with a plethora of rings and necklaces.

The centermost councilmember stands. He wears a lavender

hat with a lemon-colored robe. When he speaks, his voice carries across the room.

"Challengers and esteemed guests, for those who don't know me, I am Dezmin Dreamwader, Head of the Pruxford Council, and for tonight, your host for the Challenger's Ball. The Challenger's Ball is a tradition as enduring as the tournament itself, where the movers and shakers across Mythos gather to celebrate a test as old as time—combat. On the five-hundredth year since the tournament's inception, we have fielded one of the largest pools of challengers in nearly two hundred years. It has been longer than that since heroes have done battle in the Crystal Arena. We don't yet know the reason why the gods have blessed the Isle of Mythos with so many heroes, but in two days' time, we will all witness their power. But for now, we feast!"

Applause spreads across the room. I join in, but I can't help but notice the willful ignorance in his remarks. They don't know why we have spawned on the Isle of Mythos? I shake my head. Maybe it's because a dark wizard is coming. Did he ever think of that?

Food suddenly appears on the table, reminding me of Lord Kassidy. There must be another teleportation mage here somewhere.

The platters of food smell delicious. There are roasted meats, seasoned vegetables, bread, and some gelatinous things I'm not familiar with.

"What do you think of the city?" one of the catfolk asks us, her voice alluring. Her fur is gray and tinged with white. A hooped earring with a chain runs from her ear to her nose, and she wears a silky robe patterned with exotic flowers.

Limery answers with a mouth full of food. "Limmy likes it. Its is a very bigs city."

"The gnomes have a certain appreciation for their crystals," Don answers.

The two gnomes nod in agreement, and one responds. "It is said that the first gnome earth mage pulled crystals from the earth, forming a wall to protect his village. That wall now makes up the Crystal Arena."

"You don't say?" Randy stabs a piece of meat with his knife. "You learn some new shit every day."

Don casts him a sideways glance.

The second catfolk, a brilliant white with a large gray mustache, licks his paw and combs out a piece of food caught in his chin hair. "If you ever visit, you'll find Antadale much less of a spectacle. Our city is simple, elegant, refined."

The gnome's expression suddenly sours, and I cough to keep from laughing. While the two couples politely bicker with one another about which city has more to offer, I try to get to know the other challengers better, starting with the assassin.

"Are there many lizardfolk in Ellynmylly?" I attempt to break the ice before taking a sip of my gnomish wine. "I saw a few in Goldspire."

"You've been to Goldspire?" He hisses as he pronounces the S.

"Briefly. It's like a different world over there, that's for sure."

He nods. "It's said that all lizardfolk come from the same spawn, but it has been ages since we were one people. We scatter across the continents like leaves in the wind."

"Kind of like the trolls. Except now, there are three tribes gathered together."

"That is...most odd."

I want to break the news then and there, telling him about Valmar and everything we know, but I know it's too soon. If I can prove myself in the arena against so many challengers, they'll be more inclined to listen. One thing I know is that people respect power.

But the more challengers I see, it feels like our party has fallen behind. There are more level twenty-nines and thirties than I would have imagined.

"Hey, lizardman," Randy calls from across the table. "You mind switching seats with Don here, I'd love to talk to you about some rogue shit."

Drzz'rt whispers something to the other lizardfolk next to him, then nods.

Don sets his plate down next to me. "Randy might be crude, but he says what he means."

"I'll take earnest over pretentious any day." I shrug. "They invited a rogue to a ball, what'd they expect?"

He laughs. "Too true. It's a fitting class, that's for sure." He leans in a little closer, and I'm once again entranced by his eyes. "I heard about what happened after you left Lynchton. Damn shame, but I'm glad you made it out."

I find it hard to look away from the swirling galaxies. "How'd you find out?"

"After they respawned, Otis wouldn't shut up about how he was going to have his revenge. I've never seen Ethan so mad, I thought he was going to rip Otis's head off then and there. Practically all of us know. Well, maybe not Jude and Glenn. No one has seen them around in quite a while. What I don't get is why they attacked you? Seemed y'all were chatting it up the night before."

"You haven't heard about Valmar?"

He frowns. "That one of your troll buddies?"

While I fill in Don on the meeting at Seascape and King Orso's prediction, Randy and Drizz'rt talk shop. I'm not sure what they're going on about, but several times, one takes the other's hand and mimics a stabbing motion.

I debate whether or not to tell Don about what happened in Frostmoor with Jude and Glenn, but I elect to keep that part to myself. It sounds like news travels fast among heroes, and I don't want a super-villain team-up any time soon.

When I'm done, he sits back in his chair. "Damn, that's crazy. So, you think Ethan is in league with this Valmar guy?"

I nod.

"And you're wanting to do something about it?"

I nod again. "I'm not sure if he's in league with him directly, or his patron has something at play. Either way, he attacked us because he didn't want me uniting more heroes. So, I want to make sure that if we go to war, we're prepared."

He looks around the room before leaning in once again. "What's in it for us?"

His question takes me by surprise. "Saving the world not a good enough reason?"

"Some of you guys really embrace this, don't you?" He grins. "I'm all for fighting the good fight, but I worked too damn hard for these levels to throw them away on a lost cause. This place ain't no different than prison when you really look at it. People respect those with power. I've felt it myself. Anywhere I go, people look at me with respect—not for who I am, but for what I can do. I'm not a dirty player like some of these guys, but I'm not stupid either."

As much as I hate it, I can't argue with his logic. He sees this game for what it is. Maybe he hasn't had those special moments that make Mythos feel like more than a game. Even so, he's managed to play it well without being a giant asshole. If I can reason with him, I think he'll do the right thing.

"As heroes, we could be the presence that shifts the scales one way or the other. You've said it yourself, you're not a dirty player. When shit hits the fan, who do you want to have your back? Those that are fighting to keep their way of life, or those fighting to destroy it?"

"Look, I'll be real with you. This is the first time in years that I've had some actual freedom. Lord knows if I'll ever see it again once they pull us out for good." The galaxies within his eyes continue to swirl ever-so-slowly. "I'm as sentimental as the next guy, but not here. I like you, really, you've got bigger balls than most of these guys." He smirks. "If you want me to join you, then this is your chance to show everyone here why they can't afford to be on your bad side."

I force myself to look away, knowing that he's not talking about this dinner. He's right, though. In two days, for good or bad, they're all going to see what I'm made of.

Several people gasp as one of the gnomes at our table tosses his water in the catfolk's face. His fur drips with water, and his whiskers dip low. The cat blinks for a moment and then swipes, his claws extended. Inches before ripping off the gnome's face, a guard appears out of nowhere, lifting the catfolk in the air by the scruff of his neck.

"Both of you, out. Now." The guard grabs the gnome by the robe and drags them both toward the exit.

Each of their guests gathers their belongings, staring daggers at one another as they follow the guard. I'm guessing there's a bit of regional animosity between Pruxford and Antadale, which would explain why so few catfolk are here.

A glass chimes again, and Dezmin's voice carries over the crowd.

"And with that, here's another chance to remind you all that the no-combat policy goes for everyone, not just the challengers." A bit of laughter carries through the crowd. "Now that the main course is over—" Our plates suddenly vanish from the table, and Limery groans as his fork slams into the tablecloth. "—we'll begin the introduction of the challengers and their regional sponsors once dessert has been served."

Puddings and tarts appear on the table, and after Limery devours his, Drzz'rt passes several uneaten desserts from our departed tablemates to the imp.

"Thank yous, lizardmans!"

A shadow appears in front of me, and as I turn around, I realize it's my own. Michael the paladin stands behind me, beaming in all his holy glory.

He kneels between me and the void mage. "Don, if you don't mind, I would like a moment with the troll."

"By all means." Don moves back across the table, taking a seat next to Drzz'rt.

Michael moves into the empty seat. His hair gently waves, as if he's standing in front of a calm breeze. Whoever his patron god is, they really treat him right.

I cross my arms and lean back against my chair. "I'm guessing you're not planning to kill me in the middle of the ball."

"You're correct." He smiles, and I swear one of his teeth actually sparkles. "I carried that anger in me for a long time. You ambushed us, and though Jude might not be perfect, we had done nothing to wrong you that day. But as I have continued down my path and gained favor with my god, she has taught me forgiveness. In hindsight, I can see that had we happened upon you, the results would have been the same. It was you who braved the streets of Vanaria and brought peace between our people. For that, my god is thankful, and she has requested that I aid you going forward." He extends a glowing hand.

Alert! *You have been offered Oath of Protection. Accept?*

I'm speechless. I thought he might not be aiming for my head anymore, but I never would have expected this. Maybe this game can change people.

I shake his hand, and the oath activates. "I don't really know what to say, but thank you."

He winks as he lets go of my hand. "I will offer you my aid against the darkness, but shall we meet in the tournament, know that I will raze you to the ground with the cleansing light of Onera."

Wow, if he's this intense when he's trying to help me, I'm glad he's not still trying to kill me.

When I look over, Limery's face is covered in chocolate frosting, fruit filling, and crumbs.

He finally sits back in his chair, rubbing his bulging tummy. "Limmy is fulls."

I give him about two minutes before he passes out.

Soon after, crystal chimes again and Dezmin's voice carries across the great hall.

"And now, the moment you've all been waiting for. Everyone here tonight will get an exclusive first look at this year's challengers. We will begin with Mistville, represented by the Mistville Court."

Three merfolk at the raised table stand. Shimmering scales coat their bodies in shades of blue and green. Gills run along their necks and short tropical-colored fins streak along their heads and forearms. Their clothing is very simple, each one wearing only a sash that runs over one shoulder and wraps around their waists.

Among the crowd, two merfolk stand.

"And their challengers, Oruma Zenen and Tozzet Girok."

I analyze their stats.

Tozzet Girok

Level ???
Tidal Mage
Merfolk

The tidal mage has deep-purple scales and bright-yellow fins. His chest and back are broad, like an Olympic swimmer, and he doesn't break eye contact with the merfolk standing at the council table. I'm guessing he's a pretty powerful water mage to be competing here.

Oruma Zenen

Level ???
Mesmer
Merfolk

She's much slimmer than the mage, with turquoise scales and vibrant orange fins. A white sash covers her chest, and she also seems fixated on the other merfolk.

Next, they announce the representatives and the three challengers from Antadale. A fighter, a paladin, and most interesting of the three—a blood mage.

Lanxkuri

Level 32
Blood Mage
Catfolk

Her fur is midnight black, but not nearly as void-like as Festa Forgetooth's, the Emperor of Goldspire. She stands tall, her golden eyes radiating with pride as her tail swishes behind her. She wears a black kimono patterned with blood-red flower petals. I know the catfolk are renowned for their healers, but I'm not sure if a blood mage powers their attacks with their own blood or uses the blood from their opponents. At level thirty-two, either one is a frightening proposition.

When the triumvirate of Ellynmylly is announced, there's actually applause from various tables. A halfling, a human, and a horned lizardfolk all wave from the council table. Both Drzz'rt and the giant stand when the challengers are introduced, along with two humans and two halflings, one of which has a super interesting class.

Erbin Longfoot
> *Level 29*
> *Puppet Master*
> *Halfling*

No idea what that could be. Maybe some type of summoner?

Next up is Pruxford with thirteen challengers. Including Arty, Roddick, Reddick, and ten gnomes. The three adventurers and the drunken master monk make up the melee damage of the group. Of the rest, there are five mages, two tinkerers, a druid, and a cleric.

The gnomes in the crowd all stand, but I notice those from other regions do not.

Dezmin speaks again, this time announcing those of us from the Isle of Mythos.

"It is unfortunate that the leaders of Seascape and Vanaria were not able to make it this year in spite of having so many challengers, but we all look forward to seeing what their heroes are truly made of."

"And Limmy!" the imp shouts, still sprawled out in his chair.

There's some laughter, but Dezmin doesn't acknowledge Limery's outburst. One by one, we are introduced. When it's Taryn's turn, Breebis claps loudly, her face filled with pride. Limery raises a hand when his name is called, but he doesn't move from his slouched position in the chair. Three of the heroes aren't present—Troy Malloy, Tommy Sullivan, and Bridger Phillips.

We all take a seat again, and Dezmin delivers his final remarks.

"And there you have it, the challengers of the Quincentennial Champion's Tournament. Stop by the sporting district tomorrow to place your bets. It's sure to be a thrilling event this year, with some surprises no one will be expecting. The grand ballroom is now open. Enjoy the evening, and thank you all for attending the Challenger's Ball."

Chatter erupts as soon as he finishes, and our plates magically vanish. People begin moving toward the ballroom, but Limery has finally drifted off to sleep. I pick him up, cradling him in my arm as I go to find Taryn.

He's chatting with Breebis, a hand resting on her knee. I guess the liquid courage has put his nervousness at bay. They both smile and laugh.

I'm happy for him.

He stands up when he sees me. "Dude, some of these guys have crazy classes. I think we should hit the library tomorrow and see what we can find out."

"That's actually not a bad idea. You two gonna do some dancing?"

Taryn grins, turning to Breebis and extending his hand. "What do you think? You know us ebony dwarves have rhythm, right?"

She blushes but takes his hand. "I guess we're about to find out." She turns to me. "Are you coming as well?"

I shake my head. "As much as I would like to grace you with my moves, I think I'm going to call it a night. This one overdid it again." I gesture toward the sleeping imp in my arm. "You two have fun. We can talk strategy tomorrow."

Taryn pats me on the side and then heads to the ballroom with Breebis's arm interlocked with his. Limery snores gently, and I head for the exit. There's no telling what awaits us in the tournament, but it's never too early to start preparing.

CHAPTER 33
THE CALM BEFORE THE STORM

Unlike Limery, whose snores could rival a freight train, I have a hard time finding peace once we're back at the inn.

Just a few days ago, hitting level twenty-seven felt like such an accomplishment. After the Challenger's Ball, though, I feel further behind than ever. The catfolk blood mage was a whole five levels ahead of us, and there's no telling if any of the challengers with concealed levels are even higher.

While we were spending days traveling through Goldspire, Frostmoor, and Wandermere, the rest of the heroes were killing monsters and exploring dungeons. With how long it takes to gain a level now, it feels almost impossible to catch up.

I try to tell myself that what we gained is far more valuable than levels, but Don was right about one thing: everyone respects power.

Eventually, I fall asleep, and far too soon it's morning. Only a day before it all comes to a head.

Downstairs, Arty and his brothers are already halfway through their breakfast.

He motions for us to join them. "You left the ball early last night."

"Yeah, Limery is a glutton with no self-control." I pull up a seat across from him. "Did we miss anything exciting?"

He shakes his head. "Not really. Though, Roddick caught the fancy of a halfling that wouldn't take no for an answer. He dances about as well as a fish on dry land."

I chuckle, watching Roddick's embarrassment. "Sad I had to miss that."

Roddick's ears flush a bright red, and he seems suddenly fixated on his plate. He doesn't look up until the barmaid comes over to take my order.

After Limery and I order, I rejoin the conversation. "So, what are you all up to on the final day before the tournament?"

Arty finishes the last bite of his food and lets his fork rattle against the plate. "We're gonna hit up one of the dungeons. No better way to work out stress than stabbing things that want to kill you. How about you?"

"Taryn and I are planning to get in some research. Try to figure out what some of those classes are. You have any idea what a mesmer is?"

"Can't say I do." He frowns. "It's a shame they don't announce the brackets ahead of time. We'll take it as it comes."

The barmaid brings out our food while Reddick is still finishing up the last of his, so we've got a few minutes to talk before they head out.

"There's something that's been bugging me." I stab a piece of sausage and wave it around as I talk. "You said your parents live in Pruxford, but why are you always at the inn instead of with them or the guild?"

Arty lets out a loud laugh and exchanges knowing looks with his brothers. "Well, let's just say that at home, Mom runs the roost, so to speak. There's a little more peace and quiet, and a little more freedom, at The Puzzled Peacock."

Reddick nods in agreement. "You caught us at a strange time. We're actually on the road quite often with quests for the guild. We like a good drink or two when we visit home, and the ale doesn't flow quite as freely at our dear old mom's."

"Ain't that the truth," echoes Arty.

"Why not the guildhall then?"

Roddick pushes his plate forward. "If I have to listen to another fresh-faced recruit talking about what he's going to do, or an old-timer bragging about what he's done, I'll put a sword in my ear."

"Hear, hear!" Arty taps his fist on the table. "And it's always the same damn stories. At least we have new tales every time we return. Active adventurers stop by the guild, but we don't shit where we eat."

Light spills in from the doorway, and I turn around to see Taryn trying to sneak toward the stairs. He's still wearing his formal robes from the night before.

"Busted." He grins.

"Mornings, Taryns." Limery looks over from his plate of food, oblivious to the situation.

"I think the dwarf might have had more fun than all of us last night." Arty waggles his brow and then stands. "Save us the tale for another time. For now, the dungeon awaits. We'll see you all tomorrow."

Taryn takes a seat next to me as the others leave. "Dungeon?"

"Just some mobs." I raise my eyebrows. "So?"

He smiles mischievously. "What?"

"You clearly didn't come back last night. I need details."

"It's nothing like that." His cheeks go red. "For real. We were one of the last ones to leave the ball, but we were having such a good time, we didn't want it to end. We went back to the stable and were using Berry as a pillow to look up at the stars. I guess we fell asleep."

I shake my head. "Sounds like the plot of a YA novel."

"I'm sorry." He rolls his eyes. "Are you sad I didn't tuck you in?"

Taryn orders some food, and we sit around chatting while I wait for him to finish. Limery plays with Flubs as the catlike slime explores the room.

"So, I'm guessing you like her?" I ask.

Taryn narrows his eyes. "We doing this again?"

"I'm serious." I throw my hands up. "No judgment."

"I don't know. I mean, yes, but—" He pauses. "—it's weird, isn't it?"

I shrug. "Everything about this is weird." I hold out my arm. "This feels like my body. And when we 'go back,' that feels like my body, too. So, maybe it's only weird if you make it weird."

He laughs. "Bro, if anybody ever found out…"

"This is a top-secret government program. We all signed NDAs. I think you're fine."

"Maybe. But it's not like we're gonna be in Pruxford for long after the tournament. Still, it was nice to spend time together."

After breakfast, Taryn changes out of his formalwear, and we head to the library. It's a beautiful, cylindrical glass building that rises several stories. From the street, I can see shelves within filled with books and scrolls. If there's anywhere we can find out about some of these classes, it has to be here.

I pull the door handle, but it doesn't budge. I try again with more force, but there's no give, so I press my hands to the glass and peek inside.

"What's going on?" asks Taryn.

"Door's locked, and nobody's inside."

Limery floats down from my shoulder and places his feet against the door as he tugs.

"Library's closed today." An older gnome sits on the curb smoking a long pipe. "All government buildings are. For the tournament."

"You've got to be kidding me."

"Don't worry, I got this." Taryn crouches in front of the door and pulls out the Nimble Key. A moment later, he yelps and drops the key as a spark shoots out from the door. "Fuck." He shakes out his hand. "The door has a protection enchantment."

I lean against the wall. "Looks like we aren't getting any research done today. Might as well head to the stables and get in some training with Caustic."

"And Taryns can kiss his girlfriends." Limery returns to my shoulder, cackling.

"Hey! She's not my girlfriend. And besides, where did you hear that?"

Limery zooms overheard, laughing maniacally while repeating the same phrase. "Taryns has a girlfriends. Taryns has a girlfriends."

Taryn scowls at me, but I just laugh.

"Wasn't me," I say, grinning.

Taryn insists we practice outside of the city so that we can train without the risk of setting the borough on fire. I think it's actually to put as much distance between Limery's teasing and Breebis as possible.

Once we're out there, we take turns working on individual drills since Limery, Taryn, and I will each be on our own during the tournament.

We've gotten so used to working as a team that it feels like there are glaring holes in each of our styles when we're solo. Caustic and I lack any real burst magical damage. His poisonous gas is more lingering at his current level, and it's unlikely I'll have enough time to summon the number of horrors necessary to make Kamikaze effective. But with all my recent advancements, I'm a one-troll smash force.

Without me, both Taryn and Limery are severely lacking in crowd control abilities. The tournament will come down to the matchups we draw. Hopefully, they're random, and not designed to expose our weaknesses.

We spend hours correcting formations and picking apart tactics that we'll only ever use in this tournament. There are no breakthroughs, but by the end of the day, I've come up with some useful ways of deploying my horrors alongside Caustic, even having him drop them from the sky like bombs, and Taryn utilizes the full synergy of his pets and druid abilities.

We're stronger as a team, but hopefully, we don't get steamrolled.

After dropping the pets back off at the stables, Taryn decides to linger for a bit while Limery and I head back to the inn.

Not wanting to play over a hundred scenarios in my head that are likely to never happen, I take a small amount of sleep dust and am gone before my head even hits the pillow.

CHAPTER 34

CHANGE OF PLANS

ON THE MORNING of the tournament, we receive special instructions detailing where the challengers should enter the arena. We eat breakfast alongside Arty and his brothers in near silence. For once, the brothers don't bicker or joke. Each one seems locked inside their own head, no different from us. I guess no matter our background, an event like this hits us all the same way.

I used to get the same way before an important stream. When I was goofing around for attention, it was more about the entertainment than my skill. When I was actually trying, that's when I would get inside my own head. That's when I'd snap if things went wrong. That's what got me here.

Arty and his brothers head to the arena after breakfast, but we stop by the stables for our pets. Caustic nuzzles me, nearly knocking me over, and Limery perches on the dragon's antler-like horns.

Breebis decides to accompany us to the arena early so she can get one of the better seats. She and Taryn talk as we walk, but I tune them out. My hands are jittery with nervous excitement. I have no idea what to expect, but this will be our chance to show everyone—heroes, challengers, and all of Pruxford—just what we're made of.

Even though we arrive several hours early, the streets are full and there's already a crowd gathering outside the arena. They gawk at Caustic, whose increased size is a lot harder to play off as some elaborate costume. Guards stand sentry at the gate, alongside a pair of palace guides. One of the guides holds a clipboard, and the other operates the scanning orb that hovers between the two. The orb scans a catfolk in a hooded blue robe, and then the guards allow her through the gate.

When it's our turn, Taryn hugs Breebis good-bye. The orb scans him and his pets in turn. As soon as he's through, Limery is right behind him.

I step forward, and the orb scans me and then Caustic. One of the gnomes raises his left hand, and the guards cross their spears, barring my entry.

The gnome adjusts her half-moon spectacles. "Unfortunately, sir, the dragon may not compete with you today."

"What do you mean he can't compete?" I frown. "He's my pet."

She purses her lips, and I get the feeling she wants to roll her eyes at me. "I do apologize, but the two of you are not properly bonded. Per tournament rules, only bonded pets and companions may compete alongside a challenger."

"What the fuck?" My chest tightens, and I clench my fist to keep from losing my temper. "Is there someone I can talk to? I just hatched him a few weeks ago. There has to be some kind of exception."

The gnome presses her fingertips together. "Unfortunately, sir, these rules have been in place for hundreds of years. You are not the first, nor will you be the last, to have an unbonded pet prohibited from the tournament."

Deep breaths. Now is not the time to lose my cool. I know this is nothing personal, but not having Caustic is going to be another blow against us.

I turn to Breebis. "They aren't letting me take him in because we haven't bonded yet. Would you mind taking him back to the stable for me?"

She takes the leash. "I can, but if you don't mind, I'd like to let him watch. It might be good for him to see you in action."

"Thanks, I appreciate it." I turn to Caustic, cupping his bearded jaw in my hand. "Sorry, boy. I wish you could come, but you're going to have to sit this one out."

Caustic huffs and a small puff of green smoke escapes his nostrils.

"Oh, calm down. It's not his fault you haven't bonded," Breebis reprimands Caustic before shouting behind me as I step through the gate. "Good luck!"

I throw up a peace sign and find Taryn and Limery waiting for me on the other side.

"What took you so long? And where's Caustic?" Taryn looks around me as if he's expecting the dragon to step through the gate any moment.

I shake my head in disappointment. "We haven't officially bonded yet, so they aren't letting him compete."

"Dude, that's wack." Taryn frowns.

"Yeah, dudes, that's wacks," Limery echoes, crossing his arms.

I sigh. "I mean, I get it. It keeps things fair, but it does suck to have wasted all that training time on things I can't even use."

"Hey." Taryn guides Berry closer to me. "It might not be something you use in this tournament, but it's far from wasted. Now, let's go see what's in store."

As we make our way through the arena, it appears that most of the palace guides are now stationed here. They stand everywhere we go, like guides at an amusement park, directing us to the Challenger's Pit located underneath the arena.

When we finally find the pit, it's like a cross between an underground bunker and a jewel mine. There are dozens of rooms carved within the stone tunnels. The walls are speckled with gemstones polished to a smooth finish. The gems within the walls produce their own light, casting each room in a different glow.

More than half of the challengers are already waiting throughout the tunnels. Some gather in the alcoves, while others stand or sit by themselves. They're all dressed in battle attire, but most of them have their weapons hidden—probably to keep the rest of us guessing as much as possible.

A gnome druid sits in a corner by himself, his mossy green skin almost identical to Breebis's. He wears a blue jewel-toned cloak, and a red falcon perches on one shoulder. Two wolves, one silver and one black, stand protectively in front of him.

In another area, a tinkerer fiddles with a contraption that scurries around on metal legs like some kind of steampunk spider.

Don's unsettling void-like eyes settle on me as we pass. He nods to me while Randy cleans his fingernails with a dagger.

Over a dozen guards are positioned along the corridors in addition to several more gnome guides. Though the guards' faces are concealed behind the shimmering helms, the size difference helps to identify those that are gnomes from the other races.

A gnome in a bright-yellow robe stands in the middle of the pit, waving her arms as she gives orders and directs people. "Welcome!" She locks eyes on us as soon as we enter, speaking a mile a minute. "Tatina Tinkerton at your service, Head of the Department of Events and Entertainment, and chair of the Challenger's Tournament. Most unfortunate news about your dragon, but rules are rules, and as cruel as it may seem, you are no exception to centuries of precedent. Please find a place to wait and one of our guides will be around to begin your preparations. Do try to savor the moment, for this will be a day unlike any other!"

As quickly as she came, she disappears, greeting one of the halflings from Ellynmylly as they waddle down the ramp.

"She seems excited." Taryn grins.

I laugh. "Who knows what kind of special dust the Pruxford fairies are cooking up."

Arty waves to us from an alcove at the far back. We pass the two merfolk and a group of three gnomes on the way to join him and his brothers. Before we have a chance to talk, a guide comes over pushing a cart filled with glowing potions. A guard stands on each side of him. The potions are white, with a yellow halo that extends beyond the glass. The bottles are nestled neatly in a container lined with felt, indented to the exact size and shape of each bottle. The guide hands out the potions one at a time, first to me, then Limery. He gives five to Taryn—one for him and each of his pets.

Legendary Item. Revive Potion. *One of the most difficult and time-consuming potions to create, only one Revive Potion may be brewed by a grandmaster-level enchanter at a single time, and each potion takes one year to create. A revive potion grants one victory over death, portaling the user to a preset location with 1HP upon receiving fatal damage while simultaneously activating a full-heal and returning the body to its natural condition. A corporeal doppelgänger remains behind at the death site.*

The gnome snaps his fingers, drawing my attention back to the present. "As I was saying, we are doing things a little different this year. Instead of the customary protection spell, each of the challengers and accompanying pets or familiars are given a Revive Potion for the tournament. So instead of fights stopping when the protective shield is broken, each fight will be to the death in order for each challenger to display the full-range of their abilities." He gestures toward the potions. "Each Revive Potion takes a year to brew under the strict supervision of our grandmaster enchanters. We have been preparing for the quincentennial tournament for many years now. Since this is a single-elimination tournament, the winner of the tournament will carry the effects of the Revive Potion as part of their prize. Drink your potion, and once we return to the arena, you will be given instructions on where to set your revive portal. You will also be able to set the portal of your pets or familiars at that time." He looks at us impatiently. "Go on, drink up."

I press the bottle to my lips, swallowing the syrupy, tart liquid. A warm buzz fills my stomach and a moment later, I receive a notification.

*Alert! You have ingested **Revive Potion**. Upon receiving fatal damage, your body will be transported to your revive location where you will be rebuilt anew. If you do not have a revive location selected, the potion will not activate. Would you like to set your revive location now?*

I close out the notification for now. Limery puckers his lips as he drinks his potion, and Taryn forces each of his pets to drink theirs. Jordy is so obsessed with his that his tongue writhes around inside the bottle as he tries to get more. When Flubs ingests the potion into his gelatinous body, a glob of yellow liquid sits in his core for a second before abruptly vanishing.

Once we've all drunk our potions, the gnome takes our empty bottles and pushes his cart along.

After drinking the potions, I can't help but think about Swift's brother Draydon. He died in a tournament just like this when his protection shield didn't activate. If he'd been given a revive potion instead of a protection shield, maybe he wouldn't have died.

I also can't shake the feeling that these potions would be better saved for the battlefield. The potions for Taryn alone have taken five years to brew. I've seen the kind of power King Orso and King Favian possess. Would it not be worth it to have those with that much power charge into battle again and again to inflict as much damage as possible? Or is there a limit to how far the portal can transport someone after dying? Years of work is about to be used up for a single day's entertainment. It doesn't feel right.

"So, where's the big scary dragon?" asks Arty.

"You're not going to believe this." I fill him in on everything that happened.

"Tough break. I guess your luck ran out in the dungeon." He grins. "Though I think it evens the playing field a bit."

I laugh. "You're worried about me when there are challengers five levels higher than me competing?"

He squints his single eye, not amused. "You'll find out soon enough that levels aren't everything."

More challengers continue to filter in, and the air is noticeably more tense compared to the ball. Even Otis keeps his big mouth shut as he walks by with Ethan and Kevin. The warlock has his dreadlocks pulled up in a bun and wears a sleeveless robe that reveals his many tattoos. The sorcerer wears a billowing cape over his robe, but I can see the straps across his chest loaded with an assortment of potions.

There are no groups bigger than three people, aside from ours, and most talk in hushed whispers. Once everyone has arrived, Tatina snaps her fingers, and her voice carries through the pit.

"Greetings, challengers. In just a moment, you'll be given the official seeding for the first round of the tournament. Please note that the seeding is final. But first, we will go over a couple of announcements. First, shield mages have been stationed around the arena. Shield mages are some of the most specialized mages across Mythos, and those in Pruxford have been honing their skills across the ages. After the opening ceremony, protective barriers will be erected to keep any potential projectiles or spells from hitting the crowd. You'll notice once the matches start that these barriers can also eliminate outside noise during the matches. There will be a special seating area for challengers still in the tournament and a secondary area to set your spawn point for those who are eliminated. Both areas will have protective barriers in place. Second, every challenger, pet, and familiar has consumed a Revive Potion for this year's tournament, therefore, you are encouraged to display your full potential on the battle-field. There is no need to fear for the well-being of your fellow challengers today. Give the crowd what they came for. As a final note, no legendary potions are allowed in today's tournament. Now, please stand by for the official seeding."

No legendary potions means I can't use my Angel of Death Brandy—not that I would want to waste it here. I wonder what other legendary potions might be out there.

A couple of minutes later, we receive a notification, and there's immediate grumbling. Cursing and complaints fill the challenger's pit. Instead of being separated into brackets, we're all divided into one of four groups. A quick scan shows Limery, Taryn, and I are all in separate groups. Before I even have time to process the names in each group, Tatina's voice carries above even the loudest voices.

"Hear, hear! As always, some of you are unhappy with your grouping. Well, let me tell you, you are not the first nor the last to be unhappy with your position in the tournament. Competing in the Champion's Tournament is an honor. Were this a normal tournament with only twelve or so challengers, most of you would not even be here. But with a field of forty, there's more opportunity than ever for a dark horse to rise through the tournament. Were it not a difficult task, then the Champion's Tournament would not be known across Mythos as one of the preeminent tests of combat skill. Nothing about this tournament is designed to be easy. Now, as you can see, you have all been separated into four groups. Further instructions will be provided shortly, but know for now that two challengers from each group will advance to the quarterfinals. After that point, it will be a single elimination bracket until a champion is crowned."

I try to piece together what I can from the limited information. Four groups, ten challengers each, only two advance. Will there be a point system for those who advance, or will the remaining brackets be randomized? More importantly, is there any method to the seeding of each group?

In only a few minutes, we'll be going aboveground for the opening ceremonies. While others bitch and moan, I take a moment to look over the groups, starting with my own. Luckily, Arty is also in group one, so we can watch each other's back. Otis is in our group as well, so I'm certain he'll be gunning for me after our run-in at the ball. The two I'm most worried about are Lanxkuri, the catfolk blood mage, and Erbin Longfoot, the halfling puppet master. We're also up against Scotty Heyden the sniper, a catfolk paladin, and three gnomes.

Group two feels like the group of death. Limery and Roddick are up against Ethan, Don the void mage, Michael the paladin, Oruma the mesmer merfolk, and Tozzet the tidal mage merfolk,

Tommy Sullivan, who was one of the heroes that didn't show at the ball, a catfolk fighter, and a gnome mage.

Limery doesn't look the least bit intimidated as he high-fives Roddick, but there is a clear sense of concern on Arty's brother's face.

Reddick is in group three. Facing Drizz'rt and Kevin the sorcerer will be tough, but I'm not so sure about the rest. I haven't seen Jason and Lester since our first fight in the forest, but being in the same group means they can watch each other's backs. There's also Bridger, another hero I haven't met, and both a halfling and human from Ellynmylly, and two gnomes.

Taryn's group also looks pretty tough. There's the giant from Ellynmylly, Randy the rogue, both monks, in addition to three other gnomes, a human, and Troy Malloy, another hero who didn't show at the ball.

Gongs and cannons echo from above as the arena comes to life. In only a matter of minutes, we'll be introduced to Prux-ford. I stand there frozen, eyes shifting between Taryn, who strokes Ruby's neck, and Limery. I wonder who I should talk strategy with first. Taryn has his pets, which is enough to give him an advantage over many of the challengers. But Limery, how is he supposed to compete against the likes of Ethan and Don, let alone a tidal mage who can likely douse any fire he summons?

Fuck. This is too much to process right now. Everything is happening so fast, and I'm not sure how I can worry about every-one's matchups, much less my own. It's easy when we're together, but how can I help them like this?

A firm hand grips my shoulder. "I can see the worry in your eyes. You fear for your friends." Arty moves in front of me, his massive eye staring into my own. "They are both strong. You must learn to let go and trust in their abilities. This is meant to be chaos. Every year, the matchups aren't announced until minutes before the tournament. No one is given time to prepare."

I take a deep breath and attempt to fight off the panic attack looming over my shoulders. I close my eyes and find my center. We can do this. It's just like with Caustic back in the dungeon. He surprised me. I'm sure Taryn and Limery will do the same. We've all gone through too much for me to worry if they are strong enough.

I walk over and wrap my arm around Taryn. "This is going to be a shitshow. Good luck."

"Just another day in paradise." He embraces me and squeezes. "Besides, this is the one time we can push our limits without the fear of losing a level. One way or another, I'm going to know what I'm capable of by the time this is over."

Limery flies over to my shoulder, grinning. "Limmy and Roddicks is togethers. We's goings to make a teams." He balls his small hands into fists. "Limmy is ready to fights!"

"Showtime, challengers! Group one, you're first out." Tatina's voice calls from every direction. "Line up. Group two, you're up next."

I fall in line behind Arty, and the guide leads us out of the pit and up a ramp that empties into the arena through a beautiful crystal archway.

"Watch your back, troll," Otis says from behind me, but all thoughts of him vanish as we step into the arena.

The design of this arena is on the opposite end of the spectrum from the one in Goldspire. We exit the archway onto a plain of crystal so smooth that it looks like a frozen lake. The stadium surrounding us is massive, with two levels of stands that wrap in a circle beneath the giant pillars of crystal. Thousands of fans fill the stadium, and their cheers roar like the tide.

This must be what it feels like to be a professional athlete in front of the home crowd. My skin tingles at the energy, and for a moment, I don't think about the stakes of the tournament. I simply appreciate being here.

The gnomish council sits in an illustrious booth on the lowest level, midway across the arena alongside the other heads of state. Guards stand at the edges of the booth, and it is already protected by a transparent barrier. It's almost imperceptible aside from the occasional flare of energy that ripples through the shield.

The booth next to theirs is empty. There's also a booth on the ground floor of the arena. I'm assuming one is for defeated challengers and one is for those still competing.

The announcer's voice carries as he introduces us one by one as we parade across the arena floor. We're escorted to an area near the center, where a large circle is etched into the crystal floor. Once we all step inside, the ground shakes briefly and we ascend on a cylindrical platform of raised crystal until we are twenty to thirty feet off the ground.

Once the platform stops moving, group two enters. This time, I'm able to watch as an earth mage raises their platform from the arena floor. Limery waves to me from his perch on Roddick's shoulder.

Groups three and four are announced in turn, and the crowd continues to applaud.

"There you have it—the field of the Quincentennial Champion's Tournament! Without further ado, transform the arena!"

The two earth mages stationed in the arena get to work. The arena shakes, and the crystal floor shatters into millions of pieces. It sounds like rain as crystal continues to disintegrate until the four pillars stand like tall islands among a sea of ice-blue sand.

Then, a silvery glow forms around the edge of the arena as eight silver bubbles begin to rise from the floor. The silvery shields continue to grow, and they connect like bubbles as they touch one another. As they morph into one another and grow bigger, the shields become more transparent until the last two barriers merge, creating a massive dome that arches over the arena like a snow globe. Four smaller barriers form around the tops of each pillar.

I'm trying to understand the need for the additional barriers over the platforms when something shifts in the sand beneath us. Out of the corner of my eye, I spot more movement across the arena floor as sand continues to shift.

The crowd's gasp is audible as a massive serpentine body launches from the sand, arcing over the shielded platform of group three. The silvery-gray creature has slick scales, miniature red eyes, and a massive cyclone of teeth beneath its hooked snout.

Sand Wyrm. *Level 40. These legless, wingless dragons burrow beneath the sands of sprawling deserts. Their slick scales allow them to travel through the sand unimpeded without the need for the toxic slime other wyrms require. With magic-resistant scales, serrated teeth, and powerful elemental magic, wyrms are some of the most dangerous creatures in all of Mythos.*

The mana-infused wyrm I fought in the forest is nothing compared to the size of this one. At level forty, I wouldn't be surprised if it could eat us in one bite.

"All right, folks, what do you think of our special guests?" The crowd erupts as a second sand wyrms reveals itself. *"The first round of the tournament will be a combination of a battle royale and king of the hill format. The final two challengers left standing in each group will advance to the second round. In this mode, there's nowhere to hide. You either fight on the pillar or take your chances with the wyrms down below. A word of advice to our challengers—the wyrms always win. Fight for your place in the next round. If you fall out of the platform's protective zone, you're wyrm food."*

The three other pillars shift their positioning as the earth mages move them around the arena, lowering and then sliding them through the sand until they surround the group one pillar in a triangle formation.

"Challengers, set your spawn points to the booth beneath the council and ready yourselves. The match will begin in thirty seconds."

After setting my spawn point, I immediately summon three horrors, making sure I summon Horror of Power last for the bonus damage on my next attack. Then I equip Destroyer. This is a bash-as-many-people-as-I-can situation, so I'll save the Regeneration Triad for when I know I can use it. Beside me, Arty equips his armor, helm, and insanely-large sword.

I lock eyes with the cyclops. "Watch each other's backs and try to take the center if we can."

Everyone on the pillar has put space between themselves and the others. A shirtless Otis wields a large double-edged axe with glowing runes. There's something different about his appearance that I struggle to name.

It takes me a few seconds, but once I spot the change, I can't unsee it. His neck is way thicker than it used to be, and a patch of bristly hair runs from the back of his head to his back like a wild boar. It was probably concealed beneath the heavy fur of his vest at the ball. I'm guessing he's unlocked a Spirit of the Beast or Totem Warrior path.

Next to Otis, Lanxkuri—the black catfolk blood mage—licks her paws. In lieu of her kimono, she wears a simple red robe that stops at her knees. Her tail flicks back and forth behind her. Next to the blood mage, a catfolk paladin with golden fur wears thick armor and holds a comically-large white warhammer over his shoulder. His fur shimmers with the same radiant energy as Michael.

Erbin Longfoot, the puppet master, watches my horrors like they are a delicious meal. Only the three gnomes still stand huddled together. I recognize one as the druid from before with the falcon perched on his shoulder. The two wolves stand in front of the group, teeth bared. There's also a cleric with a long gray beard. He wears a white robe with a golden symbol over his chest and holds a mace in his jewel-covered hands. At the back, a tinkerer kneels over several contraptions that I can't quite make out from where we stand.

To my other side, Scotty Heyden holds a slender bow that's nearly as tall as he is. An arrow with a spiraled tip is nocked and ready as he crouches to one knee.

"The archer is my first target," I whisper to Arty. "After him, I'm pushing the center."

Arty nods, and the crowd joins the announcer as he counts down.

"Five."

"Four."

"Three."

"Two."

"One."

CHAPTER 35

MAKE THE CUT

I ACTIVATE Berserker Rage as soon as the timer hits zero. The shield around our platform fades, and the cheers of the crowd abruptly cut off as the dampening effect of the outer barrier keeps the noise at bay.

Otis roars from across the platform as he activates his rage as well. My blood boils as increased stats flood through me, and thanks to my Spirit of the Beast path, it will last twice as long.

Next to me, Scotty draws the arrow back even further, and orange energy spirals around the arrow shaft. A hidden piece of the bow unfolds, revealing a glass contraption, almost like a sight. As he holds the arrow steady, the charge grows stronger, and the shaft elongates until it's almost the size of a spear.

This looks like a badass attack, but I'm not going to get skewered waiting around to see if he's aiming for me or someone else. Instead, I activate Concussive Force and swing for the fences with the increased damage buff from Horror of Power.

Scotty releases the arrow just as my hammer connects with his side. His neck and legs curl around the force of my attack, and he rockets off the side of the platform. It'd be comical if not for the searing pain around my midsection as the giant arrow flies past like it was launched from a cannon. Its dense energy peels skin and flesh from my ribs.

A sand wyrm arcs through the air beside the platform, devouring Scotty before he even hits the ground.

I touch my tender ribs, but thanks to my increased regeneration, the wound is already mending.

There's a scream behind me, and I turn just in time to witness the gnome cleric sliding off the end of Arty's sword into the arena below.

Two down, six to go.

The presence of my horrors suddenly goes dull. They aren't dead, but they're no longer responding to my commands. I find them stationed in front of the puppet master like guardians, along with the druid's silver wolf. When I try to regain control of my horrors, it's like the connection has been severed. So, I summon three more and keep them by my side.

Erbin's grin as he stares at the other gnomes makes my skin crawl.

Nearby, Otis battles with the catfolk paladin in the center of the platform. His axe moves with incredible speed and force, sparks flying as the paladin manages to deflect every blow.

Meanwhile, Arty's arms glow red as he slices at projectiles being shot from the tinkerer's contraption. Each of the mechanical orbs explodes upon impact, sending gears and springs bouncing across the platform.

With the cleric gone, the tinkerer and druid stand back-to-back. The tinkerer shouts for the druid to send out his remaining wolf against Arty, but the druid refuses. His eyes burn with hatred toward Erbin. The druid lifts his golden staff, and a gust of wind pushes the puppet master toward the edge of the platform.

Lanxkuri uses the distraction to attack, grunting as she activates her blood magic. Her eyes go red, and a stream of dark energy shoots from her palm, bringing the druid to his knees. The puppet master escapes the gust of wind just before blowing off the platform and sends his puppets at the downed druid.

"Not so fast." I cast Sacrifice on the three stolen horrors, and even though they aren't under my control, they vanish into the ether, giving me a point in Dexterity, Strength, and Constitution.

The silver puppet-wolf crashes into its black counterpart, and they go for one another. The falcon dives at the possessed wolf's eyes, meanwhile the druid slowly comes back to his senses.

I keep my eye on Lanxkuri as I wait for my moment to attack. She and I are the only ones not currently engaged in active combat.

Otis decapitates the paladin, and the head rolls off the edge of the platform as the body collapses. The barbarian hovers over the body, skin steaming as he beats his hairy chest with a fist.

Stupid oaf. I switch out Destroyer for the Renewal Spear and launch the weapon like a javelin. The emerald spearhead hits Otis in the shoulder, sinking in halfway up the shaft as blood splatters from the exit wound on his chest. I watch from behind as Otis pulls the spear through his chest with a rage-fueled scream.

He turns around, heaving as he tosses the spear to the ground.

"You're going to pay for that!" He charges across the platform with an insane burst of speed, the outline of a wild boar superimposed over his body.

His axe cuts through the air with enough power that it whistles. I dodge the attack, but not before it slices through the tip of my braid, unraveling the thick black hair. I summon a Horror of Vitality, but the passive slow doesn't affect him while he's raging. Both of our rages should be up soon.

He keeps pressing. The wound in his shoulder nearly healed

when a giant glob of red liquid soars past me. It wraps around Otis's head and shoulders, forming a thick bubble. He drops his axe to tear at the liquid that clings to his face like cellophane. His fingers rip through it, but it's like clawing at water. The bubble reforms as fast as he tears it away, making it impossible for him to breathe.

I glance over my shoulder and see the shriveled, desiccated body of the paladin, all of the blood drained from the decapitated corpse. Behind it, the blood mage contorts her hands in the air, keeping the paladin's blood formed around Otis's head.

Otis drops to his knees, grabbing blindly for his axe. I want to kick it away, but I'm not getting anywhere near that blood. Finally, he grabs the weapon and swings. A stampede of wild boars similar to my spirit guide charge across the platform. One hits me in the leg, knocking me to the ground as my rage ends.

Otis swings again, his movements more erratic as the steam fades from his shoulders. With each swing, he moves slower and slower until the weapon drops from his grip. He falls to his knees, and a moment later, collapses on the platform.

I back away, keeping as much distance between me and the blood mage as possible. The puppet master must be dead because he's nowhere to be seen. Arty swings his sword wildly, fighting off the tinkerer's projectiles while keeping the two wolves at bay. Thanks to the Helm of Resolution, he's managed to gain a twenty-five percent Dexterity buff due to deflecting the rapid attacks. The massive sword moves faster than it has any right to.

The falcon screeches overhead, diving and clawing at the cyclops. The tinkerer now has five contraptions set up on the ground. They rattle and whir as they assault Arty like miniature cannons.

I smash one of the cannon's orbs out of the air and join the cyclops. "Sorry I left you hanging. Let's finish these two, but keep an eye out for the blood mage, she's opportunistic."

Arty grunts his affirmation as he splits another orb in two.

The projectiles continue to barrage us while the wolves snap at our feet. Out of the corner of my eye, Lanxkuri stands still, watching us and making this all the more difficult.

One crisis at a time.

Roots spring up from the ground, but Arty slices them before they can latch around us. The momentary lapse in concentration causes him to take several hits from the projectiles. One of the metallic orbs unfurls, and metal prongs extend from within, latching onto Arty's arm. He screams as he rips it off, pieces of flesh dangling from the prongs.

I smash another orb just before it hits him. "Fuck this, I say we charge them."

"Lead the way." He grunts.

My sudden surge catches the wolves off guard, and they retreat toward the gnomes, but not before I smash one of them in the rear with Destroyer. The splash damage from Ram's Rage carries forward, hitting the second wolf with a burst of magical damage and knocking two of the tinkerer's contraptions to their sides.

While the gnome crouches to reposition his devices, Arty leaps through the air, bringing the blade of his giant sword down like a sledgehammer between the two gnomes. Energy explodes from both sides of the weapon, tossing the tinkerer and one of the wolves over the edge.

The druid rolls across the platform toward the center. Lanxkuri groans as she activates an ability from across the platform. The gnome freezes in place, his fingers twitching like he's trying to move, but the rest of his body is stiff as a board. I don't care if it's the blood mage's doing, I bring Destroyer down on his head just the same, and then I kick the body off the edge just to be safe.

Arty gathers by my side, and we face off with Lanxkuri.

I lift Destroyer over my shoulder. "No matter how this ends, one of us advances."

He narrows his eye. "To hell with that. We finish this together."

I summon more horrors and immediately cast Sacrifice, boosting my stats. Arty and I spread out, making it difficult for Lanxkuri to focus on us both at the same time. I switch out Destroyer for Petrified Staff. The gnarled staff allows me to cast ranged physical attacks every ten seconds.

I use its ability, sending out a charge of energy that the blood mage dodges with ease from this distance. Arty attacks her from behind as she dodges, but she sidesteps the massive blade with practiced ease, raising her hand as a spear of blood shoots out, impaling the cyclops in the ribs. Her health drops by about five percent from using the attack, but Arty takes even more damage despite his high Constitution.

While she's facing away, I switch back to Destroyer and go for the kill shot. Somehow, she senses me coming, because she turns around and a beam of black energy hits me in the chest, knocking me on my back while simultaneously draining a chunk of my health.

A flash of blue trails back through the beam, and the blood mage's health returns to full.

She can attack with blood and replenish her own health the same way. This is going to be a pain in the ass.

I crawl to my feet, feeling slightly lethargic from the blood loss. Arty rushes toward me.

Destroyer feels heavy in my palm. "She's going to be—"

Arty swings his sword, and I barely manage to raise Destroyer so he doesn't take off my head. The force of the hit sends me sliding several inches toward the edge.

"Dude, what the hell?"

He attacks again, and I notice the blackness in his eyes. He's under some kind of confusion spell. I parry the first attack, then meet his sword with my full Strength. The clash echoes around us as our weapons collide.

I reposition to keep myself away from the edge when a bottle explodes between us. Hundreds of glass shards rip through my skin, speckling me with cuts like a bloody Easter egg.

The darkness from Arty's eyes fades, and he comes back to himself. "What happened?"

Before I have time to explain, the dozens of cuts burn like fire as blood explodes from the wounds in thick globules before transforming into bats that swarm us. More and more bats pour from our wounds, and my health continues to plummet. A shadowy aura spreads from each of the blood bats as they attack us.

The air teems with bats, and their aura begins to block out the sun. Wings flap and bats screech as my world descends into darkness. I swing Destroyer, but there are too many bats. With each new bite, they spawn quicker than I can kill them.

Before I know it, my health is more than halfway gone, and I'm nowhere near ready for another rage. I summon horrors, casting Kamikaze as soon as they spawn, but it's no use. Dozens of bats assault me at a time, their bites like pinpricks. The blood loss continues to mount, and it will eventually kill me or Arty. At least one of us will advance.

Then it hits me. I summon Pharos and blinding light spills out in front of me. The bats squeal as the spirit beast charges at the shadowy monsters. Some of them combust into globs of blood that fall to the floor, while others fly high into the air to escape the frost goat's light.

Next to us, Lanxkuri stands with both arms curled up by her side. Black energy radiates from her palms as her index finger and thumb form a circle. Her eyes go wide when she notices my spirit beast, but before she has time to react, Arty and I attack.

From opposite sides, his sword goes low and Destroyer goes high, connecting at the same time. His blade severs her legs, and the hit from the warhammer sends her body windmilling over the edge of the platform. She extends a glowing red palm, and a black aura surrounds her just as the sand wyrm snatches her from the air.

With her gone, I drop Destroyer to the floor, suddenly drained beyond belief.

Without warning, the noise of the outside arena returns. Cannons erupt from all sides, and the crowd cheers louder than ever.

The announcer's voice echoes around us mid-sentence. "*—and there you have it. Chod and Arty survive group one, securing their place in the quarterfinals! What a start to the first round of the Champion's Tournament!*"

I tune out the rest of what he says and go to Arty. He heaves as he leans on the guard of his sword.

I grip his shoulder and lean next to him. "I can't believe we pulled that off."

"Me neither. That attack..." He shakes his head in disbelief. "I've never experienced anything like it. If not for your goat, one of us would certainly be dead."

The platform shrinks, lowering and contracting as one of the earth mages maneuvers us around the arena. Group two's pillar rises above the others and takes center stage.

As our platform glides through the sand like a hockey puck, I spot the seating area for those who were defeated. There's a tunnel at the back of the booth that goes into the outer arena, and some of the challengers have already left. Others sit idly by while the gnome tinkerer and druid appear to be arguing.

Our pillar comes to a stop, docking against the booth next to the council. Several of the council members stand and clap as we step off the pillar. There are a half-dozen guards stationed in their booth, as well as two in ours. Once we're inside, a barrier forms around the booth.

"Let's give it up one more time for the champions of group one, Chod the forest troll and Arty the cyclops!" The crowd roars, and the announcer continues. *"Group two is sure to be just as exciting, so join me as we count down to the next battle."*

CHAPTER 36
GROUP OF DEATH

From where we sit, it's hard to see Limery in much detail. I can make out Ethan's shadow wings and Michael's gleaming armor. There's a small red dot that I assume is Limery.

Arty pokes my forearm. "Check this out."

He holds a metal tube up to his eye. At the end of the tube, there are several rows of rotatable glass lenses.

He taps one of the lenses into place with his finger. "It's a magnifying lens. You can adjust them, and they make it easier to see things far away."

I find a similar item next to my seat and hold it up to my right eye. It works like a scope, allowing me to zoom in with amazing detail based on which lens I choose. It wouldn't be a bad idea to have one of these for personal use, especially while traveling.

With the magnifying lens, I spot Limery hovering over Roddick right as the countdown hits zero and the protective barrier fades from their pillar.

Come on, Limery. Just stay out of the action for as long as possible.

Limery flies higher, and the announcer does a play-by-play of the action. I do my best to tune him out, focusing on what is actually happening, but it's hard to keep out the amplified voice entirely.

"And we're off! That's a mighty strike from the paladin, but victory won't be that easy…"

My claws dig into my palms. Come on, little guy, you've got this.

The beginning of the fight is complete chaos. Beams of energy explode, fire erupts, and metal clashes. Don summons a void portal behind the gnome mage that looks like a black mirror floating in the air. The mage's robe flutters behind her before she's violently sucked in.

A second portal spits her out off the edge of the platform. She raises her staff as she falls, and a beam of light gathers at the end, but a sand wyrm swallows the diminutive mage before the spell fully activates.

"Wow, folks! What a tactical display of void magic. One challenger down, and now the warlock is making his presence known."

Ethan takes to the air on his shadowy wings, shooting bolts of dark energy from his palms. The black lightning bolts crack with thunder as they crash into opponents.

Oruma, the merfolk mesmer, and Tozzet, the tidal mage, stay near one another. Beams of water pour from the tidal mage like a firehose, blasting against Michael's giant shield and pushing the paladin toward the edge before he's able to dash out of the way. A miniature waterfall shifts around the merfolk duo at shoulder height, forming a shield and mitigating many of the attacks thrown their way.

The mesmer's hands flash silver as she creates a clone of both her and Tozzet while Ethan targets the two merfolk with his bolts.

Black lightning rips into one of the tidal mages, and his body shatters like a broken mirror.

"You can always count on a good mesmer to bring chaos to the battlefield. Let's see if the challengers can locate the real Oruma. But wait, we've got a clash on our hands center stage. Listen to that metal sing!"

Roddick and the speckled catfolk fighter go at it. Roddick wields a shortsword and buckler while the nimble catfolk uses two shortswords. Sparks fly as the two clash repeatedly. They seem evenly matched in technique, but it's clear that the catfolk has the speed advantage. Limery summons a flame wall between the two to give Roddick a moment of respite, but the tidal mage extinguishes the fire with a whirlpool that sucks in the catfolk.

While the soaked cat fights to free himself, Michael seizes the opportunity to attack. His sword glows with radiant energy and lightning explodes into the sky as he brings down his sword on the fighter, killing him instantly.

"The paladin delivers the judgment of Onera, and the god of light has found the catfolk fighter unworthy!"

Roddick stands there with his mouth agape, but the momentary lapse proves his downfall. Arty curses next to me as Ethan flies behind the cyclops's brother. A chain of dark energy forms between the two, and the color quickly drains from Roddick's face. He tries to run, but the link between them doesn't fade. His body shrivels until he collapses to the floor.

"An essence drain from the warlock has removed another challenger from the competition. Watch out, though, now we've got an angry imp on our hands."

A streak of bright orange darts through the air as Limery goes molten, barreling into the warlock with ridiculous speed. There's a flurry of activity as the imp attacks the warlock like an angry wasp, avoiding Ethan's attacks and countering again and again.

"Goddammit, Limery! Leave him be!" I shout, knowing he can't hear me.

A shroud of darkness surrounds Ethan and a dark, clawed hand the size of his body reaches out from the void, smacking Limery to the ground like a fly. My heart drops as the imp bounces off the ground like a ragdoll.

I can't tell how low his health is, but he's not built to take hits like that.

Next to me, Arty clicks another lens into place and leans forward.

Behind Limery, one of the mesmers morphs to look like the dead catfolk and pounces, weapons drawn, toward Limery who's curled up on the platform. The catfolk has Limery in his sights when Michael appears out of nowhere, using his massive shield to protect the imp. A white glow explodes from the paladin and Limery, and the next moment, Limery is flying again.

"Would you look at that? Saved by the paladin! Who saw that coming?"

Tommy Sullivan stabs the catfolk in the back, and the clone shatters into mirrored pieces just like the tidal mage. The real mesmer teleports from across the platform, reappearing behind the hero and pressing her hands to both sides of the hero's head. When she releases, Tommy drops to his knees, screaming as he tears at his hair.

"Tommy looks to be suffering from Torment. Oruma is not holding anything back today."

Don blasts the downed hero with a bolt of dark energy. At the same time, Tozzet hits him with a water whip. The human fighter's hands drop to his sides, and he collapses to the ground.

"And another one bites the dust! Wait, look at that. The warlock is calling for backup from his patron!"

A tear rips through the air around Ethan, revealing a backdrop of lava and darkness as two demons crawl through the rift. The purple-skinned demons have horns that swirl upward like an antelope, and they crawl on spindly arms like a monkey with long, clawed hands and feet. A barbed forked tail whips behind them and they snarl, each one revealing a dangerous set of teeth. They're too far away for me to identify them, but these are definitely different from the flying demons we faced outside Lynchton.

Tozzet summons two water elementals to fight the demons, each one nearly six feet tall. They tower over the demons like a raging ocean in physical form. I expect a good fight, but the demons tear through the elementals and swarm the tidal mage, raking their claws across him and stabbing with their barbed tales until the mage stops moving.

Michael raises his sword overhead, and it glows yellow before twin beams of holy light shoot from the sky, vaporizing the two demons in puffs of smoke.

"The demons might not fear elementals, but they are no match for the Smite of a god."

Limery goes after the mesmer now that the tidal mage is gone, but she teleports away. Don follows behind her with his own teleport, somehow getting to her destination faster and summoning an orb of darkness that swallows the mesmer whole as soon as she reappears.

"Wow! There's your overwhelming proof that in short distances, Blink is faster than Teleport. And now we're down to the final four!"

Arty and I are both on the edge of our seats. Somehow, Limery is still in the thick of it. I just hope he stays out of the action long enough to secure a spot in the next round. There's no need for him to be a hero.

Ethan presses his hands together. His tattoos glow, and the air crackles as two massive balls of shadow form beside him, each one pulsing with dark energy. The shadows are so dark that they seem to swallow the light around them. A black-clawed hand breaks through the darkness. Then another, gripping at the edge of the shadow until a demonic skull resembling a horse's pokes through. The demon emerges from the darkness, unfurling the same shadowy wings that keep Ethan aloft, its hoofed feet hovering above the platform. It looks up, and blue fire blazes within its eye sockets.

Shadow demons. Fuck.

Nebulous blades form in each of the demon's hands. Just like Taryn's Shadow Daggers, they are capable of bypassing weapons and armor to inflict damage. The last time we faced these demons, a single hit from one of their blades took out half of my health. The only reason we defeated them was because of the phoenix's sacrifice. This isn't good.

"The warlock has certainly evened the odds. It appears the paladin, imp, and void mage have formed a temporary truce. This is going to be good."

Don and Michael gather side by side with Limery hovering between them as they face off against Ethan and his demons for a spot in the quarterfinals.

I hope the three of them can band together to take him out, because I don't know if any of us can defeat Ethan one-on-one with a patron as powerful as his.

Ethan unleashes a black bolt at Limery, and it crashes between the two heroes as Limery dodges the attack. One of the demons dives for Michael, swinging its shadow sword as the paladin raises his own.

I curse Michael's stupidity. As a paladin, he should know better! The demon's sword can bypass metal, and there's no telling how much damage it's about to inflict.

Somehow, the paladin's sword blocks the shadow blade, and

molten energy burns where the two weapons touch. Hot sparks erupt between the blades. The demon grows darker and Michael glows brighter until an explosion blows them apart.

Damn, I was wrong. I guess holy magic can stop a shadow attack after all. That will be useful information going forward.

Limery throws a barrage of fireballs, and Don opens a void portal in front of them. The fireballs disappear inside the void, reappearing behind Ethan and exploding against his back. The demon that had been guarding Ethan dives for Don, but the void mage blinks to the other side of the platform. Limery chases the demon, hurling fireballs but careful to stay out of the reach of the shadow blade.

Michael returns to the center of the platform, all visible remnants of the explosion gone as his armor once again shines bright. Ethan's tattoos glow a platinum blue as he fires a barrage of dark energy at the paladin. Michael crouches, raising his shield as the dark bolts fizzle out upon impact.

Meanwhile, Don continues to Blink in rapid succession like a laggy video game as both demons pursue him around the platform.

"I don't know how much longer the void mage can keep this up. That much spatial travel in such a short time has to be taking its toll." The announcer has everyone on edge as the battle continues to unfold.

I flip one of the lenses and zoom in further. Sweat beads from the void mage's brow as he continues to Blink around the platform. I don't think he can keep it up much longer.

One of the demons transforms the blade of its sword into an infernal whip. As Don Blinks, the demon flicks the weapon and it whips across the platform, wrapping around the void mage's ankle as he reappears.

Don Blinks again, but this time, the demon travels with him as he teleports away. Ethan abandons his fight with the paladin as if he knows exactly where Don will emerge and hits the void mage with a spell the moment he reappears, shrouding Don and the demon in a dense fog.

Michael doesn't move as both demons plunge their swords into the void mage. Instead, he targets Limery with a buff.

The imp goes molten once again, only this time he blazes with a bright light similar to the paladin's as he dives at the demons. Their swords are still buried in the void mage when Limery melts through the chest of one demon. Light explodes at the point of impact, and the shadow demon bursts into millions of particles of black ash.

The light around Limery fades, and the second demon takes to the air, rejoining Ethan.

Ethan nods toward Limery, and the demon flies after the imp. Limery zooms around the platform, weaving like a fighter jet as the winged demon pursues.

"Demon versus imp. Paladin versus warlock. Who will survive and secure their place in the quarterfinals?"

While Limery and the demon play their game of cat and mouse, Michael and Ethan showcase the power of light and darkness. Bolts of sinister energy crash against the paladin's holy weapons and armor. Every time holy and infernal attacks touch, they explode with violent power. Michael casts buff after buff, avoiding the damaging effects of Ethan's attacks. As the paladin's aura continues to change time and again, I realize I never knew there were so many shades of white.

In the battle of speed, Limery proves faster and more agile than the demon. As they fly by the warlock and paladin, Ethan calls the demon off. Limery doesn't notice, leaving Michael two against one.

The demon dives for Michael from behind to attack the

paladin unaware. It swings the shadow blade for Michael's head, but the blade crumbles to ash inches from the paladin's neck as if blocked by some unseen force. In an impressive display of finesse, Michael blocks Ethan's corrupted bolts with his shield and spins around, slicing the demon in two from groin to head.

The entire stadium gasps at the heroic display.

There's little time to appreciate the effort as Ethan puts his hands together overhead and a bolt of lightning so dark it shrouds the arena shoots from above. It hits the paladin with a thunderous crash, and Michael vanishes.

Cannon blasts and cheers echo around the arena.

"Oh my gods, folks! That's what this tournament is all about. It's not every day you witness a patron banishing a paladin from existence. A stunning display of power. Give it up for the winners of round two, Ethan and Limery!"

Arty and I share the same shocked expression. Limery did it! Holy shit, he did it! I jump to my feet, clapping with the rest of the arena.

After a long bout of applause, platform two descends and slides across the arena with Ethan and Limery standing at opposite sides. Limery scowls at the warlock as our barrier disappears and they dock with our booth.

Limery flies over and wraps his arms around my neck. "Limmy dids its! Limmy wons!"

"You did a great job." I pat him on the back. "I'm proud of you."

"Who knew imps were so powerful?" Ethan leans against a column and stares out at the crowd. "To hear others talk of them, you'd think they were nothing more than glorified messengers."

Limery grows hot as he sits on my shoulder. "Limmy doesn't like yous. Yous is a bad mans."

The warlock grins but doesn't look our way. "Don't you forget it."

The entire time we wait for the next match, Ethan never looks in our direction. He keeps his gaze focused on the inner arena. Maybe it's his attempt to further get into our heads. Not that he needs any help with that. He might have scrapped his way into the quarterfinals, but he did it going one against three and prevailing.

Do any of us really have a shot at beating him when he can summon demons to fight on his behalf? I honestly have no idea the scope of his power when his patron is involved.

"Look, Chods. It's Caustics." Limery grabs my horn and pushes my head to the left, pointing into the stands.

Sure enough, Caustic's large frame sticks out like a sore thumb against the sea of gnomes. I really wish he'd been allowed to fight with me. We're doing better than I could have hoped, already clinching three of the final eight spots, but a dragon is a dragon.

Putting on a good show might gain us a few new allies, but nothing beats winning. As Don said, everybody respects power.

The impossibly-hard-to-tune-out announcer's voice begins the countdown for group three. There are some dangerous opponents in this group that I know of, including Drizz'rt, Kevin the sorcerer, and Jason the mage.

I grab a magnifying lens from a nearby seat and hand it to the imp. When he holds it up to his bulbous eye, it's nearly as big as he is.

I focus mine on the platform. Everyone is scattered around the perimeter except for Jason, who stands right in the middle. A bold strategy. He doesn't wear the traditional wizard robes of most mages and sorcerers. Instead, he wears a slim-fitting black tunic and a red shawl draped around his shoulders and head like a hood. The center seems like an awfully dangerous spot for the mage to start, leaving his unprotected back exposed to an attack.

The countdown ends, and the barrier fades. Drizz'rt is the first to move, leaping toward Jason's backside with daggers clutched in both hands. A blindside attack from an assassin is going to be gruesome.

Jason kneels, and a cube of energy forms around him, blocking Drizz'rt's attack as the rogue lizardfolk stabs into the barrier with his daggers.

Energy flares along the cube and it expands, rapidly swelling beyond the edge of the platform and pushing every challenger off the ledge into the sand below. Two of the challengers die to the sand wyrms before ever hitting the ground.

Reddick survives the fall, but he only lasts a moment before a wyrm gets him too.

A moment later, cannons fire to announce the end of the match, but I can't tell who the other survivor was.

Ethan curses, shaking his head as he stares into the arena.

"Would you look at that! Our quickest round yet. Jason puts his arcane Cube of Protection to great use, but Drizz'rt, the infamous assassin, has managed to cling to the cube's exterior with his sharp claws, securing his place in the next round!"

Sure enough, Drizz'rt is latched onto the far side of the cube, claws digging into the shield's surface. Jason cancels the spell, and Drizz'rt plummets into the sand below. One of the earth mages quickly forms a one-person platform to save the lizardfolk from the wyrms, raising him back to the main platform.

The assassin and the mage exchange heated words while the crowd continues to applaud.

I send Taryn a quick message, wishing him luck. Not that I imagine he's checking his notifications right now. I'm sure he's feeling the pressure, especially after Arty, Limery, and I all advanced.

I know I would be.

When the platform docks, Drizz'rt is still glaring at Jason. The mage nods to Ethan and takes a seat in the back corner of the booth. The assassin offers Limery and me congratulations before taking a seat behind us.

Before I have a chance to ask him why he's so upset, the announcer begins counting down for the next match.

I turn my attention to Taryn. Come on, bro. You've got this.

CHAPTER 37

RAM, BAM, THANK YOU, MA'AM

The platform was like the eye of a hurricane, an eerie quiet amidst the roar of the crowd.

Taryn sat on Berry's back with Ruby between his legs. Instead of curling up, she stood on all fours as Berry shifted his feet, groaning and huffing at the other challengers.

Jordy stood in front of them, head lowered and ready to attack. Flubs tried to peek above the lip of the vial around Taryn's neck, but he ordered the slime back inside. No one knew about Flubs aside from his friends, and he wanted to keep it that way.

He gently stroked the soft fur of the jackal's ears. She was on high alert, just like Taryn. The texture of her fur was calming, and Taryn needed it now more than ever. Chod and Limery had both made it to the next round. No one would ever call him a failure if he didn't make it, but he wanted to push himself. He was a good support, but now was the time to see what he was truly capable of when his back was against the wall. He couldn't compete with many of the challengers when it came to burst damage or raw power, but if he played it right, he had a chance to outsmart them.

And for once, he could do that without fear of losing one of his pets.

His hand instinctively moved over his heart, over the carrot tattoo that rested there.

Taryn's pulse thundered in his ears as he watched the nine other challengers. To his left, there was Sam the monk. He knew precious little about him aside from the fact that he was another hero that had managed to keep a low profile. Then there was Kazzandre the giant and a gnome mage.

Kazzandre towered over everyone else, wearing studded leather armor while wielding twin warhammers that would be full-sized weapons for anyone else. He'd heard some of her adventures at the ball, and when it came to raw strength, she might give Chod a run for his money. She spun the weapons against her palms. Taryn wondered if it was out of excitement or nervousness? Perhaps both.

The gnome wore a sky-blue robe embroidered with silver snowflakes along the arms. The end of his staff looked like it was carved from ice. He'd need to be extra cautious of abilities that could freeze or slow.

To Taryn's right, Randy the rogue sported a full arsenal of knives and daggers strapped about his body. The silver thread of the wolf on his chest sparkled as it caught the light of the sun. Their eyes met, and the rogue winked before returning his gaze to the giant.

Next to Randy stood Troy Malloy, a fire mage, and a little further down was the drunken master gnome. Even just standing there, the monk wobbled like he could topple at any moment.

Taryn grinned, wondering if it was a requirement to be drunk for the class to work or if the class made the gnome appear drunk.

On the far side of the platform, a human adventurer from

Ellynmylly looked about uncertainly. Two gnomish tinkerers sandwiched him from both sides, already setting up their gear.

The countdown hit zero and Taryn summoned a ring of poisonous mushrooms around himself and his pets. His goal was to lay low for as long as possible. Berry looked threatening in his own right but the less attention they garnered, the better.

Next to him, Sam the monk narrowed his eyes at Taryn. He drew his fist back and a watercolor outline of a tiger formed over the monk's arm. As his torso twisted to unleash the attack on Taryn, a warhammer hit the monk in the side. Ribs audibly cracked, and the tiger attack wisped away as he flew off the edge.

The giant smirked at Taryn, stomping in his direction, but Taryn cast Stonewall between him and the giant, keeping her at bay for now.

"Why the hell are they targeting me? Maybe we need to look more intimidating."

Berry groaned in response as Taryn summoned more mushrooms, creating land mines of poisonous fungi between him and the others. For now, he had a narrow strip of safety protected by Stonewall and mushrooms with the platform's edge at his back.

At the other end of the platform, the gnome tinkerers joined forces, setting up a fortress of metal plates complete with mounted turrets. The contraptions fired on the drunken master, who somehow dodged every projectile shot his way.

Closer, Troy battled the gnome mage in a dazzling display of fire and ice. The occasional errant spell flew past Taryn as fireballs collided with ice daggers, creating a fine mist that streaked with rainbow in the sunlight.

The human from Ellynmylly ran toward the center of the platform as Randy chased him, his head on a swivel as chaos raged all around him. Taryn saw the patch of ice before the adventurer hit it, slipping and sliding off the edge of the platform without ever being touched.

Taryn turned his attention back to the rogue, but it was already too late. A dagger was coming at his neck too fast for him to react or dodge.

His neck stung like a pinprick, and Taryn reached for the wound, wondering how long he could survive with a dagger in the neck. His blood was surprisingly cool to the touch as he searched for the wound, but then it gurgled. Taryn realized it wasn't blood at all. The tip of the dagger had barely grazed his skin thanks to Flubs.

Taryn removed the dagger that was encased within the slime's body. In the blade's reflection, his neck barely had a scratch. Flubs had been on alert even when Taryn's attention was elsewhere.

"Thanks, buddy." Taryn stuffed the dagger into his satchel.

Randy frowned, saw the many mushrooms in front of Taryn, and then set off for less defensive prey.

Meanwhile, Troy and the ice mage's battle crept ever closer to Taryn. The ice mage had his back turned as he formed ice shields to block a barrage of fireballs.

Taryn couldn't pass up the opportunity for an easy kill. Mushrooms exploded as Jordy ran across the platform, ramming the unsuspecting mage off the side. The poor gnome flew like a soccer ball, and a sand wyrm snatched him out of the air.

"Ram, bam, thank you, Jordy."

On the other side of Stonewall, Taryn could hear the giant fighting someone. She groaned and grunted as metal clinked.

Taryn needed to get a better view of the battlefield, so he summoned more mushrooms to protect his pets and transformed into his bird form.

He flew up and perched on the stone wall, where Randy and

the giant danced in a circle on the other side. Taryn then flew higher, taking in all the action at once. Since his pets couldn't advance to the next round without him, no one was paying them much attention for now as long as they kept out of the way.

The fire mage lurked at the edge of the platform now that the ice mage was gone, just out of the action as the two tinkerers continued to assault the monk.

Might as well sow a little chaos. Taryn flew low, casting Mind Warp on one of the tinkerers before returning to his pets.

One of the tinkerers suddenly turned on the other. There were loud crashes as their contraptions and turrets fired at each other from close range, destroying the fortress they'd created. While the one tried to calm the mind-warped gnome from attacking him, the drunken monk leapt with a flying kick that sent the first tinkerer off the edge. The monk landed in the middle of the wreckage, spinning around and connecting an elbow that launched the second tinkerer off the platform to be devoured by a sand wyrm.

And then there were five.

A section of Taryn's wall crumbled as one of Kazzandre's warhammers smashed into it, giving Taryn line of sight on the raging battle between her and the rogue. The quick-footed rogue appeared to be too nimble for the giant, dodging her attacks with ease. She swung for him again, but he evaded, somehow sliding between her legs and stabbing her in the groin along the way.

The giant roared in pain as her hammer eviscerated another section of the wall. She winced as she brought the second warhammer down on the rogue that had repositioned behind her. He dodged again, this time rolling to the side and slicing behind her knee as her warhammer crashed into the platform. With each new wound, the giant moved slower, making it easier for Randy to tear her down.

Eventually, she could barely stand, wobbling like a newborn fawn as Randy circled her like the wolf on his chest. Then a fireball exploded against Kazzandre, sending the giant toppling over the edge.

Randy turned on the fire mage, snarling. "She was mine!"

Troy shrugged. "If she was yours, I wouldn't have killed her."

While the two argued, the gnome monk attacked Troy from behind, kicking the mage in the back and knocking him to his knees.

The mage stood, fists covered in flames. "You're going to pay for that!"

Randy readied his daggers as the three challengers squared off, oblivious to Taryn standing idly by. Shit was about to hit the fan.

This time, Taryn was ready for it. Troy punched and a stream of fire shot at the monk, while at the same time, Randy sprinted for the mage with his daggers tucked by his side.

"Good night, boys," Taryn whispered as he cast Endless Night.

A veil of impenetrable darkness settled over the center of the platform, preventing those inside from seeing or smelling anything. He had thirty seconds before the ability ended, and he planned to use every second of it.

Taryn pulled Lightning in a Bottle from his satchel and tossed it into the darkness. It was a one-time use item, but now seemed like the perfect opportunity. Glass shattered and thunder cracked from within as the stored lightning exploded from the bottle. With five charges inside, there was a good chance someone was taking multiple strikes, along with a fifty percent chance of being stunned.

Next, Taryn cast Lightning Bolt in the center of the dark cloud. With its ten-second cooldown, he'd be able to use it once more before the cloud dispersed. He picked a spot at random and cast Moonbeam. A stream of silver light disappeared within the cloud.

He summoned poisonous mushrooms along the cloud's edge to prevent anyone from fleeing the carnage in his direction, and when Lightning Bolt came off cooldown, he cast it again. Taryn commanded his pets to retreat to his crumbling wall and summoned a second wall for their protection before taking to his bird form. He flew high above. Hopefully, when the spell faded, no one would notice him.

The spell ended, and the three challengers picked up where they left off. Troy cast a massive fireball at the drunken master that swirled in a vortex toward the gnome. As soon as he unleashed it, Randy stabbed the mage in the back with a dagger.

The monk swayed drunkenly as the fireball approached, but his hands moved in a practiced formation. Wisps of orange energy trailed his fingertips, and he took a step back, extending his hands as the fireball hit him, then he was somehow cradling the blast. The flames rolled across his chest with the finesse of a Harlem Globetrotter and as he redirected the fireball with his off-hand, the outline of a fiery eagle soared alongside the attack.

Randy dove out of the way as the blast engulfed the fire mage.

The monk raised his hands in the air like he'd just won, but Randy looked over his shoulder, scanning the perimeter of the platform.

His eyes lingered on Taryn's walls before he looked overhead. "Son of a bitch."

The drunken master grinned as he walked across the platform, swaying as he extended a hand to the rogue. "Congrats on making it to the next round."

Randy laughed. "You are a dumb motherfucker."

The rogue extended his hand. The moment he was about to shake, Randy's entire body shimmered. Shadow copies of himself spread out to both sides, and the real Randy appeared behind the monk. He buried his dagger in the gnome's neck, and the cannons echoed from around the arena.

"Wow, folks! With a bag of tricks like that, who would have thought it would be the druid pulling the wool over everyone's eyes? Congrats to Randy and Taryn for securing the final two spots in the quarterfinals."

The crowd cheered as Taryn returned to his dwarven form. He canceled Stonewall, and his pets came running over, Berry nearly knocking the druid to the ground as he nuzzled him.

Berry growled as Randy approached.

The rogue threw up his hands. "Don't worry about me. Just paying my respects. That guy might have been an idiot, but you played your cards to perfection." He grinned. "You won't fly under the radar in the next round."

Taryn smiled. Somehow, he and his friends made up half of the final eight spots.

CHAPTER 38
FIGHTING, FRIENDS, AND FOES

Between rounds, the earth mages return the sandy floor to gleaming crystal, and the platforms disappear. The sand wyrms are once again returned to wherever they dwell somewhere deep underground. A band plays in the stands, their music amplified across the arena while giant kites shaped like dragons, phoenixes, and other winged creatures soar above the crowd.

Taryn gestures wildly as he recounts his fight for us. He hasn't stopped grinning since he joined us in the booth. "I wish I could have saved Lightning in a Bottle for a later round, but I don't know if I would have survived without throwing everything I had at them." A green string of slime reaches out from the vial and taps Taryn on the cheek. "Or without Flubs. He saved me big-time."

"You put on a show. People will be talking about that fight for years to come. I still can't believe the monk thought the match was over." Arty's eye widens slightly as he shakes his head. "Crazy. Maybe he was drunk."

The four of us laugh, but no one else in the booth seems to be paying much attention to our conversation. Drizz'rt and Randy have become fast friends, once again talking shop and breaking down their moves for one another a couple of rows behind us.

Jason and Ethan stand in opposite corners on the other side of the booth. Ethan continually stares out into the arena, while Jason sits alone in the back corner.

"Any idea what we'll be up against next?" I ask.

Arty shrugs. "I don't think any of us were expecting four battle royales to start off with, so there's no telling what they have planned. She did mention that the next round will be single elimination."

Down below, the earth mages begin redesigning the arena, this time pulling crystal from beneath the floor to form obstacles, ravines, cliffs, and rock formations across the battlefield. A water mage fills a dip in the ground with water, forming a large pond, and then an earth mage creates a bridge and several stepping-stones across it.

When they're finished, the entire arena is the battlefield, opening up a slew of possibilities for the next round.

The music stops, and the announcer's voice carries above everything. *"As our mages prepare the arena for the quarterfinals, the moment has finally come to announce the seeding for the rest of the tournament."*

Massive slabs of glass rise from the arena floor on opposite sides of the stadium like giant scoreboards. One of the mages waves his hand, and an eight-person bracket carves into the glass. As each of our names are announced, they fill in on the display.

"On the left side, we have Chod versus Arty for match one, a true battle of the brawlers, and then it's rogue versus rogue in match two as Drizz'rt takes on Randy. On the right side, Ethan the warlock will face the deceptive druid, Taryn, for match three. And for the final match of the quarterfinals, Limery the imp is up against Jason the mage."

"The deceptive druid." Taryn puffs out his chest. "That has a nice ring to it."

Randy bursts out laughing behind us. "This is really going to be a strain on our friendship, Drizz'rt."

The lizardfolk laughs for the first time since I've known him. It's unnerving the way he chirps like a dolphin as his jaws widen, revealing a set of dangerously-sharp teeth. "The deepest bonds are forged on the battlefield. I look forward to testing your skills."

"Please never make him laugh again," Taryn mumbles.

Arty grins as he cracks his knuckles. "This is a fight I look forward to."

Having all four of us in a separate bracket was wishful thinking. I doubt even Hawkin's buff would prove to be that lucky.

I wink at the cyclops. "Well, then I guess we better put on a show."

With all three pieces of the Regeneration Triad equipped, I have an additional thirty percent HP, bringing me to over nine thousand without any of my horrors. For every horror I summon, I'll gain an additional ninety health as long as they remain alive.

If I were able to summon the full sixty horrors before they started to decay, I'd more than double my resting HP. There's no way I'll have the time to pull off something like that in this tournament, but the twenty percent regeneration buff and the bonus healing from both the Renewal Spear and Horrors of Finesse make me pretty damned hard to kill.

Arty's giant eye threatens to pop out of his head when I equip the new weapons. I almost feel bad for keeping them a secret.

He laughs. "I should have known you had something up your sleeve."

"Sorry, friend, but I came to win."

The countdown ends, and I summon my horrors. There's a good fifty feet between me and Arty, and I aim to keep my distance while I continue to build up my horrors.

Arty must know my motive, because he moves in, intent on engaging me early.

As much time as we've spent alongside one another the past week, this is the first time I've tested Arty's strength directly aside from our arm-wrestling match.

He's every bit as strong as me, maybe even more so.

I parry his sword attack with my spear, and it takes everything I have not to lose my grip on the weapon. He swings again and this time, I take the hit full on against my shield. The force from the attack sends my feet sliding several inches.

For now, I play on the defensive, using the terrain to my advantage to slow the pace of the fight and let the cyclops continue to press me as I summon more horrors. I send them running off to the bridge over the pond at the opposite end of the arena, careful to keep Arty far away from them. With his Helm of Resolution, each attack he lands within a certain time frame increases his attack speed. So many horrors would be a feast for him.

After five minutes of letting Arty pressure me around the arena, absorbing hit after hit, I dash back and shake out my aching hands. "Tired yet?"

"Hardly." A red aura surrounds his legs as he closes the distance in a single jump, bringing his massive sword down on my shield once again.

Pinned underneath the shield, I summon a Horror of Vitality. The horror's passive slows Arty, and I sacrifice my horrors all at once.

With an influx of stat points, I roll out from under the shield and activate Concussive Force as I stab at Arty's ribs. He dodges, spinning and countering with an overhead strike. Thanks to my bonus stats, I'm now faster and stronger than the cyclops. I pull my weapon back and parry with the butt of the spear, but I still can't land a hit. Sparks fly as the weapons grate against one another.

I rotate the spear, parrying his attack and using the momentum to slam his blade into the ground. Arty drops the sword and pulls out a warhammer. The hammer's weight is much harder to deflect with the spear, but it gives me the longer reach. I jab it at him and when he swings, I let him knock the spear from my hand. It spins like a helicopter blade out of my palm.

As his momentum carries him forward, I roll to his blindside and activate Return to Sender from the new effect stone. The spear abruptly shifts course like it's pulled by a powerful magnet.

When it returns to my hand, I jab the spear underneath the back of Arty's helm until the spearhead pokes through his eye socket, skewering his eye like a martini olive.

The announcer's voice returns alongside the celebratory cannons. Even though he's not truly dead, I try not to look at the body of my friend. It's a sight I hope to never see.

Instead, I raise my arms and bask in the glory of the crowd. One step closer to the finals.

"For our second match of the quarterfinals, it's a battle of blades as Randy the rogue and Drizz'rt the assassin vie for a place in the semis."

The fight between Randy and Drizz'rt is like watching a dance of shadow and misdirection. The action is so fast that the announcer can barely keep up. The two rogues move with amazing finesse and speed, steel clashing in a spray of sparks as they dash around the battlefield.

From up in our booth, it's almost impossible to tell who is winning. One minute, they move in a blur, and the next their blades are ripping through shadowy silhouettes and doppelgängers.

Watching them, I realize just how valuable a good rogue can be.

Randy and Drizz'rt clash, and their blades sing. Randy activates Shadowstep and Doppelgänger, and two versions of himself split in opposite directions while the real Randy blinks behind Drizz'rt.

The lizardfolk buries his blade in one of the doppelgängers and it turns to dust just as Randy appears behind Drizz'rt, plunging his blade into the assassin's neck. The golden lizard turns to dust, with the real Drizz'rt already behind Randy. He slams both of his daggers into the rogue's shoulders.

With arms immobilized, Randy's weapons fall to the floor. Drizz'rt pulls a vial from across his chest and smashes it against the ground, where a plume of gray smoke explodes, concealing both rogues.

When the smoke clears, Randy lays on the ground with a half-dozen blades sticking out of him while Drizz'rt leans against a nearby boulder, sharpening his dagger.

"What a display of speed and deception! This fight looked to be over a half-dozen times, with each challenger two steps ahead of the other, but there you have it, a remarkable finish. Round one of the semifinals will feature Chod vs Drizz'rt. Now stand by for the second half of the bracket featuring Ethan and Taryn."

Taryn huddles in the corner of the booth with his pets, giving them a pep talk. Berry, Jordy, Ruby, and skele-cat Flubs nod along as Taryn pumps his fist and points at each of them in turn.

Right now, he's in the zone, and I don't want to interrupt his focus. Ethan, on the other hand, has barely moved from his position leaning against the column, still staring intently into the arena.

Limery scowls at him from atop my shoulder. "Limmy hopes Taryns beats the bad mans."

Ethan glances at us out of the corner of his eye. "It's important to have dreams."

Jason snickers in the back corner, but I pay him no mind.

The platform returns, and the shield fades as Drizz'rt steps into the booth. He nods at me as he takes a seat in the back row.

Taryn climbs onto Berry, and both Ruby and Flubs leap into his lap.

"Good luck!" I call out as Jordy leads their troop onto the platform.

"Good lucks, Taryns!" Limery waves.

"See you soon." He winks as he turns to the crowd.

Ethan casually joins Taryn on the platform, and it descends into the arena. The earth mages showcase some of their skill as the base of the platform widens and shrinks as it moves around the terrain. It stops in the center, and a ramp descends on each side as the challengers take their positions.

The announcer blathers on about each of them, recounting their progress in the tournament as if we all haven't been watching it unfold over the course of the day.

I lift my magnifying lens as Taryn dismounts from Berry. He sends the bear to the right and Jordy to the left while Ruby and Flubs stay behind Taryn.

I understand what he's doing, but I don't like it. Freeing up

Berry to attack for when the warlock inevitably summons demons makes sense, but it puts Taryn on the ground. If he can stand back and use his spells from a distance, he might have a shot.

When the countdown ends, Taryn summons a ring of poisonous mushrooms between him and Ethan. The warlock unfurls his shadow wings and takes flight. Reality tears and portals appear beneath both of his feet. Crab-like demons the size of a small dog crawl through the dark portal, each one has six barbed legs, pincers, and a flattened midsection covered in eyes. The dark red eyes on their shells are unsettling even from this far away.

The demon crabs fall to the ground and scatter. Jordy rams into one and launches it across the arena. It lands with a splash in the pond. Berry crushes a demon with his paw while ripping off a pincer with his teeth. Green ichor trails from the appendage, and Berry spits it out.

Lightning crashes from the sky, arcing toward the warlock. A quick flap of his wings avoids the strike, and he counters with a demon bolt of his own. The black lightning explodes against a boulder a few feet away from Taryn.

Demons continue to funnel out of the portal like ants until dozens of them swarm the battlefield. Berry and Jordy destroy as many as they can, but they aren't quick enough. Taryn casts Strong Wind, increasing their movement speed and allowing his pets to evade the swarms more easily when they need to. Moonbeam is especially effective on the demons, but the cooldown is too long. The mushrooms deal lingering damage when they burst, enough that Taryn can finish the crab-demons off with a stab from his Shadow Dagger.

"It looks like the warlock has taken a page from the druid's playbook. He seems content to stand back for now, watching and waiting for Taryn to make a mistake."

There's no way Taryn can fight off the demons and Ethan at

the same time—and Ethan knows it. He hovers with a bemused expression, occasionally firing a demon bolt but otherwise watching the chaos unfold.

Taryn casts another Moonbeam, and it hits one of the portals directly, incinerating the demons crawling through. Smoke billows up from their dried corpses, and when the smoke clears, the portal is gone.

Ethan frowns, swooping across the chaos and hitting Berry with a purple beam of energy. A purple haze forms around Berry, and his health begins to drop. Taryn reacts fast, casting Imbue and doubling the bear's size while summoning more mushrooms.

"That got his attention! Ethan is on the attack, hitting the bear with Corruption."

Unfortunately, Imbue doesn't raise Berry's health or Constitution, so it continues to trickle down. There's no way Taryn will have the time or space to cast Restoration on him.

Demons continue to crawl through the open portal faster than they are being destroyed. Jordy leaps around the rocky terrain, launching himself from a boulder headfirst and stomping crabdemons before climbing back to the high ground.

Berry is having a tougher time. Even though he's larger, the demons cling to his backside and pinch at any area not covered by his golden armor. Blood mattes the rusty fur along his legs.

Taryn casts Lightning Bolt around the second portal, and demons explode across the arena. The attack does nothing to the portal itself, though.

Ethan shoots another demon bolt at Taryn, and he dives out of the way, but it was only a distraction. While Berry fights with the swarm of demons, crushing them and tearing them apart, Ethan casts Essence Drain and a channel of purple-and-black energy forms between the bear and the warlock.

Taryn's head swivels between Berry and the portal, and I

know exactly what he's thinking. He can either use Moonbeam to buy Berry some time or he can use it to close the portal, not both.

Berry's health continues to drop rapidly when a silver streak shoots from the sky.

Moonbeam hits the portal, killing demons and sending up more smoke. At the same time as the attack hits, Taryn's remaining pets charge for the warlock.

He's going all in.

Ruby leaps toward Ethan, launching herself high enough to sink her teeth into his boot. She dangles there, refusing to let go.

Ethan blasts her at point-blank range with his free hand, and her body collapses to the ground.

"Oh noes," Limery gasps beside me.

I place a hand on his feet, feeling the same dread.

Flubs abandons his skeleton and shoots through the air like a spitball. The slime wraps around Ethan's hand but immediately turns solid. The warlock shakes his wrist and Flubs slides off, hitting a boulder and shattering into hundreds of pieces.

"Ethan refuses to abandon Essence Drain, using his off-hand to cast Frozen Touch on the slime. Is there anything Taryn can do to stop him?"

Taryn transforms into his bird form and dodges a blast as he goes for the warlock's eyes. Ethan swats at the bird with his free hand but still doesn't release his hold on Berry.

Taryn swarms Ethan again and again like an angry mockingbird. While we're all focused on Taryn, Jordy launches himself off a boulder, hitting the warlock in the back and breaking the spell.

Berry shambles a few steps before collapsing under the attacks of the demons. Ethan searches for Taryn, but he hovers high overheard still in bird form. The crowd gasps as he changes back into a dwarf some hundred feet off the ground and falls with both daggers equipped.

He lands on Ethan's back, both blades plunging into the warlock. With both weapons embedded, Ethan's health is actually dropping. He reaches for Taryn, but he can't seem to get a hold of the dwarf. Instead, he dives toward the ground as his health plummets, crashing into a cluster of crab-demons. They swarm Taryn, forcing him to let go.

Ethan unleashes a slew of attacks on Taryn while he's pinned beneath the demons. When his HP reaches zero, I avert my gaze as Ethan turns his eyes on Jordy.

A few moments later, the cannons fire.

When Ethan returns, I have to physically restrain Limery to keep him from attacking the warlock.

"It's okay, buddy. Taryn is fine. He'll be waiting for us when this is over."

Limery snarls at Ethan. "Limmy doesn't like hims."

I pull Limery aside. "Look, it's okay to be mad, but you have a fight coming up. You can either channel that anger and use it to power you, or you need to let it go so that you can focus." I pat him on the shoulder. "I'm not going to tell you what to do, just don't let it make you sloppy. Got it?"

He nods, but I can see the rage burning within his bulbous eyes. He sits on my shoulder and stews as the announcer prepares everyone for the next fight.

When it's time for them to go, he hugs me and flies over to the platform. Jason mumbles something to Ethan as he walks past, but the warlock rolls his eyes.

Me, Drizz'rt, and Ethan are now alone in the booth that once felt crowded. Soon, we'll be down to the final four.

Limery flies around the battlefield, darting back and forth before the match starts. I don't know if I have ever seen him this worked up. Maybe when he showed up with Chief Rizza and the others as we were being ambushed by Ethan and his crew, but this feels different.

I glance into the stands to check on Caustic. He's still sitting with Breebis, so I guess he's behaving himself.

Drizz'rt climbs over the seat and sits next to me. "You have fought well today. You bring honor to the trolls." He hisses as he pronounces the last word.

I acknowledge his presence before returning my gaze to Limery. "Thanks. You were pretty impressive yourself—especially against Randy. That was amazing to watch."

He ignores my compliment, turning his attention to Limery. "The little one, he is strong."

"He is. Passionate, too."

"I wish him well."

The countdown ends, and the fight begins. Jason's hands glow and arcane chains appear out of nowhere, wrapping around Limery's body and tethering the imp to the ground. He struggles against their hold, but the chains don't budge.

Limery goes molten, his entire body burning like flaming lava until the chains vanish into the ether. Before he flies away, an octahedron prism forms around the imp, locking him in place and quenching his fire.

For a moment, he seems suspended in time. Rainbows ripple through the prism as it catches the light, and then Limery's body begins to glow, at first in his chest, and then spreading out along his belly and arms until his entire body pulses with orange and yellow. Flames lick at his body and he ignites, going full molten.

Still, the prism doesn't give. Jason's hands glow, fingers outstretched as they point at one another like he's trying to contain the imp. His brow furrows, and a bead of sweat trails down his nose.

Come on, Limery. Keep pushing.

Fire bursts to life around the imp, not the flames of his molten form but something more intense. The mage falters, nearly falling to his knees, but he catches his balance. The fire burns within the entirety of the prism, concealing Limery as the flames swirl. The air around the prism shimmers from the intense heat.

A crack forms, and then the entire thing shatters. Limery hovers in the air, and fire continues to blaze around him, spinning in a circle like a miniature sun and hiding the imp from view.

"Oh gods, I can't believe this, folks! The imp just broke through an Arcane Prison using Fire Shield! That's not an ability you see every day. What more does this miniature hellraiser have in store for us today?"

Fire Shield? When the hell did he learn that? I bet the little bugger has been hiding his new ability since he hit level twenty-five!

A barrage of spells hit Limery's fire shield, but they all fizzle out on impact. Jason casts more and more, hitting him from all sides, but Limery's shield holds.

Then it expands. As it does, some of the rocky terrain gleams as it turns to glass from the heat. Once the fiery shield doubles in size, flares pop along the outer surface, licking at the air. Jason takes a few steps back, and the heat increases again, so much so that a gust of warm air hits us in the stands.

"Wow, did you feel that, folks? He's turning up the heat. Let me remind you that the shield mages have invoked every precaution to keep our wonderful guests safe from the conflict. Nothing capable of damage will pass through the barrier. And speaking of shields, Jason has just cast Cube of Protection."

I remember that spell. It was the one he hid inside back in the forest when he nearly killed Ismora. Apparently, Limery remembers it, too because as soon as it's cast, he goes on the attack. The fire shield fades, and he moves like a fireball toward the mage, summoning a flame wall on all four sides of the cube. Landing on the top of the cube, he presses his hands to the glass. His body goes molten and the entire scene is nothing but hazy, distorted heat.

Only a few seconds pass before the cube shatters, and a flame-covered Jason runs through the fire wall. He stumbles across the battlefield, searching for the pond, but Limery pursues like an arrow, latching his burning body onto Jason until the mage falls to the ground, and the cannons boom.

The crowd erupts, and I release the breath I was holding. Drizz'rt is on his feet, but Ethan shows no emotion as he stares down into the arena.

Limery doesn't wait for the platform to carry him back, choosing to fly over instead. One of the mages cancels the barrier, and Limery flies into my arms.

"Limmy dids it. Limmy is tireds." His eyes flutter, and then he's asleep in my arms.

I sit down, cradling him as he snores. You did it, Limery. You certainly did.

CHAPTER 39

CHALLENGER OR CHAMPION

THE BREAK between the quarterfinals and the semis is longer than the others. The gnomes put on some kind of show, but I pay it no attention. Limery snores in my arms while my mind runs through tactics for dealing with an assassin who can probably run circles around me.

We're so close to pulling this off. Two more wins and it could be me and Limery in the finals proving to everyone that they don't want to cross us.

I catch the end of the intermission as a group of gnomes hang-glide across the arena. Streams of brightly-colored smoke trail behind them as they make designs in the sky. The gliders barrel-roll, spin, and do loops to the delight of the crowd.

Drizz'rt shakes his head, muttering "gnomes" as if that explains everything.

The announcer goes through his usual pre-fight buildup, and I wake Limery. After the last match, he's gassed. Even though he could use the rest, I don't trust Ethan not to pull some shady shit, so I give Limery a stamina potion that will hopefully help rejuvenate him a little. He extends his small hand for a fist-bump, and then I step onto the platform across from Drizz'rt.

Regardless of what happens, there's no animosity between the lizardfolk and me. I fully expect him to test my limits, but I can't lose. I just can't. There's too much on the line.

As the platform descends, I search for the booth with the eliminated challengers. About a third of them have already bailed. Who knows, maybe they didn't want their failure on display, or maybe they've joined up with friends and family in the crowd.

Taryn sits in the front row, giving me a thumbs up with Berry and Jordy sitting to each side of him, and Flubs and Ruby each occupying one of his legs.

For some reason, the gesture takes me back to the trial, back before I knew this place existed. I had just been sentenced, and I was terrified at not knowing what awaited me. Taryn shouted his encouragement from the back of the courtroom. When I turned around, there he was, thumbs up as he towered over everyone around him, his giant afro making his presence even more imposing.

He's the only person in my life that I can say has always been there for me, even when I haven't always been the most pleasant to be around. He lifts Ruby's paw, making her wave, and I throw up a peace sign.

Behind Taryn, Arty, Reddick, and Roddick sit next to Randy, Don, and Michael. The rogue laughs and nudges Roddick in the shoulder. If nothing else happens, we've made at least a few allies from being here.

The platform stops moving near ground level and ramps descend from each side. Drizz'rt and I take our position opposite one another and wait for the fight to begin.

"Chod has made a name for himself across Mythos, but it pales in comparison to the legend of Drizz'rt. There's a saying amongst the

rogues of Pruxford that if Drizz'rt has marked you, you're already dead. Let's see how well brute strength matches up against the skills of a trained killer, shall we?"

The crowd cheers, and the countdown begins. Drizz'rt stares at me from across the arena. He wears a leather vest that reveals his slender but muscled golden arms. Half a dozen daggers are strapped to each side, and several amulets are tucked inside the vest. A shortsword hangs from his hip and more daggers are strapped along his form-fitting pants. His tail flicks back and forth like he's ready to pounce.

The countdown hits zero, and I summon three horrors in quick succession. Almost as soon as they appear, they vanish in a puff of smoke as Drizz'rt hits each one with a well-placed dagger. He's seen the buffs my horrors give me and he's not going to let me take advantage of them.

I've still got a nice health buff from the Regeneration Triad, and I keep the massive shield out in front of me as I try to close the gap. When I'm within spitting distance, Drizz'rt makes his move.

He charges straight at me, catching me off guard. I position myself behind the shield and ready my spear. He continues his push, and I jab once he's in range. The assassin spins out of the attack and runs up my shield, launching himself from the top and hitting me in the shoulder with two daggers as he backflips away.

I grimace as I pull the daggers out and the wounds continue to burn. The distraction leaves me open to two more attacks in my bicep and chest. I duck behind the shield, using it as cover as I remove the weapons buried in my body. With the twenty-percent regeneration buff, my wounds should heal without issue, but once the blades are out, nothing happens. Instead, the wounds continue to sting, and my health actually trickles down.

Dammit! I've been poisoned.

I could use my Tiger's Eye Pendant to clear the poison, but I'm sure he has plenty more coated with poison so I can't waste it. Going into a rage will cancel the poison as well, but I'm holding on to that card for now. I've got enough health that I can spare to lose a little.

For now.

Standing up, I keep as much of my body behind the shield as possible. I summon more horrors behind me, using Sacrifice before Drizz'rt has a chance to kill them.

He circles around me, keeping his distance from my spear. I'm twice his size, but somehow, it feels like I'm the prey.

Drizz'rt uses his doppelgänger ability, forming two clones to each side of him. I've seen this attack before against Randy, so I turn around, ready for the assassin's sneak attack.

Pain flares along my back as several blades stab into me. I turn around, unable to tell which of the doppelgängers is the real Drizz-z'rt when fresh pain flares through my back again.

I roar, swinging wildly with my spear to clear some space. My health drops faster than ever with a half-dozen daggers buried in my back. Drizz'rt explodes a vial at my feet, and smoke fills the area as all four assassins swarm me.

I can't see anything as the wounds in my back surge with pain and then relief as the blades are pried from my flesh, followed by more burning and a fresh wave of cuts along my arms and legs. I try to run from the smoke, but it follows me as the assassin continues to pick me apart. There's no way I can beat him on speed alone, so I need to show him something he's not prepared for.

I summon three horrors and cast Kamikaze while they surround me. The damage pushes my health into the red, but I hit Drizz'rt as well. He grunts, revealing his position, and I swing the spear until I hit something firm. I summon Pharos as soon as I do.

The spirit guide pushes back the smoke, revealing the assassin as he moves out of range. The brief encounter with the Horror of Vitality, before I exploded it, has slowed him for a few seconds. He's probably still faster than me even with a twenty-percent slow, but this is my chance. I activate Berserker Rage and go on the attack.

The poison vanishes from my body and my healing kicks into overdrive. I chase after Drizz'rt, but he uses the terrain to his advantage, jumping from boulder to boulder like Jordy. When the slow wears off, he stops on top of a giant emerald and pulls out his sword, gesturing for me to attack.

I swipe at his legs with the spear and he jumps, flipping through the air and landing behind me.

This time, I'm ready, letting the momentum of my attack carry me around just in time for my shield to block his swing. The sword grates against the metal shield, and I counter with a spear jab loaded with Concussive Force. He sidesteps it again and again as I press the attack.

Even with the added stats from my rage, at best this is a draw. As soon as it ends, he'll pick me apart again. I toss the shield aside and put everything I have into attacking, jabbing, and swinging with two hands, but I still can't manage to land a hit.

When my rage ends, I stand there heaving.

Drizz'rt sheaths his sword and takes out two daggers, spinning them against his palm. He grins. "Good effort, but it's over. There's nothing left to save you."

I stab the spear into the sand and take a few steps back, equipping Destroyer. The weight of the warhammer feels more natural than anything else I own.

I ready my next ability. "Why don't you come and find out?"

His tail flicks, and he takes a few steps in my direction—

slowly this time, like he's savoring the moment. "Do you want this to end quick, or should I drag it—"

The spear jabs through his throat from behind, and blood pours down his neck. His eyes are full of surprise as his jaw opens and closes, blood gurgling in his throat as he tries to speak.

I take a step closer, dusting sand off his shoulder. "Quick works for me."

Behind him, Arty releases the spear, and Drizz'rt topples on his face as the cannons boom.

"Would you look at that, folks! And here I thought rogues were sneaky. It looked like Drizz'rt was about to have this one in the bag, and then Chod uses Champion to summon a copy of the challenger he defeated in the previous round."

The crowd's roar is deafening. For a moment, I close my eyes and listen. There's electricity in the air, and it dwarfs anything I've ever experienced streaming or at an in-person tournament. This is special.

I open my eyes and pump my fist in the air. I'm in the finals, baby!

When I arrive back at the booth, Limery and Ethan stand on opposite sides. Limery scowls at the warlock, but when he sees me, his expression changes into a giant smile. Ethan purses his lips but says nothing.

"Chods! Yous dids it!" He shakes his small body in the air as he dances and sings. "Chods is going to the finals. Chods is going to the finals."

I take a seat once he finishes. "How are you feeling?"

"Limmy was tireds, but Limmy feels better nows."

"Good." I lean in close. "To beat him, you can't afford any mistakes. I'm sure he has some moves that we haven't seen, so keep your guard up. You're stronger than I realized, but he's cunning."

He nods, then his eyes narrow as he glances at Ethan. "Limmy is going to hurts the bad mans."

I hope he does.

Once their introductions are over, the two step onto the platform. After witnessing Limery's last match, I wonder if Ethan is nervous at all. If he is, he doesn't show it. He's as composed as ever, arms tucked behind his back as the platform slowly descends.

For the first time today, I'm completely alone in the booth. As they take their positions, my pulse races. Sitting back and watching as Limery takes on a warlock backed by some powerful being, I'm more nervous than I have been for my own fights.

I just hope Limery has enough left in the tank.

Not that long ago, I woke up to Limery's bulbous eyes inches from my own as he tried to steal my necklace. But ever since that funny, caring, annoying, mischievous, greedy little imp has come into my life, everything has changed. If only the other heroes had that same kind of experience, then maybe they wouldn't hesitate giving everything they have to keep from losing it.

The fight begins, and Limery is instantly on the attack, hurling fireball after fireball at Ethan as the warlock moves through the air on shadowy wings. His tattoos glow as he tries to counter the imp's aggression by casting spells of his own. Limery flies through the air like a hummingbird, zigging and zagging. Fireballs and dark lightning shoot across the arena as the two dance high above the ground.

Fighting solely in the air forces both to switch up their usual style. Ethan can't exactly summon demons to fight on his behalf unless they have wings, and I'm beginning to think there's a long cooldown on the flying shadow demons since we haven't seen them since the first round. Limery is without his Fire Wall that high up, but it doesn't seem like much of a hindrance so far.

Ethan is nowhere near as fast as the imp, taking several hits without landing any of his own. Limery sticks to what's working, flying circles around the warlock and attacking from all angles. He does it for so long that the announcer runs out of commentary.

The entire arena is quiet except for the whir of magical attacks. Their fight slowly rises higher and higher until they are fighting above the lower-level stands.

Limery manages to whittle the warlock down to half of his HP with no signs of slowing down.

Then forty percent.

Thirty.

Twenty.

"This matchup is unfolding in a way none of us expected. Is there anything Ethan can do or are we watching his slow but inevitable demise?"

I can't help but wonder the same thing. Did Ethan blow his most powerful abilities in the earlier rounds? My Champion ability has a six-hour cooldown, and I'm sure that some of his are much longer.

"What's this? Is Limery finally going for the kill shot?"

My chest tightens as Limery goes molten in front of Ethan.

No, no, no, no, no. Dammit! Stick to what's working. I don't like this one bit.

Limery darts at Ethan, smashing into the warlock's shoulder before zooming off. Ethan tumbles through the air before regaining his bearings, just in time for Limery to smash into him from the backside, sending him spinning once again.

Three more times, Limery hits him like a flaming fastball until the warlock is at ten percent health.

"Now finish him off."

Limery dives again, just as a shroud of black energy surrounds Ethan and a dark, clawed hand the size of the warlock's body reaches out from the void. It plucks Limery from the air, holding his flaming body still as Ethan casts Essence Drain.

A line of black-and-purple energy forms between the imp and the warlock. Limery burns brighter, but the hand doesn't release. When the warlock's spell activates, Limery's health plummets far quicker than Berry's did.

Ethan's health creeps up to twenty and then thirty percent as Limery's continues to fade.

Helpless, I clench my fists until my claws dig into my palms and blood trickles into a pool around my feet.

Limery's fire dims as his health drops into the red, and his bulbous eyes grow heavy. His body goes limp against the giant hand, and then it releases him.

I can't pull my eyes away as he falls lifelessly to the ground.

And then the cannons fire.

CHAPTER 40
THE STORM

ETHAN and I sit at opposite ends of the booth waiting for the intermission before the final match to end. A tinkerer has a contraption set up in the stands that shoots out bubbles two to three feet in diameter. An orchestra plays calming music as a wind mage sends the bubbles floating across the arena.

When they pop, the bubbles explode into a kaleidoscope of butterflies that flutter among the crowd.

The sun dips near the horizon, and the sky streaks with lilac and magenta, the perfect backdrop to the jeweled outline of the Crystal Arena. By the time our fight starts, I expect it will be almost nightfall.

The music fades, and the announcer begins our introductions.

"What a day! What a day. This has truly been one of the most exciting Champion's Tournaments in recent memory. We've seen some impressive displays of both might and magic, none greater than the two finalists about to take the stage.

"When rumors first began spreading that heroes had returned to the Isle of Mythos, I think most of us were skeptical, to say the least.

After all, it had been ages since the last hero was recorded. Many wondered if this new breed of hero could measure up to the legends that came before them. Could they right the wrongs of Mythos and tackle the challenges no one else could? After today, I think we can agree that these heroes are the real deal. So, let's all cheer for the new age of heroes, and enjoy the match between Chod and Ethan!"

We step onto the platform outside our booth, and the crowd cheers even louder. I wave to them, but Ethan keeps his eyes focused on the battlefield. Caustic leaps onto his hind legs when I wave at him, and Breebis wrestles him back to his seat. I take a quick glance at those who have been eliminated and spot Limery sitting on Arty's shoulder. The imp waves with one hand while he devours a meat skewer with the other.

After a few moments in the spotlight, I tune out the distractions. I have a fight to win, and I need everything I have focused on taking out Ethan.

We take our positions on the battlefield, and the announcer keeps going, recounting our fights in vivid detail. The sky has now faded to a deep purple, and the gemstones around the arena flicker to life like old lampposts, each one producing a dull glow.

Time seems to grind to a halt as we wait for the announcer to finish, but then the barrier surrounding the battlefield shimmers slightly as the roar of the crowd abruptly cuts off, leaving us in an uneasy silence.

There's a slight pop as I summon my horrors, followed by their grumbling.

Ethan and I stare at each other from across the platform. This is it. My chance to show everyone why they should be on our side. After watching him dismantle Taryn and then Limery, though, I doubt anyone has their bets on me.

A dark aura surrounds the warlock as he hovers several feet off the ground. His shadowy wings extend behind him, flapping gently as they hold him aloft. I wish I had a better idea of his cooldowns, so I could know what to expect. As it is, I'll have to play this like all his cards are on the table.

I hold the Shield of Vigor in front with one hand, and the Renewal Spear in the other. I'm much more comfortable with my warhammer, but with the full set active, I can drag this battle out forever as long as I can hit something to replenish my health. I'm going to need to close the gap to do so, which won't be easy considering Ethan can fly. Not to mention figuring out how to deal with any new demons he may introduce.

He hasn't summoned any of the flying shadow demons since the first round—maybe they're still on cooldown or limited to once per day. I doubt that he's shown us all his tricks, though, and I can't help but feel like there's something big he's been holding on to.

Ethan smirks. "You really think you have a shot? The druid is gone. The imp is gone. There's no one here to save you this time."

I summon more horrors as I slowly approach. "I'll take my chances."

"I admire your spirit, but this isn't a fight you can win." He laughs. "The game's over."

He moves his hands in front of him, drawing symbols in the air that leave a trail of glowing energy. When he finishes, two rifts form in the air behind him, each one about six feet tall. They pulse with an energy much more vibrant than any of the previous portals he's opened.

I grab a Horror of Finesse and toss it by the horns at the warlock. With a flick of his wrist, a beam of dark energy explodes the horror mid-air.

There's a ripping sound, like tearing fabric, as the rift grows larger. Blinding white energy spills from within, similar to the portals that connect the kingdoms. Water gushes through as the tear widens. The smell of saltwater fills the air, then the rift splits further until the portal is several stories high and thousands of gallons of water rush into the arena like a dam just broke.

I jab my spear into the ground to hold my position as water pounds me, but my horrors wash away to the back of the arena. Water splashes all around me, and I inhale the salty mist.

What the hell is he doing, summoning some kind of sea monster?

Thunder roars from the other side of the portal as it expands a final time. Two large pirate ships break through, crashing against the arena floor and dislodging some of the gemstone boulders. Massive black sails adorn each ship, emblazoned with the symbol of the Blacktide portal—two curved horizontal lines with a vertical slash going through each.

Shit, did he really just open a portal from Pruxford to Blacktide?

Each ship is full of creatures that look like trolls but with more slender frames, smaller ears, and less defined jawlines. Sea orcs. They're almost like a cross between a forest troll and a seaside troll, but with more goblin-like features. Their skin is sea-foam green with streaks or patches of black that give them a sinister appearance. Each one has a weathered look about them, and they sport a variety of facial piercings. Their noses are hooked, and their lips turn up in a permanent snarl. Short tusks help to frame their pointy jaws. Each orc wears tattered black clothing, and almost every one of them has a cutlass at their waist.

They hang over the edges of the ships, snarling and yelling, waving weapons in the air. More hang from the masts and crow's nests. These ships are massive, so it's impossible to tell how many are aboard.

Water continues to pour through the portals like a geyser. Pretty soon, I'll be swimming around the arena.

What the hell is he trying to do?

A cannon blast erupts, only this time it's from within the battlefield. A flaming projectile shoots from one of the ships and explodes against the barrier meant to protect the crowd.

On the other side, the crowd panics. Gnomes climb over one another as they race for the exits, and the guards in the council booth draw their weapons.

This is definitely not part of the tournament.

"What are you playing at, Ethan?" I shout over the boom of more cannons as streaks blast through the night.

The barrier ripples against the impact, but it holds for now.

Ethan unleashes a demon bolt, and it explodes against my shield. "You think I care about some tournament? This is only the beginning—just a taste of the terror coming your way if you continue to meddle. A storm is coming, and there's nothing that you or anyone else can do to stop it." He grins and it fades to a scowl as he flies between the masts of the two ships and points at me. "Finish him!"

Sea orcs growl as they leap over the ship's railing.

"Oh, fuck."

Nearly two dozen orcs land in the water before I have the sense to get moving. I stow my weapons and run, summoning horrors and sending them on the attack behind me.

As I look over my shoulder, there are at least fifty sea orcs on the ground, all ranging between level fifteen and twenty. They continue to spill out, and for every one that jumps into the arena, another replaces it aboard the ship's deck.

The orcs cut through my horrors almost instantly, but the passive slow manages to hinder a few of them. As they are trampled, I put a little more distance between me and the horde. There's no way I can fight this many on my own.

Cannons continue to fire, shooting some sort of magical

projectiles at the barrier. For now, it continues to hold strong with all but one of the shield mages positioned outside of the arena.

What I don't understand is that if this is an attack, why is no one helping? The guards are on alert and there's commotion in the council booth, but they aren't doing anything.

So far, I don't have a plan, so I continue running, trying to put as much distance between me and the orcs as possible.

Then I see the booth with the defeated challengers. If they join in, maybe we can push the orcs back through the portal before anyone gets hurt.

The shield mage responsible for their protection stands at attention, not a care in the world as invaders launch an attack on Pruxford.

Something large moves in my peripheral, and I look up to see Caustic clawing at the barrier. He flaps his wings, biting and clawing at the invisible shield. Breebis holds the leash, trying to pull him back, but he attacks like a rabid animal. He must know this isn't like the other fights. The barrier ripples around his attacks, and I wish he was with me right now.

Once I'm close enough, I shout at the shield mage protecting the challenger's booth. "Let them out! We're under attack."

"I have orders." He frowns, his voice stern. "No one is allowed on the battlefield until the match is over."

"Are you stupid? Does this look like part of the match to you?" I point at the hoard of approaching orcs. "What do you think happens to you once they kill me?"

He glances between the orcs and the challengers, where Taryn and Arty beat against the shield surrounding their booth, yelling for their release. I wonder if they could break it if they tried.

"Goddammit." I can hear the grunt of the sea orcs as they get close. "I'm screwed, and then you're fucked."

I reequip the Regeneration Triad and try not to think about

the impending pain. I bang the spear against the shield as I backpedal around the edge of the battlefield, trying to gain their attention so that none of them go after the idiotic mage.

They follow, and I greet the first sea orc with a spear to the throat. Ram Rage sends out a ripple of splash damage into the orcs behind him, lowering their health by a fraction. A second orc slices at me with its cutlass, but I block it with my shield and follow up with Concussive Force. The hit knocks the orc back, stunning it and sending splash damage to those behind. More try to swarm me, but I kick, jab, and deflect their attacks as best I can. Though I manage to keep them from surrounding me, cuts well up all over my body.

My health drops with each wound I take. Once the Renewal Spear has a full charge, I activate it and gain a burst of health. Every time I summon a Horror of Finesse, my next attack heals me again. Combined with Concussive Force's knockback, I'm a pain in the ass, but even with nine-thousand HP, I'm losing more than I'm gaining.

I continue maneuvering around the arena to keep the horde in front of me, but I know that I can't do this forever. Not against this many enemies.

As I run to my next position, Caustic is still going crazy against the barrier. His section of the stands has completely vacated except for Breebis. I'm thankful she's not leaving him alone, but Caustic can protect himself. I'm not so sure about Breebis.

A blade rips into my calf from behind and I stumble to one knee. If I don't use Berserker Rage now, I'm done for.

I activate the ability and the wound stitches itself together in seconds. My muscles bulge, and my health immediately begins to replenish. I swing the shield in an arc, dislocating one orc's jaw and clearing space. Once I'm on my feet, I use the shield like a battering ram, shattering bones and sending orcs flying until I have enough room to fight.

My attacks are faster, and I skewer several orcs until a pile of bodies lies around me. But not enough. It's never enough.

Once my rage is nearly over, I reposition, letting the orcs come to me. I back into a boulder I didn't see and the orcs press in on me. Curved blades tear into my skin until even my increased healing can't keep up.

My health drops, and just as my rage ends, I receive a notification.

Alert! *Caustic has initiated Draconic Convergence. Accepting Draconic Convergence will create a permanent bond between the dragon and its chosen counterpart. Do you accept?*

I accept, and a wave of anger and panic unlike anything I have ever experienced flares through me. More notifications come through, but I can't focus on anything other than the crippling pain and overwhelming emotions.

In the distance, cannons continue to fire. And then a mighty roar cuts above it all.

An anger that isn't mine continues to rage inside of me, like it's superimposed over my own thoughts. There's a heavy pressure against my body, and then orcs are ripped away. Caustic's neck whips as he tosses them aside. When he sees me alive, I feel his panic turn to relief, but the rage burns even hotter. Orcs run from the intimidating monster. He unleashes a stream of toxic gas to both sides and steps in front of me like a lioness protecting her cubs. The orcs retreat, but Caustic arches his back and spews green gas that shrouds them as they run back to the ship.

The air crackles as a fireball flies past us. Time seems to slow as the fireball hits the gas and orc body parts explode across the arena. Chunks of flesh splash into the water all around us.

I search for the source of the fireball and see Limery speeding toward me while the challengers continue to climb through one of Don's portals from the booth to the battlefield. The shield mage argues with them but doesn't try to stop it otherwise. Don allows everyone through but Otis and Kevin, closing the portal before they can step through.

"Fuck you, buddy." Randy flashes the shield mage a crude gesture as he runs toward the chaos, Drizz'rt by his side. He raises his sword. "Let's fuck up some orcs!"

"Is yous okays, Chods?" Limery presses his small hands to my face.

Before I have a chance to respond, Taryn hands me a potion. "Drink this." He looks out at the chaos. "What the hell is happening?"

Berry and Jordy stand protectively behind him.

I take a gulp of the sweet red liquid, and the pain ebbs as my health recovers even faster than normal. "This is Valmar using Ethan to make his presence known. We need to stop them before they break the barrier and get into the city."

Taryn looks out at the chaos. "I think we've got a few people down for the cause."

A massive wave carries Tozzet across the watery battlefield like he's some godly merfolk surfer. His hands glow and a larger wave swells behind him. He rides the pipeline as waves curl around him, avoiding the tidal wave as it surges past, completely obliterating the remaining orcs as they retreat. But there's still a multitude waiting for us aboard the ship.

I crawl to my feet, pointing my spear toward the ship. "Let's go!"

We come upon Scotty, the sniper, as he kneels in the water charging the same attack that he tried on me in the first round. Only this time, he succeeds. The arrow elongates and tendrils of energy curl around the shaft as he releases it. The spear-sized arrow flies like a javelin, skewering three orcs on the bow of one ship.

There's a loud explosion as part of the barrier protecting the crowd shatters. Screams and blaring alarms from outside suddenly fill the battlefield, along with the announcer's voice as he tries to maintain order among the chaos. Ballistae clank as they fire giant grappling hooks into the stands, and the orcs begin crossing using a pulley system.

"We are under attack. I repeat, Pruxford is under attack. Please remain calm and exit the arena in a safe and orderly fashion. Shield mages are attempting to contain the threat within the arena, and city guards are mobilizing around the Pruxford portal. Whatever you do, stay out of the streets. I repeat, the city is under attack. Find a safe space and remain calm until the threat is under control."

Sea orcs zip across the ropes like they've practiced this a million times. Once in the stands, they kill indiscriminately. One of the shield mages dies while trying to maintain her shield, causing another piece of the barrier to fall.

More grappling hooks land among the stands. Magic explodes as the guards, councilmembers, and heads of state join the fight.

Good. We've got enough problems down here.

Ethan hovers above the two ships, casting spells at the challengers who have decided to fight back. Some of the sea orcs have crossbows, and there appears to be at least one mage or cleric on each of the ships casting buffs on the others.

"Limery, I want you to stick with Caustic. Everywhere he blows gas, hit it with a fireball. Burn those ships to the ground."

Limery flies over to Caustic and perches behind the dragon's antlers. "Come on, Caustics! Let's burn those shipses to the grounds!"

Caustic looks at me, and I can feel his affirmation as he takes flight. I can already tell this bond is going to make everything smoother between us. It's like I can feel what he's thinking without the need for words.

The announcer addresses us directly. *"Challengers, if you can hear this, hit those ships with everything you have. Destroy their weapons and do not let any more orcs breach the barrier. The council and guards are mounting an offensive to take back the upper arena. Gods be with you."*

Caustic swoops over the ship, releasing a dense green stream of gas. A second later, Limery sets it aflame. The explosion rocks the arena and topples one of the masts, but the water pouring through the portals quickly extinguishes it.

"I got this!" Don forms a void portal in front of one of Ethan's portal with its counterpoint near Tozzet to funnel the rushing water directly to the tidal mage.

"Hit the ship again!" the void mage shouts, and Caustic and Limery take another pass. This time, they set the ship ablaze.

Taryn casts Lightning and Moonbeam, and orcs leap from the burning ships where Randy, Drizz'rt, Arty, Roddick, Reddick, and the drunken master all wait to dish out some physical punishment. I continuously summon horrors and send them on the attack.

"That's it, the barrier is almost re—" the announcer's voice cuts off mid-sentence as the shield mages manage to repair the barrier.

A few dozen orcs remain trapped on the other side against city guards and the council. Even from down here, I can see the orc bodies speckling the stands. One of the earth mages topples a giant emerald pillar, and it crushes a handful of orcs.

Kazzandre chops at the hull with her axe, wood crunching beneath each blow. She lets out a groan as one of the orcs leans over the edge of the ship with a crossbow, hitting her in the shoulder.

I'm about to toss my spear at the orc when Sam the monk runs past. The watercolor outline of a tiger forms over his arm, and the air ripples beneath his bare feet as he wind-walks up to the ship's deck like he's climbing stairs two at a time. The tiger superimposed over his arm roars as he punches the crossbow-wielding orc with enough force that it flies across the ship, cracking one of the masts.

I run to Kazzandre, joining her attack and smashing the hull with Destroyer. Together, we break through the wood, forming a hole big enough for several gnome challengers to enter. I send in a few horrors alongside them for the surprise attack.

On the opposite ship, Lanxkuri wreaks havoc with her blood magic, using the fiery corpses against those that still survive.

Jason sneaks around the edge of the arena, forming steps with his Cube of Protection as he and Tommy scale the ship. For a moment, I think they're about to attack the orcs, but then they both disappear through Ethan's portal back to Blacktide.

Ethan dodges a blast of holy light from Michael the paladin, and it sizzles against the deck of the ship. The warlock hovers in front of the portal over the ship on the right.

"This isn't over!" he shouts, as he casts a demon bolt at the paladin. Then he flies through the portal and it blips closed.

With Ethan gone, the sea orcs are no match for the challengers that remain. The smell of burned corpses and saltwater is overwhelming. We manage to take one of the captains alive, but he refuses to talk, so Taryn binds him with the vines of his Sapling Staff until one of the guards can escort him to the palace dungeon for more thorough questioning.

Once the fight in the upper arena is over, the shield mages cancel the barrier and the heads of state make their way down to the arena floor with the council to inspect the damage.

Oruma, the mesmer, points out where the portals were to the bureaucrats as Taryn and I join them.

Dezmin, the head of the gnomish council, barks out orders to a handful of palace guides that follow him around. His normally-friendly face is contorted in a mixture of despair and anger. "I want Ethan marked as a wanted man across all of Mythos. I want the Pruxford portal guarded by no less than a hundred soldiers at all times. For this to happen in Pruxford, of all places... Gods help us."

The horned lizardfolk from Ellynmylly kicks a piece of wreckage, shaking his head. "How is this possible? There's not a mage alive capable of opening a portal from Blacktide to Pruxford. There hasn't been a new portal constructed since the Age of Mages, and to open them on a whim..."

I push my way to the front of the group. With the devastation surrounding us, my word will never have this much weight again. "This is what we have been trying to tell you. Valmar is still alive. He's growing stronger. He's testing you. King Orso believes a war is coming, and he wants to be prepared when it does."

"Now is not the time," Dezmin snaps. "Can't you see we have a crisis to deal with? If you hadn't let the warlock escape, then maybe we would have answers right now."

"Me?" I clench my fists, but it's not me who shouts back.

"Enough!" Felston's voice booms over his superior, and his eyes narrow above his bulbous nose. "I've had enough of your arrogance, Dezmin. You were warned of this threat, and yet you did nothing. I told you of the behemoth in Seascape, and you chose to brush it off. You can no longer afford to bury your head in the sand. How many lives were lost today because you chose to do nothing? How much blood is on my hands because I let you? You're angry and full of hate for those that attacked our city? Good! It's about time you took this seriously. But don't you dare take it out on those who risked their own lives to stop this atrocity. If not for Chod and his dragon, and everyone else still here that fought for our entertainment today, our losses would have been much greater."

The arena is so quiet that the crackling, burning embers of the wreckage are the loudest sound.

"You're right." Dezmin sighs. "I am sorry. I failed spectacularly, and it will forever stain my legacy. I should have listened to you, Felston. Your council has always been wise beyond measure. I just hope it is not too late to right the wrongs I have made."

"What do we do now?" asks one of the catfolk from Antadale.

"We act." Dezmin snaps his fingers, and palace guides scurry in front of him. "Send a message to every kingdom informing them of what has happened. Send special instructions to Seascape, Vanaria, and any kingdom not present today that there will be a meeting in Pruxford and many heads of state are already here. Tell them we request their attendance. If a war is coming, then it is time we prepare."

Taryn and I exchange glances. War. Somehow that three-letter word fills me simultaneously with hope and dread.

EPILOGUE

THE AFTERMATH of the attack is more bureaucracy than anything, and most of the challengers leave to get some much-needed rest. Even though the other leaders aren't here yet, the heads of state have been meeting with the gnomish council since we left the arena.

Those of us that remain sit on the steps of the Crystal Palace, looking out over the city. The streets are empty except for the city watch patrolling. You'd never know the chaos from earlier just by looking.

This wasn't an invasion. It was a terror attack, and it worked. You can see it on the face of every leader, like the boogeyman they heard about for so long turned out to be real. Maybe now we can all take this seriously.

Two shield mages and an earth mage died in the attack on the arena, along with nearly fifty attendees. A second attack inside the city left hundreds more dead. The sea orcs blindsided the citizens as they funneled through the city portal. With most of the guards stationed at the arena, it was a bloodbath. No one was prepared for the attack.

Otis and Kevin disappeared, along with the shield mage responsible for the booth they were in. Nobody seems to know if he went willingly or not. No one has seen Richard the cleric since then either.

"I don't know if anyone else could have held off the orcs long enough for us to get in the fight." Arty pats me on the shoulder. "Congrats on bonding with Caustic, by the way. It couldn't have come a moment too soon."

"Thanks, I just wish we were never in this position to begin with." I laugh dryly. "All of this just to get a meeting with the council."

"We did it, though. Everyone is finally on the same page." Taryn stands in front of us a few steps down, Flubs arching from one hand to another like a slinky. "Nothing we can do now but wait for the others to arrive. Maybe explore a few dungeons in the meantime. Speaking of which, that was crazy with Caustic. One minute, he's clawing at the barrier; the next, he's flying straight through it. What kind of new abilities does bonding with a dragon unlock?"

Caustic lays on the marble platform next to me, his giant head resting in my lap. His thoughts are calm and content. It's going to be strange getting used to having his feelings merged with my own.

I smile as I stroke his snout. "I was pinned beneath a mountain of orcs, and I got a notification saying that Caustic was initiating Draconic Convergence. I guess bonding was his choice all along. The next thing I know, he was saving me, and I could kind of feel what he was feeling, if that makes sense. Like if someone could accurately explain what they were thinking, but without words, just feelings. Honestly, I haven't checked any of the other notifications with everything that has happened."

Taryn raises an eyebrow. "Well, what are you waiting for?"

I pull up my notifications, and the first thing I notice is that I have a new message. Who in the world would be sending me a message at a time like this? I focus on the icon, and the message appears across my vision.

Incoming Message (Admin): *Chad, I apologize but believe me when I tell you that this was out of my control. - Valery*

I stare at the message, wondering what she could possibly mean. Did Valery have something to do with the attack today? How is that even possible? And why? I close out the message and notice there's a tab I haven't seen before. It pulses slowly.

Message Requests.

That's odd. Let me guess, it's probably Ethan or Otis trying to get in a few last words. I focus on the tab, and it expands. When I see the name of the sender, my heart skips a beat and I find it hard to breathe. The world goes quiet, and a dull ringing fills the silence.

Message Request: Dorothy Jordan

The woman I raged at to get me sent here? What? This doesn't make any sense. How is she able to send messages to me in-game? Is this what Valery meant when she said something was out of her control?

I focus on the message, and a wall of text appears across my vision.

Incoming Message (Dorothy Jordan): *Chad, Chad, Chad. I wondered what had happened to you. Your sentence passed and I kept wondering if I'd see you streaming again. When I didn't, I thought that maybe your little stint in rehab had finally put you in your place. Maybe you'd given up being a jackass for entertainment for good. Truth be told, that thought brought me solace.*

Imagine my surprise when I get a call from someone claiming to be the head of Mythos Gaming telling me he has a once-in-a-lifetime opportunity for me.

Funny how the world works, isn't it?

Now, I know the truth as to why no one has heard from you. Looks like little ol' daddy saved your ass again, didn't he? Not that I should be surprised. There's no such thing as justice in this world. You got to run away to this game, while I continued to deal with the fallout of your actions.

After you humiliated me on the stream, my crying face became a meme. After the trial, it went viral. Imagine that—your lowest moment posted across the internet for laughs, haunting you everywhere you go.

And when your little band of troll followers no longer had you to entertain them, they joined my stream, harassing me to the point that I had to shut it down.

But now, here I am, and I finally see what the fuss is all about. You got lucky being sent here. But I wouldn't get too comfortable, Chad. Payback's a bitch.

My entire being feels like I'm encased in ice. Caustic stirs, now able to sense my unrest.

I don't understand how any of this is possible. How is she here? And more importantly, why? What possible reason could Mythos Gaming have for bringing her into this world?

ACKNOWLEDGMENTS

Congratulations! *You have finished* Sentenced to Troll 5.
    5 of 6 completed.
    +1 stat point to distribute.
    +1 Review to leave.

Thanks for reading! I hope you had as much fun reading about Chod and his adventures as I did writing them. This adventure is just getting started. If you enjoyed the book, please consider leaving a review. Reviews and word-of-mouth are the lifeblood of indie authors. The more positive reviews I have, the more likely it is that others will take a chance on this series.

To all of the people who helped make this book possible, you have my deepest thanks. Cindy, you wade through the trenches and the books are always better for it. Caroline, your encouragement and support helps make the tough days not so bad. Davey, this one's for you, brother.

This book wouldn't be what it is without my team of beta readers. Paul Tuson, Loren Foster, Sami Taylor, and Tom Nemes helped make this a better story.

And to all of my supporters over on Patreon, thanks for sticking through the thick and thin. I can't wait to send out the signed copies of this one.

Gold Tier: Michael Percell, Robert Schaefer, Eric Sprague

Silver Tier: Nick Kelly, Sami Taylor

Bronze Tier: Cindy Koepp, Rachael Osterhout, Rickie Brookes, Roxanne Baechler-Gill

As well as all of the Wood Tier patrons.

If you're looking for more books similar to my own, check out LitRPG Books.

About the Author

S.L. Rowland is a cozy fantasy and LitRPG author known for crafting immersive worlds filled with adventure, heart, and a touch of humor. A lifelong gamer and fantasy enthusiast, he draws inspiration from tabletop RPGs, video games, and the fantastical. When he's not writing, he enjoys weightlifting, hiking with his Shiba Inu, and enduring the heartbreak of being an Atlanta sports fan.

SLRowland.com

Patreon-For signed paperbacks, advanced chapters, exclusive short stories, art, merch, and more.

Newsletter: For updates on new releases, sales, and behind the scenes content!

Email: slrowlandauthor@gmail.com

Find out more at https://linktr.ee/SLRowland

ALSO BY S.L. ROWLAND

Tales of Aedrea

Cursed Cocktails

Sword & Thistle

The Halfling's Harvest

There Be Dragons Here

Pangea Online

Pangea Online: Death and Axes

Pangea Online 2: Magic and Mayhem

Pangea Online 3: Vials and Tribulations

Sentenced to Troll 1-6

Path to Villainy: An NPC Kobold's Tale

Collected Editions

Pangea Online: The Complete Trilogy

Sentenced to Troll Compendium: Books 1-3

Sentenced to Troll Compendium 2: Books 4-6